LIFELINES

AN ANGELS OF MERCY NOVEL

CJ LYONS

Also By CJ Lyons:

Angels of Mercy Medical Suspense:
LIFELINES
CATALYST
TRAUMA
ISOLATION

Lucy Guardino Thrillers:
SNAKE SKIN
BLOOD STAINED
KILL ZONE
AFTER SHOCK
HARD FALL
BAD BREAK
LAST LIGHT
DEVIL SMOKE
OPEN GRAVE
GONE DARK
BITTER TRUTH

Renegade Justice Thrillers featuring Morgan Ames:
FIGHT DIRTY
RAW EDGES
ANGELS WEEP
LOOK AWAY
TRIP WIRE

Hart and Drake Medical Suspense:
NERVES OF STEEL
SLEIGHT OF HAND
FACE TO FACE
EYE OF THE STORM

Shadow Ops Covert Thrillers:
CHASING SHADOWS
LOST IN SHADOWS
EDGE OF SHADOWS

Fatal Insomnia Medical Thrillers:
FAREWELL TO DREAMS
A RAGING DAWN
THE SLEEPLESS STARS

PRAISE FOR NEW YORK TIMES AND USA TODAY BESTSELLER CJ LYONS:

"Everything a great thriller should be—action packed, authentic, and intense." ~#1 *New York Times* bestselling author Lee Child

"A compelling new voice in thriller writing…I love how the characters come alive on every page." ~*New York Times* bestselling author Jeffery Deaver

"Top Pick! A fascinating and intense thriller." ~ 4 1/2 stars, *RT Book Reviews*

"An intense, emotional thriller…(that) climbs to the edge of intensity." ~*National Examiner*

"A perfect blend of romance and suspense. My kind of read." ~*#1 New York Times* Bestselling author Sandra Brown

"Highly engaging characters, heart-stopping scenes…one great rollercoaster ride that will not be stopping anytime soon." ~Bookreporter.com

"Adrenalin pumping." ~*The Mystery Gazette*

"Riveting." ~*Publishers Weekly Beyond Her Book*

Lyons "is a master within the genre." ~*Pittsburgh Magazine*

"Will leave you breathless and begging for more." ~Romance Novel TV

"A great fast-paced read….Not to be missed." ~4 ½ Stars, Book Addict

"Breathtakingly fast-paced." ~*Publishers Weekly*

"Simply superb…riveting drama…a perfect ten." ~Romance Reviews Today

"Characters with beating hearts and three dimensions." ~*Newsday*

"A pulse-pounding adrenalin rush!" ~Lisa Gardner

Edgy Reads
Cover design: Toni McGee Causey, stock photo courtesy of Deposit Photos

Library of Congress Case # TX0007032572

CHAPTER 1

MONDAY, JULY 1, 6:45PM

JULY FIRST, THE MOST DANGEROUS DAY OF THE YEAR.

Transition Day, the day newly graduated medical students arrived to begin their internships, freshly scrubbed, wearing long white lab coats instead of their short student jackets. And absolutely no smarter than they were on June 30th.

Dr. Lydia Fiore knew all about the dangers of Transition Day. People died on Transition Day.

Starting her new job today, of all days, was not a good omen.

Yet, here she was, pacing outside Pittsburgh's Angels of Mercy Medical Center, its shiny steel and glass patient care tower looming over her.

She blinked hard, tried not to imagine herself running along the beach, the Pacific stretching out to infinity beside her. She'd left Los Angeles behind. Pittsburgh was home now.

She stopped beside the main ER doors, beginning to wonder if this was such a great idea after all. Her stomach did a tumble and roll, like being sucker-punched by a wave off the coast at Malibu, dragged under by your own stupidity.

Lydia remembered her own Transition Day, back in L.A. Her time on the streets working as a medic had given her an edge—an edge quickly erased with her first failed resuscitation.

Ain't no cure for death, the ER's charge nurse, a woman who had been in the trenches for thirty years, had told her back then, smirking at yet another intern's ego successfully sliced and diced.

What Lydia never understood until now was that as harrowing as med school, internship, and residency were, nothing in life was more terrifying than stepping into the role of attending physician. Boss. The buck stops here. The one in charge, the one responsible, the one most likely to be sued if anything went wrong.

The screech of brakes, honking of horns, blare of sirens, and stench of diesel fumes smothered her in a blanket of humidity. Pittsburgh smelled a lot like L.A. Shoving her jagged bangs back from her face, she bounced on the balls of her feet, ready to take the plunge.

Attending physician. As in: attending to the needs of all the patients and their loved ones and the staff and the residents and the medical students and, if there's time, catch up on charting, quality assurance, research, lecture preparation, public relations, committee meetings, continuing medical education, and oh yeah, don't forget to be nice to the volunteers and auxiliary members while you're making those life and death decisions.

An air-conditioned breeze escaped through the ER's open doors, bringing with it the familiar sounds of urban trauma. Footsteps clattering, a baby crying, voices colliding.

A siren's call to Lydia. Her toes curled in anticipation, eager to push off from a high cliff. Ready or not, this was her new life.

AS LYDIA WAS GETTING THE SIGN OUT from Mark Cohen, the attending she relieved, a petite, red-haired woman in her twenties joined them, waving her trauma radio to catch their attention.

"Fourteen-year-old, full arrest coming in by squad."

Mark frowned. "I'll stay, see you started."

"No. Mark, go home." He'd just finished working a twelve-hour shift and looked exhausted. Lydia was certain she could handle anything Pittsburgh had to offer. It wasn't like she'd be on her own. There were residents, other attendings, a hospital full of sub-specialists. "I'll be fine."

"All right, if you say so." He turned to the red-head and made introductions. "Nora Halloran, your charge nurse for the night. Nora, have you met Lydia Fiore, our new attending?"

"Nice to meet you, Dr. Fiore."

"It's Lydia, please."

Nora didn't waste time shaking hands. Instead, she donned a pair of polycarbonate protective glasses, making it clear she intended to personally supervise the new attending's first major case. She nodded to Mark, then hustled down the hall, rounding up her troops.

"I guess this is yours." Mark handed Lydia the trauma radio, the symbolic passing of the baton that accompanied all shift changes. "Call me if you have any problems. Good luck."

Lydia clipped the small radio onto her belt and tugged the drawstrings of her scrub pants tighter. Her pulse revved up in anticipation as the familiar weight settled on her hip. She jogged the first two steps then slowed herself to a fast walk, heading toward the ambulance bay to meet the paramedics and her first patient.

"Fourteen-year-old male found in full arrest at Schenley Park," a medic called out as they rushed a sandy-haired teen strapped to their stretcher down the hall. The second medic rode on top of the gurney, straddling the boy, performing chest compressions amidst the remains of a Buck Cherry t-shirt that had been cut away to allow placement of EKG electrodes.

They quickly arrived in the critical care room. Lydia helped her team transfer the teenager to the ER's bed.

The first medic, Trey Garrison according to his name tag, glanced up, revealing a pair of vivid hazel eyes that locked onto Lydia's gaze. Bagging oxygen into the boy's lungs, he didn't falter in his rhythm as he shifted places so Lydia could check breath sounds with her stethoscope.

The hum of contentment mixed with adrenaline sparked an electrical tingle that radiated throughout her body. She loved it when a resuscitation flowed almost effortlessly, as if it was choreographed. Trey read her mind, handing her an ophthalmoscope before she could ask for it.

"His friends said he was fine, then suddenly got a frightened look on his face, jumped up, ran about twenty yards and collapsed. One of them began CPR at the scene. We found him in v-fib, shocked him without results, one round of epi, shocked again and loaded with lidocaine." Trey's tone was grim, with good reason. The prognosis of an arrest unresponsive to epinephrine and defibrillation was worse than poor.

Ain't no cure for death.

"Drug use? Any past history?" She glided her hands over the now naked teen's body, searching for any trauma or other reason for his sudden collapse. Her vision tunneled to center on her patient, her focus drowning out all sounds except the information her team provided. In the zone.

"Friends said no, but we saw a couple empty cans of beer. They said he's healthy."

"Shock him at 360," she ordered, "then load him with amiodarone."

"He'll be due for another round of epi," Trey's partner put in as he hauled his stretcher out of the room, freeing up space for Lydia's team to work. He returned to stand in the corner. She felt his, Trey's, and Nora Halloran's gazes on her as she finished her assessment. Wondering about the new doc in town, no doubt.

Lydia backed away from the bed to gain a better perspective—

the big picture. A nurse delivered the shock to the electrode pads. No change, still v-fib.

"His name is Theo Pearson," Nora announced, pulling a thin nylon wallet from the pocket of his shorts. Lydia spared a glance at the charge nurse. She was petite, shorter than Lydia's five-five, and looked pretty young to be in charge of an ER this size.

Lydia watched the monitor as the amiodarone was pushed, followed by another round of electricity. Her foot tapped in time with her own pulse in an unconscious attempt to spark Theo's heart into the same steady rhythm. The dancing green lines that represented the electrical activity in his heart spiked erratically before finally resolving themselves into a regular pattern.

"V-tach. Do we have a pulse?" she asked.

"No pulse," Trey announced after palpating the carotid area. Trey's partner resumed CPR, relieving the nurse.

Lydia bounced on her toes, doubt breaching her defenses, releasing a stream of nervous sweat trickling down the back of her neck. Ventricular tachycardia was theoretically better than ventricular fibrillation, but no pulse was still dead.

She sped through the possible causes of arrest. For a healthy fourteen-year-old, drugs like cocaine or crystal meth were high on the list. Until the tox screen came back there was little she could do except run the cardiac arrest protocol.

Much as ER docs loved guidelines and protocols, Lydia knew they were really a mask to hide the real truth about medicine on the front lines—that doctors pretty much made it up as they went along.

Except Lydia was running out of ideas. And time. "How long has he been down?"

Trey answered her after glancing at the overhead clock. "Coming up on seven minutes."

She squeezed one hand tight into a fist, then released it as if flinging away pessimistic thoughts. Damn it, she hated losing. Even worse, losing a kid.

"Hang a amiodarone drip, defibrillate again at 360 and give another epi." She moved to the head of the bed, brushing against the broad-shouldered paramedic.

After the jolt of electricity finished arcing through her patient, she performed a complete reassessment. When in doubt, start from the ABC's: airway, breathing, circulation. She needed to find something to treat. The boy had been without oxygen for too long; if she was going to get him back it had to be now.

The odds were against her and her patient. Full arrest in the field, not responding to electricity or meds—Lydia had better odds winning the lottery without buying a ticket.

"He's back in v-fib," Nora announced.

She was losing him. Lydia leaned forward to listen to his breath sounds again. Then, stopped, sniffing. What was that, Pine Sol? No, it smelled more like a new car. She straightened and looked at Theo's face. Around the tape of the endotracheal tube, beneath his nose and around his mouth, a red rash like prickly heat mottled his skin.

"Hold that epi," she told Nora as the nurse was preparing to push the stimulant into the IV. "Get me propranolol, one milligram."

The room quieted. Lydia tore her attention away from her patient and saw Trey staring at her. He stood, arms crossed as if waiting to complete his own assessment on the new doc.

"Dr. Fiore, I don't think that's what you want," Nora said in a tone implying that Lydia was clearly out of her league.

Lydia straightened, met the charge nurse's gaze across the table, the patient between them. Everyone was silent, watching to see who drew first blood.

Nora stepped closer, laid one hand on the patient's arm as if protecting him from Lydia.

"Do as I say. Give him the propranolol."

"That's not AHA protocol, Dr. Fiore," Nora said in a firm

voice, her cheeks flushing so that they almost matched her red hair. A nurse didn't out-trump a physician, especially not an attending physician, yet everyone in this tight-knit team clearly deferred to Nora's authority. "American Heart Association has set guidelines for a pulseless arrest."

Pittsburgh charge nurses were no different than L.A's. They truly believed in protocols—just like they lived for paperwork, preferably done in triplicate.

Lydia grabbed the vial of propranolol from the crash cart and filled a syringe with the proper dose. "We don't have time to argue."

"Epinephrine is the drug of choice—" Nora put in.

"If you give him that epi, he's dead."

CHAPTER 2

IT WAS KIND OF NICE FOR ONCE being the person who knew it all, Amanda Mason thought as she watched the new Emergency Medicine interns report for their first shift. Unlucky stiffs had been assigned the overnight shift. Seven to seven. The witching hours. She hoped they'd brought their roller skates.

Amanda was a fourth year medical student doing her first elective of her senior year. But since she'd been in the ED—it was an Emergency Department, not a room—many times during her third year clinical rotations, it was familiar territory. It didn't hurt either that her roommate, Gina Freeman, was a third year Emergency Medicine resident and had shown her the ropes.

"Um, do you know where the suture sets are?" an intern asked, his eyes already glazed over, shoulders slumped under the weight of a lab coat bristling with hemostats, trauma shears, tape, EKG calibers, *One Minute Consult to Emergency Medicine, Nelson's Antimicrobials* and a *Harriet Lane Handbook.*

"Sure, follow me." She led him to the clean storage area, stocked with bins of various suture material: nylon, chromic, vicryl, even old fashioned silk, all available on a dizzying variety of needles. "What are you sewing?"

"Chin lac. I want some 5-0 nylon."

"Here you go." She handed him a small, green foil packet of Ethilon. He was kind of cute despite the worry lines creasing his mouth. Not too much older than she was, maybe twenty-six or so. "Are you interested in pediatrics? I saw your *Harriet Lane.*"

"Pygmy medicine? No, I'm straight EM." He turned to look at her, his thousand-yard stare fading, replaced with a gleam and a rakish smile. "I'm Jim Lazarov."

Amanda decided to ignore his derogatory comment about Pediatrics, her chosen specialty. It would be rude not to, and even though she was far from her South Carolina home, she still heard Mama's voice ringing through her mind, telling her a lady always minded her manners. "Amanda Mason. Current emergency medicine extern and future pygmy medicine practitioner."

"Extern" or "acting intern" was what fourth year medical students on elective assignments were called. Made them sound better to patients than "student doctors." With her blond hair, blue eyes and what her brothers called a "Barbie doll" face when they were in a teasing mood, Amanda had a hard enough time with patients taking her seriously without constantly reminding them that she was still only a student.

Jim shook her hand, dropping it as her words sunk in. "Student? Guess that makes you my scutmonkey. You should be sewing this smelly homeless lady instead of me."

"I'm a fourth year," Amanda protested. "I have my own patients."

"But I out rank you," he said with a pointed nod at her short lab coat which marked her as a student.

"And I out rank you," came a voice from behind them.

Jim jumped. Gina, Amanda's roommate, stood there, no lab coat, just hospital scrubs with nothing other than a pen and her ID badge to weigh her down.

"Why aren't you in there suturing Mrs. Madison like I told you, Lazarov?" she snapped, hands on her hips, straightening to her full five-ten which put her even with Jim. Gina liked being as tall as most men, never stooped or slumped, even arranged her multitude of braids so that they made her look taller and highlighted her high cheekbones. "You do know how to do a plastics closure, don't you? Because if she has a scar—"

"C'mon, she just an old homeless hag." Jim didn't meet Gina's gaze, clearly intimidated by the tall black woman, yet still compelled to talk back.

Amanda cringed as she watched—you didn't talk back to Gina, not if you knew what was good for you. And never about patient care. Gina didn't have the people-sense God gave a gopher, but she didn't let anything get in the way of her job. Oh boy, Jim was in for a night of scut duty now.

Gina's glare deepened. She stepped forward, not touching Jim but close enough that he rocked back, hitting the wall behind him. Her gaze trailed over him. The intern was dressed nicely—they all did on their first day, Amanda had noticed. But something about the tailored cut of Jim's clothing seemed to pique Gina's interest.

"Where'd you go to medical school, Lazarov?"

He shuffled his leather loafers. "Here. Pittsburgh."

"But you never did a rotation here at Angels? How'd you manage that?"

"Worked at North Hills, St. Mary's, Monroeville mainly," he mumbled. Amanda felt embarrassed for him, but she couldn't pull herself away. Watching Gina in action was fascinating. "Did one rotation at the VA. Dermatology."

Lines creased the corners of her eyes as Gina's frown deepened. "So you spent med school partying in the suburbs, learning everything you know at hospitals that dump all their non-paying patients, the complicated cases, and the stuff that's just too bothersome to deal with on a Friday night on us."

"Um, I guess so."

"Guess what? You're in the real world now. *My* world. And

no patient who crosses through that door gets a wallet biopsy. Every patient is a person and every person gets the best you got. You understanding me, Mr. Lazarov?"

He snapped to attention. "Yes'm."

"Once you're done with Mrs. Madison, there's a guy with cerebral palsy in room five that needs disimpacted and his decubiti debrided. Go. Now!" she added when Jim didn't jump fast enough.

Jim sped away, clutching his suture tray to his chest, bumping into a laundry cart before successfully navigating his way into the exam room. Gina fell back against the wall, laughing.

"You didn't have to torture him like that." Amanda felt the need to defend Jim—after all, next July first, that would be *her* bumbling her way through her first shift, trying hard not to kill anyone.

Gina merely grinned. "Sure I did. Most fun I had all day and these interns need to know who's boss. Especially a spoiled rich kid like him. Did you see those shoes?"

"You're one to talk," Amanda said, eyeing Gina's own four-hundred dollar sneakers. "Y'all are richer than God."

"Hush. Keep talking like that and I'll tell your momma about the hordes of men parading through your bedroom door," Gina said using a cartoonish southern accent and patting her ebony cheeks as if she were about to swoon. "I declare, it's just shocking."

"Liar," Amanda said with a flounce and a toss of her head. "I haven't had the pleasure of entertaining a gentleman caller since I started on the wards last year. You, however—"

She stopped as she noted a crowd of nurses and residents gathering outside the open door to the trauma room. Gina noticed as well, tapping a nearby nurse on the shoulder. "What's up?"

"It's the new attending," the nurse said. "Her first code and she's killing the patient."

"A code? Hey, why didn't anyone tell me?" Gina asked, pushing her way through the crowd. "I'm supposed to be command doc now that I'm a third year resident."

Amanda followed after her, not wanting to be left out of the fun, but certain that the EM guys never got the wobbles like she did any time there was a major case or full arrest. Emergency Medicine specialists were like surgeons—they lived for the adrenaline rush.

Given a choice, Amanda would take a nice, fat, healthy baby to cuddle rather than plunging into a trauma with its blood, guts, and gore.

CHAPTER 3

LYDIA REACHED FOR THEO'S IV, propanolol in hand. She was all too aware that a crowd had gathered, watching her. Sweat matted her scrub top to her back.

Two more people pushed inside the room, a tall black woman wearing scrubs, carrying only the bare essentials, just like Lydia, and a blond haired medical student. They both ignored Lydia to turn and look at Nora for answers.

"What's going on?" the black woman said as she quickly glanced at the code sheet and saw Lydia's orders. She challenged Lydia with a hard stare. "I'm Gina Freeman, third year Emergency Medicine resident. Third years usually run the codes around here. Probably because we know how to follow protocol."

This was turning into a downright mutiny. Great way to start her first shift. Gina and Nora stood side by side, blocking her from Theo's IV. The medical student hovered in the background, looking worried.

"Out of my way. Now." Lydia's voice surprised her—it had dropped, sounding low and dangerous, the same tone of intimidation she'd learned to ignore when gang-bangers tried it on her.

To her surprise, it was Trey who broke the impasse. The paramedic touched Nora's arm, nodded to her as if pulling rank. "Let her give it."

Nora took two stiff steps to one side, her posture straighter than a Marine gunnery sergeant's. "Dr. Fiore, I will have to report this to Dr. Cohen. If this boy dies because of your actions, I cannot let myself or my nursing staff be involved."

Lydia ignored the charge nurse and reached around Gina, who stood glaring, arms crossed in defiance. She pushed the cardiac medication into her patient's veins, eyes focused on the monitor above him. *Come on*, she urged, willing the boy's heart to resume a survivable rhythm.

The room grew quiet as the seconds stretched out, the only sound the whoosh of oxygen the respiratory therapist pushed into Theo's lungs. Ten seconds, twenty.

"I'm giving the epi," Gina announced.

"No," Lydia said firmly, her gaze locked on the monitor tracing, the syringe still clenched in her sweaty palm as her foot tapped out the seconds. She knew she was right, she had to be—but was it already too late for Theo Pearson?

Gina reached for the IV. Lydia batted her arm away, covering the IV with her hand.

"If you give him that epi, you'll kill him," she told Gina. "Look at his face, see that rash? Take a whiff of his skin and clothes. He's an inhalant abuser. Probably some kind of room deodorizer. The solvents make the heart hypersensitive to epinephrine. That's why he had such a frightened look on his face—his own adrenaline was poisoning him."

"The fight or flight reflex," Trey said, his hazel eyes fastening onto Lydia's face with an intensity that made her blink.

"That's right." She tore her gaze away from him as the luminescent green tracing on the monitor changed. The band constricting her chest relaxed. She exhaled and focused on the monitor. No longer the chaotic jumble of electricity that was v-fib, normal beats began to appear. First one, then a cascade of others followed.

"I have a pulse," the medical student yelled.

"Check his blood pressure and let's get him on a drip." The team now rushed to follow Lydia's orders, energized by the near-miss and the save. "I don't think we'll be needing this." She took the syringe of epi from Gina. "Why don't you go check on the interns, make sure everything's going okay."

Gina straightened, her jaw locked as if she was afraid of what she might say. She exchanged a glance with Nora before stalking from the room.

The rest of the staff looked at Lydia as if she'd just performed a heart transplant with a plastic fork and spoon. The same admiring expression Lydia's mother, Maria, used to get from her favorite customers. Right after she fleeced them with her best flim-flam mumbo-jumbo psychic spiel. Maria always defended herself, saying she saved as many lives as any priest or physician, that she inspired her clients, gave them hope, dreams.

Lydia shook off memories of her mother. This wasn't one of Maria's fairy tales spun for an unsuspecting mark. This was reality and Lydia knew exactly how close she'd come to losing Theo.

Once everyone had left, she leaned against the stainless steel sink, the silence of the empty trauma room embracing her. Her hands clenched against the rim of the sink, she bowed her head, took a deep breath in, held it for a second, her pulse echoing through her body, then released it.

The door opened and Trey returned. "Forgot our monitor cable." He rescued his equipment. "Good call, doc."

"I got lucky," Lydia said, pushing away from the sink, irritated that she'd spoken the truth. But it *was* only luck that there had been enough clues to lead her to the correct diagnosis.

"You know what they say. Smarter to be lucky than lucky to be smart."

Lydia shook her head, rolling her eyes. That was what Maria

had always said as well. "Too bad I don't believe in luck."

She believed in skill, knowledge, facts and the passion to use everything she had to fight for every life that passed through her hands. If that wasn't enough, she didn't know what was. Hoped she never had to find out.

Trey paused, one hand on the door, his eyes half narrowed as if he wasn't sure if he liked what he saw. "Guess if you're smart enough, luck doesn't matter. Anyway, it was a good save."

He was right. Instead of kicking herself for almost losing Theo, she should be grateful things turned out the way they had. "Thanks, Trey."

"See you around, doc."

She didn't bother to hide her smile as she watched him leave, admiring the broad shoulders and well-defined muscles his short sleeved uniform emphasized. Nice to know she seemed to have earned the respect of at least one medic in town. And a handsome one, at that.

Her smile broadened as she basked in the glow of her success. After growing up in L.A.'s foster care system, clawing her way through UCL.A. medical school and not just surviving but thriving during her grueling emergency medicine residency at the busiest trauma center in the country, Lydia was ready to handle anything Pittsburgh could throw at her.

No, she was more than ready. She was going to knock 'em dead.

Figuratively speaking, of course.

CHAPTER 4

"HOW EXACTLY DID THIS HAPPEN, MR. PERCH?" Gina asked the thirty-something Penn Dot worker with the strange, stellate shaped laceration in the center of his forehead. She'd already numbed the area and was picking out tiny bits of crumbly grey material, trying to decide on the optimal approach to putting Mr. Perch's head back together.

"Well, now," Mr. Perch answered, his voice a bit muffled by the sterile drape and the Jack Daniels he'd imbibed earlier. "It was my girlfriend."

"Your girlfriend? Did she hit you with something?" Satisfied that she'd debrided the worst of the damaged tissue, Gina began irrigating the wound.

"Nah, of course not. Sally wouldn't never hurt a flea. See, she's been steppin' out on me, seeing another guy. Rodney's his name. That's all I hear about anymore. How Rodney's so strong he can pick her up with one hand, smash a beer can on his head. So I showed her."

Nora came in, carrying Mr. Perch's tetanus booster. She gave a small shake of her head as she listened to Mr. Perch's story. "How did you show her?"

"I went over to her place and a put a cement block on the

back of my truck and I broke it with my head. I'd seen it done a thousand times on TV, knew it couldn't be that hard. Except, they must use a different kind of block or something."

"Or something," Gina said, starting to re-align the edges of the gaping hole in his forehead. A corner-stitch with vicryl and a few well placed horizontal mattress sutures brought everything together nicely.

"Nice job," Nora said appreciatively.

Gina grinned. She prided herself on her plastics closures. "Mr. Perch, maybe you need another approach to win Sally back. Something more romantic."

"Romantic? I just smashed my face open for her, what's more romantic than that?" He let out a small yelp as Nora gave him his tetanus shot.

"Maybe a walk in the country?" Gina offered, more concerned with tying her knot than Mr. Perch's love life.

"Nah. Sally gets hay fever."

"Ummm, how about poetry?" Nora suggested. "Write her a poem, tell her how you feel about her. Women are suckers for poetry."

"A poem?"

Gina had to hold her needle away from his skin as Mr. Perch wrinkled his forehead, obviously thinking hard. As hard as a brain pickled with whiskey would allow.

"I like that. I can do that."

"Just hold still for a minute and I'll have you patched up almost good as new. There'll be a bit of a scar, but women love interesting scars."

"Thanks, doc. You're the best. Both of yinz. A scar—what rhymes with scar? I know. NASCAR. Sally loves her NASCAR."

"WE'VE GOT A TRAUMA COMING IN," Nora announced, poking her head into the exam room where Lydia was guiding the medical student, Amanda, through a spinal tap on a chubby six-week-old baby.

"What is it?"

"Pedestrian versus car. Doesn't sound too bad. The medics report only a few abrasions on the patient. They're ten minutes out."

"Call the trauma alert. I'll be there as soon as I'm done with this." Lydia carefully positioned the spinal needle between the baby's lumbar vertebrae. "Until then, Gina can run it."

"You're the boss."

Lydia wasn't surprised when the charge nurse stayed to observe. It was pretty obvious Nora still didn't trust her, despite her saving Theo Pearson earlier. She inserted the spinal needle and the baby barely flinched.

"Shouldn't she be crying or fighting?" Amanda asked, her worried tone emphasizing her Southern accent.

"Absolutely. I much prefer them with energy to fight when they're this young." It was almost one in the morning and so far things had gone fairly smoothly during Lydia's first shift. Halfway home. Other than her earlier resuscitation, this baby was the sickest patient she'd seen all night.

The needle slipped into the baby's spinal canal with a small pop. She quickly withdrew the stylet, allowing the cerebral spinal fluid to flow into the collection tubes.

"Go ahead and push the antibiotics," Lydia told the nurse. She held up a tube with a few drops of fluid in it for Amanda's inspection. "What do you think?"

"It should be clear, like water. Cloudy fluid like that indicates meningitis."

"Right. Call the Peds ICU, tell them we have a customer for them." The nurse moved to the phone and Lydia turned back to

Amanda. "Next time, you do the tap. See one, do one, teach one."

Amanda beamed. She carefully wiped the Betadine from the baby's skin before re-fastening the diaper. "Do you think she'll be all right?"

"We got to her early." They almost hadn't. Lazarov, one of the interns, had wanted to discharge the baby with a diagnosis of colic, but Lydia had caught the family in time. "I hope so."

Lydia caught Nora's eye. The charge nurse was watching from inside the door, arms crossed over her chest, but nodding in grudging approval. "Amanda, do you feel comfortable explaining everything to the parents? Staying with them until the peds guys get down here?"

Amanda nodded. "No problem."

Lydia joined Nora in the hallway. "About earlier," she started.

"Dr. Fiore," the charge nurse interrupted, obviously with a rehearsed speech, "I can't have communications breaking down in the middle of a resuscitation. It's my job to protect the patient at any cost—"

"I'm sorry. I should have made my thoughts clear." Lydia didn't add that no one had given her a chance. Didn't matter. She was the command doc, it was her job to make sure everyone was on board. "I apologize."

Nora clamped her mouth shut, finally relaxing her arms, letting them fall to her sides. "It was a good call," she allowed, a smile tugging at her lips. "None of us are going to forget it anytime soon."

Their radios went off, a symphony of electronic chirps announcing the arrival of the trauma patient. Together they jogged back to the trauma bay, grabbing Tyvek gowns and gloves as they entered.

"What have we got?" Lydia asked.

A young man strapped to a back board by neon orange belts lay on the bed, his neck immobilized by a c-collar. The team, with Gina at the head of the bed in the position of command doc, was cutting off his clothes with trauma shears. Lydia recognized the same paramedic, Trey Garrison, hovering nearby, watching the respiratory tech bag oxygen into the patient.

"Twenty-eight-year-old pedestrian struck by a slow-moving vehicle. Patient developed loss of consciousness and profound respiratory distress en route," Trey announced. He reached out to adjust the face mask, securing a tighter seal. "Pulse ox was 100% the entire time, but he started having difficulty breathing."

"Respiratory distress? So much for our nice, stable patient." Lydia's heart rate bounced up a notch. "Was he thrown? Hit his head?" She joined him, ignoring Gina's glare. This wasn't a case for a resident.

"Not according to witnesses."

Lydia quickly assessed the man's airway and breathing. He had a small abrasion on his face, nothing serious, and no signs of any foreign body that he could have choked on, yet he was struggling to breathe, taking one ragged, irregular breath, then pausing before fighting for the next.

"No pneumothorax or chest trauma. The only injuries I could find were a few scrapes where his hip collided with the bumper," Gina said, not yielding her position at the head of the bed. Lydia finished her exam and had to agree.

"Rapid sequence intubation protocol," she ordered, noting with approval that the nurses had the equipment and medications ready. "I'll do this one, Gina."

Gina reluctantly stepped to one side. Lydia raced through the differential diagnosis as she moved to take control of the man's airway and help him get the oxygen he was so desperately hungry for.

"We'll need head injury precautions. He might have an epidural. Keep an eye on his vitals. Draw a trauma panel, tox screen and blood alcohol. We'll get an arterial gas as soon as he's tubed. Who's on for surgery?"

Nora answered. "Seth Cochran is the resident on call for

trauma. He hasn't answered his page."

The charge nurse sounded defensive. No wonder, if it took them this long to mobilize their trauma team. The trauma surgeons should have been here already, even though this had been billed as only a level two alert. That still meant potentially life-threatening injuries.

"Who's the trauma attending?" Lydia asked.

"Dr. Weiss."

"Forget Cochran, get Weiss down here."

The team flowed around her in the controlled chaos common to any resuscitation. Lydia slid the metal blade of the laryngoscope to lift the patient's tongue. A pool of secretions blocked her view. She reached out blindly and the suction catheter was slapped into her hand before she had to ask. After suctioning the excess saliva, she was able to intubate the young man without any difficulty.

She glanced up to see that it had been Trey who had assisted her. His frown deepened despite the monitor showing an oxygen saturation of one hundred percent. Couldn't get any better than that. But instead of improving, the patient's blood pressure plummeted.

"Where's trauma?" she asked again. Back in L.A., they'd already be down, working with her to stabilize the patient.

"They never answered. I'll page them again," Nora said.

"Gina, help me do another secondary survey." Together they examined the patient from head to toe once again, searching for any additional injuries. Lydia did a FAST exam with the portable ultrasound, looking inside his abdomen and chest. Still nothing to cause his difficulty breathing. Which meant nothing she could fix.

Lydia gently laced her fingers through the patient's thick blond hair, palpating the skull below. No signs of a fracture, no reason for him to be comatose, unless there was a hidden brain contusion or bleed. But that didn't fit the picture—his blood pressure would be high, his pulse low—the opposite of what she was finding. An alarm sounded, its irritating beep jangling her nerves as it signaled a fall in blood pressure.

"We must be missing something. Did the surgeons answer?" She tried without success to keep the frustration from her voice. Her patient was deteriorating and she had no idea why.

"Dr. Weiss is in the OR," Nora said. "He's sending his resident down."

Lydia didn't need any snotty-nosed resident second guessing her, but it was better than nothing. She moved out of the way of the X-ray techs who were shooting films of the cervical spine, chest and pelvis.

"I can't get a pressure," Gina said as the monitor alarm grew piercingly ominous.

"Hang two units of Oneg. DPL tray," Lydia ordered, staring at the monitor, trying to make sense of the readings it was giving her. "Where the hell is that surgeon? Is this how you people usually run your traumas?"

"Our doctors have the best resuscitation rate in the city," Nora told her coldly, reminding her once more that Lydia was the outsider here.

Trey opened the lavage tray without contaminating anything on it as Lydia snapped on a pair of sterile gloves. The medic frowned, giving her a quick nod of encouragement. She was grasping at straws and he knew it. But if straws were all you had, that's what you went with. No way she was going to give up without a fight.

Lydia dumped Betadine over the patient's abdomen and stabbed a lavage catheter into the space around the intestines, hoping to find a source of blood loss to explain his condition. The fluid she withdrew was stubbornly clear. No help there.

"Heart rate's bradying down," Gina announced.

The entire team, including Trey and his partner, looked to Lydia. She rocked back on her heels, her gaze raking over her patient, head to toe. Right now she had no answers. Could it be spinal shock? If so, she had to be careful not to give him too much fluid. But if the shock was caused by blood loss, then fluid was what could save his life. Her stomach twisted as she tapped her foot, frustrated she couldn't pinpoint the injury killing her patient.

"Atropine half a milligram. Push that blood. Call CAT scan, we'll need a head, spine, chest and belly," she ordered, going for the shot-gun approach.

Nora rushed to the phone as the X-ray tech returned with the films taken earlier. Lydia flipped the films onto the view box, happy to have an excuse to turn away from her bewildered team and to have a few moments to think. She bounced up and down on her toes as she scrutinized the films.

The X-rays were distinctly unilluminating. "Everything looks good. No pnemothorax, no widened mediastinum, no obvious cervical spine fracture." Even the pelvis, which had impacted the car's bumper, looked normal. Gina joined her at the view box, nodded her agreement.

"What the hell is going on here?" Lydia examined her patient once more. He was blond, tanned, muscular. Looked healthy, like he worked out and took good care of himself. No tattoos, no needle tracks, no surgical scars.

"Labs are back," Nora announced. "All normal, blood alcohol is only point oh-six."

Gina glanced at Lydia as if daring her to manufacture a diagnosis from the normal findings.

Lydia turned away. She didn't have any answers and everything she did seemed to only make things worse. She stripped her Betadine-stained gloves off, twisting them into a tight ball and dumping them in the trash before grabbing a new pair. Damn it, she must have missed something—but what?

"I lost his pulse!" Gina called out.

Rushing back to her patient's side, Lydia quickly assessed his airway as Trey began CPR. The tube was in place, the oxygen hooked up, no problems there. The monitor showed a flat line—not even something she could shock.

"Epi, push another unit of blood, let's needle his chest." She needed to both discover the cause of his deterioration and treat it simultaneously. If she didn't move fast, he would be dead.

Lydia spiked a large-bore catheter through the man's chest wall. Nothing—no rush of air that would indicate a collapsed lung. Gina did the same to the opposite side. Nothing there either. Lydia wasn't totally surprised—the man's oxygen level was still normal, and it was the first thing that should have fallen if he had dropped a lung.

She grabbed the labs. What had she missed? But everything looked good, except for a mild metabolic acidosis.

Nora spoke up from her position at the chart table. She was holding a driver's license in her hand. "Dr. Fiore, I think you should know who your patient is," she said, sounding shaken.

"I don't care who he is," Lydia told her, her voice sharper than she'd intended. "I just want to find out what's wrong with him so I can treat it." She'd exhausted every standard resuscitation protocol. Time for the not-so-standard.

"High dose epi," she ordered. The patient's heart persisted in its standstill. "Let's look at his heart again." She reached for the ultrasound transducer and halted CPR just long enough to scan the cardiac region. No evidence of fluid around the heart, structurally it looked normal. It simply refused to beat.

She paced back and forth, feeling as trapped and helpless as her patient. She tried not to look at the clock, but she knew he'd been down too long. A body could only go without oxygen for a short time and her patient's time had been up awhile ago. It galled her to admit defeat, but her patient was dead. She only wished to hell that she knew what killed him.

You're not God. There would be no miracles here tonight. "Stop CPR, check his pulse," she ordered in a low voice.

Garrison pulled back from the table, his fingers on the carotid pulse, watching the clock's second hand. Lydia held her breath, her eyes fixed on the monitor, willing it to spark to life. Nothing.

The rest of the team remained silent. Everyone avoided Lydia's gaze, stepping away from the table and into the shadows along the edge of the room.

"No pulse," Trey said after feeling it for a full minute.

"Any objections to calling it?" Lydia was surprised by how normal her voice sounded. It sounded like she knew what she was doing, was in command. It lied.

One by one the staff shook their heads. Gina and Trey were the only ones who met her gaze. The resident with a defiant look; the medic with one approaching sorrow or disappointment, she wasn't certain which. "Okay, time of death 12:56 am."

As soon as the words left her lips, a wave of exhaustion plowed into Lydia. Her scrubs stuck to her skin, soaked with the sweat of her failed efforts to combat death.

She reached out for her patient. Gently, she laid his hands over his abdomen before disconnecting the bag from the endotracheal tube. The nurses would do the rest, prepare him for his family to view. But Lydia needed to touch him one last time, to reassure herself she'd done everything humanly possible.

A religious person might have sent a prayer to speed the soul on its way, but she'd never had much faith. Not in people, not in religions, and not in the God who watched as the world spun out in tragedies like this. All she could do was say goodbye. And promise herself that she'd find out why he died so it wouldn't happen again.

"Who the hell keeps paging me?" a voice thundered from the hallway. "Can't you people handle a simple trauma?"

Lydia left the room. A tall man in surgeon's scrubs, still wearing a paper hat fresh from the OR, stood outside the door. His name tag hung from the pocket of his scrubs and read: Elliot Weiss, Chief of Surgery.

"What took you so long?" She had to tilt her head back to

meet Weiss's eyes. "Where's your resident? Why did no one answer our pages?"

The surgeon stopped and crossed his arms over his chest, glaring down at her. "And you would be?" he asked in a haughty voice.

"Lydia Fiore, the new ER attending."

"Dr. Fiore, for your information, my resident was called to a code in the surgical ICU. Life and death situations take precedent over traffic accidents with minor injuries."

"You're too late to help my patient, so I guess we won't be needing your services after all, Dr. Weiss." She fought and lost the battle to keep the sarcasm from her voice. Her knees trembled; she felt ready to fall down as adrenaline fled from her body.

Weiss ignored her accusation. "If you don't need me, then why the hell do you people keep paging me?" He held his beeper in front of her face to prove his point.

"I paged you, Dr. Weiss." Nora joined them in the doorway. She wiped her hand against her face as if erasing the lines left behind by her trauma mask. "I'm so sorry," she said in a quiet voice, holding out a worn leather wallet for his inspection.

Lydia glanced up at the sound of Nora's voice. She knew that tone—it was one she'd used more times than she could count. A tone of preparation, of foreboding. What was going on here?

Weiss took the billfold and glanced inside. His tanned face turned ashen as he took a ragged breath. He blew it out, collapsing in on himself, as if without the air propping him up, he was less of a man. The wallet fell from his limp fingers, thudding to the floor.

"No, it can't be." He pushed past them into the trauma room. "Jonah!"

Lydia looked at Nora, then bent to retrieve the wallet Weiss had dropped. The driver's license belonged to a Jonah Weiss, address on Shady Avenue.

"His son," Nora said.

CHAPTER 5

HIS SON.

Lydia leaned against the cold tile wall, blinking back memories, knowing exactly how Elliot Weiss felt—a collision of anger and fear that quaked your hands and sent blood pounding through your head. A few breaths later, she steeled herself and pushed off the wall. She opened the door to the resuscitation room. Weiss had pulled the drape back from his son's lifeless body.

"What the hell have you done?" He whirled on her. The color had drained from his face, yet his eyes sparked in the glare of the overhead lights.

"Someone get me a scalpel and a thoracotomy tray. I need to crack his chest." He pounded his fist on his son's sternum. "Damn it, Jonah, come back." The words emerged in a strangled whisper. "Why are you just standing there? Move it!"

She approached the distraught father and placed a hand on his arm. "He's gone. There was nothing we could do."

He slapped her hand away, his entire body jerking with the movement. "You killed him, you killed my son."

A large man, Elliot Weiss towered over her, his blue eyes blazing. He clenched her arms, his weight almost pulling her off balance. Suddenly he released her, stepping back as if she was contaminated.

"Get out of here," he muttered in a low voice that quickly escalated. "Get out of my sight, get the hell out of my hospital!"

Lydia held her ground. He wasn't a surgeon right now, he was a grieving father whose son had been wrenched from him without warning.

"We did everything possible." She hoped her voice didn't betray the nagging uncertainty she felt about Jonah's death. Had she missed something? Something that might have saved his life?

"Leave now," he replied, his voice a low growl as he turned back to his son's body. "Just leave me with my son."

Lydia stepped toward the doorway. Wished she could deny the flush of humiliation that burned her cheeks when she saw the ER staff waiting beyond, staring at her. Was it just a few hours ago she had proven herself, earned their admiration? Now they looked at her with pity and contempt. Even the medics.

"I hope you're proud of the job you did here tonight, Dr. Fiore." Elliot Weiss's voice carried clearly despite the fact he didn't raise his head or look at her, his gaze remaining focused on his son's corpse. "Because I guarantee, tonight is the last night you will practice medicine in this hospital."

She kept walking, her footsteps small, sharp taps against the hard floor, carrying her stiffly held body past the staff, past Trey and his partner. Nothing else she could do except go on to the next patient.

And try hard not to kill them.

AMANDA SAT IN THE LOW SLUNG VINYL CHAIR in the waiting area. The Millers had left, a pediatric resident guiding them up to the ICU where they could see their baby. She felt so bad for them. They were such nice people, had done all the right things. She'd tried to comfort them, praise them for bringing in their daughter right away instead of waiting, but they didn't care about any of that. What they wanted from her was the one thing no one could give them: a guarantee that their baby would live.

She leaned forward, started to stand. Her left leg crumbled, pins and needles shooting through it. She dropped back into the chair, glanced around. No one seemed to notice her sudden clumsiness.

It was a fight to keep her face expressionless as she bent down and massaged her lower leg. She could barely feel her fingers kneading her calf muscles through the thin cotton of her scrub pants. Feet fall asleep all the time, nothing to worry about, she told herself. It didn't mean anything.

She would have believed herself if her leg going dead on her wasn't the latest in a series of strange occurrences. Sudden dizzy spells where she'd see double and the room would spin around her. An uncontrollable twitch along her quadriceps muscles, jolting through her, keeping her awake at night, making her muscles cramp and buckle during the day at random intervals.

Stress, fatigue, the poor diet and long hours of a medical student. That's all it was. She'd carefully observed her symptoms, researched them all, chiding herself for having the infamous med student syndrome, known to the lay world as hypochondriasis. None of the symptoms followed any known pattern, none fit into any syndrome or disease process she could find.

It was all in her head. Was that better or worse than having real symptoms?

Amanda dropped her hands, stared without blinking at the dingy grey linoleum until its patterns swirled like anvil clouds, harbingers of the storms that routinely swept through her coastal hometown. She loved those storms, kept a chair beside her window back home so she could watch the dance of wind and lightning. The next day the sky would be a crisp, radiant blue, scrubbed clean, as were the sweet grass marshes and sandy beaches. The next day everything would be fine as always.

Her mouth suddenly dry, she licked her lips, swallowed and denied the taste of fear burning her throat. Everything would be fine. Just fine.

She forced herself to smile. A smile on the outside left you smiling on the inside, Mama would say. She couldn't afford to be sick—not money-wise or time-wise—therefore, she wasn't sick. That's all there was to it.

She kicked her leg against the floor, the pins and needles finally fading. Bracing herself on the chair, she stood, stomped her foot a few times before trusting her weight to it. Then she gingerly walked through the waiting room, past the triage nurse and back into the ED.

"Where have you been?" Gina said, rushing down the hall at her usual head-long pace. "You won't believe what happened. The new attending killed Dr. Weiss's son."

NORA PACED THE HALLWAY, finding it difficult to ignore the muffled sounds of grief penetrating the closed door of Trauma One. She stopped with her hand on the door, ready to go in to try her best to help Dr. Weiss, when footsteps sounded behind her.

"Is he still in there?" Seth Cochran, the fourth year surgical resident on call for trauma, asked.

Seth looked tired, even more than usual for surgeons who routinely maxed out their allotted eighty-hour workweeks. His brown hair was rumpled, a side effect of long hours spent wearing surgical caps, his cheeks sunken and eyes red-rimmed. He adjusted the drawstring on his scrub pants, kept his gaze cast down, not looking directly at the closed door, as if death were contagious.

"We're going to need the room. But I hate to disturb him," Nora said, choking back the urge to ask the questions she really wanted Seth to answer. Like why he looked so bad, why he hadn't answered the trauma alert, what was going on with him?

"I didn't even know Weiss had a son."

"Jonah. His name was Jonah."

Seth jiggled his trauma shears, spinning them on his fingers like an Old West gunslinger. He still didn't look her in the face. His cheeks were flushed. Like he was sick or something. Nora almost raised a hand to feel his forehead, even though he would hate the public display of affection.

"Why didn't you answer your page?"

"Busy. You know how it goes. Can only be one place at a time." He shifted from one foot to another. "How long do you think he'll be?"

Insensitive even for Seth. But he'd been acting funny for a few weeks, spending more time with the dog than with Nora. She'd thought it a good idea, their getting a dog together. After all, they'd been dating for almost a year, living together for three months. It had seemed like the natural next step. Short of the "M" word, of course. She loved to fantasize about a wedding, about babies—rambunctious boys all looking like Seth with his dark Huck Finn eyes and Tom Sawyer mischievousness.

Until a few weeks ago, it felt like that was exactly where she and Seth were headed.

The door opened before she could muster the courage to simply flat out ask him what was wrong. Elliot Weiss emerged, taking care to shut the door behind him as if their voices might disturb Jonah.

"Nora." He let her name hang in accusation. "How could you let her do this? That woman, Fiore."

"Dr. Weiss, believe me, we did everything we could."

He was shaking his head before she finished. "No. I don't

believe it. She missed something. She killed my son."

Nora had no idea what to say to that. She glanced sideways down the hall, glad that Dr. Fiore was busy in the OB-Gyn room, out of sight. If she knew what was good for her, she'd stay there all night.

"Is there anything I can do?" Seth put in.

Weiss brushed his hands on his scrubs. "Keep an eye on everyone upstairs. Check Lipton's post-op orders on our bowel resection. And for godsakes, don't kill anyone."

He stalked down the hallway, Seth and Nora following a few steps behind. "Nora, get me Mark Cohen on the phone. And Tillman."

"Oliver Tillman? The CEO?" Nora rushed after him. Surely he didn't expect her to wake the head of the hospital at two-thirty in the morning? Why? They couldn't do anything to Dr. Fiore in the middle of the night, it took the entire Executive Committee to censure a physician. Nora wasn't even sure that Lydia Fiore had done anything wrong. Despite her youth, she seemed as good as any of the other ED physicians, better than some.

"Of course, Oliver Tillman," Weiss replied, rounding on her with a piercing look that forced Nora back a step. "I want that woman out of here. Now."

Nora knew Weiss was used to getting his way whenever he threw his weight around in the OR. But this wasn't the OR, this was her department and she was damned if she was going to start a witch hunt.

She grabbed the phone and dialed Mark Cohen's home number. Mark could handle Weiss, maybe keep Tillman out of this. For Dr. Fiore's sake, she hoped so.

CHAPTER 6

"WE NEED TO TALK." Lydia glanced up from her laceration repair to see Mark Cohen standing beside the curtain. She'd known that sooner or later someone would call him. She'd hoped it would be later.

"I'll just be a few minutes." She was surprised at how normal her voice sounded. As if nothing had changed since she'd last seen him, nine hours ago.

"Meet me in my office when you're done." He sounded tired and the look on his face definitely wasn't the same friendly grin which had greeted her at the start of her shift.

Of course, that was before she let the Chief of Surgery's son die.

Her breath caught, couldn't make it all the way down her lungs. It was as if a malignant mass pressed against her heart and chest, threatening to choke her. And it kept on growing, twisting her gut, an unbearable pressure.

Forcing herself to ignore it, she continued the rhythmic movements of placing stitches, taking care to evert the wound edges and exert just the right amount of tension on the nylon. The middle-aged drunk would have little to no scar—if he ever sobered up enough to notice.

It was a little after four in the morning. Emergency departments were usually at their quietest then, but tonight was exceptionally somber. Lydia was glad to have found this quiet corner and an even quieter patient, discounting his occasional snore, to occupy her time. To keep her out of range of the whispers and stares that were becoming more hostile. To give her time to think.

She'd lost patients before—hell, every physician had—but none where she felt so confused about the outcome. There had been plenty of cases that made her angry or sad. Abuses of the system, abuses of the flesh. But in none of them had she felt this burden of accountability. If only she knew why Jonah Weiss died... A tremor of uncertainty shook her hand holding the needle-driver.

She'd lost patients before, but she'd never faced the possibility that she had killed one.

It took her two swipes with the scissors to cut the last suture. Mr. Elizar didn't notice, his blissful slumber undisturbed. Finally, she went to face Mark Cohen.

Lydia paused outside his office, took several deep breaths, forcing away the black spots that kept circling her vision. Then she knocked and entered.

As Chief of Emergency Services, Mark rated an office suite just down the hall from the administrative wing of the hospital. Unlike his neighbors in administration, he had no plush carpeting, his desk was a scarred and battered relic, and his only other furniture consisted of ceiling-high bookcases that lined the walls and two mismatched, shabbily upholstered chairs. Instead of expensive artwork coordinated by interior designers or fancy framed diplomas, the little free space on his walls was crammed with colorful originals done in watercolors and crayon, courtesy of his six children. His desk was covered with stacks of files and binders, but Mark seemed to have a distinct gift for creating order from chaos.

He sat at his desk, watching a video playing on a small TV/DVD player. Lydia cringed, realizing it was the tape of the Jonah

Weiss resuscitation.

Cameras in the trauma rooms began filming as soon as the lights were turned on, standard procedure for a teaching hospital like Angels. The videos would be reviewed at the weekly Morbidity and Mortality conferences where protocols and procedures were discussed and mistakes dissected.

He'd just gotten to the part where she had told Nora she didn't care who her patient was. Her voice sounded shrill and the expression on her face when he paused the playback was edged with desperation.

She looked away from her own image frozen on the screen. That wasn't how it was. Surely she hadn't snapped like that, come so close to losing it.

"I'll be finishing your shift," Mark said, his gaze still on the TV screen.

"I can finish my shift." She sounded defensive, weak. It wasn't like she was going to kill anyone else in the next three hours—at least she sure as hell hoped not. She planted her feet flat on the floor and sat up straight, facing him with what she hoped was a fearless expression.

"No, you can't." The tone of his voice allowed no argument. "Effective immediately, you're on probation. No patient care except under my direct supervision."

"You're treating me like a medical student? That's crazy. For how long?"

"Until the Executive Committee meets on Friday and decides whether or not to terminate your privileges."

"Terminate?" Things were far worse than she thought. She'd been expecting a chart review, a good hammering during next week's M and M. But getting fired? "You can't do that. Mark—"

He held up a hand and her protest sputtered to a halt. Probably for the best since she had no idea what to say anyway.

"It's not up to me. I'm sorry. This comes from the top. Oliver

Tillman, our CEO. The Executive Committee will also be considering any further action in addition to termination of your employment."

Lydia considered that, knowing it wasn't his fault. With the hospital's CEO involved, her fate was out of Mark's hands. She might not only be out of a job, but if a complaint was filed with the State Medical Board, she might be out of a career. She gripped the wooden seat frame as her thoughts spiraled out of control. Probably a malpractice or wrongful death action as well. Meaning her life as she knew it was over. July first, the most dangerous day of the year.

Mark sighed and rose to turn the TV off, ignoring the remote control. His posture was stooped. He hesitated before turning back to her. "I've reviewed the tapes of both of your resuscitations tonight," he said, returning to sit behind the desk. "That was a good call on the Pearson boy."

She looked up. His voice was more familiar now, no longer the grim reaper delivering bad news. He sounded almost encouraging.

"I also reviewed your dictation and the nurses' notes from the Weiss case. You want to give me your version of what happened?"

Here was her chance to clear her name. If only she knew what *had* happened in that resuscitation room.

"When the initial call came in things didn't sound so bad," she began, remembering the baby with the fever and presumed meningitis. Before she left, she needed to call the ICU to check on her. "I called a trauma alert anyway," she went on, "because of the mechanism of injury. The next I heard the patient was in the room. He'd deteriorated en route and the medics didn't have a chance to call in."

Mark nodded, things like that happened, you couldn't always control them. "What did your initial assessment reveal?"

She raised her hands in frustration, then quickly dropped them back in her lap and grasped them together, forcing them into submission.

"I couldn't find anything to treat. I wanted to take him to CT and scan him, but he arrested before I got him there."

Mark was silent for a few moments. Lydia knew it sounded weak. Maybe she'd be better off letting the tape and her actions speak for her. Then she remembered the look on her face when he had paused the tape. She'd lost control of the situation. One thing ER doctors and surgeons had in common was a need to always remain in control.

"Take me through what you were thinking," he broke the silence.

"Spinal shock, severe cerebral contusion, epidural, retroperitoneal bleed, aortic dissection, but nothing fit the clinical presentation." She paused, her mouth dry, wishing for a glass, a sip, a taste of water. "Will there be an autopsy?"

There had to be. Her palms were sweating but she didn't wipe them on her scrubs, instead kept them clenched so tight that her fingers went cold and numb. A post-mortem exam was her only hope to find out what had caused Jonah Weiss's death. But if the results revealed she was at fault, her career was over.

She rocked forward in her seat. She needed to know. She couldn't live with herself not knowing, much less continue working with this doubt clouding her mind. If she was to blame, what would she do without medicine? The words blurred in her mind. If she didn't have her work, what would she have left?

"Elliot Weiss requested an autopsy," Mark said. "It's scheduled for nine this morning."

That surprised her. In L.A. it took weeks to schedule a routine autopsy; even homicides often had to wait a few days. The thought of the autopsy frightened her but at least she wouldn't be kept waiting to learn if she was guilty.

"Weiss has also contacted the District Attorney's office," Mark continued, his voice once more emotionless. "Depending on the results of the autopsy, a criminal complaint may be filed."

Lydia's heart stuttered. Losing her job was bad enough, but going to jail? "Criminal charges? You can't be serious. I've never heard—"

"Negligent homicide, involuntary manslaughter." Mark's words battered at her defenses, but she held herself straight, kept her gaze on him even if his face did waver out of focus. "I suggest you retain an attorney. Since you're on probation, you won't be able to use the hospital's legal services."

A lawyer? What did he expect her to do? Flip through the yellow pages and let a perfect stranger with a bold-print ad take control of her destiny? Not likely.

Mark came around his desk and propped himself on one corner, ignoring the cascade of reports sliding to the ground. "This isn't going to go away, and it's deadly serious. You could lose everything, Lydia."

She nodded numbly, her lips compressed so tight she could feel the blood drain from them.

"I know you don't know anyone here in Pittsburgh," he continued in a fatherly tone, "so I put together a list of some reputable attorneys." He handed her a sheet of paper. She glanced at it, unable to force the characters into focus. "The name at the top, Michelle Cohen, is my sister. If you don't think there's any conflict of interest, I would highly recommend her."

She looked up at him, the enormity of her predicament weighing on her. "Do *you* think there's a conflict of interest?" she asked, dreading yet needing his answer. "Mark, do you think there was anything else I could have done? Would you have done anything different?"

"Honestly, Lydia," he finally replied, "I think you performed admirably."

She sat up straighter, his words lifting some of the weight from her. Some, but not all. "Then how the hell can Tillman and the Executive Committee treat me worse than a common criminal, presumed guilty?"

"Pittsburgh isn't L.A. Especially when it comes to men in power, like Elliot Weiss. And," he cleared his throat, obviously not enjoying being forced to play the heavy, "the autopsy may prove both of us wrong."

Silence settled between them. Lydia unclenched her hands, laying them flat on her thighs and holding them still, restraining the slight tremble vibrating through them as the impact of his words hit home.

It was going to take a miracle for her to get her privileges back even if the autopsy revealed she hadn't missed anything. There would always be that shadow of doubt, just enough for the powers-that-be to rule against her. Better safe than sorry, they would say. Can't take the risk of something like that happening to one of our children.

"Go home, Lydia," Mark said. "Get some rest."

She pushed herself up to standing. It took more effort than she would have imagined. "I was supposed to do a ride-along with Med Seven on Wednesday."

Mark looked at her, eyes narrowed in concern. "Don't you want to take some time off?"

"To do what? Feel sorry for myself, brush up on my waitressing skills?" The edge in her voice startled her. "Sorry. I don't mean to take it out on you. But I need to keep busy. I could go as an observer. Hands off, no patient care."

"We occasionally arrange for civilians to ride with the squads," he replied, obviously not thrilled with the idea.

"Please, Mark." She hated that it came out sounding like begging. "I need to feel like I'm still doing something."

"All right. But absolutely no patient care, do you understand? If I hear of you so much as putting a Band-Aid on someone, I won't be able to defend you. Breaking your probation could mean immediate dismissal."

She nodded. Hard to believe how much a routine ride-along had come to mean to her. She stood there a minute, trying to center her thoughts on where she needed to go next, what she needed to do. The door swam in her vision, seemed an impossibly long way off. Finally she focused on one foot, then the other until she was out the door. Her body moved with an unfamiliar stiffness, her bones replaced by brittle shards, ready to shatter.

Lydia refused to think of the possibility that Jonah Weiss might be her last patient. Refused to think that he was the last person she would ever treat.Refused to think that she might never practice medicine again.

CHAPTER 7

NORA HUNG UP THE PHONE, laughing, and turned to Gina who was finishing some charting. "Got one for you, Gina."

"What is it?"

"Ankle injury. Triage says it's pretty swollen."

"Give it to Lazarov. Even he can't kill a sprained ankle."

"Sorry. Patient asked for you personally."

"Me?"

The sliding doors to triage opened and a nursing assistant appeared, pushing a man in a wheelchair, one leg up, ice packs lined up from foot to knee.

"Mr. Perch, what happened?" Gina asked, joining them.

Mr. Perch gave her a smile and waved at Nora who took over for the nursing assistant and wheeled him into an exam room. "I took your advice, Nurse Nora. That's how I hurt myself."

"You hurt your leg writing poetry?"

Gina and Nora each took one of his arms and leveraged him onto the table. He grunted, expelling a cloud of whiskey and stale cigarettes. At least he hadn't messed up her laceration repair, Gina saw as she checked him out.

"Well now, Sally is so mad at me, I figured she would just tear up any letter I sent her. But she drives the Liberty tubes every day to work, so I figured I'd write my poem, I call it *Ode to NASCAR*, and put it some place where she could see it."

Gina exchanged a glance at Nora. "You didn't."

"Yep. Climbed part way up the mountain and was just starting to spray paint the first line on the entrance to the tunnel when I lost my footing and slid the entire way back down."

Nora turned away, her face scarlet and shoulders shaking with laughter. Gina fought to keep a straight face as she examined his leg. He didn't seem in too much pain, but he was still drunk enough that he probably couldn't feel much anyway.

"You definitely have a sprain, Mr. Perch. And I think you broke one of the bones in your foot. We're going to get some X-rays and get you all patched up. You won't be able to drive for awhile." Given his tendencies to drink and drive, that was probably for the best.

He grinned. "You're the best, doc. So along with a broken heart, I've got a broken foot? Sounds like that might make a good poem on it's own, don't it?"

Both Nora and Gina violently shook their heads. "No more poetry for you, Mr. Perch."

"Why don't you take Sally to the fireworks on the Fourth?" Nora suggested.

Gina shot a glare at Nora—sending this guy to a fireworks display was an invitation to get half the city burned down. "Maybe instead of fireworks, you could just stay home and cook her dinner?"

Oh hell, now she'd probably just condemned Mr. Perch's entire neighborhood. "Or you could call for carry-out?"

LYDIA CHANGED BACK INTO HER STREET CLOTHES, slunk out

through the ER's rear entrance, and dragged her feet along the empty street, her only company the birds stirring among the gravestones in the cemetery beside the hospital. The cemetery was old and large, taking up several city blocks and surrounded by a high wrought iron fence. Ancient maples and oaks spread blankets of shade over the graves, giving the sprawling acreage of green grass and white granite a serene appearance.

She turned the corner, heading toward the inexpensive motel where she was staying, and was immediately deluged by the sounds of traffic on Penn Avenue. Busy even at this early hour, not quite six am. The heavy-sweet scent of fresh bread drifted up from the bakery on the corner. Usually that smell would have her salivating, gnawing with hunger, but this morning it made her feel unaccountably alone.

The feeling didn't dissipate after she ducked into her motel room, decorated in muted shades of orange and brown sure to inspire despair. She gazed longingly at her climbing gear and long board propped up in the corner—no chance for a run at some Mackers or even the hint of an ocean breeze, not here. Pittsburgh's three rivers offered no hope of a fix for her surfing jones.

She stripped free of her jeans and threw on running clothes. There was no way she'd be able to sleep, not with her mind spinning faster than a hamster on its wheel. Movement, sweat, pounding feet were her best chance of a cure.

Tucking her room key into her pocket, she ran out, heading across Penn and back past Angels of Mercy into the residential area beyond it. The houses lining both sides of the street were quiet, peaceful. Yellow brick rowhouses, modest two story framed homes with postage stamp yards, the occasional red brick tudor-wannabee thrown in for variety.

The sun finally revealed its profile above the collection of rooftops. Roses and peonies scented the air, vying for attention with riotous color. More than one early-rising housewife was out sweeping her front stoop, squinting suspiciously at the strange woman pounding the broken pavement.

It was hard to accept that this idyllic contentment was reality for so many. To the people living here, the world Lydia grew up in would be the stuff of sensationalistic news specials, horror films, and nightmares. Her childhood was spent living on the streets of L.A. with her mother, Maria. Typical of their unusual mother-child relationship, from the time Lydia was a toddler it was always "Maria", never "Mom", "mother", or "Mommy." Maria was the child and Lydia the one forced to care for them both, to fight and scrabble to protect what little they had.

After Maria died, Lydia was shuffled around L.A.'s foster care system until she was emancipated, sent back out on the streets to fend for herself with a garbage bag filled with her possessions and two hundred dollars in her pocket. That was back when she was eighteen. Felt like a lifetime ago.

Sometimes, Lydia still lay awake at night wondering what it would have been like if her mother hadn't been killed, if they had settled down, actually lived in a house, a real home. She didn't think she would have minded having a home with a big tree stretching its branches over her porch, watching out for her.

Maria would have hated it, spending every night in the same place. As a child, having a home was all Lydia had dreamt of. Even now, thirty years old, eighteen years after Marie's death, she still sometimes woke with an aching emptiness in her stomach, fragments of images from her dream home haunting her.

Pittsburgh was her chance to finally make those dreams come true. The enormity of what she might lose if she was found responsible for Jonah Weiss's death hit her hard. She'd been in fights before: street fights requiring dirty tricks and cunning, fights to save patients with all her knowledge and skill, fights to stay in control despite emotions swirling all around her.

Nothing like this, though. A fight where none of her defense mechanisms would save her, where her survival depended on the opinions of strangers. She paused on a street named Rosetta, doubled over, catching her breath. It hurt too much to breathe, to inhale the morning scent of pancakes and sausage and sunshine.

She ground her heel into the pavement, pushing off into a punishing sprint, racing around the corner and back toward the more familiar sights and sounds of traffic and exhaust fumes.

Maybe she should have cracked Jonah's chest. It wasn't indicated in blunt trauma cases like his and the odds were a million to one that he would have survived, but she could have tried. Or maybe if she'd pushed the blood faster–or had she killed him with too much fluid, too fast?

Her thoughts twisted like a moebius strip. No matter where she started, she always ended back at the same place. With one dead man. Her patient. He'd deserved the best she could give him, and she couldn't convince herself that was what he'd received.

Damn it, what had she missed? There had to have been something.

She kept running until the sun was well above the rooftops and the city streets were congested with morning rush hour traffic, the sounds of horns blaring and brakes squealing drowning out her thoughts. Then she returned to her motel room, showered and changed, preparing for the inquisition.

CHAPTER 8

GINA LEANED BACK AGAINST THE DESK at the nurses' station. Seven am. A clear board, other than patients waiting for beds upstairs. Perfect way to end a shift. "Anyone seen Lazarov?"

"Who?" the clerk asked, already shrugging out of his lab coat even though his replacement hadn't yet arrived.

"The intern. Mr. GQ."

"I asked Therese to instruct him in the fine art of cleaning up after a Code Brown," Nora said. She handed her trauma radio over to Rachel, the charge nurse on days, and joined Gina. "Jackass thought he could leave it for my nurses to deal with."

The thought of Lazarov getting his manicured hands and Brooks Brothers shirt dirty made Gina smile. "Guess he's found out rule number one of life in the ER: scut rolls downhill."

"And interns are at the bottom of the food chain."

They were interrupted by the sight of Mark Cohen accompanied by a nervous looking college-aged kid. "Gina, Nora," he said. "Are you two back on tonight?"

"No, boss," Gina answered, watching as the kid almost knocked over a tray of urine specimens. Nora quickly straightened the tray, moving it out of harm's way. "We're both off."

"Oh well, I'll have to find someone else. This is Bob Brown," he gestured to the kid. "He's a student from Pitt, going to be shadowing some of our night shift workers for an article he's writing."

"Self-reported Stress Levels in Night Shift Medical Workers," Bob volunteered, reaching a hand out to shake. "It's for my honor's thesis."

"Nice to meet you, Bob," Nora said. "Are you pre-med?"

"Yes ma'am. Not sure about much else, not yet at any rate."

Gina smiled, maybe here was one way to make sure Lazarov actually got some work done during a shift. "You need someone to tag along with? Why not Jim Lazarov?"

"I hadn't thought of an intern," Mark said, "but it's a good idea. No one's more stressed than they are, especially this early in the year." He explained to Bob, "Our start of the year is July first, the day the new interns start. I'll talk to Jim. In the meantime, let's get you a volunteer jacket and visitor's pass."

"Nice meeting you, ladies," Bob said as he trailed after Mark like a lost puppy.

"They make them younger every year," Gina muttered.

"We were never that young," Nora said with a laugh. "You headed to Grand Rounds?"

"Soon as Amanda gets here." Gina yawned and stretched. Grand Rounds was from eight until eleven, two hours of lectures followed by the dreaded yet much anticipated Morbidity and Mortality. Most of the ED attendings not on duty, many of the nurses, some medics, and all of the residents and medical students on service would be in attendance.

Most of the residents slept the first two hours, unless the attendings kept them awake with an inspired lecture, or less-inspired and more mean-spirited pimping: the arcane tradition of asking esoteric questions no one knew the answers to. Then came the M and M case review. The residents involved in the case would be grilled, roasted in front of their peers in a perverted sort of cannibalistic ritual. Scutmonkey served fresh with a side of humble pie.

"I'll save you guys seats. Want to do lunch after?" Nora glanced both ways, leaned forward. "I want to talk to you about what happened. With Dr. Weiss's son. Do you think we screwed up?"

Gina rubbed her wrist, thinking. The case puzzled her as well. As nice as it had been to see the cocky new attending get busted down a notch, she hated to see any code go sour. "Not our problem. Interns may be at the bottom of the food chain, but attendings are the ones who take the heat when things go wrong. I'm betting that Dr. Fiore's first day was also her last."

Nora looked worried, as if she cared about what happened to the new attending. That was Nora—a natural-born Mother Hen who liked it when all her chicks played nice. "That's exactly what Dr. Weiss said."

"Like I said, not our problem."

Amanda joined them, moving a bit slow after the long night. Good thing she was going into Pediatrics. Gina wasn't sure if her soft-spoken roommate had what it took to survive the pressure-cooker of an Emergency Medicine residency. "Where have you been?"

"Up on Four, checking on my meningitis baby in the Peds ICU," Amanda said, combing her fingers through her shoulder-length blond hair, which was looking a bit stringy.

"He doing all right?" Nora asked.

"She. And it looks like she'll be fine. Thanks to Dr. Fiore picking up on how sick she was. Jim Lazarov was about ready to send her home, told her parents she was just colicky." Amanda shook her head in disapproval. The new intern was obviously not making a good impression on her either.

"Hey, why didn't Seth come down for our trauma?" Gina asked Nora. The charge nurse and Seth were practically engaged—Gina figured Nora would be getting a diamond any day now.

"Although maybe it's lucky he didn't, otherwise Weiss would be blaming him."

Nora frowned as she led the way to the auditorium where Grand Rounds were held. "Weiss said something about Seth being at a code in the Surgical ICU."

"Still, you'd think he would have at least answered his page or sent someone else."

Amanda broke in. "Did you say a code? Upstairs in the ICU?"

"That's what Weiss said."

"That's funny. The charge nurses were giving report while I was in the ICU and they were saying it was a miracle, they'd gone all day without a code despite it being July first."

"Too bad we weren't as lucky," Gina said, noting the puzzled look that crossed Nora's face. Lately Gina had been hearing some strange rumors about Seth missing pages when he was on call. One medical intern had even told her she'd seen Seth one night last week wandering the stairwell barefoot.

Gina wasn't about to meddle. Before he began seeing Nora, Seth had had quite a reputation among the nurses and staff, thanks to his Hollywood good looks and a couple of incidents involving naked bodies in storage closets and call rooms. It had taken him several attempts before Nora agreed to go out with him last year. But since then he'd settled down and hadn't given her any reason to worry.

Until now.

"I'm sure Weiss was mistaken," Gina said. It wasn't like her to soft peddle anything, but she couldn't stand the look of anxiety on Nora's face. "Probably trying to cover his own ass for no one showing up to a Trauma Alert."

Nora was looking at the floor as if the auditorium's beige carpet could give her answers. "Yeah. You're right. Probably."

CHAPTER 9

AT A QUARTER TO NINE, Lydia pulled her Ford Escape into the parking lot behind the squat concrete building on Penn Avenue that housed the Allegheny County medical examiner. If you missed the small sign out front, you could have easily mistaken the bland, single-story white stucco building for an office building, home to orthodontists and estate appraisers.

The guard at the front desk scrutinized her California driver's license before giving her a visitor's badge. Getting a new driver's license was on her list of things to do, along with getting the Escape's oil changed after the long haul from California, and finding a place to live.

Unfortunately, she was running through realtors faster than a crack addict through a dime vial. For some reason none of the real estate professionals could understand her lack of enthusiasm when they insisted on showing her houses wildly out of her price range. They heard "doctor" and thought Porsche, whereas Lydia was on a 72,653 mile, four-year-old Ford budget.

She waited while the guard called one of the morgue assistants to escort her back to the autopsy suite.

"Dr. Fiore?" A young woman wearing a maternity top and

scrub pants approached. "I'm Jan Dombroski, Dr. Steward's assistant. If you want to come with me."

She led the way down a corridor lined with linoleum flooring faded to an anonymous, dingy grey. Once beyond the double doors leading to the inner sanctum, the familiar smells of Ozium and bleach greeted her. Smells that said hospital, that represented her comfort zone, the closest thing to a home Lydia had had for years.

"This your first time here?" Jan asked. Despite her advanced pregnancy and work environment, she bounced along the corridor with the energy of a teenager.

"Yes, I'm new to town."

"Dr. Steward is one of the assistant medical examiners. He's scheduled to do your case."

They entered a brightly lit room festooned with hanging plants. Lydia had no idea what kind of plants they were, but seeing them made her think of the roses and peonies that had perfumed her morning run.

"You want any coffee? Dr. Steward is reviewing the patient's medical records, so it will be a few minutes."

Jan poured them both coffee and sank into a plastic molded chair at the small round table. Lydia joined her. A small aquarium bubbled in the corner with a large hand printed sign hanging over top of it reading: *DO NOT FEED THE FISH*!

On the door was posted a more official sign: *NO FOOD BEYOND THIS POINT*. The opposite wall held four video monitors, each labeled with a different autopsy suite.

"Are you expecting anyone else?" Lydia asked, hoping Elliot Weiss wasn't planning to attend. She didn't think she'd be able to face Jonah's father, not here, under these circumstances. Seeing Jonah again would be hard enough.

Jan shrugged. "We weren't expecting you, although the physician of record is always welcome, of course." She reached over and flicked on the monitor labeled: CLEAN ROOM #2. "You can watch over the monitor, or if you'd like, you can dress in."

Lydia needed to see this in as much detail as possible. "Where do I change?"

"There are sterile overalls in the anteroom." Jan pointed the way with her free hand. "Just put them on over your street clothes. I'd wait until we're ready. Even with the AC running full blast, it still gets pretty hot in them. Oh and don't mind Dr. Steward–he won't like you coming in."

Had Steward already formed an opinion about the case? Or her culpability? "Why's that?"

"He doesn't like anyone messing with his routine. He's one of the best forensic pathologists we have, very thorough, very meticulous. The DAs love him, he's great on the witness stand. In fact he does a lot of the criminal cases. But he has his own way of doing things. And he takes his time, which," she glanced at the clock hanging over the sink, "is why we're running late."

Thorough and meticulous, sounded like exactly the kind of Medical Examiner Lydia needed. Someone who could explain Jonah Weiss's death. She liked this Isaiah Steward already.

"How long have you worked here?"

"Going on ten years now."

That surprised Lydia given how young Jan looked. Jan put a hand onto the table and maneuvered her way to a standing position once more. The motion seemed effortless, as if she was used to carrying so much extra weight.

"Is this your first baby?"

Jan smiled and rubbed her gravid belly. "Lord, no. She's number four. Everyone thinks it's a strange job for a pregnant woman. But I think it's kind of fitting. Working here puts everything in perspective."

Lydia sipped her coffee. She felt the same about her job. Being a diener, or autopsy attendant, was probably one of the world's oldest professions. At least as old as medicine. As long as people have been dying, other people have been trying to discover why and how to prevent it.

"It's a good job, interesting, I'm always learning something so I don't get bored. 'Course when I'm like this," Jan gestured to her belly, "I don't do any of the heavy lifting. Basically my job right now is to keep Dr. Steward in line–believe me, that's hard enough."

Jan left. She appeared again on the monitor as she entered the autopsy area and rolled a chart table into position beside a long metal table with a drain at one end and a water tap at the other. No plants, no fish in this room, everything was shades of steel, cold and sterile.

On the table, shrouded in plastic, lay a body. Jonah Weiss. It was all too easy for Lydia to envision him lifting an accusatory finger and pointing it at her.

She gulped down the rest of the coffee. It gave her something to do besides looking at Jonah's corpse.

Jan returned with a sheaf of photocopies. "You can keep those if you like," she said. "I'm going to get Dr. Steward. He'll backed up all day if we don't get started."

Lydia reviewed the reports. There were copies of her dictation, the labs, and the nurses' notes from last night's resuscitation. Also included were the police report and EMS run sheet which she hadn't had a chance to see before.

According to witness statements, Jonah Weiss had been at the Ironworks, a bar in Squirrel Hill not far from his home. The bartender had served him two beers and stated that he did not appear intoxicated. Jonah and his friends were watching the second game of a west-coast Pirate doubleheader which had gone into extra innings. His friends said Jonah had complained of a headache and left to return home at about twelve forty-five in the morning. As he was crossing Murray Avenue he swerved directly into the path of a car turning onto the street.

The car, a '97 Cadillac Seville, was driven by a Madeline Pierce, a 62 year-old widow who was returning home from visiting a sister in Youngstown. Mrs. Pierce stated she had watched Jonah almost complete his street crossing but then, inexplicably, turn back and swerve directly into the path of her car.

Lydia glanced up from the reports, watching the fish swim lazily in their tank. She thought about the headache Jonah had complained of before the accident. It could have been caused by a leaking aneurysm in his brain. Maybe encephalitis or even a tumor?

Or maybe she was grasping at straws.

The door opened. A thin black man wearing a crisp white lab coat and metal rimmed glasses entered.

"Dr. Steward." She rose. Never hurt to play nice with the guy who happens to hold your fate in his hands. "I'm Dr. Lydia Fiore from Angels of Mercy. I'm here to observe the Weiss autopsy."

Steward looked over the rims of his glasses, peering at the hand she offered as if it was a contaminant in one of his specimens. Then his gaze rose to her face. No doubt about it, she wasn't welcome here.

"I know who you are," he said in a voice perfectly suited for the tenor solo from Handel's Messiah. He ignored her hand, left it hanging there.

"You need to know that I don't care what agenda you may have," he continued. "I will find out what killed Jonah Weiss."

Lydia frowned, confused. Agenda? He acted as if this was somehow personal to him. "I have no idea what you're talking about. All I want to know is why my patient died."

His eyes narrowed, and he stared at her for a long second. "You mean you don't know who Jonah Weiss was?" He sounded skeptical, as if everyone here in Pittsburgh was on intimate terms with the late Jonah Weiss.

"I know he was Elliot Weiss's son. But I didn't learn that until after he was dead. Why, is it important?"

Steward gave a small shake of his head. "Jonah and his father haven't–hadn't," he corrected himself, "spoken in years. You've never heard of GOAD?"

"No. What's GOAD?" Lydia asked, surprised by the medical examiner's attitude. Shouldn't they be focusing on Jonah's resuscitation?

"Jonah's group. Gays Organized Against Discrimination. He's been all over the news with it, was planning a big rally on the Fourth."

"Believe me, Dr. Steward, I don't have any idea what you're talking about. I just moved here from L.A. a few days ago."

He still looked distrustful but turned to the door. "All right then, if you say so."

"Dr. Steward," she called. His back went rigid. He glanced over his shoulder, peering at her over the top of his glasses. "You sound like you knew Jonah Weiss personally. Isn't it a conflict of interest for you to perform his autopsy?"

The glacial stare returned. "If you're implying that I am biased in anyway, I can assure you I am not," he said in measured tones. "All I want to know is what killed Jonah and who is responsible. I requested this case because I can be the best advocate for the deceased. But yes, I did know Jonah. And no, it won't interfere with my judgment in any way." With that he stalked from the room.

Lydia stared after him. Mark Cohen had been right about Pittsburgh being a small town. She was definitely very much the outsider here. A sitting duck about to take the blame for Jonah's death.

CHAPTER 10

LYDIA WAS IN THE LOCKER ROOM, climbing into a pair of white protective overalls when Trey Garrison entered. "What are you doing here?" she asked.

His stride broke for a moment as if he was startled by her question. Then he grabbed a pair of disposable coveralls from the shelf. "Same as you, I expect."

Paramedics didn't routinely attend autopsies. Never, in fact, in her experience. If anything went wrong it was the attending physician who took the blame, not the medics.

She zipped up the coveralls. They hung from her frame, the crotch falling almost to her knees. Trey was having the opposite problem—the one-size-fits-all Tyvek overalls were too short and too tight across his chest and shoulders.

"Why didn't you tell me Jonah was complaining of a headache before he was hit by the car?"

He jerked up straight, the Tyvek groaning in protest. "I did."

"No, you didn't."

"I'm sure we did. Besides, it wouldn't have made a difference if we hadn't."

"He could have had a leaky aneurysm, a tumor, increased

intracranial pressure from a subdural—"

"None of which you could have fixed. Besides, all of those would have presented with different symptoms. Don't try to blame what happened on me or my crew."

Lydia had been about to open the door to the autopsy suite but swung back around. "Do you really think I'm here to find a way to blame you?"

He stared at her for a long moment, eyes narrowed. "Been done before. You've obviously dissected my run report already, looking for ammunition."

"I need to know what killed my patient."

"*Our* patient," he reminded her, stalking past her and opening the door himself.

Lydia got a glimpse of Jonah's naked body lying beneath the spotlight in the room beyond. She stood frozen, let the door swing shut again.

Whatever happened on the other side of that door would decide her future. And she had absolutely no control over it.

Ain't no cure for death. If she had caused Jonah's death, she would deal with it, could deal with it. Steadying herself with one deep breath, then one more, she reached out, banished the tremble from her hand, and pulled the door open.

Steward glanced up, scowling at the intrusion, before resuming his discussion of Jonah's physical characteristics, finishing his preliminary measurements and photographs. Trey stood against the wall, looking like a lean, mean snowman in the white coveralls.

Jan was beside the chart table taking notes. She had positioned a portable digital scale to her side and a metal specimen table directly behind her. She silently handed Lydia a disposable face mask complete with plastic splash shield and gestured for her to stand beside the scale. Her own mask was a bulkier, reusable one that resembled a purple gas mask, designed to protect against the smallest of particles. Someone in a whimsical mood had drawn cat whiskers on the respirator that covered her nose and mouth.

"There's a voice activated recorder, and we're taping," she whispered, "so please don't talk unless it's absolutely necessary."

Lydia nodded, wondering if Elliot Weiss would ever watch the tape or if it was just for the lawyers' benefit. She stood beside Trey. He inched away, posture rigid, eyes narrowed in suspicion.

Steward impressed Lydia. He was very thorough and moved at an efficient pace. He and the autopsy tech quickly examined, measured and photographed the few external injuries present. Then the tech made the Y-shaped incision and removed the chest plate, cutting through the ribs with a pair of heavy duty shears that could have come from Sears' garden department.

She shifted from one foot to the other as the dissection continued. Jan took each individual organ as the other autopsy tech removed it from the body, weighed it, then handed it to Steward, who examined it on the specimen table. Steward kept a running commentary on his findings and totally ignored Trey and Lydia.

Once the chest was done, they moved on to the abdominal cavity. The tech removed the stomach and handed it to Jan for weighing.

Lydia's stomach rumbled in a most unfeminine way. Jan didn't seem to notice, but Trey's stoicism cracked with a ghost of a smile visible in his eyes. She couldn't help it. Autopsies always made her hungry. A combination of anxiety and the tediousness of the proceedings. Despite what they showed on TV, post-mortems were usually boring affairs.

Jan placed the stomach onto the scale with a squishy plop. Lydia straightened, now totally alert. She reached out a hand to block Jan from retrieving the organ. The morgue attendant looked up in surprise. Lydia didn't blame her–something was wrong here.

"Wait," she said, interrupting Steward's monologue as he commented on the lung tissue in front of him. Trey stepped forward, all traces of his smile gone.

There was abrupt silence as everyone turned to stare, or in Steward's case glare, at Lydia.

"What's wrong?" Trey asked, his mask muffling his voice into a low growl.

Lydia leaned forward to sniff at the specimen on the scale. "Can't you smell that?"

"Stop the recorder," Steward ordered.

Jan brushed her respirator down with the back of one gloved wrist and inhaled deeply. She frowned. "There's something. I'm not certain what," she said. "Must be something he ate." She glanced over at Lydia with a motherly smile. "Usually, I just try to ignore that smell."

Lydia shook her head. She couldn't deny what she'd sensed. A sharp, almost rancid odor. Unnatural. She took another smell. "No, this is something else. Bitter almonds. It smells like bitter almonds." She turned to Steward, hoping for confirmation. "Do you smell it?"

He scowled at her, hard to do when all she could see around his protective gear were his eyes hidden behind thick lenses. "Surely you're not implying that our trauma patient here is also the victim of cyanide poisoning?" he scoffed. "Dr. Fiore, if you think it is that easy to evade any responsibility you have for this man's death–"

"Just see if you smell anything," she interrupted.

Trey brushed up against her, craning his head over the table and inhaling. He shook his head. "I don't smell anything."

Steward carefully placed the lung tissue in its container and stalked over to the scale. He lowered his mask, leaned forward and sniffed delicately.

Lydia was bouncing on her toes—cyanide! "How on earth does a pedestrian hit by a slow moving car end up dying of cyanide poisoning?"

Steward didn't even bother to answer her question. "I don't smell anything," he said, leaning over the scale.

It was obvious he thought she was crazy. Couldn't blame him. She'd never even come across a case of cyanide toxicity before. When it did happen, it was almost always with smoke inhalation or self-inflicted—not getting hit by a car. But there was no denying it. The smell grew stronger with each breath she took. "Try again, please. I'm not making this up."

Steward dramatically took a deeper inhalation. Then he shook his head. "Nothing. Now, could we please get back to work?"

"More than half of the population lacks the gene to smell cyanide," she reminded him, recalling the fact from a distant biology class. There was something there–she was certain. "And look how red his lung tissue is." She pointed to the specimen Steward had begun to examine. "Shouldn't it be darker blue from the lack of oxygen?"

Steward peered at the lungs. They were two reddish blobs of tissue shimmering under the fluorescent lights. When he turned back, his frown had deepened into a scowl. "How on earth would Jonah Weiss have ingested cyanide?"

"I have no idea, but it fits," she said, feeling light-headed as the weight of guilt lifted. "The headache he complained of, the sudden respiratory distress....No wonder everything I did had seemed to make things worse. There are very specific antidotes to cyanide toxicity and without them death is certain after any significant exposure."

"If there is cyanide present, there must be some explanation," Steward said doubtfully. "It is not necessarily the cause of death. Did you have him on a nipride drip? Something that could have been metabolized into cyanide?"

"No, of course not."

"Don't look at us," Trey said, his tone defensive. "We ran a basic trauma protocol: O2, saline, monitoring. No drugs."

"Still, a drug misadventure is the most likely reason. One of your people hung the wrong medication."

"No. When he arrived he was in respiratory distress but he was never cyanotic," Lydia argued. "That's because the cyanide was already in his system, displacing oxygen from his red blood cells. It explains why our labs were normal. He had plenty of oxygen, it just wasn't doing him any good."

"An interesting hypothesis," Steward said with sarcasm. "It certainly would take you off the hook, wouldn't it, Doctor?"

It was Lydia's turn to glare at him. "All I'm asking is that you keep an open mind and run the analysis. You said you were the victim's advocate, unbiased. Doesn't that mean you have to investigate every possibility?"

He hid his reaction by raising his mask once more. "This isn't a possibility; it's an impossibility."

"What would it hurt, doc?" Trey surprised Lydia by taking her side of the argument. He'd done the same last night, she remembered. The paramedic seemed like a natural born peace-maker. When he wasn't doubting her motives, of course.

"We'll check his tissues and fluids for cyanide." Steward gave in. "But it might be pointless–cyanide is difficult to test for under the best of circumstances."

"But you'll try?" Lydia persisted.

"I wouldn't get your hopes up. It's probably a post-mortem contaminant," he said. "It was a few hours before my people got to the body, you know."

Steward refused to concede Weiss might have been poisoned. Jan had said he wouldn't draw any conclusions until he had all the evidence before him. So why did Lydia get the distinct feeling that he'd already judged and condemned her?

"Let's get back to work here," he snapped.

The remainder of the autopsy was unenlightening. There was no obvious injury she had missed, but neither was there an obvious cause of death. The microscopic and toxicological analysis of the tissues would take days, maybe even weeks. Unless Steward could document the presence of cyanide, she would have nothing to defend herself with at the Executive Committee's inquiry. Everyone would assume Jonah died because of something she had done or failed to do.

Back in the locker room, Lydia peeled off the Tyvek overalls and tossed them in the trash can. Trey was right behind her.

"Hey, let me buy you lunch," he said, hopping on one foot when his leg got caught in the clingy material.

She paused, one hand on the door. "I thought I was the bad guy—trying to blame you and your crew for my mistake."

"Sorry about that. It's happened before." He finally plopped down on the bench and pulled his foot free. "It's just lunch."

Lydia rubbed one hand over her belly. Lunch with a handsome medic would be nice, but she couldn't. "I'm late for an appointment."

"Sure you're not just blowing me off?" His grin was infectious and she found herself mirroring it.

Until she remembered why she was here. "Have to go see my lawyer. Try to save my job."

"Why? If you're right about the cyanide, then Jonah's death wasn't your fault." He was standing now, dangerously close—near enough she couldn't help but wonder how a man trapped all morning sweating in Tyvek overalls could smell so good.

"Even if there was cyanide present, I won't be able to explain it. The hospital Executive Committee will react just like Steward—thinking I screwed up. They'll assume I'm trying to pin it on anything else. After all, why would anyone want to kill Jonah Weiss?"

He twisted his mouth as if considering her words. She wasn't sure if he was serious or if he was mocking her. She had the feeling that other than protecting his job and patients, Trey was rarely serious about anything.

"In that case, you're screwed. Might as well let me buy you lunch."

"Sorry, no. I really am late." She opened the door but he caught her arm. She yanked it away—she didn't like to be touched unless she invited it. Six years in the L.A. foster care system had seen to that. It had also taught her to pick her battles carefully because she was guaranteed to lose most of them.

Trey glanced down at his empty hand then dropped it to his side. "You're not going to try to do anything stupid, are you, doc? "

"I don't know what I'm going to do. But I have to try something." Was this fight worth fighting? Did she really need this job that much?

"Why? Like you said, it probably won't save your job anyway."

Her mind was made up. "It has nothing to do with my job. Jonah was *my* patient. I'm not giving up until I know what the hell killed him."

CHAPTER 11

AMANDA SNUCK OUT OF THE DARKENED AUDITORIUM during the second lecturer's question and answer session. Her eyes watered with fatigue and boredom.

The first lecture hadn't been bad. Recent advances in the early detection of acute myocardial ischemia. A few too many statistics, but at least it was practical. But the second lecture... A yawn overcame her as she pulled the door open and slipped into the bright hallway. Utilization review and changes in ICD coding.

Basically the last hour had been a strident accountant flashing power point slides jammed with columns of indecipherable codes and haranguing them about the money being "hemorrhaged" because doctors insisted on writing down their diagnoses in words rather than the prescribed ICD numerical codes.

Who the heck needed that after being up all night? Amanda used the restroom down the hall from the auditorium. It was brightly lit, not as bright as sunlight, but still it felt good after being cooped up in Grand Rounds for two hours. She splashed cold water on her face, trying to convince her body that it didn't need sleep.

She had a feeling it was an argument she would be losing on a regular basis over the next several years. If she'd become a physician assistant instead of going to medical school, she would already have been pulling in a good salary for the past two years, be working regular hours, able to help her family instead of draining money that they didn't have and couldn't afford.

The cold water helped to break her endless chain of worries about her parents taking out a second mortgage, about the student loans that would be coming due after graduation next year, about the transcription job she had to give up since starting her clinical rotations. She looked up, water sparkling on her eyelashes, dripping from her chin. The woman in the mirror looked back and neither of them had any answers.

"Nothing to do but just keep on doing," Amanda said, her voice sounding tinny in the empty room. "That's what Mama would say."

She dried her face, pulled a sealed foil packet from her lab coat and quickly swallowed the three pills inside. Dr. Nelson said to take her vitamins at breakfast, so she figured this was close enough. During her last check up at the research clinic, he had hinted that she was on the medication side of the double-blind placebo controlled study of his new nutritional supplements, said that if she was, she could expect to feel more energy, less fatigue.

Amanda glanced at the mirror one last time before leaving, half convincing herself that she could already feel the vitamins working.

A crowd milled around the coffee and donuts—the hospital's idea of a complete and nutritious breakfast. She saw Gina, assumed Nora was near by, and started to edge her way through the throng of medical students, residents, interns and nurses. Not attendings. Attendings didn't throng or crowd. They proceeded around the corner to the physician lounge nestled between the auditorium and the cafeteria, heads bowed together as they discussed attending-level-very-important-and-vital academic topics. There they would get coffee, tea, cappuccino, bagels, donuts, eggs, hash browns, pierogies, toast or whatever they desired, all prepared fresh and served to them at warp speed so they wouldn't be late for M and M.

Amanda would be lucky if she snagged a donut before they vanished. In four short years, that would be her with the attendings. How the heck could she learn everything she needed to know in so little time? Dr. Fiore had only been an attending one day, yet she'd been able to diagnose a baby with meningitis just by walking down the hall and hearing it cry. And she wasn't even a pediatrician.

Amanda knew they made Dr. Fiore leave her shift early because of what happened with Dr. Weiss's son. She hoped everything was all right, that Dr. Fiore would be back soon—she'd learned more in one night from her than in her entire EM rotation last year.

"Hey, scutmonkey." A hand grabbed her by the elbow just as she was about to snatch a donut. She whirled around. It was Jim Lazarov.

"I told you my name is Amanda," she said, too tired to be polite and not liking his forward manner or arrogant tone. Gina had been right about him.

"I don't care," he said, enunciating the words slowly as if she were too stupid to understand. "You're a scutmonkey and a poacher."

"What are you talking about?"

"You poached my patient, stole my procedure."

"You mean the spinal tap? Dr. Fiore pulled me into the room, I didn't even know it was your patient until I spoke with the parents." Remembering the Millers steeled her backbone and she faced him head on. "While we waited for the resident from the Pediatric ICU, after we admitted your patient for a life-threatening illness that she may still die from, and after you told the parents to take her home because she had colic."

Jim narrowed his eyes, stepped forward, into her space. "There was nothing wrong with that baby when I saw her. I examined her head to toe. And that doesn't change the fact that you stole a procedure from me. You owe me."

He'd picked the wrong scutmonkey to try to intimidate. Amanda leaned forward, now she was the one encroaching into his space. "I don't owe you anything. You owe Dr. Fiore a thank you and the Millers an apology. They're on the fourth floor in the PICU. And the baby is doing fine, by the way, if you even care."

With that she spun on her heel and strode away. Only to stop short when she saw Gina standing a few feet away, watching and listening, grinning like a wicked step-sister.

"What?" Amanda snapped, trying to ignore the flush of embarrassment that she was certain made her cheeks glow like two red hot coals.

"Way to go," Gina said. "Not bad for a scutmonkey."

Nora joined them, shooting Jim a glare that made the intern go pale in the face and stumble away. She handed Amanda a donut. "Here, you've earned this."

Gina steered them back inside the auditorium. "C'mon. Let's go see who's getting their ass kicked this week."

LYDIA RUSHED UP THE PORCH STEPS to the grey Victorian that housed Michelle Cohen's law practice, ten minutes late for her eleven o'clock appointment.

Apparently, the neighborhood of Squirrel Hill seemed to have outlawed parking garages or lots. Forced to circle the block several times, she'd finally found a spot on a side street. Now her once crisp linen shirt clung to her in a mass of sweaty wrinkles, ruining any chance for a good first impression.

A man's voice carried clearly through the large leaded windows that opened out onto the wide veranda. A strange sing-song rhythm. Was he was praying?

A handicapped accessible ramp wove up to the other side of the porch. Lydia futilely smoothed the wrinkles on her shirt, opened the heavy oak door, then stopped short.

In the center of the reception area stood a tall, thin man, arms outstretched wide as if awaiting crucifixion. His head was tilted back, he would have been staring at the ceiling if his eyes weren't closed. A beatific smile filled his face.

The first man's smile was in sharp contrast to the sound of another man shouting over his shoulder as he was escorted from the office on the other side of the tiny reception area. "No way are we going to let those faggots dictate to us! You get us that permit or there's gonna be hell to pay!"

"Your will be done," the first man intoned, then snapped his head up and his arms to his side like he was finishing a jumping-jack. He beamed down at Lydia but his gaze was out of focus, still engaged in other-worldly communication.

The second man joined him, shaking the first's arm while including Lydia in his glare. He wore jeans and a wife-beater—the better to display his collection of swastikas, flaming crosses, and other skinhead tattoos.

"Dr. Fiore?" the young man who had escorted the Nazi-wannabe from the inner office asked as he took his seat at the receptionist desk. He looked like a parody of an earnest law student, down to the polka dotted bow tie. "Please have a seat. Ms. Cohen will be with you in a minute."

"A doctor?" the tall man asked, his attention zooming in on Lydia. His eyes were a piercing grey, the color of a molten lead. "You are a practitioner of the arcane art of healing?"

Lydia glanced at the receptionist and found no help there. He hid his grin behind his hand as he studiously read a letter.

The skinhead frowned, again tugging the tall man's arm. The tall man seemed rooted to the oak floor. "We don't have time for this, Matthew."

"Always time for a convert, Hampton," the tall man assured his companion in dulcet tones. He turned his stare onto Lydia and she had to think twice to not squirm under his penetrating gaze. "You think you can save a life?"

"I try."

The man's smile widened. "Don't you understand it all lies in God's hands? No mere mortal can change or influence his plans. So," he tilted his head, staring at her as if she were a rare zoo specimen, "why do you even try?"

"Someone has to."

He arched a superior eyebrow infused with righteousness in her direction. "Futility. True believers have no need of your feeble attempts to intercede in the Creator's grand design."

"You can go on in, Dr. Fiore," the receptionist said.

Lydia had no choice but to turn to the side to pass the man when he did not relinquish his position in the center of the small room. His tattooed companion snickered at her, also not giving way, forcing her to brush past him face on. What kind of lawyer was Michelle Cohen if these were representatives of her clients?

"Here's Dr. Fiore, Mickey," the receptionist made introductions.

Lydia stopped inside the doorway, still hesitant. The room faced the front porch. Two large windows were open, allowing the summer breeze to ruffle through lace curtains. A Queen Anne desk whose legs had more curves than a ballet dancer's calves sat upon a brilliantly polished oak floor. Michelle Cohen looked to be in her late forties. She had wiry copperish hair with the slightest hints of grey in it, lively hazel eyes and a freckled nose.

"Do you want tea or coffee?" the receptionist asked, herding Lydia into the room.

Lydia shook her head. "Nothing for me, thanks."

"No thanks, Danny." The receptionist left and Michelle

pushed herself back from her desk, deftly maneuvering a titanium-framed wheelchair forward to greet Lydia. "Call me Mickey," she said, thrusting her hand out.

Lydia shook it, then sank down into one of the two leather chairs that sat in front of the Queen Anne desk. Mickey's legs were encased in black silk slacks and a pair of black low-heeled pumps. No obvious signs of atrophy that Lydia could observe. Either the attorney hadn't been wheelchair bound for long or she didn't need it all the time.

"Mark's message said you're involved with Jonah Weiss. If it's about the protest, then I'm sorry but you're out of luck. I'm already representing other interests."

Lydia stared at her without comprehension. "Other interests?"

Mickey laughed and returned behind her desk. "You just met him." She nodded toward the reception area. "Matthew Kent. The leader of the Sons of Adam." She continued, obviously misreading Lydia's look of confusion, "So you see, I really can't help you if you're looking for a permit for July Fourth. Conflict of interest, you know. Who are you working with?"

"Working with?" Lydia echoed. What did the Fourth of July have to do with Jonah Weiss or his death? Isaiah Steward had mentioned the holiday as well.

"What's your agenda?" Mickey squinted at her. "You don't look like you'd be from the Nation of Islam, but I've been wrong before. Maybe Right to Life? Homemakers for God?"

Lydia shook her head, now certain she was in the wrong place.

The lawyer frowned. "You're not here about the protests on the Fourth, are you?"

"No, sorry."

"But I thought Mark said it was about Jonah." She rocked her wheelchair back and forth while scrutinizing Lydia. "Did Mark tell you what kind of lawyer I am?"

"No, why?" Lawyers specialized, just as physicians did, but Lydia didn't think there was that much difference.

"Dr. Fiore, I work for the ACLU. I represent parties whose civil rights are being violated."

"A civil liberties lawyer? ACLU? You're the guys who defended the KKK's right to hold protest marches in black neighborhoods."

"Constitutionally they have that right, so yes the ACLU defended them in that case. I've worked for Holocaust survivors and the NAACP as well as the KKK. I handle all sorts of clients whose politics I may disagree with." Mickey shrugged. "Like Matthew Kent and his organization, the Sons of Adam. Our homegrown version of the Branch Davidians. The Constitution must be protected. I consider it my primary client."

"I don't think I qualify then." What had Mark been thinking, sending her on this wild goose chase? "My case has nothing to do with the Constitution or my civil liberties."

"Mark left a message on my machine saying that you needed help and it had to do with Jonah, so I just assumed–well, never mind what I assumed. I do apologize."

"I always teach my residents that the first rule of medicine is to trust nobody and assume nothing," Lydia told her with a smile. Despite their rocky introduction, she liked Mickey Cohen. Her warm attitude was refreshing after Isaiah Steward's chilly reception.

"That's basically what they teach us in law school, too. So, why are you here if it's not about the GOAD protest?"

"I'm here because I'm the physician who attended Jonah Weiss when he died early this morning." That sounded better than saying she was the doctor everyone thought killed Jonah Weiss. But not by much.

"Jonah's dead?" Mickey's smile faded fast as the wheelchair banged into a desk leg. "God, I just spoke to him yesterday." Her glance moved to focus on something far in the distance. "What happened? You were there?"

Lydia told Mickey of the events surrounding Jonah's death, including his father's accusations and her new suspicions that his death was due to cyanide poisoning. Going through everything aloud, she suddenly felt foolish. How flimsy the whole thing sounded. She had no proof or evidence, only bizarre theories. Even more absurd was the idea that her future depended on proving that a murderer was roaming the streets of Pittsburgh.

Mickey leaned back in her chair, absentmindedly popping small wheelies, bouncing the front wheels off the hard wood floorboards. Then she tilted the chair back in perfect balance for several moments before bringing it down with a soft thud.

"I think maybe it's a good thing Mark sent you to me," Mickey finally said.

"You mean you believe me?"

"Let's just say I'm not making any assumptions that Jonah's death was accidental."

"But if you're a civil liberties lawyer, how can you help me?" Lydia protested, although she was elated to finally have someone on her side.

"I know who all of Jonah's enemies are."

CHAPTER 12

MICKEY SENT HER ASSISTANT, DANNY, out for sandwiches while she and Lydia continued their discussion.

"GOAD is a group Jonah organized while he was a law student," Mickey was telling Lydia when Danny returned with a paper sack stained by grease and emanating a tantalizing aroma. He stepped out and quickly came back with a handful of pills and glass of water then stood by and watched until Mickey gulped them down. Lydia enjoyed watching how the earnest young man, barely into his twenties, took such attentive care of his wheelchair-bound boss.

"Gays Organized Against Discrimination. Jonah worked part-time for Carnegie Mellon and was upset by their refusal to offer same sex partners benefits. So he formed GOAD, sued them, and now CMU has one of the best policies in the nation. And Jonah's career as a gay rights activist was born–which is pretty much when his relationship with his father fell apart.

"Elliot Weiss could handle a gay son as long as he was discreet, but not one who was on the front page constantly. Jonah was involved in one protest after another, repeatedly arrested and refusing bail so that he could use his court dates as a public forum."

"Sounds like he was pretty militant."

Mickey took a bite of an over-stuffed Reuben and nodded as she wiped sauerkraut off her chin. "Militant is an understatement. Jonah's private life was a mess, but when he was in the spotlight he felt like he had everything, like he was finally in control of something."

Lydia peered underneath the piece of pumpernickel topping her sandwich. She had ordered French fries and coleslaw with her turkey and provolone and was surprised to find them included inside the sandwich.

"Primanti Brothers," Mickey explained. "It's a Pittsburgh institution. Try it, you'll like it."

Lydia mashed the sandwich down into an edible height and took a bite. Messy, but delicious.

"You sound like you knew Jonah fairly well," she said after taking a second bite and washing it down with iced tea.

"I was his advisor in law school. You didn't know you were dealing with an academic, did you?" Mickey said with a wistful smile. "I quit teaching after I was diagnosed with MS a few years ago. Now I work part time for the ACLU–most of it can be done from right here in my home, so my bad days don't slow me down as much." She shrugged, making light of the hand fate had dealt her.

"Assuming there wasn't some diabolic plot for revenge on behalf of the university, who would want to kill Jonah Weiss?"

"That's the problem. Jonah has a lot of enemies."

"But, murder? That sounds personal."

Mickey pushed back in her chair again. "Anything to do with GOAD is personal to Jonah. You see, Jonah is—was—one of those rare people who could recruit followers to his cause and inoculate them with the same passion he felt."

"He had charisma."

"And more. Jonah inspired the people who came to him, almost in a religious way. But he was also a narcissist and demanded those close to him keep proving their faithfulness by sacrificing more and more of themselves in the name of the cause."

"Maybe someone he pushed too far? A scorned lover, perhaps?" Lydia suggested.

Mickey hesitated for a moment. "He and Isaiah Steward were involved until a few months ago."

Lydia choked on her tea. "The medical examiner? The one who did Jonah's autopsy? How could he possibly call himself a neutral party–he should never have been allowed near that body!"

She remembered how Steward had seemed to judge her, immediately assumed she was responsible for Jonah's death. Maybe instead he was nervous about her being there, probing, asking questions. What if Steward had killed Jonah? If so, then he was in the perfect position to ensure no evidence remained. "What happened? Why did they break up?"

"Jonah and Isaiah were leaving the Ironworks one night when they found some skinhead kids vandalizing Jonah's car. Jonah immediately went on the offensive and confronted them. He punched one of them, dislocated the kid's jaw and then broke his arm. Isaiah was trying to break them apart, but Jonah kept yelling at him to join him. Then things got ugly.

"One of the kids pulled a gun on Isaiah. They held him back while they beat Jonah, forcing Isaiah to watch."

Lydia imagined the scene, trying to picture how the fastidious Steward would have reacted. "They broke up because Isaiah was upset with Jonah for escalating the violence?"

Mickey nodded. "He felt it was Jonah's fault for attacking the kid. If they'd just walked away the only damage would have been to the car. The cops agreed."

"So the skinheads, they got off?"

"Except for the injured kid, the rest ran. After Isaiah told the cops that Jonah was the one who had hit the kid—"

"They weren't going to press charges."

"Right. Jonah blamed Isaiah for not siding with him and

publicly denounced Isaiah as a coward and traitor to their cause. That pretty much ended things."

Lydia thought about that. "The Ironworks is the same bar Jonah was at last night before he died."

"It's a gay bar, few blocks from here. Pretty low-key place except when punks get it in their heads to go gay-bashing."

"Or maybe slip some cyanide into a gay rights activist's drink?"

Mickey grimaced. "Maybe. Except we have no proof."

"We may never get any. Not if Isaiah Steward was involved. The evidence could have already been destroyed."

Mickey dropped her gaze to her desk blotter but nodded.

"Should I talk to the police? Let them handle it?"

"With what as evidence?" Mickey asked. "I can't see that they'll get involved until we have something definite, like laboratory confirmation that there was cyanide present."

"And if Isaiah Steward is involved?"

Mickey frowned at the doodle she was drawing and shrugged. "Then it's too late to do anything about it. We can only wait and see what the tests reveal."

"He could get away with murder."

Mickey laughed. "Listen to you. You've already got the poor man tried and convicted and we're not even certain that a crime has been committed. Assume nothing, remember?"

"I'm certain. I know I didn't do anything wrong, that I didn't kill Jonah Weiss. His injuries were minor–and cyanide poisoning is the only thing that fits everything that happened."

"Knowing and proving something are worlds apart," Mickey persisted, rationally.

Lydia glared at her. This was her life they were gambling with, but the attorney only smiled back. As if this was an academic mock trial.

"My best advice to you at this point is to wait for the lab

results. If they're positive, the Medical Examiner will rule Jonah's death a homicide and the police will take over. But you're not going to do any good investigating a crime you can't even prove was committed."

"You think I should do nothing?" Anger tightened her throat and she had to swallow twice before her mouthful of sandwich would go down. "I can't do that. You don't understand, my entire future is at stake here."

Mickey shook her head sadly. "I do understand. Take my advice. Go home. It's out of your hands."

Lydia tapped her foot. There had to be something she could do. She wasn't going to sit back and watch everything she had worked so hard for go up in flames. "What if the tests come back negative for cyanide?"

"Then we'll figure out something. There are other jobs besides the one at Angels. Hell, maybe we could sue them for wrongful termination." Mickey reached out and offered her hand from across the desk. "Believe me, Lydia, I'll do everything I can to help you."

Lydia took the lawyer's hand, feeling numb. Mickey seemed satisfied as long as she had a legal position to pursue, but Lydia wasn't.

She left the office in a haze. She could lose everything. But she refused to believe it could come to that–she wouldn't let it, damn it! There had to be a way to find out who poisoned Jonah Weiss.

CHAPTER 13

DIGGERS TAVERN WAS HOUSED in a large two-story brick house. The building had once been a boarding house for gravediggers at the cemetery across the street, built just after the turn of the century to replace the old building that had burnt down in 1902. That building had replaced another, which had replaced another, all serving the same purpose since the 1700's. Once the Angels of Mercy cemetery closed to new inhabitants in 1952, Diggers had outlived its usefulness as a hostel and been converted into a restaurant.

Diggers' main clientele were hospital workers from Angels, who appreciated its small windows and poorly lit interior where it was difficult to distinguish night and day. Patients and their families tended to steer a wide berth away from the ominous, looming building and walked on past to the bright colors of the Burger King or Eat n Park down the street on Penn Avenue.

Nora forced herself to hide her disappointment when she spotted Seth having a leisurely lunch with Lucas Stone, one of the neurologists at Angels. She'd paged Seth that morning, and he'd told her he would be busy in clinic, too busy to join her for lunch after Grand Rounds. Thankfully, Gina led her and Amanda to a table on the other side of the room in what had formerly been the smoking section. The area still reeked of tobacco, as if the walls continued to exhale it long after patrons could. Closest thing to a nicotine fix Gina was going to get until they went back outside, Nora thought with satisfaction. Maybe she could finally convince her to quit for good.

Amanda gave Seth a little wave before Gina yanked her hand down and steered her into a chair facing the wall. Nora saw what her friend was doing but rebelled against Gina's attempts to put her in the chair with its back to Seth. Instead she took the opposite seat, facing Seth and Lucas dead on.

Seth acted like he didn't even see her. Poor Lucas looked awful. She hadn't seen him since his divorce was finalized. Maybe Seth was just trying to cheer him up. Maybe that's why he'd blown off Nora's lunch invite.

"I'm having a beer," she announced to the waitress, ignoring Amanda and Gina's looks of surprise. "A Rolling Rock. What?" she asked, staring past them as Seth and Lucas stood to leave, Seth angling himself so he didn't have to look in their direction. "I'm entitled. It's almost noon. And I'm not on again until tomorrow morning."

Amanda yawned, covering her mouth politely and ordered a Dr. Pepper. "I'm back on tonight."

"Poor baby," Gina said, ordering a posh Swiss mineral water even though they all knew the closest she would get was Perrier. "Wait until you're a resident. Eighty hour work weeks."

"What happened with Dr. Weiss's son?" Amanda asked. "I can't believe Dr. Fiore messed up. She seems like a really great teacher."

"She must have missed something. I know I didn't," Gina replied.

Nora yanked her attention away from Seth and back to her own tablemates. "Don't blame my nurses. I double checked all the meds and the blood packs—no mistakes, everything was in order. But...."

She trailed off, distracted as Seth almost ran into a seated man in his haste to escape. He caught himself, pivoting to avoid a waitress and suddenly was looking right at her. She tried to smile but felt it falter when he spun away and was out the door before Lucas finished paying the check.

"Well hell, what the heck was that all about?" Nora muttered.

Amanda craned her head over her shoulder to see. "Who's the cute guy Seth was having lunch with?"

"Lucas Stone, neurology. Don't even think about it," Gina told her, "he's on the rebound, just got divorced. And he's an attending." Gina tugged her cigarettes, some rancid smelling Turkish brand, from her jeans. "God, I need a smoke."

Amanda sighed, sipping through her straw at her Dr. Pepper. "Doesn't hurt to look."

"You know, Nora," Gina continued, tapping her cigarettes against the tabletop. "Only two reasons for a guy to be hanging out with his best friend and avoiding his girlfriend. And one of them comes with a little blue box from Tiffany's."

"Shut up, Gina." Both turned to stare at her. "He's not going to ask me to marry him. I thought maybe—I hoped—but he's been acting so strange lately. Now, I don't know what to think."

"Strange how?" Amanda asked.

Nora felt her cheeks burn and took a drink of her beer to cover up. "Like he hasn't touched me in almost two weeks. No matter how hard I try—and believe me, I've done everything except jumping him in a supply closet."

"Why not try that?" Gina said. "He'd probably like it."

"I think he is going to ask you to marry him," Amanda said, rolling her straw around the edge of her glass. "Guys get superstitious about stuff like that. Like wearing the same socks when they're on a winning streak."

"Guys think turning down sex is romantic?" Gina scoffed. "Nah, I say he's sick. Or stressed out. Junior year of surgery is as tough as it gets."

"I have three brothers," Amanda argued. "Their idea of romance is getting the oil changed in your car or walking the dog when it's raining. Or the ultimate, holding off on sex until a special occasion. To them it's making a commitment."

Nora took another swallow of beer, thinking about it. "He has been kind of jumpy lately, not sleeping well. You really think that he's getting ready to propose?"

"You said you two had a big date planned for the Fourth, didn't you?" Gina asked.

Amanda bounced in her seat, clapping her hands. "He's going to ask you during the fireworks. Oh Nora, it's going to be so beautiful. Trust me. Everything will be fine."

A smile crept over Nora's face as she felt her worries lift. Amanda was right. After all, Seth was the only man she'd ever shared her secret with, yet he'd done all right with the knowledge that she'd been a rape victim. He'd accepted her for who she was now, not what had happened almost three years ago.

She shook her head, her smile widening into a grin as she imagined fireworks and Seth kneeling before her, a ring in his outstretched palm. How could she ever have doubted him?

They lingered over their lunches, dissecting Grand Rounds and the Jonah Weiss resuscitation. Even talking about possible ideas for a wedding. Amanda made Nora promise to call her as soon as Seth asked. Gina had laughed, saying she was fine waiting until the next day, after they finished celebrating the end of Seth's vow of celibacy. While they waited for the check, Gina left to go have a smoke.

As Nora watched her track down their waitress first, she knew Gina was paying their check. She smiled, saying nothing to Amanda because the perennially impoverished medical student would be embarrassed. "I wish she would quit that filthy habit," she said instead.

Amanda just shook her head. "At least she only smokes outside."

"Right, that's what half our patients say as well." Nora eyed Amanda. They were the same age, both twenty-five, but sometimes Amanda seemed much younger, naïve. "What's up with you and Jim Lazarov?"

Amanda blushed, confirming Nora's suspicions. "At first I thought he was kind of cute, but—"

"But you're going to stay the hell away from him, right? I've heard rumors from a few nurses over at North Hills. Believe me, you do not want to get involved with him."

Amanda straightened. "No way. Not after the way he treated the Millers. That poor baby."

"How about the way he treated you?"

"Well, that too. But really, it's not worth discussing."

"Not worth discussing? Amanda, he grabbed you. Gina and I saw it if you want to report him—"

"Nora, it wasn't like that. You're over reacting. He's just an insecure bully. Believe me."

Maybe she was over reacting, reading something into the intern's behavior that wasn't there. She hoped so. "If you say so."

CHAPTER 14

LYDIA OPENED THE DOOR OF HER MOTEL ROOM and was greeted by a wave of humidity and the smell of mold. The maid had been and gone, but had forgotten to turn the air conditioner on. Or maybe it was how management saved money; the sauna discount.

She cranked the AC on high, stripped and changed into running clothes. Tucking the old-fashioned motel key—a real brass key on a large fob—into her pocket, she grabbed a water bottle from the twelve pack she'd bought at the Giant Eagle and ran out the door.

Her feet pounded the pavement in a furious rhythm. An ambulance raced past her, heading toward Angels, and she thought about Trey Garrison.

Something about the paramedic with those gorgeous bedroom eyes made her nervous. The way she seemed to be always checking his reaction to her actions, looking for approval, the way her pulse jumped when she knew he was looking at her, the way it became hard to focus on anyone else when he was nearby.

A black SUV almost side-swiped her when she stepped off the curb. She jumped back, re-focusing on the traffic around her instead of on Trey. Clearly, the man was dangerous—just thinking about him had almost got her killed.

Any other time, a romantic encounter would be nice and Trey Garrison would top her list of potential partners. But right now she had to fight to save her career. Tonight would be spent ferreting out everything the internet had to offer on cyanide, GOAD, Jonah Weiss and Isaiah Steward and the Sons of Adam.

"Help!" a cry came from the alleyway beside a large brick building called Diggers. "Someone, help, he's having a heart attack!"

Lydia stopped, looked around. No one else nearby and she had left her cell phone recharging back in her room. She sprinted down the alley and into the loading area behind the bar. A man lay on the pavement beside an open dumpster. Another man stood over him.

She stopped a few feet shy of the men. Something was wrong here. Something about the way he stood, rigid, hands at his sides, weight forward. Then she spotted the black SUV parked farther down the alley. The same one that had almost hit her a few minutes ago. A man, features hidden by the tinted glass, sat in the driver's seat, the engine revving as if he were waiting for something.

She reached in her pocket for her pepper spray. And realized it wasn't there–she had the damned motel key, not her own key ring.

She pivoted, ready to run back the way she came. Behind her, a fourth man slammed the dumpster lid down, and shoved it hard, blocking her path. At the sound, the prone man jumped to his feet, miraculously cured.

The first man had a shaved scalp, nasty acne and wore a t-shirt reading: Gays Organized Against Discrimination. The second's tee was another GOAD shirt, advertising a benefit to raise money for AIDS research. The man beside the dumpster wore a plain black polo, but still managed to capture her attention as he drew a short, retractable baton and swung it in an arc towards her head.

As soon as his arm went up, she struck. She shot her fist into his armpit, followed by a sidekick to his knees. He dropped the baton and fell to the ground.

"What the hell!" he bellowed. "Get the bitch!"

The first two men, both with close-cropped hair and tattooed arms, came at her. Neither held weapons. Lydia feinted toward one. He swung out with a roundhouse he telegraphed from a mile away. She slammed her fist into his solar plexus while ramming a knee into his groin. He blew his breath out in an audible whoosh and folded over, clutching at his crotch, blocking her from the other man.

She finished him with an elbow to the back of his head and pivoted to face the others. Dumpster man was still scuttling along the pavement, flailing for his blackjack.

Which left Number Three. She centered her attention on him, keeping the others in her periphery as best she could.

"Fire!" she shouted, hoping the noise would make it past the closed door of the bar. "Help, fire!"

Number Three was a good six-four, built like the cross between a Rams linebacker and a Rwandan gorilla. No way she was going to beat him. Not without a very large gun. Even then, he looked like bullets might bounce off him. But, she didn't have to win. All she had to do was open a path to either the rear door of the bar or back to the street.

"Scream all you want," he said, stepping forward. "No one can hear you."

He launched a quick jab that threatened to decapitate her if she let it land. Ducking under his guard, she shot out her hand with the key, aiming for his eyes. He turned at the last moment and all she accomplished was a deep gash along his cheekbone. Painful, but not the incapacitating blow she'd wanted.

He wrapped her in a deadly bear hug. She immediately reached down with her other hand, dug her fingers into his groin as she hooked her leg behind his knee. His scream almost hit mezzo-soprano as his arms relaxed enough for her to break free. Just in time for Dumpster Man to sweep her feet out from under her with his baton. She flew sideways, sprawling, slamming face first into the concrete, most of her weight landing on her right forearm and elbow.

Pain zapped through her, blurring her vision. Someone, Number Three she guessed from his weight, wrenched her left arm behind her, twisting her wrist viciously.

"Hey, what's going on here?" a woman's voice broke through Lydia's haze of pain.

She looked up just as the other two men tackled Gina Freeman, the ER resident. They pulled her away from the back door of the bar, one man holding her in a choke hold with his baton. Her face was already turning purple, her mouth opening and closing as she gasped for air.

"Let her go," Lydia shouted, raising her head. "She can't breathe."

Number Three slammed her back down onto the concrete, face turned away from Gina and the others. He leveraged his weight between her shoulder blades.

Her vision swimming with red spots, Lydia fought to breathe. Number Three leaned forward, his right hand planted in front of her face as he bent his head down.

"Someday I'm going to kill you for that, bitch," he whispered in a rasp punctuated by his own gasps of pain and exertion.

She forced her head up, mouth open trying to gulp any oxygen to be found. Number Three laughed at her feeble attempt, then finally relented. He eased his bulk off her and hauled her to her feet. Pain crashed down, doubling her over with the effort to breathe as she drank in the air. Slowly her vision cleared and the ringing in her ears subsided.

It took all her effort to swing her head far enough to check on Gina. The man with the baton had relented. The other man held a hand against Gina's mouth while restraining her arms behind her back.

"What do you want?" Lydia's voice was a hoarse whisper but it carried as much venom as a Mojave rattlesnake.

Dumpster Man, the one with the baton, appeared in her vision, listing slightly, favoring the knee she'd kicked. He bared his teeth, wrapped his fingers around her throat and squeezed.

"Shut your mouth, bitch," he told her. "Unless you want your friend to get hurt. All we want to do is talk, understand?" He lowered his hand. Lydia took a deep breath, then nodded slowly. A trickle of blood slid into her eye and she blinked furiously.

"Gina, are you all right?" she called out.

The man with the baton slapped her. "I told you to shut up. Your friend's fine. She'll stay that way as long as you behave yourself. We don't appreciate you stirring things up. We heard you're spreading rumors that Jonah Weiss was poisoned. We know for a fact there was no poison. Heard it straight from the coroner's office. So you might want to just head on back to L.A. unless you want to see someone get hurt–like your friend here."

He paused for a minute, giving her a hard stare and time to think about what he said. "Stop meddling in things that don't concern you and we'll all live happily ever after. Any problems with that, Dr. Fiore?"

A groan came from Gina's direction and Lydia fought to turn her head again, to assure herself that Gina was all right. The man in front of her grabbed her chin between his fingers, forcing her to focus only on him. She choked down the hot bile of fury rising in her throat, forced herself to drop her gaze, and nodded. She couldn't risk Gina getting hurt.

"I can't hear you. I asked you if you had any problems with us going our separate ways. Do you?"

"No." The word came out a strangled whisper.

"Good. Then we won't be meeting again. But don't worry, we'll be keeping an eye on you, Doctor. Make sure you keep your side of the bargain. Don't even think about going to the cops. We'll know it if you do."

Lydia raised her eyes to meet his gaze. A small act of defiance she couldn't repress. The man took a step back under the weight of her glare.

"Let me give you a small demonstration of what will happen if you don't do as you're told." He nodded to Number Three who pivoted her to face Gina.

The man who held Gina forced her down until she was kneeling between him and the man with the baton. Her eyes locked onto Lydia's, pleading, tears brimming over.

The leader raised his baton and with frighteningly quick efficiency struck Gina's head. Lydia cried out and tried to lunge free but Number Three held her fast. Gina's eyes rolled up, then fluttered shut and she slumped forward. Her captor released his grip. Gina hit the pavement, lifeless.

Lydia ignored the searing pain as Number Three twisted her arm behind her, focused only on reaching Gina. "Let me go!"

"Don't forget, we'll be watching." The leader slapped the baton against his open palm and nodded. Number Three shoved her to the ground. They ran from the alley, their footsteps and laughter fading quickly.

Lydia raced to Gina. She was conscious, clutching her head, groaning in pain. Then she began retching, vomiting. Lydia joined her on the cement, gently pulled her back away from the puddle of stomach contents, her fingers searching Gina's scalp. There was already a nice goose-egg of a hematoma, but no skull fracture that she could feel. But who knew what was going on beneath?

Lydia hauled Gina upright and half-carried her to the back door of the bar. She wrenched it open. "We need some help out here!"

Gina grabbed her arm, eyes at half-mast. "Who were those guys?"

CHAPTER 15

HELP ARRIVED IN THE FORM OF A WAITER, Amanda, Nora, and two radiology residents who looked a little faint at the sight of blood. Gina gave them points for even daring to venture into the sunlight—most radiologists were like vampires, hiding in caves and vanishing into the night.

Nora took charge, calling for towels to use as pressure dressings and wanting to call an ambulance.

"No way," Gina said, now standing on her own. Well, half standing and half leaning against the wall. "Angels is right across the street, it's faster to walk."

"What happened? Should we call the police?" Amanda asked, draping one of Gina's arms around her shoulders and guiding her down the alley.

"Ask her." Gina glanced in Lydia's direction. Christ, even moving her eyes hurt. "She was the one they were after."

Lydia shook off Nora's arm but did take the towel the charge nurse pressed into her hand. She held it against her own bleeding scalp. Her lip was split and swollen and her arm was already bruising up. Gina watched Lydia's gaze dart around, as if searching for hidden danger, then she took another breath, shoulders heaving, and seemed somehow to shake her fear away. By the time Lydia turned to face Gina, her face had that same calm, thoughtful expression she'd had in the ED last night. All-seeing, all-knowing, like this was nothing new for her. Gina hated her for that. And envied her.

"They said they were friends of Jonah Weiss," Gina said when Lydia remained silent.

"Beating unarmed women won't bring him back," Amanda said, her accent deepening with indignation.

"I'll call the police as soon as we're in the ER," Nora told them.

"They said they'd come back if we did," Gina said. She hated the quaver in her voice. And the tears drying on her face. Not to mention the stench of vomit that floated like a cloud around her.

Lydia led the way to the street, her gait steady. Gina found her own sense of panic edge away as she watched Lydia's control. She stroked the inside of her left arm, the repetitive motion calming.

"You just got here, how the hell did you piss so many people off so fast?" Gina asked as they waited for the traffic on Penn to slow so they could cross the street.

Now Lydia focused on her, a slow smile creeping over her face. "Talent."

Gina couldn't control her chuckle. Damn, laughing made her head pound, but she felt less scared and that was good.

"Think you could teach me those moves some day? I couldn't do shit, but you were kicking ass."

Lydia gave a one-shouldered shrug. "Remnants of a misspent youth and an ex who was a Grav Maga instructor." She stepped out into a gap in the traffic, leaving the others to follow.

"If you won't call the police, at least call Jerry," Nora said. "He'll know what to do."

Jerry. He'd be all over Gina, wanting to mother and protect her. The thing she hated most was that she'd love it. That feeling of being safe and secure, able to surrender the need to think, to make decisions—it was addictive.

"Who's Jerry?" Lydia asked.

"Jerry Boyle, Gina's boyfriend."

Thank you very much, Amanda. "He's not my boyfriend."

"No, he's just the guy who's hang-dog in love with you and sleeps in your bed more nights than not."

Gina glanced at her roommate, raising an eyebrow despite her headache and instantly regretting it. Woohoo, little Southern gal showing some backbone there. Amanda was constantly surprising her that way. "He's not my boyfriend."

"They why call him?" Lydia asked.

"He's a cop." Gina couldn't help but notice Lydia's look of distaste. So, the new attending didn't seem to mind getting mugged by gay rights activists, or even possibly causing the death of the Chief of Surgery's son, but talking to a police officer got her upset?

Hmm...maybe she would let Jerry come over, take care of her tonight. While he was at it, he could find out everything there was to know about Lydia Fiore.

AFTER HAVING THE PRIVILEGE OF EXPERIENCING Angels of Mercy Medical Center from the other side of the curtain, Lydia decided that being a patient pretty much sucked. Definitely not as much fun as being the one in charge. It didn't help that she had no identification on her, much less insurance information. After almost an hour trying to process her, the registration clerk was clearly frustrated.

"Phone number?"

"Just let me think a moment." Her voice came out harsher than she intended, but her knees were still wobbly and the adrenaline flooding her system left her gut wrenching with nausea. It took all her strength to sit still and try to answer the clerk's questions. "It's the Pilgrim Inn, down a block on Penn. I can't remember the number."

"Address?" The woman wouldn't stop badgering her. All she wanted was a minute to think. Her elbow was already swelling, but she could move it all right, so nothing broken. And her legs were scraped to hell and back.

"I don't know. Look it up." The clerk glared at her. Lydia softened her voice, reminding herself that hopefully she'd someday soon be working with these people again. "I'm sorry, I just don't remember."

She decided to play up the patient card and lowered the towel to reveal the blood there. Scalp lacs always bled like stink. Might need stitches or staples. Her head thudded relentlessly as she tried to concentrate on what she'd seen of her attackers. Nothing made sense.

They knew about her suspicions that Jonah had been poisoned—which meant someone present at the autopsy. Isaiah, Trey, Jan and the other assistant. Or someone they mentioned it to. Elliot Weiss? No, that made no sense.

Maybe someone overheard her conversation with Mickey? She remembered the open office windows, curtains billowing in the breeze. The two men in the lobby when she'd arrived. From the Sons of Adam, Mickey had said.

Either way, it was an awfully short list of suspects.

"What in God's name have you gotten yourself into?" Gina asked as the clerk walked away. She swung her legs over the side of her gurney. The heel of one of her Jimmy Choo sandals had been snapped off. She crossed her ankles, frowning at the gaping hole it had left behind with a mournful expression.

Gina was waiting for her head CT—she'd had all of her insurance information and so had already been seen. Lydia had refused treatment, thinking it would get her out of here faster, but the all-powerful clerk still had to register her in order to release her Against Medical Advice. She could just walk away, but she hated leaving Gina alone. She'd wait until either Amanda or Nora returned. They'd gone to expedite Gina's CT, otherwise they could be here for hours.

"So, those guys, they sounded like you knew something more about Jonah's death."

Why couldn't Gina have gotten the retrograde amnesia that came with most concussions? Losing those few minutes in the alley might save them both grief. Lydia hopped down from her own gurney, pain thudding through her arm and head, and began pacing. Moving was the best way to keep her mind clear.

"Think they'll come back? Those friends of Jonah Weiss."

Lydia wheeled on her, leaned close and kept her voice low. "Those were no friends of Jonah Weiss."

CHAPTER 16

GINA'S SANDALS CLATTERED TO THE FLOOR. "If they weren't friends of Jonah Weiss, who the hell were they?"

Lydia hesitated. The small curtained alcove was hardly the place to be discussing this. "I'll tell you later."

"We could have gotten killed out there. I deserve to know why."

Seemed like Gina's stubborn streak rivaled Lydia's own. Gina stared at her, condemning her with silence. As she had every right to. It was Lydia's fault she'd gotten hurt.

Lydia swallowed hard. Gina had no idea how lucky they'd been—it was obvious the ER resident came from money, probably never witnessed violence before first hand.

"Gina, you need to be careful what you say and who you say it to. Those guys weren't gay rights activists and they sure as hell weren't friends of Jonah's."

Lydia started pacing again, thinking furiously. When she'd first been ambushed, she'd suspected Isaiah Steward since he had been Jonah's lover and had connections with GOAD—that was before she got a good look at her attackers.

Now the thought seemed humorous. But the truth could potentially be much, much more dangerous.

Her attackers had had tattoos on their arms. A 14 and an 88, as well as intricate Celtic crosses surrounded in flames with swastikas in the center.

"Why did those not-gay, un-friends of Jonah want to hurt you?"

Lydia's head throbbed with every blink. She brushed back the curtain, tempted to wheel Gina up to CT herself, anything for a little peace and quiet so she could think this through, figure out what to do next. She understood Gina's fear and anxiety–the adrenaline rush of the attack only served to heighten those feelings. Her own pulse still surged, refusing to quiet down to its normal rhythm.

"What kind of cop is your boyfriend?" she asked instead. Whoever he was, Gina's cop should be a safe bet. Most right-winged, Aryan Nation supporters didn't date black women.

"A damned good one." Pride surged through Gina's voice. "He's a detective for the major crimes squad."

"Does he have any tattoos?"

"Tattoos? Are you nuts? What kind of question is that?"

"Just answer it."

"No. He's a good, Irish-Catholic boy, doesn't drink or smoke either—I'm the one with all the vices. Wanna see my tats?"

Gina tugged down the waistband of her designer low-riders. Lydia barely glanced at the Chinese lion tattooed over her hip. Gina obviously thought it made her cutting edge. Just like her smoking did. Easy to buck the system when you have money to fall back on when the system bites back. The resident, despite her wise-cracks and tough façade, obviously had a lot to learn about the real world.

Lydia inhaled deeply, forced her clenched fists to open. "I'm sorry you got mixed up in all this. Really, I am."

Before she could say more, Amanda returned with a wheelchair to transport Gina to radiology. Lydia had been surprised to learn that the soft-spoken medical student was Gina's housemate, but somehow it made sense when she saw them together. Opposites who complemented each other. Amanda was still upset, sparing only a quick nod at Lydia as if uncertain how to treat the attending who had fallen so very far and fast.

"Don't leave," Gina called over her shoulder. "You still owe me an explanation."

"I think you owe us all one." Trey Garrison pushed aside the curtain. He turned, allowing Gina and Amanda to pass. "You okay, Gina?"

"Yeah, I'll be fine." Amanda wheeled her into the hallway and out of sight.

Trey had changed into street clothing, a pair of khaki cargo shorts and a wrinkled, moldy-smelling Relay For Life t-shirt. His hair was speckled with white paint, which also streaked his hands. His eyes narrowed as he took in Lydia's blood and grime-streaked shorts and jog bra.

Then he frowned. To Lydia's surprise, he took her arm, scrutinizing the bruises already beginning to form there. "You get checked out? You might need X-rays. Or stitches." His fingers delicately parted her hair, examining her scalp.

"I'm fine. Just waiting to sign out AMA." She backed away from his ministrations.

He looked down at her and for the first time she realized how tall he was. And how warm and mesmerizing those hazel eyes were.

"Why are you here?" she asked. It sounded like a challenge—she didn't mean it that way, but she also didn't need a nursemaid.

He stared at her for a long, hard moment before deigning to answer. She met his gaze, could sense him judging her. "Nora Halloran figured this has something to do with Jonah's death. She knew we both went to the autopsy, so she called me. Said you weren't talking, didn't want the police involved." He pursed his lips in a disapproving frown. "Thought I could talk some sense into you. So, I'll do you a deal. Leave me clean up that cut and tell me what happened."

Without waiting for an answer, he clasped her left hand and led her to the large scrub sink in the far corner. His hand was large, virtually swallowing hers, but he held her lightly, as if guiding a wild animal who might bolt at any moment.

"That's some deal—what do I get out of it?"

The curtain was still open. Several nurses and residents watched, anger in their expressions. Lydia couldn't blame them. Killing the Chief of Surgery's son and getting one of their own hurt was a sure recipe to becoming a *persona non grata*.

"I got to level with you, doc." Garrison yanked the curtain shut. "I checked you out. You've got a reputation for being," he paused, his fingers dancing through the water, checking its temperature, "kind of tenacious."

She looked up at that, unable to stop the smile crossing her face. "Tenacious?"

"What? You didn't think a working man knew fancy words like that?"

Now she chuckled. "No. I don't think 'tenacious' was the word anyone out in L.A. used. Try pig-headed."

He shrugged, pressed his hand against her back, bending her over the sink. His fingers were gentle as they smoothed her hair back from the wound.

"Actually, stubborn as a mule was what your residency director said. With a temper that got you in trouble more than once. Point is, you're the kind of woman who doesn't stop until she gets what she's after."

She lost track of his words as she allowed herself to relax under his hypnotic touch. Her muscles unclenched, adrenaline leaching from their fibers, leaving her sore and aching.

"You got a problem with that?" she asked when he paused to grab some Hibiclens soap.

"No. But you will. Pittsburgh ain't like L.A. This city is good at keeping secrets. If certain people want something buried, it's going to stay buried."

He rubbed the pink soap into a thick lather, then soothed it into her hair. It stung a little, but only for a moment. She breathed in the candy-apple scent.

"Just an abrasion," he commented as he rinsed the soap. His hand circled her eyes, automatically protecting them with the same motion parents use bathing their children. "Lost some skin, but nothing to stitch."

She allowed her head to rest in his strong, open hand. This felt good–almost, well, too good. A familiar warmth stirred in her pelvis as she remembered another side effect of adrenaline–it made her horny as hell.

Not the time or place, she told herself, gently disengaging his hand and standing upright. She dried her hair with the towel he gave her.

"Are you telling me it doesn't matter who killed Jonah Weiss? That you don't care why he died or that someone might get away with murder?" she asked, using the damp towel to dab at the multitude of abrasions lining her forearm.

He was standing too close, but he didn't back away. For a moment she thought he might, thought she'd scared him off. Instead, he raised a hand and tucked an errant strand of dripping hair behind her ear. "Not if it means you might get hurt."

She found it hard to breathe, the air around her was perfumed by his testosterone. Her eye level was right at the notch at the top of his breast bone, that deliciously sensitive v of skin. Her tongue darted out to lick her lips. She forced herself to step sideways, out of range of his intoxicating male scent.

He bent to open a small refrigerator, giving her an excellent view of his well-shaped ass in those almost-too-tight shorts. Nice legs too. He straightened and handed her an ice pack, his grin telling her he knew exactly what she was thinking. And that he liked it.

"What happened out there, doc?"

"Call me Lydia," she said, rubbing the ice pack along her wrist and forearm. "I worked the streets as a medic, just like you."

"Yeah, I heard that you put yourself through school." He paused but didn't look away, kept staring straight into her eyes. "And that you came out of the foster care system, lived on the streets before that."

"Stop looking at me like I was raised by wolves. It's not like it sounds. I just had an—" How to describe Maria to this stranger? "I had an unconventional mother. That's all." She felt his gaze on her, raised her chin. "Some days I wish I stayed out on the streets. More fun, less lawyers."

"No, you don't. I saw you last night. You live for this."

"Yeah." She managed a half-smile. "Too bad I might be out of a job. Permanently."

Trey leaned forward, weight on his palms, one hand brushing hers on the crisp white sheet. She shivered. This was getting way too intense. The way time slowed when he stared at her like that, dismissing the rest of the universe.

Or maybe it was just the adrenaline.

Before she could decide, he slid his hand over top hers, shifted his weight so that he now stood directly in front of her, their legs touching. She met his gaze, tilting her head so that their mouths hovered mere inches apart. His hand feathered up her arm, coming to rest on her shoulder.

"This is probably not such a good idea," she said.

His hand reached her hair, stroking it back from her face, fingertips brushing against her cheekbone.

"Your call," he told her, the words emerging with a whisper of breath.

"To hell with it." She framed his face in her hands and pulled him close.

Their noses bumped in that awkward real-world first kiss kind of way, but he immediately adjusted. Anticipating her movements, just like he had last night in the trauma. His lips pressed against hers and a shudder raced over her body. She opened her mouth beneath his, loved that he kept his eyes locked onto hers, enjoying even more the warmth of his body as he leaned into the embrace.

Her toes curled and tingled as she hooked one leg behind his, pulling him closer still. He lost his balance, catching himself with one hand on the gurney, the other wrapped behind her head, gently cradling her. Lydia felt her eyes closing despite of herself. Damn, he was one hell of a kisser. Made her think maybe there was more to keep her here in Pittsburgh than just her job.

A man's voice shattered the moment as the curtain rattled back. "Someone here call for the cops?"

CHAPTER 17

NORA FOLLOWED BEHIND AMANDA as she pushed Gina's wheelchair into the elevator, clutching Gina's ER chart so tightly the metal threatened to slice into her palms. Slice her wide open, let all her fear and terror and ugly memories spill out for anyone to see.

Amanda hit the button for the second floor, radiology, and the doors slid shut. Nora took the opportunity to take a deep breath, her first since she'd heard Lydia shout for help and ran out to find Lydia and Gina covered in blood. They were both all right, she reminded herself. Both all right.

She knew their blood was still on her hands, despite washing them twice already. You couldn't see it, but she knew it was there. She fought the urge to rush from the elevator, try to wash her hands again. Had the feeling that once she started, she might not stop until she had scrubbed herself raw. As if scrubbing her skin could scrub clean her memories.

It wasn't like she could say anything—Seth was the only person she'd ever told about the rape almost three years ago. Besides, she was over it. She just needed to take charge of her emotions, that was all...

The elevator stopped and they emerged on the second floor.

The CT tech Nora had harangued into jumping Gina's spot in the queue was waiting outside the scanner room. She sent the tech and Amanda into the scanner with Gina who was still protesting that she didn't need a scan, but obviously loving the attention.

Nora continued down the hall to the scanner control room. A few minutes to gather herself together, that was all she needed. Just a little peace and quiet.

She went in and was surprised to find Seth and Lucas there, huddled over the console as they viewed a patient's head CT.

"How's it look?" Seth was asking. He sounded anxious, bent forward, squinting at the grey and white images, his back to her.

Lucas zoomed in on an area, then announced, "It's clear. Nothing."

"I thought you were in clinic," Nora said. Her voice sounded harsh, stretched tight.

Both men jumped. Seth whirled around, now standing with his back against the screen, blocking it from her. Lucas hit some buttons, erasing the images, and swiveled in his chair.

"Nora, what are you doing here?" Seth asked.

She gestured over her shoulder to the scanner behind the thick glass beyond. Gina was climbing up onto the exam table and the tech was preparing the machine. "Gina and the new ER attending were attacked behind Diggers."

"Attacked? Were you there? Are you all right?"

Seth wrapped her in his arms. She was scared and upset and, as much as she wanted to, the last thing she needed was to break down, not here in front of Lucas. She pushed Seth's arms away. "I'm fine. Gina took a hit to the head, has a mild concussion."

She glanced over her shoulder, saw that the tech had Gina positioned. "At least, I hope that's all it is. Lucas, would you stay and read the films? I hate to wait for radiology. Might take forever."

"Sure, no problem," he said absently, his gaze locked on the women in the scanner room. "Who's the blonde with Gina?"

"Gina's roommate. She's a fourth year medical student doing her ER rotation."

The control room door opened and Amanda entered.

"Lucas?" Seth waved a hand to get the neurologist's attention. "About that patient we were discussing? What time do you want him in the sleep lab tonight?"

"Oh, right. That patient. Nine o'clock."

Nora saw the way Lucas's eyes widened at the sight of Amanda. Wondered if that was a good idea for anyone—Lucas was still getting over his divorce and although Amanda was the same age as Nora, she really was just a kid.

"Amanda Mason," Nora made introductions after Seth nudged her, "this is Lucas Stone. He's a neurologist and is going to read Gina's CT for us."

"Nice to meet you, Dr. Stone," Amanda said. She moved into the small, dark room, leaning against the console so she could both watch Gina through the window and have a view of the computer images once they were generated. "I appreciate your helping out."

Lucas tilted his head. "South Carolina?"

"Why yes," Amanda said with a smile. "That's amazing."

"I went to school at Emory," Lucas replied. "Medical school I mean, before I came back home. Here, to Pittsburgh."

Good lord, the man was practically stuttering. And was that a blush Nora spotted crossing Lucas's face? Men, they were all alike. Bring a pretty girl into the picture and they all turned into animals.

She shook her head, trying to shake away her foul thoughts. Spotting a wall mounted canister of hand sanitizer, she globbed some on her palms and rubbed her hands until they turned red.

Seth turned to Nora, one hand stroking her hair as if he needed to remind himself what it felt like. It'd been days since he touched her like that. She remembered what Amanda said and didn't think she could wait until the Fourth, she missed him too much. And after what happened today, she needed him.

"I have to get back to clinic. Are you going to be all right?"

He sounded like he meant it, but at the same time he was edging away from her, not waiting for her answer. She wanted to say so many things, but one glance at Lucas and Amanda and she simply answered, "I'm fine. See you tonight?"

He straightened, one hand already on the doorknob. "I thought you were working tonight?"

"I'm off. Switching to days tomorrow." He frowned, looked puzzled. "You asked me to, remember? So that we could both have the Fourth off?"

"Oh. Well. Right." He looked to Lucas, then glanced out the window at Gina. "If Gina has a concussion, won't she need someone to stay with her tonight?"

"I hadn't thought of that," Amanda said. "I'm back on at seven. Maybe Jerry?"

Nora felt Seth's stare on her, weighting her down. "I can do it."

"Great. I'll see you tomorrow then."

He planted a quick kiss on her forehead. And damn it all, she wanted more. So much more.

The CT tech crowded into the room and slid into his place at the console, starting the scan.

Nora tapped Lucas's arm. He and Seth had grown up in the same neighborhood together, had known each other for years. "What the hell is going on with Seth?"

He flushed, shrugged and looked away, concentrating on the images of Gina's brain flashing on the screen.

"I think he's going to propose," Amanda said, swinging her leg with a jerking motion.

Lucas scrunched his face, as if caught between saying something and saying nothing, and avoided Nora's gaze.

"No bleed or fracture," he finally announced.

"She's all right?" Amanda asked.

"She should be fine. Just fine." He cleared his throat. "Nora, you already know what to look for tonight. How about if you take Gina back down to the ER while I explain the signs and symptoms of increased intra-cerebral pressure to Amanda?"

Amanda gave her a pleading look. Nora shrugged, hands palm up. Amanda should know better, nothing could ever come of it. Not while Amanda was a student. Lucas was an attending, making him strictly off limits.

She grabbed Gina's chart and followed the tech into the scanner, leaving Amanda and Lucas behind.

THE MAN IN THE CONSERVATIVE NAVY SUIT looked too young to be a detective with the Violent Crimes squad—Pittsburgh's equivalent to L.A's elite Robbery Homicide Unit.

"Jerry Boyle," he introduced himself after apologizing for interrupting. Trey moved back, placing space between himself and Lydia, but close enough to hear everything.

Lydia looked at Boyle skeptically. "Could I see some ID, please?"

He fished a wallet from his pants pocket. His hair was dark and his eyes were brown, radiating kindness and empathy. Good eyes for a cop to have—all the better to fool you with.

"Nora Halloran called me. Said my—said that two doctors were assaulted. You're one of them, right? Dr. Fiore?"

Lydia scrutinized his credentials. He was who he said he was. "Yes. Gina is up in CAT scan, but she should be back any minute. I can go find her if you like."

She jumped down from the gurney, pain jarring through her arm, head and assortment of bruises, and almost made it past Boyle. He shifted his weight, nothing threatening, but enough to block her path.

"Actually, Dr. Fiore, Nora said I should speak with you." He flipped open a small notebook. "What happened?"

Lydia cursed Nora's maternal instincts. Over protective and interfering—good qualities in a charge nurse, but the last thing Lydia needed or wanted. Her heart was racing again. Just holding Boyle's badge and ID had jumpstarted a cascade of anxiety she was powerless to stop. She backed up, pressed against the gurney.

Trey seemed to notice her discomfort and slid over to stand at her side. Another one with maternal instincts—well, after that kiss, maybe they were more like territorial instincts.

"Dr. Fiore?" Boyle persisted.

No flight of fancy was going to sidetrack the detective or get Lydia off the hook. Should have feigned amnesia, but it was too late now. Sooner or later, she had to trust someone. She just wished it didn't have to be a cop.

She took a deep breath and told him about the attack behind the bar. Objective observations, no conjecture, just the facts. Including the threats about what would happen if she or Gina went to the cops.

Boyle was a good listener, didn't interrupt, took a few notes but kept his focus on her. Trey on the other hand went rigid, his hand reaching out to squeeze hers as she described being beaten.

"Sounds like you gave as good as you got," Trey said when she finished. Was that a hint of pride in his voice? "If Gina hadn't showed up—"

"Her and her damn cigarettes," Boyle muttered. Lydia glanced at him in surprise, watched as he re-composed his mask of indifference. "Er, I mean—"

Lydia felt compelled to defend Gina. After all, it was because of Lydia that she had gotten hurt. "It wasn't her fault, she was just in the wrong place at the wrong time."

"My specialty," Gina herself called out, flinging the curtain aside as Nora wheeled her in. "Good news. My brain is normal." She glanced at Boyle. "No jokes from the peanut gallery. I see you two have met. So did you solve the case, rustle up the bad guys yet?"

Boyle seemed nonplussed to have his personal life collide with his professional. He glanced at each of them, then crossed over to Gina, looking like he wanted to scoop her up. Instead, he reached down a hand to help her to her feet and guide her over to the gurney. "You're sure you're all right?"

"Of course."

Boyle turned to Nora. "That true? The doctors cleared her?"

Nora smiled. "She's fine. They're working on her discharge papers now. She'll need someone to stay with her tonight. I can do it if you're busy."

"No, no way, I'll—" He took a deep breath, slowed down. "I mean, thank you, but I can handle it. I appreciate the offer."

"No problem." Nora beamed like a mother hen who had seen all her chicks come home to roost. "Dr. Fiore, are you going to tell us what exactly happened out there? I think we deserve an explanation."

"It's no good, Nora," Gina said, swinging her legs from her position on the gurney, one arm wrapped around Boyle's. "She wouldn't tell me anything. Said she'd only tell Jerry—if he didn't have any tattoos."

"Tattoos?" Boyle and Trey chorused. They squared off, looking each other up and down like alpha dogs—and alpha males—did. Lydia shook her head at the scene. This was getting out of control. She shut the curtain, wishing for more privacy.

"In L.A, I knew a few cops who sympathized with the Aryan Nation."

"Aryan Nation?" Trey said. "I thought you said they were members of GOAD?"

"I said they wore GOAD t-shirts." Lydia sighed, tried to think of the best way to explain everything. It was hard to do since most of what she had were theories and speculations. “The Sons of Adam, they’re like Pittsburgh’s version of the Aryan Nation, right?”

Boyle’s fingers clamped down on the thin mattress he leaned against. “Yeah. Why?” he asked with a long pause between his words.

“I think they might have murdered Jonah Weiss.”

CHAPTER 18

AMANDA WATCHED NORA WHEEL GINA AWAY and turned back to Dr. Stone. His eyes were on her and she was surprised to see him blush and look away. With his sandy hair and fair complexion, it made him look like a teenager.

She slid away from the console and into the chair beside him, spinning the chair close enough that their knees touched. He jumped, and there was that blush again. She'd seen Gina do this when they went club-hopping—make guys stutter and drop things—but she'd never been able to do it herself. A warm glow danced over her. It was kind of fun, this feeling of excitement and power.

Not to mention the naughty certainty that her mother would definitely disapprove.

"Should I call you, Doctor?" she asked, making her voice drop like Gina did when she was talking Jerry into doing something he didn't want to do.

Lucas Stone pushed his chair so hard away from her that he ricocheted off the rear wall. A clipboard hanging there fell, hitting him on the shoulder before it clattered to the floor.

Amanda laughed. Time to get serious. He was an attending,

after all. But he had started it, asking her to stay behind.

"Call me?" he squeaked, cleared his throat. "Call me."

"Yes, if Gina shows any signs of increased intracranial pressure." He stared at her, raising the clipboard like it was a shield and he needed protection. "From her concussion?"

"Er. Right. Actually, Ms. Mason—"

"Amanda, please." There was no rule that said an attending couldn't call her by her first name.

He heaved in a breath as if it was his last one. "Actually, Ms. Mason, I asked you to remain behind so that I could see when you would be free for a clinic appointment."

She blinked. "Free for a what?"

"Neurology clinic. And we'll probably need to schedule some tests. MRI, MRA, maybe an LP. What other symptoms are you exhibiting?"

"Symptoms?" She bounced to her feet. What an idiot, thinking he'd been flirting with her. "I assure you, Dr. Stone, I have no symptoms that you need to concern yourself with."

He stood, facing her, his gaze narrowed and she knew he knew she was lying. Too bad. A gentleman wouldn't just come out and start dissecting a lady's health like that, so blunt and clinical like she was a lab rat or something. Just as a gentleman would never call a lady a liar.

"You're lying," he said, his voice low, throaty. The kind of voice she'd dreamed of hearing when a man asked for her hand in marriage—serious, committed, earnest. "I saw you stumble, you have a mild foot-drop, and that tremor in your leg—"

"How dare you!" She spun on her heel, glad her foot was only half asleep and she didn't lose her balance. The rapid movement did make black spots dance before her eyes, but the door wasn't that far away and she made it out without stumbling.

He followed her. "How long since you lost feeling in your fourth and fifth toes, Ms. Mason?" he called after her.

Amanda risked a glance over her shoulder. No one was around, thank God. No one except Stone looking self-righteous in his pristine white lab coat, arms crossed over his chest like he was Marcus Welby Jr.

"Has it extended up your lateral gastrocnemius yet? It will. When it does, come see me."

"Dr. Stone." She stopped and faced him once more. Couldn't believe she'd ever thought he was handsome. Arrogant was more like it. "I can assure you that if I ever do develop any symptoms requiring evaluation, you'll be the last man on earth that I'd come to!"

There, that was telling him. Glad to leave with her dignity intact, she pivoted, only to catch her toes on the carpet. Her legs crossed, arms flailed, and she fell to the floor in a thud.

Stone was there in a flash. Gee, he moved fast. Almost fast enough to catch her. Not that that would have salvaged her pride. She ended up sitting on the floor, her blouse twisted and half-undone. She fumbled with her buttons as he knelt behind her and raised her back onto her feet as if she weighed nothing at all.

"That was your right foot," he said, wrapping one arm around her waist and leading her to a nearby chair like she was a child. "Your foot drop was in your left."

"It moves around, comes and goes," she admitted. Then she bit down hard on her lip. She wasn't going to say anything. Talking about it made it real. Too real. He was looking at her with such an expression of concern that it was frightening. "It's nothing, really. Doesn't cause me any problems with patients, honestly."

"Honestly," he echoed her, his voice low again, very, very serious. "You need to tell me everything. Now."

"DR. FIORE, YOU NEED TO TELL ME EVERYTHING. Now. Why do you think the Sons of Adam killed Jonah Weiss?" Boyle demanded.

Lydia suddenly found herself in her least favorite place: the center of attention. She began to pace, anxious enough without feeling their stares, but Trey stepped in front of her, taking her arm.

"Those crazy sonsofbitches are the ones who tried to kill you?"

"I don't know, not for sure." She shook off his hand, surprised by the vehemence of his anger. "Tried to warn me, not kill me. If they'd wanted to kill me, they had plenty of chances."

"Why would they want to kill Jonah Weiss?" Trey asked.

Doubt flooded over her. It all felt like it made sense in her mind, but spoken out loud she realized how few facts she actually had. "Maybe it was his ex-lover, Isaiah Steward. All I know is that someone killed him."

"Steward?" Boyle put in. "The medical examiner? What the hell is going on here?" He left Gina's side to face Lydia.

Great, two angry males to deal with. And one of them a cop. A dream come true. Lydia blew her breath out, ready to explain when the curtain was whisked open once more.

"They told me Dr. Fiore is here?"

A tall, buxom middle-aged woman with a helmet of blond hair stepped into the center of the room. Her gaze darted from one person to the next, waving her phone at each of them as if anointing them. Finally she looked at Lydia, her hopeful expression failing.

"Dr. Fiore? I'm Carol Wierschesny. From Three Rivers Realty? We spoke earlier, but you weren't answering your cell, so I took a chance and came here, thought you might be working. I've a fantastic property that just came on the market, it'd be perfect for you, but we need to move fast." She spoke all this in a rapid fire staccato, heels clacking as she zeroed in on Lydia. "Here, look at these photos." She thrust her iPhone out. "Isn't it fabulous? And what a steal, only one point two."

Lydia barely glanced at the photos of the mini-mansion.

White columns, solid brick, looming out from its perch on top of a hill, the house reminded her of a Poe story more than a home. Unless maybe it was a home for the criminally insane. "Mrs. Wierschesny, I told you that's out of my price range—"

Carol obviously came from the Dale Carnegie school of never taking "no" for an answer. "My associate is working right now to get you pre-qualified for a 110% loan, so you'd walk away from the table with no cash down and money in your pocket. Isn't that fantastic?" Her shoe slipped in a puddle of bloody water and she stopped short. "I'm sorry, have I come at a bad time?"

Nora came to Lydia's rescue. "Yes. No cell phones in the ER, you'll need to take that outside. Now." Despite the fact that Nora was dressed in street clothes, the realtor obeyed, returning her iPhone to her Prada purse and backing away.

"Really, Dr. Fiore, I can't guarantee this listing will still be there tomorrow—"

"I'm not interested, Mrs. Wierschesny." Lydia closed her eyes for a brief moment, wishing the real estate agent gone.

"Lydia," Nora said, taking her arm. "Let's go down to the locker room and get you cleaned up."

"We'll meet you at Diggers," Boyle said. "Where we can continue this in private."

Lydia glanced back over her shoulder, saw Gina holding Boyle's arm as she tottered into her broken sandals. Carol Wierschesny wasn't taking the hint and practically jogged after them as Nora guided her to the women's locker room.

"Authorized personnel only," Nora told her, shutting the door in the realtor's face.

"I'll call you tomorrow, Dr. Fiore!"

Lydia collapsed onto a bench half laughing, half crying. "I'll never be rid of that woman."

"So, just fire her."

"I already have—twice. I never knew realtors were like a

herpes virus, coming back to haunt you when you least want them."

Nora sat down beside her. "Sounds like some guys I've dated." They were silent for a few minutes. "Listen, Lydia, I need to know something. Gina's a friend. I know she thinks she knows it all and acts like, well, you know, but if she's in danger—"

"Those guys have no idea who she is," Lydia assured her. Then she frowned, hoping it was true—had she used Gina's name during the scuffle? She couldn't remember for certain. "I am so sorry she got mixed up in all this. It's my fault she was hurt."

"She says you saved her."

Lydia shook her head. "They wanted to teach me a lesson. If I hadn't been so stubborn, they never would have hit her like that, would have let us both go with a few scrapes. I was angry and it made me stupid."

Nora sat for a moment, staring at her. "Just so it doesn't happen again. Let's get you some clean scrubs to wear."

Her tone was business-like as she scurried around the room grabbing a top and pair of pants for Lydia. Lydia had the distinct feeling that she'd lost even more ground with the charge nurse. She ran through a quick shower, changed into the scrubs and she and Nora walked over to Diggers.

It reminded Lydia of some of the coffee shops she and her ER cohorts back in L.A. had haunted. Architecturally it couldn't be more different, but the atmosphere was the same: booths and tables where groups could congregate and discuss the events of the day without risking being overheard, hearty food that was dirt cheap, a jukebox with an eclectic collection spanning three decades of cover tunes and re-mixes. Home sweet home.

Boyle had appropriated a private room behind the bar. Spread out over a large plank table were plates of pierogies, salsa, soggy nachos and baskets of French fries. Trey jumped up and pulled out a chair beside him for Lydia.

She debated taking another seat, didn't like the way he

assumed they were partners in crime, so to speak, but it wasn't worth the effort. She needed all the good will she could get from this crowd. After everyone ordered, Boyle rapped his knife against his iced tea glass.

"Dr. Fiore, I'd love to question you in private, but since we've already begun this discussion under less than optimal circumstances—"

"Shut up, Jerry," Gina said, elbowing him. "Lydia. Tell us what's up. What really killed Jonah Weiss?"

Lydia choked down a mouthful of onion pierogie—they reminded her of the empanadas she used to buy from street vendors in L.A.—and explained about her suspicions that Jonah was poisoned. "Even if there is cyanide in his tissues, it will be hard to prove. A lot of times it doesn't show up."

"Cyanide?" Boyle said, back in cop mode, his tone skeptical. "Are you certain?"

Nora sat directly across from Lydia, a frown furrowing her face, digging deep crevices in her freckled forehead. Trey had taken Lydia's hand, she hadn't even noticed it until now. She would have shaken free, but it felt good.

"Doesn't sound like the way the Sons of Adam operate," Boyle continued. "A burning cross and lynch mob would be more like it. Why do you think they're behind it?"

"The guys who jumped us. They wore GOAD t-shirts but all three had tattoos of a Celtic cross with a swastika in the center, and two of them had tattoos with the numbers 14 and 88."

He frowned. "Gang tats I know. But 1488? What's that, a date?"

"Fourteen stands for the fourteen words of the white supremacist creed. Eight stands for the eighth letter of the alphabet."

Nora counted off the letters. "H."

"Right. Eighty-eight. Heil Hitler. I used to see tattoos like that on the skinheads and Aryan Nation men who came through my ER in L.A."

"Jeez Lydia," Gina said, "I think you're going for some kind of record. Haven't even worked a full shift and already you've managed to piss off the Chief of Surgery, an Assistant Medical Examiner, and both the gay-rights fanatics *and* the local skinheads."

Trey didn't appreciate the levity. His lips tightened into a flat line of disapproval. "You could have gotten killed."

"He's right, Doctor," Boyle said. "These guys are not to be taken lightly. Their first leader, Sarah Kent, died in a police chase last year. She had enough explosives and weapons in her car to start a small war."

"So why haven't you arrested them? Shut them down?" Gina asked.

"Out of my hands. The ATF raided their compound—twice since Sarah Kent died—but have come up empty. I'm sure they and the FBI are watching them, but it's not in my jurisdiction. There's nothing we could do." Boyle raised a questioning eyebrow at Lydia. "Until now."

"I can identify them," she said, knowing what he wanted. "If you need me to." It wouldn't be easy. Going into a police station or even testifying in court was not on her top ten list of favorite things to do.

"How about you, Gina?"

Gina hung her head, shaking it. "I didn't—I couldn't. I can't remember anything, it's all a blur. I didn't even notice those tattoos Lydia saw."

Nora patted Gina's arm. "That's all right, sweetie. That's perfectly normal after a trauma. You know that."

Boyle seemed ready to forget the police work, his hand inching towards Gina's, but then he cleared his throat and focused on Lydia. "So let me get this straight. First, you thought Jonah was poisoned by his ex-lover who also is in position to hide the evidence. And now, after you were assaulted by three men with Aryan Nation tats you're blaming the Sons of Adam. Hate to say this, Lydia, but we do have more than one fringe hate-group here in Pittsburgh."

"All I know is what I saw and what my gut instinct tells me."

Boyle's sigh emerged as rough as a growl. Trey straightened and glared at the other man. Lydia tried to ignore them both and started over, from the beginning this time.

"Jonah's father is threatening to get my medical license revoked and press criminal charges, so after the autopsy I went to meet my lawyer. Her name is Mickey Cohen and—"

"I know Mickey," Boyle said. "Does work for the ACLU."

"Right. She's also friends with Jonah, mentored him through law school. She's the one who told me that Isaiah was his lover."

"Ex-lover," Trey put in.

"Ex-lover. Anyway, when I was in her office there were two men there. Mickey told me they were from the Sons of Adam. One was praying, trying to convert me or something."

"Tall, pale eyes, wispy blond hair?" Boyle asked. Lydia nodded. "Sounds like Matthew Kent, the new leader of the Sons of Adam. Sarah was his wife."

"He seemed pretty harmless—from a physical violence point of view. Not the kind to be planning a religious war."

"Matthew preaches nonviolent conversion of the masses. His wife took a more militant view of things. We've heard there's a rift in the Sons of Adam—some of them still want to follow Sarah's teachings of justified violence."

"The other man with Matthew, Hampton was his name," Lydia continued. "He was a true blue skinhead—the clothes, shaved head, and he had the same tattoo as the three men who attacked us. A Celtic cross surrounded by fire with a swastika in the center."

"Was he one of your attackers?"

"No. But I couldn't see the fourth man, the one driving the SUV."

"Gina, did you?"

The ER resident shook her head, her eyes darkening as if the true impact of what happened earlier was just now hitting her.

Boyle pursed his lips. "I'll try to run down the tat, see if it's unique to the Sons of Adam. Maybe this Hampton is trying for a power play, taking the organization back to Sarah Kent's more militant path. Can you give me a basic description of the men who attacked you?"

She started with the first two and finished with Number Three—the one she had gotten the best look at. "At least 6'4", he wore jeans, black high-tops, a GOAD t-shirt. He was white, pale complexion with nasty acne, very muscular. I wouldn't be surprised if he was on steroids. His scalp was shaven, no piercings that I could see, he had a eighty-eight tattooed on the back of his left hand and another tat, the one that they all had, on his right bicep. He recently got out of prison—"

"How the hell can you know that?" Boyle asked, looking up from his notebook where he was furiously scribbling.

They were all looking at her with skepticism, even Trey. Rubes. Maria would have taken them all for everything they had within minutes. Lydia pushed her chair back, squeaking it against the wood floor. "Same way I know Trey's mother still does his laundry. Or that your mother has red hair, Detective Boyle."

Trey straightened. "Hey. How'd you know that?"

Lydia sighed. "You ran out of your house wearing only shorts and your sneakers, but you have no socks despite the fact that those shoes look new. You grabbed your t-shirt from where you left it wadded up in your closet or truck—from the smell and wrinkles, it's been there awhile. But your shorts aren't wrinkled, they still have a crease pressed in them. So, my guess is that you take your laundry over to your parents' house and your mom does it—but you haven't had time lately and you ran out of socks."

Trey blinked. Everyone stared at Lydia as if she were a side-show freak. Gina spoke up. "Is that true?"

"Yeah. I don't have a washer or dryer—" Trey shook his head. "Yeah. She's right."

Gina leaned forward, elbows almost knocking over her glass. "Do me next."

Lydia glanced at the resident. Gina didn't realize it but she was the easiest of the bunch. Those calluses on her middle fingers—old, healed, thank goodness, but they spoke of an eating disorder. Which meant a need for perfection, control, someone who was still a child at heart, who would rebel—all of which Gina had already revealed in the short time they'd known each other.

"You're a perfectionist," she finally said, taking the easy way out. Never embarrass the client, Maria always said. Make them feel good about themselves. "You come from money," she nodded in the direction of Gina's expensive shoes, "but you want to give something back, so you chose emergency medicine."

"Wow. You're right. How do you do that?"

"It's nothing. My mom taught me. Get close enough to a person to shake their hand and you can learn a lot about them just by observing."

Boyle was still eyeing her. He understood the implications, that she'd spent time as a grifter. As soon as he got back to his station, he'd be running a background check on her, she was sure.

"Wanna tell me what your story is, Dr. Fiore? Did you get into this much trouble out in L.A.?"

"I don't go looking for trouble, Detective. But I don't run from it either."

"So I see." His gaze took in her assortment of scrapes and bruises. "And my mother?"

That he asked surprised her. Most cops she knew would have maintained the illusion that they were in control, knew what she was doing and how she did it. They wouldn't succumb to curiosity and risk appearing weak.

Lydia couldn't resist the smile that snuck up on her. She was warming to Boyle, despite his chosen profession.

"As soon as Nora and Gina entered the room back in the ER, you changed. Your posture straightened, your language became formal, no swearing, less contractions, your attitude respectful, you weren't nervous about demonstrating affection towards Gina. The way a man acts when he's around his mother if he comes from a close-knit family. It was an easy guess that what triggered your response was someone who looked like your mother. So since Nora has red hair…"

"Mrs. Boyle does too," Gina finished for her. "And she does. I always thought you had a thing for Nora, Jerry. Now I know why."

"I don't have a thing—" Boyle interrupted himself, took control. "Enough parlor tricks. Dr. Fiore, can you come to the station house tomorrow, look at some photos?"

"Why don't you have a sketch artist do it, like on TV?" Gina asked.

"That's TV. We don't have that kind of money, not for a simple assault."

"I'm doing a ride-along in the morning but I can come after."

"That will work. It will take me time to convince the feds to share their surveillance photos of the Sons of Adam." He brightened. "If I can get them interested, then maybe they'd foot the bill for a sketch artist, if we need one. Can you think of anything else helpful?"

"Hampton and Kent were talking about the Fourth of July, and Mickey said something about a protest."

Boyle jerked his head up at that. "Word just came down today. A judge upheld their right to protest at GOAD's rally downtown on the Fourth."

"The only people who knew I suspected Jonah was poisoned were Isaiah Steward, his staff at the ME's office, Trey, and Mickey. There's no way the ME's office would have released that information, right?" She looked to confirmation.

"As far as the public knows, Jonah died as a result of the car accident," Boyle confirmed. "His father tried to get the DA to force us to investigate it as a homicide, but that won't go anywhere until the ME's report is final. Right now it's an open case."

"Who else could have known that Lydia suspected he was poisoned?" Nora asked.

"Maybe Kent or Hampton overheard me talking about Jonah's death, and sent the goons in the GOAD shirts to cement my suspicion that Isaiah was behind it?" Lydia answered.

"Deflecting suspicion from the Sons of Adam. They weren't counting on you recognizing those tattoos," Gina chimed in, leaning forward in excitement.

Trey was tapping his empty beer bottle on the table in an agitated staccato. "So now you're the only eye-witness. I don't like the sound of that."

Lydia bristled at his over-protectiveness. "I can take care of myself."

He and Boyle exchanged glances, obviously not convinced. She ignored them, focusing on her now cold food, shoveling it in. It tasted like white paste and she wasn't hungry but it was better than continuing to dwell on what might have happened today.

She reached for her tea and gulped it down, her mouth suddenly dry. Images of the attack flashed through her mind in a flurry of motion and blood. She brushed her hand over her scalp, wincing. Stared across the table at Gina and swallowed hard against a wave of fear and guilt.

The hardest thing about what happened today was knowing that it could have been so much worse.

CHAPTER 19

AFTER BOYLE FINISHED WRINGING OUT ALL THE INFORMATION Lydia could give him, Trey insisted on escorting her back to the Pilgrim Inn. If she hadn't been running on reserves, she would have found the energy to be irritated. "I don't need any help. I'm fine."

"So you keep saying," he said, glancing over her medley of bruises and scrapes. "I don't think you understand how dangerous the Sons of Adam are."

"And you do?"

He stopped, leaned against the wall of her motel, scanning the parking lot as he spoke. "Not me. My dad. Last year in fact, almost to the day."

"What happened?"

"He was involved in the high speed chase that killed Sarah Kent. My dad is—was—a sheriff's deputy, was the first to intercept her. The pursuit led into the city and by the time it was over he'd rolled his vehicle, Sarah Kent's car exploded, and an off-duty city cop was burned pretty bad."

"Your dad? Was he okay?"

"Broken pelvis, dislocated hip. Then he had a heart attack while in the hospital—the stress of it all. Ended up retiring from the force." His gaze returned to her. "The point is, my dad got into the crash because he was maneuvering to block Sarah. When she realized there was no escape she started speeding right towards a schoolyard where a bunch of kids were playing, would have killed them all if he hadn't stopped her. That's the kind of people the Sons of Adam are."

Suicide bombing didn't quite fit the impression she'd gotten of Matthew Kent earlier that day. But she'd only met him for a few minutes. They arrived at her room and she unlocked the door, Trey still hovering, watching her every move.

"I don't think you should stay here," he told her. "We should pack up your stuff, move you."

Okay, enough of this already. "Where?" she asked him pointedly. "Your place?"

"Ah, no, er—I don't really have a place." To her surprise, he looked away. "You were right about that. My job—before I became a District Chief a few months ago—was pretty crazy hours, rotating shifts. So I moonlight a couple places. One of them is remodeling homes and usually I just crash wherever I'm working." He shrugged, defensive now. "I mean, what's the good settling down? There's always something better down the road."

Another wandering spirit—just like Maria. One more reason not to get involved with him.

"Right," she muttered, turning the key and pushing the door open.

She flicked the lights on. The musty smell had intensified with the AC running on high all afternoon. The room now felt like summer in the Arctic Circle. She stepped inside, shivering, and turned to tell him goodbye. Trey was right there, beside her, eyes scouring the room as if searching for an enemy.

"You want to look under the bed, too?" she asked, leaning against the door jamb as he pushed in front of her. Seemed like she'd inherited a Knight Errant. Not that she needed one.

He turned a full circle, looking around the room.

"Where's the rest of your stuff?" he asked, nodding to her long board propped in the corner beside the backpack bulging with her climbing gear. She'd packed her clothes in the same luggage she'd used when she was younger, shuttling from one foster home to the next: three black plastic garbage bags. "In storage?"

"No. I travel light."

She held the door open, hoping he'd get the hint. Instead, he leaned over the dresser, peering at the photos in their cardboard frames propped up against the mirror and the cheap charm bracelet laid out in front of them. First thing she'd done with her first paycheck way back when was to buy nice frames, one silver and one Brazilian heartwood, but the faded photos didn't look right in anything but the sweat-stained cardboard holders with their flaking fake gold leaf trim.

"Don't touch those."

He jerked his hand away, gave her a strange look. She realized she'd yelled—old habits die hard.

She didn't care about her other stuff, learned fast that anything you owned was fair game in the foster care system, but she'd fought more than one bloody battle to protect that bracelet and those two photos.

"This you and your mom?" he asked, his voice funny—it had that same gentle cadence he'd used in the ER when cleaning her wounds.

She nodded and stepped closer, snatching the photos from the dresser, her pulse soothing into a steady rhythm once she held them. "They're all I have left of her."

This was getting all too weird, having him here, touching her stuff. She was already teetering on the edge. After what happened in the alley, not being able to protect Gina, it was a good bet that this was going to be a sleepless night filled with images of blood and cops and running and screams and...Maria. Panic was creeping up on her, edging beneath her defenses, ready to pounce. She needed to get

Trey out of here before it attacked.

"Were you guys migrant workers?" he asked, gesturing to the oldest photo, one of her when she was six, pretending to help Maria pick lettuce in the fields.

He appeared oblivious to her agitation. Or maybe it was a misguided attempt to lull her back into calm. He had no idea that talking about Maria and her childhood was the last thing that would accomplish that.

"For a while. We moved around a lot, did a lot of things."

"She was a beautiful woman. You look like her." He traced his finger down her arm as she clutched her photos tight against her chest.

Lydia flinched against the flare of sexual heat that accompanied his touch. In the past she'd found that filling her bad nights with meaningless, adrenaline-fueled sex was an effective way to defend against the panic. No fuss, no muss, just lots of hot, sweaty sex—best exorcism around.

So here they were. He wanted it, she could tell. She wanted it, she needed it. But…she couldn't. She wouldn't. Not after the way he had treated her today.

Tenderness, compassion—they weren't part of the exorcism ritual. Neither was allowing someone to get close, and here she'd let him into her inner sanctum. What the hell had she been thinking?

"It's getting late," she said, forcing her voice to sound normal. Or as close to normal as it could with anxiety churning her gut, colliding head on with the sexual need throbbing through her veins—a perfect storm brewing inside her. "I have a ride-along first thing tomorrow."

His gaze locked onto her eyes. He stood motionless for a long moment. That was one of the things she liked about him. Unlike Lydia with her kinetic hyper-drive in constant high gear, Trey could stand still. Not just stand still, be still. Calm radiated from him, inviting her to share his easy-going tranquility.

He stepped past her to the doorway, then turned back, giving her one more chance.

Flirting with disaster, she wrapped one hand around his head, standing on tip-toe to bring his lips to hers, their bodies pressed together, her childhood memories trapped between them, and she stole one more kiss. This one wasn't as frenzied or awkward as the one in the ER. It was a quiet, deep sharing that left her trembling when she finally gathered enough strength to push him away.

"Goodbye," she said, gripping the door so he wouldn't see her hand shaking. She choked back her regret. But she had to protect herself, protect her secrets, and letting him stay tonight was just too damn dangerous.

His smile was wide, revealing a dimple in his left cheek that was new to her. "I'll see you in the morning."

"What?" His words jolted through her. Last thing she needed was Trey Garrison and his sex appeal disturbing her ride-along. "No, I'm riding with Sevens tomorrow. Not Med Five."

He nodded, eyes crinkling with merriment. "I'm a District Chief—I ride with whoever, whenever I want. You don't think I'm going to risk setting you loose on any of my guys, do you?"

With that, he was gone. Lydia shut the door, leaning against it for a long, long minute, the rattling of the air conditioner the only sound. This was new territory for her—a kiss that left her light-headed, a touch that soothed and offered comfort, a man who maybe she could trust?

Disturbed and baffled, she carefully re-positioned her photos on the dresser where they would face her bed. The second one was her favorite, she and Maria at the Santa Monica pier just a month or so before Maria was killed.

Her fingers brushed against the image, knocking it over. Sweat broke out over her and the whooshing of her heart filled her ears, so loud she wanted to cover them with her hands and scream to drown out the sounds she knew would soon be following. She spun away, placing her back against the wall, arms wrapped around tight her chest, forcing herself to breathe.

It was the moldy, musty smell the wheezing air conditioner left in its wake that finally sent her over the edge. She slid to the floor, body rocking, knees to her chest, one hand covering her mouth to silence her screams. Just like she had eighteen years ago when she was twelve years old, hidden behind the musty drapes of a dark confessional, listening helplessly as her mother was murdered.

CHAPTER 20

AMANDA HAD STARTED HER SHIFT THAT NIGHT thinking maybe she'd been wrong about Jim Lazarov. The intern had been charming at first, even tried to teach her a few things—despite her already knowing them. Then she realized that he was just showing off for the attending and a pre-med college student who was observing, doing some kind of article on stress in night-shift workers. The student seemed nice enough, but Jim spent all his time giving him a tour of the ED, leaving her to do all the scut work.

It made for a frustrating night and she was already battling exhaustion. Amanda wasn't about to say anything to the attending—that would have been a breach of protocol that would have done her more harm than good. So she did the work, still managing to get some interesting patients that the nurses set aside for her, irritating Lazarov to no end.

"Hey, there," the soft-spoken college student said, having somehow shaken free of Jim. "I'm Bob. Bob Brown. Can I join you?"

"I'm Amanda." She was headed out to the ambulance bay to wait for Med Five who was transporting a nursing home patient. "Sure, but it's nothing interesting. Just a LOL-DFD."

"What?"

"A little old lady, done fell down. Usually with these nursing home patients that translates to a broken hip and direct to Ortho. But we need to check her first, make sure there's nothing else going on."

"The ortho guys won't do that?" Bob asked as they stepped out into the humid night air.

"Are you kidding? Orthopods don't even know what end of a stethoscope to use." She remembered who she was talking to and clamped a hand over her mouth. "I'm sorry. Please don't use that in your article—my mama would kill me for speaking out of turn like that. I didn't mean it, I'm just tired."

"I won't tell your mother if you don't," he said. "Besides, we don't always do exactly what our mothers want. Look at me, my mother wanted me to go into politics. But you have to follow your own path, right? Even if it means going it alone."

Boy, did she ever know how that felt, a thousand miles away from home, the first one in her family to even make it to college. At least her family supported her in her ambitions. "Well, don't ever give up. You have to follow your dreams. You owe that to yourself."

His smile returned, edged with flashing red lights as the ambulance pulled up. "You're absolutely right. Thanks, Amanda."

NORA LET HERSELF INTO THE BLOOMFIELD TOWNHOUSE she and Seth rented. It was a nice place—the entire row of houses had originally been built in the 1920's and boasted high ceilings, gorgeous woodwork, and red oak floors. The sound of claws skittering across the wood floors greeted her as a yellow lab bounded from the kitchen.

"DeBakey, down," she told the dog who instantly obeyed, tail thumping against the floor, eyes locked onto Nora's face in anticipation. "Good boy, good puppy," Nora crooned, scratching the dog's neck as he leaned against her, hoping for more loving. She obliged, even though she knew the kid next door they paid to watch DeBakey would have already taken him for a run and played with him. "Seth?"

She knew he wasn't here, but called his name anyway. Had he come home at all? DeBakey's empty food and water bowls gave her her answer. She quickly fed the dog, debated eating something herself, but the thought of food made her jaw clench with nausea as she remembered what happened at lunch.

She leaned against the kitchen counter, eyes closed, listening to the dog slop down his food, fighting the urge to scream. Images of her own attack layered over images of Gina and Lydia.

She forced her eyes open. Every breath she took smelled of Seth, reminding her of his absence, everywhere she looked was some brightly colored memory. She and Seth on vacation in Cancun. At a Pirates' game. At Kennywood, riding rollercoasters. Laughing, having fun, with everything to look forward to.

DeBakey finished, then came and nudged her expectantly. Nora gave in and took him for a long walk that just happened to wander past Seth's favorite haunts—the sports bar on Howley, the Liberty Avenue bookstore, and Arsenal Park.

She'd already stopped in at Angels after leaving Diggers, searching the hospital from top to bottom. No sign of Seth and no one was expecting him. There were no patients in crisis who couldn't live without him, no marathon operations in progress. And no Seth.

Lord, she didn't want to be alone tonight. Even if all he did was hold her, that would be enough. More than enough.

The park was a perennial hit with DeBakey who sniffed the ground and waggled his butt like he'd never, ever been here before and thought whoever had built a dog run inside the city park was just the bestest human ever. He was the only dog there tonight, but he didn't seem to mind, chasing squirrels while she watched from the swings beside the enclosure.

Finally, the sun began to set and it was time to go home. Still no word from Seth. Nora began to wonder if maybe Amanda was wrong, maybe he wasn't really going to propose, maybe she wasn't going to have the fairytale wedding she'd dreamed of. Some people just weren't cut out for a happily-ever-after, maybe she was one of those…

She jumped off the swing, banishing her doubts with thoughts that maybe Seth was waiting for her at home.

She looked at her cell phone for the twenty-sixth time. Still no messages. She'd already called and left two messages, as much as she wanted to call him again, she stilled her fingers. She was stronger than that, she was a grown woman, she could handle one night alone.

"DeBakey," she called, drawing some stares from a few kids playing nearby.

Poor dog, that's what happened when you let a surgeon name an animal. DeBakey didn't seem to mind being named after a pioneering cardiac surgeon. He galloped to her side, sitting when she stretched out her palm and waiting until she attached the lead again.

She scratched the dog's ears. "Let's go home."

It was almost dark when they turned the corner onto her block. Nothing stirred in the heavy humidity. The porches and stoops were empty, no signs of life. Nora stopped, fear clenching her chest. DeBakey stood at alert beside her, head swiveling as if trying to pinpoint the danger. Finally, he gave up and let out a small, confused whimper.

Tonight had nothing in common with that New Year's Eve almost three years ago. Nothing at all. That night had been crisp and cold, roads covered in black ice, she'd been a little drunk and so had her date, so they'd splurged on a cab ride to end the evening. Nora had been living in East Liberty then, had kissed her date, Matt Zersky, goodnight. It had been their second date and they really hadn't clicked, but she couldn't skip the chance to wear her new dress and go out for New Year's, not after missing Christmas with her family because of work. Matt had rode off in the cab and she'd walked up to her apartment building's doors, and...

DeBakey gave out another whimper, pressing his wet snout beneath her palm, jolting her from the memory. Nora blinked, pulled herself back to the here and now. Out alone at night in the dark wasn't the time or place to let her mind wander. She needed to stay alert, stay in control.

She wrapped DeBakey's leash around her hand, keeping him close, forcing her feet, numb with fear, to propel her down the block and up the steps to her house, half expecting Seth to come running out to meet her.

But he didn't. The house was dark, empty.

Only after leading the dog through every room, checking every shadow, locking the doors and windows, and insuring that she was truly alone, did she let the dog free of his leash. DeBakey ran to his water bowl, lapping most of it onto the floor, but Nora didn't mind. She stood, one palm pressed against her throat as if reminding herself not to scream.

She closed her eyes, wished Seth was here. Angry at herself for the weakness, for the needing. And wondering where he was.

CHAPTER 21

AFTER WORKING THROUGH HER PANIC ATTACK, Lydia washed away the remnants of fear with a long, scalding shower. The hot water stung her assorted abrasions but felt good against her clenched muscles.

She threw on her "No Fear" t-shirt to sleep in, liking the subliminal message. Not that she was counting on getting any sleep, not tonight, not after what had happened in the alley earlier. Her breath escaped her with a whoosh that echoed around the empty room. As a doctor she knew all about post-traumatic stress, as a kid the county had put her through counseling and cognitive behavioral therapy. None of which was protection against rebel memories that would side-swipe her when triggered.

Sometimes it was the sound of a woman singing, sounding like Maria. Others it was the smell of musty velvet or furniture polish. Violence, like what happened today, coupled with the same feelings of helplessness as she'd watched Gina get hurt—well, that was a surefire promise of a long, dark night haunted by visions of the past.

If she wasn't going to sleep, she might as well get some work done. She pulled out her laptop and soon was devouring information on cyanide poisoning. It was a relief to see that what she had told

Isaiah Steward was true: only a small percentage of the population, mainly women, could smell cyanide. And her doubts about cyanide causing Jonah's death were also quelled. Every symptom, even his lab findings, fit the profile of cyanide ingestion.

Next she googled Isaiah Steward. And was impressed by his distinguished career. Hardly what she'd expect from a killer—of course, in books it was always the least likely suspect who turned out to be the diabolic psychopath, wasn't it?

The GOAD website was plastered with photos of Jonah: in court, leading marches, preaching to the masses, even a slick, posed photo worthy of any Hollywood head-shot. It didn't add more insight into the man other than what Mickey had already told her, that the organization was Jonah's life.

A sharp rap came at the door before she could move on to Matthew Kent or the Sons of Adam. She jumped up from the bed, looking around for something she could use as a weapon.

"Who is it?" she asked as she grabbed her keychain with its pepper spray.

"Dr. Fiore?" a man's voice answered.

She peered through the spy-hole but it was too smudged with decades of grime to distinguish much other than the fact that the man was white and at least six feet tall. Craning her neck, she tried getting a look through the slit in the curtains. He was dressed in jeans and an oxford shirt, cuffs rolled up to reveal an absence of tattoos, and most importantly, no weapon in his hands.

He knocked again. "Dr. Fiore, I'm Pete Sandusky. I'm a reporter and need to talk to you. About Jonah Weiss's death."

His voice grew louder, trying to force her to open the door in order to shut him up, she knew. "No comment," she shouted through the closed door. "Goodbye, Mr. Sandusky."

Damn, she should have known sooner or later the press would get involved, come calling. Probably Elliot Weiss called them himself, the better to run her out of town all the faster.

"Dr. Fiore, I really think you want to talk with me."

Sandusky obviously wasn't going to give up easily. Lydia glanced at her laptop, now filled with her favorite screensaver: the surf off Diamond Head. Maybe she could use Sandusky—he'd have access to local knowledge she'd never find on the internet.

"Please open up."

"Give me one good reason," she said, already grabbing a pair of jeans and changing into a bra and tank-top.

There was a pause, as if Sandusky had never been asked that before. "How about a chance to clear your name?"

Until the lab results from Jonah's autopsy came in, there was little hope for that, but Lydia opened the door. "I need to see some ID."

He shifted his weight, not into a fighting stance, but to pull a business card from his back pocket. He was in his mid-thirties with dark hair cropped short enough to reveal a hint of salt and pepper gray in a George Clooney kind of way.

"Wait here," she said closing the door on him. Sandusky's business card didn't list any newspaper or news outlet that she'd ever heard of. Instead it proclaimed him the owner and proprietor of RiverDredge.com, with the motto of "we uncover anything and everything."

She didn't like the sound of that. Grabbing the phone, she dialed Mickey's home number and was surprised when Danny, her office assistant, answered.

"It's Lydia. Could I speak with Mickey please? I have a little situation here." As she spoke she realized she'd also better tell the lawyer about the attack earlier today—but if Mickey's clients, the Sons of Adam, were involved, then she might see a conflict of interest and drop Lydia's case.

"Can it wait until tomorrow?" Danny said, his voice hushed. "It's been a long day and she's not doing so well."

"I'm sorry. Is there anything I can do to help?"

"No. Thanks. I've got it covered."

"You live with her?" Lydia blurted out. None of her business, but curiosity got the better of her—especially after seeing the solicitous way Danny treated Mickey, a woman twice his age.

"I take care of her, in exchange for room and board. I live in the apartment upstairs." He cleared his throat. "What did you need?"

"There's a guy here asking questions about Jonah's death. Name of Pete Sandusky. He says he's a reporter, but—"

"He's an internet blogger. Pittsburgh's equivalent of Matt Drudge. Mickey says he'd rather make news than actually report it. The more sensational the better."

"Great. Somehow he tracked me down, says he won't go away until I talk to him."

"I'd come over, kick his ass for you, but I can't leave Mickey."

"No, that's all right. I'll take care of it myself. Thanks." Lydia hung up, squinting at Sandusky's card one last time. Maybe she could use the blogger, see what he knew and who he learned it from. She grabbed her keys and opened the door again.

"What makes you think my name needs clearing?" she asked, blocking his view into her room by pulling the door shut behind her.

"Because you opened the door," he said with a chuckle. "Lets find a place to talk. The Eat n Park down the block?"

Better there in public than her motel room—which she was certain why he'd chosen it. To put her at ease. She nodded and started walking in that direction, barely slowing as Sandusky grabbed a laptop from the back of a black Mercedes two door.

"We could have taken my car," he said, hustling to keep up with her, his shirt already showing sweat stains.

"It's a nice night for a walk," she said.

"Yeah, if you're an Amazon tree toad." He switched the laptop from one hand to the other. "This global warming is for shit. It get this hot and humid in L.A?"

Right. Like he really was pounding on her door in the middle of the night to discuss the weather. "What do you know about Jonah Weiss's death?"

"More than most, less than you."

She pursed her lips. She'd seen the evening newscasts featuring prominent GOAD members pronouncing Jonah a great leader. None had offered any hint that his death might be anything than a tragic motor vehicle accident. No mention of her or an autopsy. Yet here she was, walking down the street with a reporter-slash-gossipmonger dogging her heels.

The Eat n Park wasn't crowded, the dinner crowd already vanished, making it easy to get a quiet table in a secluded corner. Lydia sat with her back to the wall and her view of the rest of the room unobstructed, leaving Sandusky to take the side of the booth festooned with fake ivy.

He leaned back, manspreading without apology, his gaze feasting on her features as if she were an all-night buffet. "What are you?" he finally asked after they both ordered coffee. "Hispanic? American Indian? Black?" He frowned when she ignored his oh-so politically incorrect question. She was used to it—officials back in L.A. were always trying to pigeonhole her, frustrated that since the only family she knew was her mother she really had no clue about her heritage. Then Sandusky smiled. "I know," he said with a leer. "Creole. Am I right?"

"Tell me how you found me." She changed the subject.

"Guy I play golf with is a friend of Elliot Weiss. He called and told me about Jonah, suggested I might take a look into your background. Hinted that you're responsible for Jonah's death, not the car accident. I tried to check out the ME's report but it's not available yet—which tells me either he was right or there's more going on than a simple traffic fatality. Then I asked around Angels and learned you were brought in after you and another doctor were mugged today.

"Not believing in coincidence, I conned an admissions clerk

to tell me where you lived—not hard, actually since you had already pissed her off. And, voila." He spread his arms wide as if waiting for applause.

Lydia simply stared. He was obviously keeping something back. A lot of something. "Did you happen to notice that the Medical Examiner performing Jonah's autopsy is his former lover?"

He leaned back, a smile creasing his eyes, nodding appreciatively as he puffed himself up. "What do you think my lead story tonight was? Sure to ruffle some feathers in the ME's office as well as GOAD."

He pronounced it "gonad" with a leer that told her he thought the juvenile joke was clever. She had the feeling that was what Sandusky liked best: ruffling feathers, rattling cages, inciting riots. Making insipid jokes at others' expense. And he was vain enough to want his hard work appreciated—she'd happily use that against him. "So what do you know about Isaiah Steward and Jonah Weiss?"

"Well," he drawled, settling in and propping his feet up on the bench beside her. "You obviously already know about Isaiah and Jonah being a couple." He said the last with a fake lisp and paused as if expecting her to laugh. "Anyway, apparently Isaiah was trying to make amends. I have a witness who places him in the Ironworks, talking 'earnestly'," he used finger quotes, "with Jonah the same night he died."

"When? What time?" Lydia leaned forward. Even though Jonah had died after midnight, cyanide could take anywhere from fifteen to thirty minutes to act, so he would have ingested it earlier.

"He left right before Jonah did." He squinted at her. "Why? What do you know?"

"Nothing." It was the truth. She knew nothing, had no facts, only supposition. "Did you tell the police?"

He snorted. "Are you nuts? They don't play ball with me, so I squeeze their balls by screwing them every chance I can get. Power of the press, baby. Hey," he continued, finally catching her scowl of distaste, "it's the American way. Free speech and all that."

"Does free speech include shielding a killer?" she snapped, her fatigue and irritation getting the best of her. "You need to tell the police."

"You think Isaiah could have had something to do with Jonah's death? Then why the hell were you telling the cops that the guys who attacked you and Dr. Freeman were from the Sons of Adam?" He wagged a finger at her when she remained silent. "Don't try to deny it. I have sources in the ER at Angels who overheard you."

Lydia pulled back as far as she could, half tempted to bolt from the confining booth. Sandusky merely stared, waiting for her answer, confident that she'd oblige him.

"First, tell me about the Sons of Adam."

He clucked his tongue. "Now, Lydia. Don't play games with me."

"I'm not. I'll tell you what happened today if you tell me about the Sons of Adam."

"Well, if it's the Sons of Adam you want to know about, then I'm your man," Sandusky said, obviously trying his best to impress Lydia. "After his wife was killed—'murdered by mongrel government forces' in the Sons of Adam's parlance—Matthew Kent asked me to write her biography. I've gotten even closer to them than the feds. And it's all right in here." He patted his closed laptop. "You give me your story and I'll tell you whatever you want to know about the Sons of Adam."

Lydia didn't trust him, too slick, too fast-talking. Not to mention the fact that she actually knew nothing she could prove. "You first."

He shrugged and she knew he wouldn't tell her everything—he'd given in too quickly. Still, anything was better than nothing. "Fine."

He flipped open the laptop and turned it on. Soon a slide show of photos was on the screen. The first was a striking black and white portrait of a blond woman. Her expression was both regal and disdainful, as if condemning the world. "Sarah Kent founded the Sons of Adam with Matthew acting as spiritual advisor, keeping peace in the ranks, swaying new converts, the public voice of the group.

"But Sarah was the brains and made all the decisions. And for her," another photo, this time showing Sarah in combat gear, holding a machine gun, looking fierce, "it was less about saving souls than preparing the world for the second coming. She called it the Revelation, said the world must be cleansed before it could occur."

"Cleansed how?" Lydia asked.

"Cleansed by fire, blood—whatever it took to rid the world of the unbelievers, heathen, gays, blacks, Jews," he met her gaze, tipped his head slightly, "you, me. You name it. For Sarah, if you weren't part of the solution, meaning one of her followers, then you were part of the problem."

Photos flashed past: Matthew preaching to a crowd, Matthew and Sarah together—him standing in her shadow, a group of people raising a barn. "They live on a compound out west of here. They're not one of those back to nature groups, they don't shun technology. Matthew uses podcasts and his YouTube channel to spread his sermons on the internet. Instead, they preach independence. And hatred. Of the government, of anyone who doesn't look like them or think like them."

"So pretty much anyone who doesn't believe what they believe is fair game?"

"For Sarah, yes. But she died last year. The feds learned she was carrying a load of weapons and explosives, put out a warrant for her. There was a high speed chase and kablooey."

Another photo, this one showing a burnt wreckage of a car, a glimpse of a crumpled police car resting on its side, and two damaged houses. Then funeral pictures. Matthew Kent appeared devastated, supported by a younger man whose face was turned away from the camera. Beside him stood the man she'd seen earlier at Mickey's office. Lydia pointed to the picture. "Who's that?"

"The kid? Ezekiel, Kent's son."

"No. The skinhead."

"Alonzo Hampton, Sarah's right hand. Aryan Nation, ties to the KKK, Michigan Militia, Nation of God, and about any other militant right-winged racist group you can name. He wants to take the Sons back to Sarah's way, wage war on their enemies, start a second Revolution. Purify through blood and fire, all that jazz. But right now, Matthew is too sympathetic—the grieving widower and all—so until lately most of the group have supported him. Plus, Matthew is much more charismatic."

Lydia nodded, she'd seen that first hand—a people person Hampton was not.

"Your turn," Sandusky said.

"Guess I have no choice," she said, knowing he'd simply use his hearsay evidence with or without her corroboration. "But it's off the record." She told him about what happened in the alley and seeing the tattoos.

"Why would the Sons of Adam want to throw suspicion about Jonah's death onto GOAD?" he asked when she finished. He was rubbing his fingertips over the surface of the laptop as if he couldn't wait to start posting his theories and accusations for everyone to talk about. "Unless there is more going on than a simple car accident."

"I can't comment on a patient's case," she said, spreading her palms out flat on the table top, rocking it.

"Then I guess we're right back where we started. With everyone blaming you for Jonah's death." He bared his teeth in a wolfish grin. "Gee, it sucks to be you, doc. Good thing you've got me on your side."

Right. Just as long as it got him the inside scoop to a sensational story.

CHAPTER 22

GINA WOKE. AGAIN. She was panting, twisting in the sheets as if they were strangling her.

"Shhh, it's all right," Jerry said, his arms wrapping around her, pulling her into his embrace.

At first she fought, ready to bolt, but his steady breathing helped her to focus. She was in her own bed. At home. Safe. With Jerry. Safe.

She squinted until the red numbers on the clock radio came into focus. One-twelve. Her heart was pounding in her head so hard her teeth ached and she was covered in sweat. She pried Jerry's hands loose. "I'm going to take a bath."

"Want company?" he asked, his hand trailing across the bed, joined to hers until the last possible moment.

Tears stung her eyes and she knew she was going to lose it. "No."

Naked, she crossed the floor, groping for the doorknob in the darkness. She banged into the dresser and cursed. Jerry was immediately there, steadying her.

"You all right?" he asked, guiding her to the door and across the hall to the bathroom. He flicked on the light and examined her closely. "You don't feel sick or dizzy or anything?"

She stood there, shaking her head, unable to speak. The crack of the baton against her skull, the feel of the pavement slamming into her face, the terror and certain knowledge that she was going to die, that there was no sense in trying to fight, best just to lie there in the dirt and let it happen, pummeled her.

Her body swayed, as if she couldn't even fight gravity. Jerry lowered the lid to the toilet, sat her down, cold porcelain against her naked skin shocking her.

She had surrendered. In the alley, she had given up, let those men win without even putting up a fight.

She licked her lips, almost tasting the scorching tar that she had landed face down in, could smell the stench of decaying food, exhaust fumes, her own blood. Her stomach lurched, she would have vomited if she had anything left to throw up, but she'd already purged in secret after coming home from Diggers.

Still, how good it would feel, to try. The familiar sting of bile scratching the back of her throat, overwhelming her tastebuds, drowning out the nasty thoughts, providing some sense of control…

"Gina. Talk to me. Are you all right? Should I call a doctor?" He knelt on the tile floor, placed his palms flat against her cheeks, tilting her head up. God, she couldn't remember ever seeing him so worried.

The sight of his face, feel of his hands pressed against her flesh brought things back into focus. She blinked twice, trying to force the tears back and for a moment succeeding.

"No." She drew in a breath. "I'm fine." Then she fell against his bare chest, crying so hard her body rocked against his. He let her go for a few moments, then scooped her into his arms and carried her back to bed.

AT THREE IN THE MORNING, the Pediatric ICU was as dark and quiet as it ever got. The nurses and doctors still ran from one critical patient to the next, but with hushed footsteps and whispered urgent commands. Alarms still blared but were quickly silenced. Lights illuminated each patient's bed creating paths of shadows between.

Amanda skirted the shadows, preferring the light, weaving through spaces surrounding critically ill children until she reached Shannon Miller's bedside. The six-week-old was in an flat, open crib, much smaller than the standard patient bed, leaving a generous swath of darkness between her and the next child.

Shannon lay flat on her back, wrists and ankles pinioned to the mattress with soft felt restraints. As barbaric as it looked, Amanda knew it was a good sign. It meant the baby had begun to fight, and her nurses feared her ripping out the large intravenous catheter that ran directly into her heart.

"You keep on fighting, Baby Girl," she whispered as she stroked one finger along Shannon's palm. The baby grabbed on tight, didn't seem to notice the spasm the shook Amanda's hand. Damn it, this was not happening. She willed her hand to stop shaking.

And it did. Just fatigue, she told herself, flushed with victory. Lucas Stone was wrong. There was nothing wrong with her. Nothing that a month's worth of sleep and good eating couldn't cure, anyway. That would do her more good than any of the arrogant Dr. Stone's fancy, over-priced tests.

Above the baby, a computer screen silently revealed her vital signs in neon flashes of color marching across the monitor. Amanda bit her lip, translating the numbers as she lay her hand over the baby's scalp. Everything looked good. Best of all, the baby's soft spot was nice and flat and she actually tried to move to snuggle against Amanda's palm.

"You're going to be all right," Amanda whispered. The sleeping baby pursed her lips in a smile.

Feeling as if a weight had been lifted from her, Amanda exited the PICU, glad to embrace the brightly lit glare outside its doors. She'd left the ED to grab a sandwich from the cafeteria, had gulped it down while on the way up here to check on Shannon, but now had to get back to work. Before Jim Lazarov noticed she was gone and signed her up for more scutwork.

The biggest challenge of the night was fighting her exhaustion. She hadn't gotten any sleep today, not with Grand Rounds and everything that had happened after, and now she was dragging.

She treated herself to the elevators, instead of the stairs. This time of night they wouldn't be too slow and besides, the stairs creeped her out when no one else was around. As she waited in the elevator lobby, she turned and leaned against the wall, looking through the large picture window there. This side of the building faced onto the cemetery, the corridor stretching out before her had surgeon's offices lined up against the outside wall so that they could enjoy the view and resident call rooms on the windowless, inside wall.

A spotlight highlighted a large marble angel standing guard over a family plot. Wind shifted the branches of the trees on either side of her, casting the angel's body in shadows that made her seem as if she was ready to swing the sword she held over head. Amanda smiled and gave the angel a wink as if they were co-conspirators in their battle against disease. *Watch over Shannon and all the little ones.*

She could almost swear the angel winked back. That's how tired she was.

Movement down the hallway caught her attention. Someone coming out of a call room. Poor guy, paged at three in the morning, was her first thought. Then she looked again. The man was naked, stark naked. She felt her eyes bug wide and heat flamed her cheeks but she couldn't look away.

It was Seth. He was staring right at her but didn't seem to care that she saw—well, everything. The door to the room he had just left opened and a blond woman, one of the nurse anesthetists but Amanda didn't know her name, popped her head out, blowing him a kiss as he walked away.

"Come back any time, lover boy," she called out.

Seth didn't turn to acknowledge her, just kept staring straight ahead, then he vanished into another call room. The blonde caught Amanda's eye, gave her a gloating smile and wave as if this was an everyday occurrence, and returned to her room.

Amanda stood, one palm placed flat against her chest, blinking in disbelief. Oh Lord, oh Lord, what was she going to do? She had to tell Nora—didn't she? No, she couldn't, she just couldn't, it would break her heart.

The elevator doors opened and she backed into it, eyes still fixed on the now empty corridor where Seth had been. What on earth was she going to do?

CHAPTER 23

THE NEXT MORNING LYDIA'S BRUISES had progressed to an iridescent purple tinged with cobalt. Her pants covered the scrapes and bruises on her legs, but her arm was another story. The night spent curled up in the bathtub had not been kind to her already sore muscles. Any movement triggered a new flash of pain.

She'd dressed in navy cargo pants and a L.A.F.D polo shirt from her days on their Disaster Medical Action Team. The Masters of Disaster. Part of her job in Pittsburgh was supposed to be implementing the same type of quick response, mass casualty team. If she still had a job.

The word "Physician" was emblazoned on the back of the shirt. Technically, she wasn't a doctor today, only a spectator. To hell with it. If it bothered anyone, they could find her something else to wear. Just because she was only observing didn't mean she wouldn't be prepared. She slipped a pair of trauma shears over a hemostat and clamped it to her belt, then thought the better of it and shoved them out of sight into a side pocket.

The room was a mess, pillows and comforters tumbled in a pile on her bed. It looked like she'd had an orgy on her unslept bed instead of huddling all night in the bathtub—her last refuge on really bad nights.

Safest place when bullets were flying. That's what her mother had always said when they'd found themselves bivouacked in neighborhoods fraught with drive-bys and gang violence. With help from her usual clients and the occasional sugar daddy, Maria always managed to get them back to the relative calm of Venice Beach pretty quickly. She couldn't last long away from the beach, said she'd wither away to nothing too far from the ocean.

Lydia glanced in the mirror, pushing aside the memory of her night spent curled up in the bathtub, one hand reaching out to a ghost. She was a grown woman, long past time to put aside her childish fears. It had been more than a year since she'd last succumbed to the panic.

She squinted at her image. Except for the scabbed abrasions on her forehead, the bloodshot eyes and dark circles, no one would ever guess there was anything wrong with her life. She flashed a fake smile at her reflection, favored her long board propped up in the corner with a wistful glance, wondering what the surf at Lunda Bay was like today, and left. At least she'd be spending the day with a handsome paramedic. Trey was certain to keep her thoughts off things like being attacked yesterday, her fight to save her career, and the questions surrounding Jonah's death.

The Advanced Life Support Headquarters was on a narrow street in Shadyside, right across from an elementary school. Lydia liked the look and feel of the building immediately. Old brick ringed with arched windows on the second floor and three bays. A house with pride and history. Two medics were in the driveway washing a rescue rig. She pulled around to the side alley and parked in a visitor's spot.

"Thought you might change you mind," Trey greeted her as soon as she entered the cavernous vehicle bay. Although she was fifteen minutes early, he and a thin, muscular blond man with a wispy goatee and wraparound Oakleys were waiting alongside Medic

Seven. "Scott Dellano, meet Dr. Fiore. She's come all the way from L.A. to show us how to do things right."

"That's not true," she protested. What had flown up Trey's butt this morning? Problems mixing business and pleasure? If so, he needn't worry. She could be professional. Forget about the heat he stirred in her. Well, at least not think about it, anyway.

Then she noted the way Dellano hitched up his pants and straightened his radio. No, it was more likely simple pride. Although the EMS brass had been involved in her selection as their new medical director and training advisor, that didn't mean the rank and file would be happy with her putting them under a microscope.

She plastered a smile on her face and stepped forward, extending a hand to Dellano. "I'm only here as an observer today. And call me Lydia."

Like so many other Pittsburghers, Dellano ignored her hand. His eyes were masked by the dark lenses of his sunglasses but one eyebrow arched as he glanced at Trey. "Guess'n we'll have to give you something to see, then."

With that laconic statement, he opened the door to the rig and situated himself in the driver's seat. Trey escorted her to the rear and climbed in behind. "Remember, no patient contact." It was an order, not an observation. "This is one of the busiest departments in the state. Overall, we have thirteen ALS units, five rescue squads and respond to over 60,000 calls a year. We may not be L.A., but we're not a bunch of rednecks either."

He lapsed into silence as the radio squawked with their first assignment. Lydia did her best to keep out of the way, not easy given that her every fiber twitched with the yen to work with Trey and Dellano. They were an efficient team, rarely needing more than a few words to communicate with each other. She realized this was probably due to Trey's leadership of the ALS team as a whole. From their conversation, she gathered that he often worked with different shifts to make sure the Pittsburgh EMS maintained its reputation as one of the best in the country. Second to L.A., of course. Now she understood his cool reception. She was on his turf now and he wasn't about to let her forget it.

Despite her efforts, the silent treatment continued into the morning. Neither man was rude, but it was clear they resented any break in their routine. It was ninety degrees in the shade outside, but Lydia was trapped inside a glacier on wheels.

"YOU'RE LATE," Jim Lazarov announced to Gina when she arrived in the ER the next morning. Her head was pounding like a jackhammer, and she was already edgy from lack of sleep, hadn't even changed out of her street clothes yet.

"Excuse me?" she asked in a slow drawl as she sipped her Krispy Kreme coffee and slouched against the nurses' station, her back to the patient board. Jim was strutting, kept looking over his shoulder at a skinny guy in his late teens or early twenties who was wearing a pink volunteer's jacket and a visitor's pass. Right, she forgot the college kid she'd saddled him with last night. Bob something.

"My shift. It was supposed to be over at seven. Six minutes ago," he said when she remained silent, merely staring at him over the brim of her coffee cup.

"What, you can't handle six minutes without someone supervising you?" She turned her attention to the kid beside him. "And how was your night?"

"Fine, ma'am. Jim showed me a lot."

Jim looked like he was torn between sniping at her and making nice to the civilian. "Bob, this is Gina Freeman, one of the other EM residents." She noticed that he didn't explain that she was a *third* year resident, his boss.

"We've met already. Did you get to see everything you needed, Bob?"

"I'd like to get up to the operating rooms and ICU," Bob said, shoving his hands deep into his jacket pockets as a chagrined expression appeared over Jim's face, as if he'd just lost his chance at stardom. "Er, if that's all right."

"No problem." Gina said. Amanda emerged from a patient room, accompanying an elderly woman to the restroom down the hall. The college guy immediately perked up, even came close to breaking out into a smile as he watched her pass by.

"I could do it tonight. Amanda could cover me until we finished." Jim was practically simpering in his eagerness to get out of actual work.

"No, you're needed down here." Gina took a slow, lingering sip of coffee, enjoying the moment. "Amanda can give Bob the grand tour. Does that work for you, Bob?"

"Yes ma'am," he said eagerly.

"I don't have time for chit-chat," Jim broke in. "It's past time for me to get out of here. I've cleared the board for you. Just two drunks sleeping it off in obs, a few lacerations the suture tech is taking care of, and a bounce back of yours. Guy needs med clearance for a psych eval."

"Who is it?"

"Perch, Thomas Perch." Jim circled his finger around his temple. "The guy's nuts. Said he wouldn't let anyone but you touch him. That's all. I think you can handle it from here."

It sure as hell wasn't Gina's idea of a clear board. "That's all?" she asked in a tone anyone less clueless and self-absorbed would have immediately ducked for cover upon hearing.

Clueless Jim just ignored her, kept on walking away, the college kid following him. She raised her empty cup, ready to throw it at Jim—impudent bastard, an intern trying to give her orders—but Amanda rushed forward, caught her in time. Nora was right behind, shaking her head at the intern as the doors closed behind him.

"Oh boy, is he ever gonna pay tonight," Gina swore.

"You heard Mr. Perch is back?" Nora asked.

"Yeah. Let me get changed and I'll take care of him first. Poor guy, wonder what happened between him and Sally?"

Nora shook her head, chuckling. "If Sally's smart, she ran away from home."

"How's your head?" Amanda asked.

Nora was also watching, waiting for Gina's answer. Why was it everyone assumed one little bump on the head was going to turn her into a quivering mass of jelly? Lydia Fiore took a worse beating and no one seemed to think she was ready to fall apart.

"Fine. Barely feel a thing," she lied. "You have anyone to sign out, Amanda?"

"Nope. I'm good."

Amanda followed her into the locker room. She was moving slowly this morning, almost in a daze—and she wasn't the one who'd gotten hit on the head last night.

Gina changed into a pair of scrubs. "I'll see you tonight, then."

"Another night with Jim—I can hardly wait," she said, fluttering her hand over her heart as if she were ready to fall into a southern swoon. "My heart's all a pitter pat at the mere thought."

She hung up her lab coat in her locker and grabbed her bag. Gina finished getting ready and they returned to the nurses' station where Nora waited with a handful of ibuprofen.

"Here, looks like you need these." She handed them to Gina.

"Thanks, but I'm fine," Gina said. She'd already downed three Aleve. Any more and she'd burn a hole through her stomach lining.

"You might change your mind after you check out Mr. Perch." Nora rolled her eyes. "Sounds like he really has lost it this time."

"What's up?"

"See for yourself."

Gina grabbed Mr. Perch's chart and entered the psych observation room. Nora followed, a smile lurking beneath her professional mask of neutrality. Amanda trailed after, curious as always.

"Mr. Perch," Gina started, not at all helped by Lazarov's scrawl of "delusional, psych admit" on the chart. "Hi again. What brought you in today?"

The man appeared to be dressed in the same clothing as yesterday, only more disheveled appearing, his jeans and Steelers' t-shirt both stained and marred with tiny scorch marks as if he'd stubbed out cigarettes on his clothing. He sat with his broken foot in his walking cast propped up, someone had taken his crutches away—probably Jim, afraid that they could be used as weapons.

"More trouble with Sally?" Nora asked.

"Yes. No. I tried to explain to the other doctor," he said in a frustrated tone, "I've got a bomb inside me and I'm gonna explode! I need someone to stop it, put the fire out."

Gina plastered her oh-you-are-so-very-crazy smile on her face, and remained calm. Maybe Lazarov was right in his assessment. "This bomb, it's inside you?"

"Yes'm."

"And there's no other bomb outside of you, one that could hurt anyone else?"

"No. I don't want to hurt anyone else. I was only trying to—well, see, you said about women loving fireworks, so I asked Sally. But she threatened to call the cops on me if I ever called her again, called me a stalker, said we was over for good!

"So I got a bit drunk. Again. I thought with the Fourth coming and all, I'd just show her. So I swallowed them all and went to her house so she'd see me explode bigger than the fireworks on the Fourth, show her how much I really do care and she'd be so sad and sorry to see me go. But guess'n they was duds. Cuz even though I tried and tried, they didn't go off. So's now I want them out before they do go off." He looked up at Gina with pleading eyes. "You gonna get them out of me before they explode, doc?"

Gina blinked. Nora put her hand up to hide her own smile but Amanda stepped forward and sat down beside Perch on the bed. Gina restrained her impulse to get Amanda away from this loon, but something about his story troubled her.

Amanda lay her hand on his knee. "Don't worry, Mr. Perch. Dr. Freeman is the best there is. Now what exactly did you swallow?"

Perch blew out a sigh of exasperation that swirled around them, threatening to intoxicate them with the alcoholic fumes concentrated in his exhalation. "I told the first doctor. Let's see now, there were two cakes, a few gerbs, strobes and snakes, I can't remember how many poppers, four fountains, and two flying spinners and one pinwheel."

Nora straightened beside her, tapped Gina on the arm. "I think he's serious. Those are fireworks. My dad used to put on a big show for the neighborhood and those were some of the kinds he'd have."

Fireworks? What the hell was she supposed to do with a fireworks ingestion? Who knew what were in those things? Gina squatted down until she was eye level with her obviously still inebriated patient. "Mr. Perch, did you swallow a bunch of fireworks?"

"Hell, no. What'cha think I am, crazy?"

Gina relaxed and straightened again. She jerked her head toward the door and started out, followed by Amanda and Nora. "We're going to get you some help, Mr. Perch."

"Of course I didn't swallow no fireworks. I took all the wrappers off first. All I swallowed was the explosives inside." He gave out a loud belch, the odor of sulfur and grain alcohol creating a palpable cloud in the small space.

Gina stopped, spun on her foot, her jaw dropping. Amanda froze, eyes so wide she looked like a Kewpie doll, and Nora was caught between a grin and an expression of dismay.

"You swallowed the explosives?"

"Yep. Then when I got to Sally's house, I downed a bunch of Everclear and tried to light up, like those fire-eaters at the circus. It would have been a real good show, if'n I'd remembered my Zippo. So when I forgot, I tried punching myself in the stomach to make them go off, but that didn't work, and Sally wasn't home anyways, she was at her new man's place, and the neighbors were threatening to call the cops, so I decided to come here and get them all taken out."

"Well," Nora said, no longer able to mask her laughter, "now that makes perfect sense."

"You hang on there, Mr. Perch," Amanda said, patting him on the shoulder. "We're gonna come up with a plan."

Gina said nothing, just shaking her head, banging the oh-so-helpful chart against her thigh as she marched out of the room.

"Why the hell do the crazy ones always find me?"

CHAPTER 24

FINALLY, ABOUT 9:30, Lydia got her chance to thaw the mobile iceberg she found herself trapped inside. They were called to a multi-vehicle collision outside the Squirrel Hill tunnel on the Parkway and were the first on scene. At the center of the five car pile-up was a small Ford Focus crushed from both ends like a beer can ready for the recycling bin.

Trey and Lydia swung out of the rear with the gear. Trey shaded his eyes, pausing to survey the scene before calling for additional units including a rescue rig equipped with hydraulic extrication equipment.

Traffic streamed past, horns honking and drivers rubber-necking, sometimes swerving so close that if Lydia reached out a hand she could touch their cars. The cops were busy trying to control the walking wounded. She approached the Focus. A young girl was in the driver's seat, hopelessly wedged in, the doors accordioned shut around her.

"Can't do nothing until Rescue gets here to cut her out," Trey said, continuing on to where a woman and her son, trapped in a minivan, screamed for help.

Lydia didn't follow him. If they were screaming, they were in better shape than this girl. Her color was dusky and her neck swollen.

She had no seat belt on. The steering column was bent and the airbag had blown out with enough force to snap her head back, maybe injuring her trachea.

This girl needed help. Now.

Lydia jogged forward, then halted. Mark Cohen's words rang through her. If she even so much as touched a patient, she'd be forfeiting any chance she had at saving her job at Angels. She took another step. The girl pleaded with her with wide eyes, making no sound, desperate as she struggled for air.

Lydia stood frozen, ripping her gaze away from the girl, staring instead at her own empty hands. A car sped past, its horn blaring. Lydia turned her back on the girl. What good was having a job if she wasn't allowed to do it?

She raced back to the squad and grabbed a turnout coat, several endotracheal tubes and a bag-valve mask.

Dellano saw her and left Trey to join her at the Focus. "What do you think you're doing?"

"Saving her life. Stabilize her c-spine for me," she ordered, throwing the turnout coat over the crumbled hood and front windshield. She turned her face away and used her good elbow to shatter the already cracked glass that was bowing inward.

Black smoke billowed from below the hood, choking her with the stench of burning oil. Ignoring it, she climbed onto the turnout coat, crawling through the space where the windshield had been in order to reach her patient.

"What the hell! Hey, Trey!" Dellano called, but Trey was busy extricating the other victims from the van. Dellano scowled at Lydia as he reached through the side window to control the girl's cervical spine.

"I've got one chance at this," she said, deciding upon which ET tube to use. "If I can't tube her, we're going to have to trach her and that will be a bloody mess."

As she spoke, she cautiously inched her way forward over top the bent steering wheel. It wasn't the most comfortable position in the world with the wheel and turn signal lever poking beneath her ribs. She felt the girl's neck. It was swelling at an alarming rate. Although the girl now was actively fighting to breathe, no sound came.

Lydia inhaled, the stench of gasoline and smoldering plastic assaulting her. *Dear God, just give me this. I don't care about the job or anything else, just let me get this right.*

"She's a gonner, doc," Dellano said as the girl turned a deep shade of blue.

Lydia tuned out the sirens, horns, air-brakes and voices colliding around her, focused only on the task at hand. It was a delicate maneuver under the best of circumstances. It would be a small miracle if this worked now, but there was no other choice.

Heat radiated through the Nomex turn-out coat. She pried the now unconscious girl's jaws apart and reached in with her left hand, extending her fingers as far as she could. She'd had problems before doing this on large adults, but this girl should be small enough–there, her middle finger brushed against the familiar ridge of tissue that guarded the airway.

Threading the ET tube past her finger and the epiglottis, she listened closely as she slowly eased the tube down the airway. If the girl's larynx was crushed, the tube wouldn't be able to pass through the vocal cords.

Lydia held her breath, straining to hear a whisper of air amidst the cacophony of noise. Her entire universe shrunk to a small circle with the girl's face in the center. Then a slight whoosh sounded from the tube and she let out the breath she was holding. *Yes!*

She pushed the tube in a little farther then clamped down, bracing it in place. With her other hand, she attached the bag and began to force air into the girl's starved lungs.

"Listen for me, will you?" she asked Dellano.

The paramedic nodded in approval, Lydia's reflection

bobbing up and down in his Oakleys. He grabbed his stethoscope and with one hand placed it in his ears. "Sounds good. She's pinking up. Jeezit, doc, I never saw anything like that."

"We need to secure the tube." Her hand was already cramping in its precarious position. "If it comes out, she's dead."

Dellano fumbled in his pocket for a roll of tape while still supporting the patient's neck with one hand. Lydia heard Trey run up from behind them–there was no mistaking his bellow.

"Get the hell down from there! The engine's on fire!"

This she already knew. The heat radiating through the turnout coat was hotter than the Mojave in July. But she couldn't move without endangering her patient.

"So put it out already!" she yelled back at the paramedic.

The whoosh of a fire extinguisher answered for him. Trey climbed up from under the hood and emerged beside her.

"Damn it, doc. You made me get my uniform dirty," he complained in a friendly tone as he reached through the window and took the tape from Dellano. With one swift movement, he secured the airway. Lydia shook the blood back into her cramped hand while squeezing the bag with the other.

"Gee, that's too damned bad. Now how 'bout if you get me a set of vitals and an IV going?"

The two medics exchanged glances. Dellano smiled and nodded. Trey eyeballed their now-pink and conscious patient and nodded also.

"Sure thing, Dr. Fiore. Whatever you want."

Her cell phone rang. Before Lydia could free a hand to reach for it, Trey grabbed it from her side pocket.

"That could be the tox report on Jonah," she reminded him.

He shook his head, listening to the person on the other end. "It's your friendly neighborhood real estate agent."

Lydia cursed. "Tell her I can't talk. Tell her I moved back to L.A."

"Actually Ms. Wierchesney, Dr. Fiore won't be requiring your services," he said in an official tone. "She's signing a purchase contract as we speak. Who am I affiliated with? Rare Gems Realty. That's right, bye now."

He flipped the phone shut. "She won't be bothering you again."

"Thanks, Garrison."

His palm brushed her thigh as he returned the phone to her pocket, sending a tingle up to her pelvis. It didn't help that he was smiling again, showing off that irresistible dimple of his.

Dellano arrived with the Ked-board and IV supplies, saving her before she made a fool out of herself. Thank goodness.

The rescue unit made fast work of the extrication, using their hydraulic equipment to peel the Focus's roof off like the lid on a sardine can. Trey and Lydia stayed with their patient in the rear of the ambulance as Dellano drove them to Angels.

"Second IV's in," Trey said, looking up as he hooked the IV up to a bag of saline. "How's she doing?"

"Not bad. Easy to ventilate, no signs of crush syndrome yet. I think she's going to be all right."

"Thanks to you and that airway maneuver."

"Yeah," Dellano put in from the front seat. "That was a slick trick. Where'd you learn it?"

"A Canadian nurse. They've been using digital intubation on their premies for years. It's a bit harder on adults, especially if you either have really big hands." She reached for Trey's free hand to illustrate. "Or really small ones." She placed her palm flat against Trey's. Her fingertips barely reached to his second knuckle.

"I don't know how you do your job with such small hands," Trey said, intertwining his fingers with hers.

He smiled, his eyes widening to reveal flecks of gold mixed with the hazel in his eyes. She smiled back and squeezed his hand before releasing it. Being out in the field, hands on, saving a patient—the rush made her feel a bit light-headed. Even though every passing block brought her closer to the termination of her career.

Dellano backed them into the ambulance bay at Angels and they rushed their patient into the ER.

Nora and Gina met them in the trauma room. Lydia turned over control of the girl's airway to Gina while Trey gave the bullet.

"Nice work," a deep voice sounded from beside her.

Lydia's shoulders tensed as she glanced up. It was Elliot Weiss. Gina nudged her and she backed away from the patient. He shot her a glare, then bent to concentrate on the patient.

"Looks like a difficult intubation. Rapidly expanding tracheal hematoma." Elliot listened to the girl's lungs, nodded in satisfaction, and straightened. "Nora, get me a C-spine, chest, pelvis X-rays. Load her with Decadron and clear me an OR," he ordered. "Ortho can meet us there, deal with her fractures after I've finished repairing her trachea."

Trey practically rammed the EMS gurney at Lydia, forcing her to grab it before it hit her. He was trying to steer it and her out of the room.

"Wait," Elliot called. Lydia froze, the gurney rolling over her foot as Trey urged it forward. "Who intubated this patient?"

"I did," Trey said before Lydia could answer. He left the gurney, turned to face Elliot, blocking the surgeon's view of Lydia.

Nora caught Lydia's eye, gave a small shake of her head as Lydia opened her mouth to protest. Lydia closed her mouth but moved to stand beside Trey, reluctant to let him be the sole target of Weiss's fury.

Elliot crossed his arms, staring at Lydia as he addressed Trey. "You did. Right. Why don't you walk me through the procedure?"

Trey shoved the gurney to one side and stepped in front of Lydia, joining Elliot at the head of the bed. "It's a tricky procedure," he said. "But with the rapid swelling and progressive respiratory distress I thought it safer than attempting a field cricothyroidotomy."

Elliot nodded, his lower lip curling, still obviously skeptical. "Go on."

"I used a pediatric ET tube, and digitally intubated, using my middle finger to palpate the epiglottis, guiding the tube between the vocal cords."

Trey waved his hand up, demonstrating with an raised middle finger. Lydia elbowed him in the back, wishing he'd stop playing games with Elliot. Now that he'd taken credit for the intubation she couldn't speak up—it would only get them both in trouble, lying about a patient's care. But damn it, she wished he hadn't gotten involved. She could fight her own battles.

"It's tricky when you have big hands and long fingers like mine," Trey said. "But it worked. Guess I got lucky."

"You're right," Elliot said, his gaze directed over Trey's shoulder to lock onto Lydia. "Someone got lucky. Dr. Fiore, I believe I saw you assisting in the ventilation of this patient."

"Just helping out during the transfer," Gina interjected.

"Force of habit. Sorry," Lydia said, forcing the last word out.

"Sorry doesn't cut it. The Executive Committee meets in two days. Until then, I'm revoking your probationary status and citing you for violating its terms. If you so much as touch another patient or step foot in this hospital again before the Committee has rendered its decision, I'll have the hospital attorney take legal action and also send a letter of censure to the State Medical Board." He paused, leering down at her, his face twisted into a glower. "Do I make myself clear?"

Trey hunched his shoulders and looked ready to take a swing at the surgeon. Lydia put a hand on his arm, restraining him, and stepped forward, absorbing the full weight of Elliot's glare.

"I understand you perfectly, Dr. Weiss." She let her statement speak for itself. Understanding was not the same thing as agreeing or accepting his authority over her. His eyes narrowed and she saw he realized that as well.

"Get out of here. Now. Go home, go start looking for a new job, back with the fruits and nuts in L.A."

His raised voice drew the attention of everyone in the room who'd been trying hard to pretend to ignore the exchange. Lydia took another step toward him, raising her chin so that she stared him straight in the eyes. Dark crevices burrowed into the skin below his eyes, making him look cadaveric. She tried to stop herself, knew she shouldn't push this man so obviously haunted by the death of his son, whose only solace was found in the hospital and his work, but she couldn't help herself.

She smiled, a wide, toothy, saccharine smile. "I'm afraid you won't be able to get rid of me that easily. Pittsburgh is my home now, Dr. Weiss."

With that, she spun on her heel and marched from the room, ignoring Weiss's sputtering threats and the ER staff's stares.

CHAPTER 25

AS SOON AS WEISS AND HIS PATIENT were safely up in the OR, Nora and Gina joined Lydia at the nurses' station where Trey was finishing his run report.

"Don't mind Elliot," Nora said. "He's not himself. Insisted on working despite everything—he's even taking call tomorrow."

"The man's an asshole," Gina shared her opinion. "Hey, you should have been here earlier. We had this guy he swallowed a bunch of firecrackers."

"Firecrackers? That's a new one. I had a guy in L.A. who gave his wife a bunch of nitroglycerin pills to try to blow her up."

"Same idea. Only turns out firecrackers have all sorts of shit in them, bunch of nitrates, so the guy started to crash." Gina was bouncing on her feet.

"Methhemoglobinemia?" Lydia asked, now interested. It was a rare but often fatal condition requiring fast thinking.

"Yep. I had Amanda on the phone to the poison center, Nora here doing a gavage and charcoal—"

"So *not* my favorite procedure," Nora said, gesturing to the charcoal stains covering her scrub jacket.

"And I'm running to the pharmacy, grabbing all the methylene blue we have."

"How's the patient?" Trey asked as he handed Nora his paperwork.

"Up in the CCU for observation, but he's going to be fine." Gina gave a slight frown. "Well, except he'll probably be facing a stay in Western Psych. But was that a cool case, or what?"

Dellano appeared in the doorway after taking their equipment to the rig. Lydia and Trey stood, ready to leave.

"Good save, Gina," Lydia told the ER resident. "You should think of writing it up for the Annals."

"That would be great. Would you help me with that?"

Everyone stopped and stared. First at Gina, then at Lydia. If Elliot Weiss had his way, Lydia would never be allowed to touch another patient, much less supervise a resident. A fact that Gina, self-absorbed as she was, hadn't registered. Or was the EM resident merely an incurable optimist?

Trey cleared his throat, coming to Lydia's rescue as the awkward moment lengthened. "We'd better get going."

"Right," Nora said, shooting a glare at Gina. "We'll see you later."

"What?" Gina was saying as Trey ushered Lydia out of the ER. "What'd I say?"

Twenty minutes later, they sat around a table at the Eat N Park, finishing a celebratory late breakfast-early lunch. To Lydia's surprise, Trey was a vegetarian, ordering a fruit plate while she and Dellano chowed down on double-bacon cheeseburgers and home fries. She'd forgotten how much she missed this—life on the streets. It was one of the things that had most attracted her to the Pittsburgh job, the opportunity to both work hands-on with medics and take shifts in the ER.

Despite her parting words to Elliot Weiss, it was an opportunity that was fading fast. "Guess I should be going," she said, staring at her mustard streaked plate as if she could read her future in the dregs of her meal.

"You don't have to go anywhere," Trey said. "Weiss isn't my boss."

"Bad enough you might have to take the heat for that intubation, I'm not letting you two jeopardize your careers—"

"What the hell, doc," Dellano interrupted her. "You saved that kid's life. You're our good luck charm, we can't finish the shift without you. You want someone to die or something?"

Trey laughed. "Exactly. You're stuck with us for the duration. Besides, I want to learn more of those tricks they taught you out in L.A." He turned to Dellano. "You about done stuffing yourself, Gecko?"

Dellano wiped his milk mustache off with the back of his hand and grinned. "Yep. Ready to roll."

The two men stood, looking down at her expectantly, as if this was a rite of passage. Lydia hesitated, then joined them. What the hell, she was only observing. On the next run to the hospital she'd wait in the rig, out of sight of Elliot Weiss.

"Gecko?" she asked as they returned to the medic unit. "Like the lizard?"

"Yeah." Trey rolled his eyes. "Like the lizard."

"My girlfriend gave it to me. 'Cause of the way I climb."

She brightened. "You climb? Where? Free or sport?"

Dellano threw the keys to Trey and joined Lydia in the back. As he extolled the virtues of local climbing havens and they compared stories, the radio crackled and came to life. "Med Seven, woman with chest pain, Friendship Fellowship Church. Please respond."

"Med Seven responding, Code Three." Trey hit the light and sirens. Dellano and Lydia prepared the equipment they would need as the ambulance careened through the narrow streets. They arrived with a screech of brakes. Dellano pushed the door open. Lydia helped him maneuver the gurney piled high with gear out of the squad.

Friendship Fellowship Church was an old-fashioned frame building painted a brilliant white that glowed against the backdrop of the dingy yellow brick row-houses crowding around it. They bounced the gurney up the steps and through the polished oak front doors.

The interior was sparkling white with gleaming hard wood floors and oak pews. Sunlight streamed through a stained glass window at the opposite end, the beams of color intersecting at a spot on the floor below the altar.

Lying to one side of the kaleidoscope of color, one hand clutching her chest, the other reaching out as if to grab the streams of sunlight flowing from above, was a black woman in her late fifties. Gathered around her, crooning prayers, was a group of five women ranging in age from their late twenties to wrinkled seventies. A pile of abandoned cleaning supplies lay to one side.

"What happened?" Trey took the lead. Lydia held her tongue, reminding herself she was only observing.

"We were just starting to clean the altar," one of the older women told Trey. "We come every Wednesday. Wanda," she gestured to the patient, "was the first one here, just like always."

Lydia helped Dellano lower the cot and slide the woman onto it. Without being told, she placed an oxygen mask over Wanda's face. She didn't like the woman's anxious expression or the way she was gasping for breath, but her color was good. Trey gently pushed the patient's hands aside and unbuttoned her dress front so that he could place her on the monitor.

"It's okay," Lydia whispered to her, stroking the woman's thick grey curls away from her sweat-sheened face. "We're here to help you."

"Ma'am," Trey continued his questioning of the older woman, Maryam, even as he jotted down his first set of vitals. "What happened when she got sick?"

"Well, we'd only just started when she began to complain of

her chest hurting. We thought it was the heat," Maryam fanned herself with her hand, "and we sat her down, gave her some nice lemonade. She tried one of her pills, but said it just gave her a headache."

"What pills?" Trey asked. Lydia admired the way he remained patient with their rambling witness. "Does she have a history of heart problems?"

Wanda herself nodded vigorously. She reached into her dress pocket and handed a small amber bottle of pills to Trey.

"High blood pressure," Wanda's friend continued, her hand patting Wanda's with each word. "Angina too. She doesn't like to bother the doctor. Usually when she has one of her spells she takes a pill and it passes."

"Nitroglycerine," Trey read from the bottle.

Dellano glanced up from the EKG tracing. "Everything here looks good, just a touch of sinus tach."

Trey leaned forward and pulled the mask away from Wanda's face. "Honey, has anything like this ever happened before?"

She shook her head. "No. Can't breathe," she said with a gasp between each word.

"Pulse ox is 100%," Dellano put in. "Can't do better than that." He began the IV. Wanda didn't even flinch with the needle stick. She seemed much more concerned with where her next breath was coming from.

"Lung sounds clear, no signs of pulmonary edema. Heart sounds good too," Trey said, pulling his stethoscope away from his ears and rocking back on his heels. "What do you think, Lydia? Inferior wall MI?"

She finished strapping Wanda to the cot and they began moving down the aisle. "Maybe. Or a pulmonary embolism."

A blood clot to the lungs could cause this degree of respiratory distress, but there was nothing they could do to treat it here in the field. Trey nodded his agreement as they rushed Wanda out to the squad and quickly loaded her inside. Dellano jumped into the driver's seat and steered with one hand as he called in report to Angels.

"They said to go ahead with the MI protocol," he said when he'd finished.

Wanda made a choking noise, raising her hand to her mouth. Lydia grabbed an emesis basin from the shelf while Trey pulled the oxygen mask away. Wanda began to vomit, spasms wrenching her body until she collapsed back against the mattress once more. Lydia emptied the basin and its contents into a red biohazard bag.

Trey grabbed a can of nitroglycerine from the drug box. "As long as her BP is stable, we'll stick with the nitro. Open up, Wanda. I'm going to spray this under your tongue." He wiped Wanda's mouth for her.

"Wait," Lydia said. "What's that smell?" She sniffed. "Burnt almonds. Subtle, but definitely there."

Trey raised the nitro to Wanda's mouth. "Whoa, doc. No way–"

Wanda held her mouth open, waiting for her medication. The veins below her tongue weren't the dusky blue Lydia expected in a heart patient. Instead they were cherry red. Damn.

She grabbed the nitro from Trey's hand, dropping it back in the drug box. "Nitro will only make things worse. It's cyanide."

Trey obviously wasn't convinced. "Lydia, you aren't even supposed to be here, much less touching a patient or countermanding orders—"

"Trust me, Trey. Do you have a cyanide kit on board?"

"Top shelf," he said, leaning forward and sniffing at Wanda's mouth himself. "You sure about this, doc? I mean, it's wacky–"

She stripped the cover off the small Styrofoam box. "It all makes sense. Normal oxygen level but her breathing's getting worse, normal EKG, the smell of bitter almonds, and when's the last time you saw veins that red in a patient with a PE or MI?"

"We have to follow protocol. I can't just ignore my orders."

"I'm giving you new orders." She popped open one of the two vials of hydroxocobalamin.

"Right. New orders from a doc who's officially not even here. We'll lose our licenses and you'll never work again. Hell, if Weiss has his way, you could end up in jail." Trey's hand tightened into a fist. "What if you're wrong? What if she really is having a heart attack?"

She drew up the hydroxocobalamin, tapped the air bubbles from the syringe before glancing up at Trey, felt the weight of his stare. Wanda was oblivious. Not unconscious yet, but concentrating all her energy on breathing. Lydia wrapped her hand around Trey's fist, prying his fingers open. "I'm not wrong. Trust me."

He blinked slowly, looked down at their patient losing her battle to pull oxygen into her lungs. Dellano turned from the front seat and looked over his shoulder. He met Trey's questioning stare and nodded his assent.

"All right," Trey said.

Lydia pushed the hydroxocobalamin, hoping they weren't too late. She popped a second vial, for a total of five grams of the antidote. Finally, Wanda opened her eyes. Her breathing eased, and she appeared less anxious.

The rig stopped, then reversed into the ambulance bay at Angels of Mercy. They hauled the gurney out and rushed down the hall to the treatment room.

"Wanda, did you have anything to eat or drink this morning?" Lydia asked while transferring Wanda over to the hospital's bed.

"A glass of lemonade while I was waiting for the others, then another that Maryam gave me." Wanda's breathing was better, enough to allow her to speak without gasping.

"Is this our chest pain?" Mark Cohen entered the room, his eyes going immediately to the monitor where the patient's vitals were flashing in neon colors. "Looks pretty good," he said, bending over Wanda. "Guess the nitro helped. How do you feel?"

Trey shook his head, opened his mouth to explain, but Lydia spoke up before he could commit professional suicide. She wasn't about to let him take the rap for her decision. Not this time.

"We think she's a victim of a cyanide overdose. She responded to five grams of hydroxocobalamin and 100% O2." Her words came out in a rush as she realized the enormity of what she was saying.

Mark glanced up in astonishment, his face flushing with anger. "You gave her what? I ordered a MI protocol!"

Dellano rushed into the room, the red biohazard bag clutched between his hands. "Thought you might need this."

"He'll explain everything," Lydia said, pushing out of the room.

Trey followed, right at her heels as if he too had just realized the implications of Wanda's response to their treatment.

"It was the lemonade."

"I'll call dispatch, have them send another ALS unit and police."

"Have them call the church, warn them," she said, racing to the medication room. She punched her access code into the locked drug cabinet. Thank God, Mark hadn't canceled her code yet. She grabbed all four cyanide kits and rushed back to the nursing station.

"No luck. There's a fire out in Homewood with some guy taking potshots–got everyone tied up. They can't raise anyone at the church either."

"Hey," a voice came from behind them. Lydia whirled to see Nora blocking their path. "You can't take those. Dr. Fiore, what do you think you're doing?"

Lydia brushed past her, clutching the antidote kits. "Ask Mark," she called back over her shoulder. "Better yet, call the pharmacy and stock up on more of these. Fast."

CHAPTER 26

TREY DROVE LIKE HE WAS RACING SATAN HIMSELF, taking corners on two wheels and barely pausing to check traffic before plowing through intersections.

"How long do we have?" he shouted over the blaring siren.

Lydia didn't dare tear her gaze away from the window where she watched for oncoming traffic. "If they drank any before we got there to pick up Wanda–"

"We might be too late," he finished grimly. He pounded the horn as an old man in a Cadillac blocked both lanes, maneuvering through a left-hand turn at a leisurely pace. "Out of the way!"

The man gave them a nonchalant wave as he completed his turn. Trey cut the wheel hard, bouncing over the curb as he sped down a narrow alley. They emerged out the other end in the midst of more traffic and a melee of squealing brakes and horns. Trey ignored them, weaving between cars, driving down the turning lane, until finally screeching to a stop in front of Friendship Fellowship Church.

Lydia jumped out before the unit came to a complete stop. She ran into the church, her hands sweating so badly they slipped against the cellophane wrapped cyanide kits. Inside the door, she stopped. Her panting breaths echoed through the silence.

Gathered around the altar were the motionless bodies of four women.

Her footsteps thundered across the wood floor as she raced to the first woman. No pulse. She swallowed hard, refusing to give up. She crawled over to the next victim. Also dead.

Trey entered the church, arms filled with IV's and a tank of oxygen. "Jesus."

The word reverberated through the high-ceilinged room, floating out the stained glass windows showering colors on the women gathered below. He ran to another victim, this one lay face down in a puddle of vomit. He turned her over. "She's dead. Christ, are they all dead?"

"Those two are gone," Lydia said, forcing her voice to remain calm. No worse than any other mass casualty response. The pounding of her heart made a liar out of her.

Her hands trembling, she reached for the last victim. Maryam, the woman who had helped with Wanda. She lay face up on the altar, one arm stretched out toward the cross. Dead.

"Where's the last one?" she asked, her gaze scouring the empty space. "There were five."

"Maybe she went for help, maybe she's okay." Energized by the possibility of finding a survivor, Trey jumped to his feet.

"You look through the pews, I'll check in back."

He began to jog up and down, craning his head to look beneath the rows of heavy oak pews. Lydia spotted a door behind the altar and rushed through it. It was apparently the changing room for the choir. Stacks of sheet music lay on the table. Crimson robes crowded racks lining the room. One of the racks was overturned, releasing an avalanche of blood-colored robes. She heaved it back into place.

The last woman lay in a heap on the floor. In her hand was the receiver of the wall phone, its cord twisted around her wrist.

Lydia knelt beside her, desperately feeling for a pulse. There was none. Pressure built behind her eyes as the thin facade of professionalism that barricaded her feelings cracked and burst, releasing a torrent of anguish.

She rocked back and forth, cradling the dead woman against her body. Why? Who had done this and why?

Trey ran into the room. "I can't find–oh." The breath rushed out of him. He sank to the floor, still clutching his futile IV supplies.

She turned to him, choking back tears of frustration as she fought to regain her composure. It took more than a few moments. "I guess we should call the police."

He nodded but didn't move. She gently removed the woman's head from her lap, glanced at her hands, surprised not to see blood there. Trey reached for her, wrapping his arms around her, pulling her to him. He wasn't crying but he was shaking, shuddering with each breath. In a way, coming from a guy like him, so obviously used to being in control of every situation, it was worse than tears.

Lydia held him for a long moment. "I'll make the call. You stay. Watch over them."

She waited until she was back outside in the smoldering sunshine before pulling her cell phone from her pants pocket. It was hot out, well over ninety, the heat swimming off the pavement in shimmering waves. Lydia couldn't stop shivering.

She turned her back to the church and called the police. After explaining to the 911 operator why it wasn't a true emergency and specifically requesting Jerry Boyle, she was put on hold.

As she listened to the public safety tips repeated by a mechanical too-chipper-to-be-human voice, she watched two boys, one white, one black, circle the ambulance from opposite directions. Several people crowded the stoops of the yellow brick row-houses, most of them staring at the stranger in their midst. No one other than the two boys dared to approach, the rest settling for a wary, watchful waiting.

Boyle picked up just as she reached the ambulance. She slouched against the front bumper, as she outlined what had happened.

"Don't touch anything," he ordered. "We're on our way."

She hung up. The two boys still watched, hands on their hips in identical postures, staring at her. "Yunz gonna make the siren go off?" the black one asked.

She shook her head, started back to the church.

"Hey's there dead bodies in there?" the white one called after her.

His voice held a hint of anticipation that stopped her cold. She looked back over her shoulder at him. His pale grey eyes stared at her, challenged her to provide him with a thrill on this lazy, too-hot-to-move summer day.

She said nothing, shaking off creepy-crawlies that sped over her skin, then trudged up the steps and opened the heavy oak door. Trey now perched on one of the pews near the front of the church, hands folded in prayer, bearing witness to the lives that had ended this morning.

The police finally arrived and escorted them back outside into the blazing heat. "Don't go anywhere," the uniformed officer told them. "Not until the detectives say it's all right." He spoke as if it was an everyday occurrence to find five dead ladies inside a church.

They sat on Seven's back bumper, shaded by the ambulance's shadow as more police cars, several unmarked cars and finally two medical examiner vans pulled up. Crime scene tape festooned the outside of the church as if announcing a pot-luck dinner.

About forty minutes later, an older man came by, the pastor Lydia assumed, and was escorted inside briefly. He emerged, shaken, holding a handkerchief to his eyes. She and Trey watched as an officer let him sit inside one of the squad cars with its A/C running, head bowed as he spoke on a cell phone.

"Next of kin notification," Trey said.

Lydia shrugged. Somewhere along the way, she had lost the energy or will to speak. She'd been to crime scenes before, had handled the chaos of disasters with relish, but this was different. She had been talking with these ladies minutes before they died.

Her legs ached, she wanted to move, to run, to escape this nightmare. If it hadn't been for Trey, she probably would have.

Memories from when she was twelve echoed through her mind, mixing and melding with the scene she'd left behind her in the church. Another church, another time, but somehow they felt the same.

Evil.

CHAPTER 27

NORA WAS ON HOLD WITH EMS DISPATCH, trying to find out if she needed to make preparations for a mass casualty alert. Her insides were knotted, and after a sleepless night, she was already on edge. She'd called the pharmacy, had the remaining three cyanide kits the hospital had in stock in addition to supplies of thiosulfate and amyl nitrate on hand. But she had no idea how many people had been in the church or how many victims might be arriving.

"Any news?" Mark asked after seeing Wanda safely up to the Cardiac Care Unit. He bounced on his toes, drumming both palms on the counter of the nurses' station as if it was a bongo drum. A lot like Lydia Fiore that way, the two of them seemed incapable of standing still. Nora wished she could get rid of the pent up energy chasing through her insides that easily. But someone had to take charge, stay in control.

Mark bent over the counter, craning his head as if he could reach through the phone and find the answer he wanted. Nora held her hand up as the EMS operator came back on the line.

"Cohen, what the hell kind of operation are you running down here?" Elliot Weiss's angry bellow announced his arrival. Everyone at the nurses' station stopped what they were doing, all eyes on the surgeon. "First, that new doctor let my son die, and now I hear she almost killed another patient! I'm calling the District

Attorney, getting charges pressed."

Mark moved in slow motion. He stopped his drumming, pushed himself upright, his face going stony as he pivoted to face the much taller man. Mark's feet were wide apart, a fighting stance, a remnant of his former days as a boxer. Nora, on hold again, held one hand over the receiver of the phone.

"You'd be wasting the DA's time if you did that, Elliot," he said in a calm voice so low that Weiss had to lean forward to hear. "She didn't almost kill anyone, she saved a patient's life."

"Maybe. Maybe not."

The two men stared at each other, neither backing down as the operator returned, diverting Nora's attention. "We now have confirmation," the operator told her. "Five dead, no survivors."

"Thanks," Nora said before hanging up. Mark jerked his head up, ignoring Weiss to look at her.

"How bad?" he asked.

She shook her head, her stomach feeling hollow.

"No one? Lydia couldn't save anyone?"

"No," Nora said. She felt her face go stony, her muscles locking into a familiar mask of calm. "They were too late."

Weiss slapped a palm against the countertop. "Do you see now? That woman's a menace. I'm calling the Executive Committee to put a stop to this once and for all. We'll have Fiore's hearing today."

"IF ONLY ONE OF THEM HADN'T LIKED LEMONADE, if only they hadn't all drunk it at the same time, if only..." Trey was repeating himself, but Lydia understood why. Maybe sooner or later, with enough repetition, it would make sense. It all seemed so calculated, yet also so very random.

They sat on the ambulance's rear bumper. Around them the rest of the street had come to life, drawn to the activity surrounding the church. People asked Trey if he knew what was happening. He said no, they were only on standby. People tried to talk to Lydia as well, but she ignored them. She was fresh out of answers.

The heat and weight of the crowd's accusing stares drove Lydia and Trey inside the ambulance. They sat in front, facing away from the church, the air conditioner blasting.

Finally, word must have leaked out because several women began to cry. Others gathered around them, offering comfort. Then the food came out and with it the children. The crime scene evolved into a block party. People climbed porch roofs, hung out of upstairs windows, craning for a good look.

"I've been doing this job going on eleven years now," Trey said, easing his seat back and stretching his legs onto the dashboard. "I've seen some strange shit, thought I'd seen it all. But this morning has to beat everything."

Lydia nodded. She hadn't said anything since they left the church. She knew he was trying to comfort her, but she felt too numb to respond.

"I'd much prefer a disaster, some kind of mass casualty response where at least I knew I had a chance to try to save someone, anyone. This is too insidious, too quiet. Too personal." He was talking to himself. Lydia sat in silence, her body rigid, fists drumming against her thighs.

"Why them?" she finally said. "That's what we need to figure out."

Her last syllable still hung in the air between them when a sudden pounding on the door made them both jump.

It was Boyle. Trey rolled down his window, saying, "You took your time."

"Wanted to make sure the scene was processed correctly," the detective said. His shirt was plastered to him with sweat, his tie drooping in the heat, but he kept his jacket on. "I'd like to get statements from each of you separately. Trey, if you can talk with my partner, Janet Kwon? Lydia, come with me, please."

Lydia reached for the door handle, was surprised when Trey lay a hand against the back of her neck, squeezing against her balled-up muscles.

"Hey, it's going to be all right," he told her.

She hunched her shoulders, shrugging his hand away and pushed the ambulance door open. She jumped down from the ambulance, pain jolting through her bruises, bringing her back to full alertness.

"You all right?" Boyle asked, one hand on her elbow.

"I'm fine." Thoughts that had been cascading through her brain coalesced. "Look, this has to be the same person who killed Jonah."

"I spent the morning talking to everyone I could track down who was in the Ironworks the night Jonah died," he said, increasing her respect for him. Behind those puppy-dog brown eyes, there was a sharp brain at work. "Despite the fact that we still have no confirmation that Jonah was murdered."

"I think that's beside the point now." She nodded at the church.

He led her to an unmarked white Impala. "Yeah, well. If it wasn't for you, we wouldn't have gotten a head start on all this. Thanks."

"No. Don't thank me. If I'd picked up on it earlier, I could have saved them all." She gazed at the closed church doors for a long moment, shook herself free of regrets. "How's Gina? No problems last night?"

"You know what they say about doctors making the worst patients?" he replied with a crooked smile. "Gina takes the cake. But other than a headache and a few bruises, she's fine." He looked her up and down. "I'd say you look worse than she does."

Before she could say anything, a Lincoln Town Car pulled up alongside them. A heavyset black man wearing a ribbon-laden police uniform jumped out of the driver's seat.

"Are you Dr. Fiore?" His eyes were puffy and red-rimmed as if he'd either been drinking or crying. "I'm Commander Harold Owens of the Pittsburgh Police Bureau. I'd like to speak to you, if I may."

Boyle nudged her. "It was his wife you saved. Wanda."

Owens was in his late fifties, medium height and carrying twenty pounds of extra weight that strained the seams of his uniform jacket. He marched around the car and took her hand before she could offer it.

"I wanted to thank you for what you did for my wife," he said, his voice catching.

"Your wife, Wanda, she's all right?"

Owens closed his eyes as if giving a brief prayer. "Yes, she'll be fine, thanks to you. They're going to keep her in the ICU overnight just as a precaution."

His Adam's apple jumped and his shoulders hunched as if he sought privacy, still turned from them, his eyes searching for something beyond the white-washed house of God.

"We've been going to that church for over twenty years. Used to live here in Friendship. I knew all those women. All God-fearing, good Christian women, each and every one of them. I'm going to have to face their families and they're going to ask me why this happened and I won't have an answer."

"I'm sorry. I wish I could have done more." Lydia didn't know what else to say.

"I won't rest until I have the answers." He nodded to the church. "For them."

"Yes sir." She believed him. "Did she say what happened?"

"Right now I'm more interested in what you have to say. What made you suspect cyanide?"

"I smelled it."

Owens looked at her in disbelief. "That's it? You had nothing else to go on? What if she'd been having a heart attack?"

Lydia shrugged. "It didn't add up to a heart attack."

"But how did it add up to cyanide poisoning? Something I've never come across in thirty years of law enforcement."

"Dr. Fiore also believes Jonah Weiss may have been poisoned in a similar fashion," Boyle put in. Now the weight of the Commander's skepticism fell on him.

"Weiss? That the one the DA was all hot to trot about? Wanted a case opened before the ME's findings were in?"

"Yes sir."

"And you were involved in his case as well?" He scowled at Lydia as if she was a suspect.

"He was my patient."

"Too many coincidences. Boyle, you know how I feel about coincidences."

"Yes sir. I'm already looking into Jonah's death and any ties to what happened here."

Owens nodded absently, his gaze now fixed on the church doors as they opened and two men wheeled a gurney out. A body bag lay on top of it. "That could've been Wanda. If you hadn't been there, she would have died." His voice dropped to a harsh whisper. "Like the rest of them."

The sight of the body brought out the reporters from their air-conditioned vehicles. Several of the more aggressive reporters ignored the crime scene barricades and surrounded Owens and Lydia, crowding in with their microphones as cameras flashed.

"Commander Owens, is this the doctor who saved your wife?"

"Doctor, how did it feel to find the bodies?"

"What do you think happened here?"

The questions flew from all directions. Lydia spied one familiar face in the throng, Pete Sandusky. He made a "call me" motion with his fingers. Lydia backed away, stepping on Boyle's foot. He took her arm and shepherded her around to the passenger side of his car.

"There'll be an official statement shortly," Owens said in a tone of authority. He seemed to grow several inches taller as he faced off with the reporters. "Detective Boyle is in charge of the investigation. Dr. Fiore will not be available to answer questions as she is a potential witness." He emphasized the last with a glower at the reporters. "I would like to publicly thank her for saving my wife's life. I would also like to extend my deepest sympathy to the families of the other victims. That is all."

Boyle opened the passenger door for Lydia, then slid into the driver's seat. After cranking the engine and fiddling with the air conditioner, he turned to her. "Let's go somewhere quiet where we can talk."

Suddenly she was twelve again, a terrified little girl covered in her mother's blood, looking up at a large man in a dark suit who was driving her away from the last place she'd seen her mother alive. Lydia blinked hard, barely noticing the scenery as Boyle drove them down the block and parked in a vacant loading zone.

"I did some research on you," Boyle started. He removed his seatbelt, twisted himself to sit facing her. "Your mom was murdered when you were a kid."

Lydia said nothing, merely nodded. *Never talk to cops*, had been Maria's mantra. Ingrained in her since she was a toddler.

"Police report said you were covered in her blood, in shock. Refused to talk. It's still an open case, although the working theory was that she'd conned the wrong person."

Lydia inhaled, expanding her chest until her seatbelt bit into her skin. "That was eighteen years ago and two thousand miles away, Detective. What does it have to do with what's happening now? I told you everything I know already."

"Not willingly. Not until after Nora Halloran called me in.

Not until after Gina got hurt." Anger colored his voice. He broke off, pinched his nose and rubbed one hand along his forehead before continuing. "I'm sorry. I'm not blaming you for what happened. But I need to know that you've told me everything. Before someone else gets hurt."

Silence as his words hung between them. Lydia shifted in her seat, trying to fight free of the heat and humidity and weight of emotions building in the car. Leaving L.A, coming to Pittsburgh was supposed to have been her chance to leave her past behind, to find peace, a home.

So much for that plan.

Her stomach was clenched and her breath grew shallow. Just sitting here talking with a cop and she was close to panic. She closed her eyes, trying to forget that Boyle was a cop, trying to find room in her lungs for oxygen. After counting to five slowly, she was able to draw in a deep breath, to block out the memory of Maria's blood, the smell of it choking her as she bit down on her clenched fist to keep from screaming, certain that if she made a sound...

She started over, counted to five again. The colors of blood and stained glass danced in her vision. "What do you want to know?"

"Did you see anything?" His voice was soft, as if he faced a rabid dog or crank head instead of one tired woman.

She licked her lips, tasted blood. Her vision darkened as if veiled by the velvet drape of a confessional, smelling of must and mildew and mold. She tried to answer him, felt as if she were being garroted, her throat closing tight. Finally, she was able to force the words out.

"I saw the man."

Boyle jerked upright, reaching for his notepad. "When? Where? Give me a description."

Once started, Lydia couldn't stop, didn't know if she'd ever find the courage to say this again. As she spoke, she felt as if she had grown small, shrunk like Alice in Wonderland, looking at the world through the small slit in a curtain.

"He was big—very tall and big. Muscular. Like the guys on Venice Beach. Maria loved the beach. Said she'd die if we ever left it for too long. Guess she was right."

"Maria?"

"My mother." Her eyes burned from not blinking. She stared straight ahead, unable to look at him, would have been blinded if not for the tinted windows.

He shifted in his seat, the scratch of his pen the only sound. "Go on."

A sigh escaped her. She had never, not in eighteen years, told a living soul this. Fear seized her, making her heart stall for a long moment, as if the man was there in the car with them, ready to turn on her. Ready to kill her.

"He had a uniform and a badge and a gun and a large black stick. That's what he used. To kill her. The stick. I was hiding, stayed quiet just like she told me. He beat her and beat her and she screamed and then everything stopped. I looked out and she was lying there, blood everywhere. He was gone. I ran out, tried to help her, I tried, I tried, but…"

Her throat knotted and she couldn't swallow, couldn't speak. The silence built. Neither of them moved. Boyle had stopped writing.

"I ran. Ran away," she said, her voice a mere croak now. "Found the priest. But when we got back, she was gone. It was too late."

Suddenly she could breathe again. She filled her lungs, released the air and inhaled once more. The air was heavy, hard to move, smelled like fake pine trees and the citrus scent of his cologne. She managed to turn her head far enough to meet Boyle's gaze. "I never told anyone that before. Now you know everything."

She hoped he was satisfied, because she didn't have any more to offer.

He stared at her, dismay clearly written on his features, overwhelming his cop's mask of neutrality. His hands opened and closed and opened again until he finally ended up rubbing his palms on his pants, leaving sweat stains in their wake.

"I wasn't—I meant—" He took a breath, tried again. "Lydia, I wasn't talking about your mother. Or what happened in that church eighteen years ago. I was talking about today. What happened in the church. Here. Today."

Embarrassment flooded over her, leaving her feeling light headed and feverish.

"Of course. Of course you were talking about today," she said in a rush, hating the look of sympathy on his face. How could she have made such an idiotic mistake?

Boyle wouldn't let it go. Seemed to understand her need to share her burden even if she didn't. "You think your mother was killed by a cop."

"I saw him."

"There are other people who carry guns and badges who aren't cops," he argued. "Security guards, park rangers..."

She shrugged. It wasn't the time or place to second guess eighteen years of memory. "It doesn't matter now."

"Lydia, maybe you need to talk to someone about this. It's obvious that what you saw in the church today has unearthed some pretty powerful feelings." His puppy-dog earnest stare was back.

"Thanks, but I'm fine." She wrapped her arms around her chest, warding off any further questions. "Did you find anything in the church?"

"We have prints from the lemonade. Those might help. And after this," he jerked his head back in the direction of the church, "I can get Homeland Security involved. Domestic terrorism, possible hate crimes. They'll want to talk with you, have you look at pictures and the like."

Oh joy. More cops. "Anything you need. Just let me know."

He put his seatbelt back on and started the car up. The vents spewed out a blast of hot air that quickly turned cold. Lydia found herself sweating yet shivering at the same time as Boyle drove them back to the church.

"Look," she said as they approached the ambulance. "Please don't—I mean—"

"What you told me about your mother has no bearing on my case," he said. "No need for me to include it in my notes or discuss it with anyone." He paused, throwing the car into park and turning to look at her. "But if you ever need to talk, I'm here."

Yeah. Right. "Thanks," she said because he seemed like a nice enough guy.

"Lydia," Boyle called as she opened the car door and slid out. "Be careful." He held a business card out towards her. She turned back to retrieve it, then jogged to the ambulance where Trey waited.

When she hopped in and pulled the door shut, Trey looked at her with a frown that narrowed his eyes. "You all right? You look like you've seen a ghost."

CHAPTER 28

AMANDA SAT IN THE PATIENT'S CHAIR, trying not to squirm. She was angry and her anger built with every minute she was kept waiting. The nerve of the man! He couldn't take no for an answer, that much was obvious.

A mischievous grin crossed her face. She knew how to outsmart him.

Finally the door opened. "It's about time," she said, trying to keep her tone civil and failing. *Sorry, Mama.*

Lucas Stone didn't acknowledge her, his face buried in the chart the nurse had created. He slid into his chair and finally looked up. "You haven't changed into a gown."

"Take your history." She sat back, crossed her ankles and waited for him to start asking his questions again.

He stared at her, both eyebrows lifted in incredulity, then gave her a half smile and nod. "All right, I'll play along. When did you first start exhibiting these symptoms?"

"March 23rd," she answered triumphantly, springing to her feet.

"Wait. Where are you going?"

She whirled on him. "The only reason I'm here, Doctor, was because of the message you left saying you'd tell the Dean about my symptoms if I didn't come to this clinic appointment. An appointment which not only wasted my time, but also the twenty dollar co-pay required by the student health insurance took a good bite out of my food budget for the month, by the way."

"I'm sorry," he interrupted, gesturing for her to sit down again. "When you refused to speak with me last night, I didn't see any other way—"

"I do not take kindly to strangers meddling in my affairs, Dr. Stone. Especially strangers with no manners and an abrupt attitude. I'm a full grown woman and I can take care of myself."

"Look, Amanda, this is important. Stay. Please. I'm just trying to help."

Her hand was on the doorknob. "Honestly, you're as irritating as a hoard of sand fleas. And it's Ms. Mason."

That brought him to his feet. "Ms. Mason," he said, using an irritatingly authoritative tone that reminded her of a car insurance commercial. "I am concerned about your health and well-being. As a physician I would be remiss if I did not ensure that you had adequately addressed these concerns, especially as they may interfere with the care of your patients."

"They don't and they won't. For your information, I am under a physician's care. Dr. Nelson."

"Nelson? The guy's a quack. Always looking for the fountain of youth in those concoctions of his—he doesn't even bother to get FDA approval."

"He doesn't need to, they're vitamin and nutritional supplements, not covered by the FDA. But he is a serious scientist, still does the research and clinical trials before releasing any of his work to the general public. He's double boarded in both allergy and internal medicine with a doctorate of pharmacology."

"So he's a MD/PhD, a mud-phud, who cares? The guy's still a quack."

"He's my physician." She turned the doorknob, opened it a

crack. Then she played her trump card. "And now that you've begun a chart on me and taken your history, you are too, Dr. Stone." She smiled sweetly. "Which means no more threats of going to the Dean. Patient-physician privilege prevents you from telling anyone about my symptoms."

He stood there, jaw dropped open, looking like a little boy who'd just had his favorite toy stolen. Amanda's smile widened. This felt great, giving the arrogant attending a little of his own back.

"Good day, Dr. Stone." She opened the door and stepped over the threshold.

He followed her, took her arm. "Wait, don't go."

Shrugging his hand away, she kept on walking. "Have a nice day," she called over her shoulder with a wave. Knowing he'd be watching, she put a little extra sashay into her gait.

SCOTT DELLANO OPENED LYDIA'S DOOR as soon as Medic Seven pulled into the driveway at Angels and stopped.

"I'm sorry," he said, helping her down from the passenger seat. "I know you tried." He shifted on his feet awkwardly as Trey approached. Lydia turned to go inside. "I wouldn't go in there, doc."

"What's wrong now?" Trey asked.

"Heard some stuff I don't think Lydia needs to deal with right now. Why don't you leave us take you back to the House or drop you off somewhere?"

"What did you hear?" she asked.

The young paramedic flexed his arms, running his hands over his close-cropped hair. He bounced on the balls of his feet, looking as if he'd rather be anywhere else.

"C'mon Gecko, what gives?" Trey prodded.

"They're saying she did it."

Lydia stared at him, stunned. "They think I poisoned those women?"

"Uh. Yeah."

She blinked at the paramedic, hoping she'd heard him wrong, unable to find words to protest the ridiculous accusation. Trey had no such problems.

"Bullshit!" He pounded his fist on the hood of the ambulance. "Who said that? Where are they?"

"Why?" she asked quietly. "Why do they think I would–"

"To cover up whatever you did wrong with Jonah Weiss." Dellano spoke at a rapid fire pace as if getting the words out faster would lessen their pain. "That today's ride-along was a chance for you to hide your tracks, take the blame away from you so Dr. Weiss would drop the charges. That you could have slipped some cyanide into Wanda's IV when you flushed it, and more into the jug of lemonade." He looked up sheepishly. "It's just people talking, that's all."

"We were with her the whole time," Trey protested. "No way she could have poisoned those church ladies."

"I know that!" Dellano snapped. "I didn't say I believed them, just thought Lydia ought to know before she hears it from someone else."

"Maybe it's easier to believe than a killer sneaking cyanide to innocent people," she admitted. She'd been in the wrong place at the wrong time and the coincidence was going to be difficult for some to believe. Especially when no one here really knew her. Only one way to remedy that. She stepped past Dellano, headed into the ED.

"Lydia, wait," Trey called.

She shook her head, squared her shoulders. Had to face the rumors sooner or later. Better do it now so everyone could see how absurd the idea of her killing anyone was. Anger scorched her throat as she thought about how hard she had worked to save Jonah and the women at the church. How dare they?

Maybe she didn't need this job after all. To hell with them and to hell with this city. She had had quite enough of Pittsburgh.

A crowd gathered around the nurses' station. Lydia paused, listening to assess how bad the damage really was, hoping Dellano had exaggerated.

"It's too weird," one of the X-ray techs from Jonah's resuscitation was saying. "Any you guys ever hear of anyone round here being poisoned with cyanide?"

"Poison is a woman's weapon," a young blonde dressed in the peach colored scrubs of a nursing assistant put in. "Remember that nurse out west who killed her patients? Just to get the attention from trying to save them, like she was hero or something."

"Maybe that's why she left L.A," another assistant said. "They kicked her out, hushed it up."

Before Lydia could step forward and protest the groundless accusations, Nora emerged from the med room, scowling.

"Back to work, all of you," she snapped. "Next person who utters a word about Dr. Fiore is going on report." She stared at the crowd, hands on her hips. Still muttering among themselves, the crowd quickly dispersed.

"Thanks," Lydia said as she entered the nurses' station. "I owe you one."

Nora looked up, surprised. She shook her head and bent down to retrieve a stray scrap of paper from the floor. "No thanks necessary. On my shift, people work. They don't gossip. Especially about things they know nothing about."

She dropped the trash into a wastebasket, gave Lydia an appraising look. "Did you bring my cyanide kits back?" she demanded. Then her voice softened. "Looks like we might need to keep some handy."

"Sorry. I left them on Med Seven."

"Never mind, I'll charge them to the EMS account. Pharmacy already restocked us anyway." She picked up a chart, set it back down again before looking at it. "Lydia, I'm sorry all this is happening to you. And about what I said last night—I know it wasn't your fault Gina got hurt."

Lydia shrugged. "All I can say is this town really knows how to throw out the welcome mat."

Gina joined them, carrying a stack of charts to the nurses' station. "Did you tell her about Weiss?"

Nora scowled. "No. Not yet."

"He's calling the Executive Committee in to meet," Gina said. "Today."

"Today?" Lydia felt her shoulders hunch with anger. "Without even telling me? Don't I get to defend myself?"

"That's not how the Executive Committee works," Nora said. "It's not like a court of law or anything."

"No, but they can revoke my privileges, report me to the State Medical Board." Lydia kicked her foot against the baseboard. "Will Weiss be there?"

"He's the Vice-Chairman." Nora hastened to add, "but Mark's on the committee as well. He'll be there to defend you."

Lydia remembered how excited she'd felt, working with Trey and Dellano to save that girl's life earlier. Now it seemed so long ago.

"C'mon," Gina said. "You're not going to let Weiss win without even putting up a fight, are you, Lydia? That's like letting the people who killed Jonah and attacked us yesterday win."

Lydia looked away, saw an old man shuffling down the hall, leaning on an IV pole, his patient gown swaying in the breeze. He looked so lonely. All her life she'd fought her own battles alone—was she really going to trust the battle for her career to a near-stranger?

"When and where do they meet?"

CHAPTER 29

TREY WAS WAITING FOR LYDIA outside the nurses' station. "We've been pulled out of service," he said as they walked back toward the ambulance bay. "Got to go in for stress debriefing. Thought maybe you'd like to come along."

"You go ahead. I want to check on Wanda. And I have a meeting I have to be at later on."

He stopped, tilting his head to stare at her appraisingly. The gold flecks in his eyes flashed again. Funny how they were invisible most of the time. "I'm no touchy feely kind of guy, but–"

"Critical incident stress debriefings are the best way to prevent post traumatic stress," she finished for him. "Believe me, Trey, I practically wrote the CISD manual. Don't worry about me, I've been through worse. I'll be fine."

His eyes narrowed. Lydia smiled to prove her point. Truth was, as helpful as the CISD meetings were and as much as she encouraged everyone to participate, she hated the damn things. Trapped in a room, unable to do anything except talk until everyone broke down and acknowledged their feelings, vented and bonded. Ugh. Talk about torture.

Trey relented, held out his hand. "Give me your keys. I'll have one of the guys drop your car by. We'll park it in one of the spots beside the security office and leave the keys with them."

"Thanks," she said, meaning more than merely ferrying her Ford.

He took the keys, his hand closing over hers for a warm moment. "No problem. Mind if I check up on you later? Just to make sure you're all right?"

"I don't think missing one debriefing is going to send me over the edge," she said, easing her hand out and trying to ignore the tingling his touch ignited elsewhere in her body. It was too distracting having him near, making her notice things like the tang of his sweat or the way his nostrils flared when he looked at her a certain way–as if he had a hard time breathing when she was too close. Or the way his gaze kept moving from her eyes to her lips before he forced it back.

He gave her a boyish half smile. No dimple this time—thank goodness. She was too tired to fight that devil's charm.

"After I finish with my meeting, I'll probably go for a run," she told him.

"All right then." Did she detect a hint of disappointment in his voice? "I'll see you later. Take care."

Lydia found herself staring at his ass—and it was a very, very nice ass to stare at—as he left. She shook her head, trying to unscramble her brain. She had no time to get involved with a man; it was the last thing she should be worried about right now, she told herself as she climbed the steps to the fourth floor Cardiac Care Unit.

Between the flood of adrenaline and the leftover bruises from yesterday, her muscles cried out for movement. A few miles in this heat would release the nervous, keyed up energy that crawled beneath her skin, worse than a meth addict's imaginary insects.

She found herself looking forward to a good, long run–far better than any stress debriefing.

Wanda Owens was in a private cubicle in the fourth floor Cardiac Care Unit, awake and watching a soap opera. Listening to it at any rate, the picture was filled with snow and wavering to the point that Lydia couldn't make out anything. Wires like purple licorice whips twisted from under her gown and connected to the telemetry unit at her bedside.

"Do you want me to fix the picture for you?" Lydia asked.

Wanda clicked the TV off. "Don't bother. My glasses were left behind and without them, I can't see farther than the nose on my face. Besides, with these drugs they have me on, I can't concentrate on much of anything."

"I don't know if you remember me from this morning—"

"Sure I do. How could I forget the angel who saved my life? Those two sweet boys with you?"

Neither Trey or Gecko would appreciate the "boy" description, but the image made Lydia smile. "Sorry, no."

"Too bad. When I get out of here, I want to bake them a sweet potato pie. Especially that blond one, he's way too skinny. You too– think I'll make you two!" She playfully pinched Lydia's wrist.

Lydia reached down and took Wanda's hand. "I'm so happy you're going to be all right."

Her voice broke, surprising her. Even worse were the tears she blinked back. She turned her head, regained control. All she could think of was the image of Wanda's friends lying on the floor of the church.

"It's okay. I know," Wanda whispered, all pretense at cheerfulness vanished, tears slipping silently down her cheeks. "All day I've been trying to think why God would spare me and take them. And you know what? I can't come up with any reason at all except it was their time and he wanted them home with him. Hope he's a good listener, 'cause that Maryam, she'll talk his ear off."

Lydia glanced down at the older woman, surprised by how comforting her words were. She was the one meant to be reassuring her patient. Still, she couldn't resist the pull of Wanda's grandmotherly eyes and soft tone. She'd never had a grandmother of her own.

Wanda's grey-streaked curls feathered out against the white sheets. Her face was relaxed, confident that her faith had all the answers she needed.

But it wasn't enough for Lydia. Every time she thought of Jonah and those women, fury twisted her gut.

Wanda's fingers gripped Lydia's. "You're not a believer, are you?"

Lydia shook her head, not trusting her voice.

"Never mind," Wanda continued, patting her hand. "God knows what's in your heart. He sees everything. Otherwise, He'd never have sent you to me today. They tell me you're a doctor, that if it wasn't for you I would have died as well. If that isn't proof of God's mercy, I don't know what is."

Lydia's mouth tightened as she choked back a retort. There was nothing merciful about what happened in that church. No evidence of God's hand at work–just the opposite.

"Where did the lemonade come from?" She changed the subject.

Wanda frowned. "I wonder if they found that nice man. He could maybe tell them who did this. He came up as I was opening the church this morning. Very polite. Said Mr. Ibrahim from the grocers down the way had sent him. Said it was too hot for us to be working so hard without refreshment. Which is exactly like Mr. Ibrahim–nicest man, came over from Nigeria. But, I guess it wasn't really Mr. Ibrahim who sent him, was it?" She glanced at Lydia as if hoping for answers.

Whoever sent the lemonade knew the women would be working there today, knew the neighborhood. Must have been watching, planning for a while.

"I'll try to stop back later," Lydia told Wanda.

"Don't worry about me. You take care of yourself, you look worn out. I'll be praying for you, Dr. Fiore."

Lydia didn't bother telling her not to waste her time.

CHAPTER 30

GINA WATCHED WITH SATISFACTION as one more patient's name was deleted from the board. Nora joined her where she stood at the nurses' station, leaning against the counter, head tilted as if admiring a painting at the Louvre. A sparkling clean masterpiece, not marred by any patient's name.

"What are you doing?" Nora asked after a moment of silence.

"What am I doing? Look at that board. Have you ever seen such a thing of beauty?"

"Gina, it's the middle of the afternoon on the day before a holiday—of course the board is empty. People are leaving town, taking off for a long weekend."

"Party-pooper. See if I ask you to have your picture taken in front of my pristine board."

A new name flashed across the board. In neon green, signaling a direct admit to OB. Which meant Gina wasn't responsible for the patient. Still, it ruined her beautiful board. She sighed. "Stupid pregnant lady. Couldn't she have been seen at the clinic?"

"It's almost four, the clinic's closing. C'mon, Queen of the Board, we're going to be late."

"Late? For what?"

Nora started down the hallway leading toward the administration wing of the hospital. "For the Executive Committee meeting."

Gina balked, forcing Nora to retrace her steps. "No way. You know how Weiss can be, and the others—you don't want any piece of that. Why do you want to get involved anyway?"

"We can't let them fire Lydia, take away her license when she didn't do anything wrong."

"Face it, Nora. Lydia's shark bait. You can't expect me to put myself on the line alongside her."

"You were in that room that night." Nora somehow managed to meet Gina's gaze dead on, despite the difference in their heights. "Do you think we did anything wrong? Any of us? Are you willing to let Lydia take the heat for Jonah's death and those other five ladies?"

"No. Of course not." Gina faltered. She despised being coerced into anything, hated when Nora went all Mama-bear on her. But even more she hated the thought of a bully like Weiss winning. "Okay. I'll go. But don't expect it to make much of a difference. To the people in that room, one charge nurse and one EM resident aren't going to add up to much."

"At least Lydia will have someone there for her."

"Yeah, right. For what good it does her."

LYDIA HATED HOSPITAL ELEVATORS, with their stench of fear and urine. She always took the stairs whenever possible and usually got where she needed to go faster. Today she bolted down the steps leading from the CCU, anxious to get to the Executive Committee meeting. She fought the urge to look over her shoulder, flinched when steps above her sounded, announcing someone else behind her on the stairs.

She glanced up, relieved to see the pink jacket of a hospital volunteer disappear through the door leading to the ICUs.

Just a candy striper—or whatever they called the volunteers here. She turned to continue her progress down the next flight, chiding herself for letting her nerves get the better of her, and almost ran right into Pete Sandusky. He was wearing scrubs. Pilfered from the ER no doubt, designed to let him skulk through the hospital without interference.

"What are you doing here?" she said, forcing her fists to relax.

"Looking for you, doc," he said with that half-smile that seemed designed to irritate her. "Wanna fill me in on what happened at that church today?"

"No comment." She tried to edge past him without resorting to physically pushing him and succeeded.

"Word on the street is that those women died of cyanide poisoning. Seems like you'd feel good about being right about Jonah. Any word from the ME on confirming that?"

He trotted beside her as she continued down the steps at breakneck pace, ignoring him.

"Okay, I'll take that as a no. So want to tell me why the hospital Executive Committee is getting ready to send you down the river?"

Lydia stopped, her hand on the door to the ER. "Is that what Elliot Weiss told your golf buddy? Tell him not to believe everything he hears. I'm not giving up."

"You still believe the Sons of Adam had something to do with this?"

"That's for the police to decide, not me."

"Guess it's too bad that both Matthew Kent and Alonzo Hampton were with me all morning. Giving me an exclusive behind-the-scenes peek at their demonstration tomorrow. They've got marches organized all over the city, targeting mainly black neighborhoods and culminating in a rally at the Point during the fireworks display. Hampton hinted that there'd be a lot more to see than just a fireworks display." He chuckled. "After my next blog gets posted, he might just be right. Dead black women, dead gays, the Sons of Adam marching. This is going to be a Fourth of July to remember."

"Sandusky, you can't really be planning to incite a race riot? Even you wouldn't sink that low."

He wagged an eyebrow at her as if he enjoyed wielding power over the fate of the city. "Freedom of the press, doc. First amendment and all that jazz."

"That's crap and you know it."

"You really don't get it. Wake up and smell the coffee, why don't ya? We live in an age where information is power."

"Half-baked conspiracy theories are not information."

"Maybe not, but it's what the people enjoy. I let them make up their own minds about what to believe. When you're ready to tell me your side of the story, give me a call."

Lydia pushed through the door into the ER, chiding herself for letting Sandusky get to her. She stopped at the security office to get her car keys and tell them about Sandusky's trespassing. As she left, she couldn't stop a self-satisfied smile at the thought of the arrogant reporter being escorted from the hospital, hopefully without his story.

She ducked down the hallway on the other side of the nurses' station, heading toward the conference room. To her surprise, Gina and Nora were there, standing outside the door.

"What are you guys doing here? Testifying?" That's all she needed, more people weighing in on everything that had gone wrong with Jonah's resuscitation.

"We're here for you," Nora said quietly, opening the door and ushering Lydia and Gina inside.

Lydia stubbed her toe on the carpet, she was so stunned. Gina and Nora had only known her for two days, two of the worse days of her life. That they would take the time—it almost made her think she might have a chance to leave this room with her career intact.

She walked into a large conference room, with tall-backed executive-style leather chairs and real paintings, not cheap knock-offs, hanging on the wall, giving Lydia a glimpse of some of the wealthy patrons who had supported Angels of Mercy through the century and a half it had been in existence. Scowling portraits of Andrew Carnegie, George Westinghouse, Henry Clay Frick, and Henry J. Heinz all glared down at her, challenging this street-kid from L.A. to prove her worth to them.

"Dr. Fiore," the woman at the head of the table said. "I'm surprised to see you here."

Lydia stopped in her tracks, Gina bumping into her. "Hey, isn't that your real estate lady?"

"Hush." Nora led Gina to empty seats against the wall.

"Good afternoon, Mrs. Wierschesny," Lydia replied, plastering on a smile almost as fake as the realtor's hair color. Doomed, she was doomed.

"This is most unusual." A strident woman in a white lab coat and scrubs was standing, fists planted before her on the large Brazilian cherry wood table. "I protest."

"This is an unusual case," Mark Cohen put in. "We need all the facts we can gather before deciding the fate of a fellow physician. Dr. Fiore, Dr. Freeman, and Nurse Halloran were all present during the resuscitation."

"You mean failed resuscitation," the woman muttered, taking her seat.

Mark was brave enough to meet Lydia's gaze and acknowledge her with a nod from his place on the other side of the conference table where he sat with the department chairmen. Lydia took a seat at the far end of the table, Gina and Nora at her back. The other physicians banded together on one side of the table, all wearing variations of the home team uniform of white coats and stethoscopes, a striking contrast to her stained cargo pants and polo-shirt.

"Dr. Fiore," Carol Wierschesny said, gracing Lydia with a neutral smile, "we appreciate you and your colleagues taking the opportunity to make yourself available to us for questions. But you must understand that all committee deliberations will take place in private."

"Yes. Thank you for the opportunity to present my case."

Carol, who it turned out was the committee chairwoman, made introductions. The hospital administrators wore various shades of charcoal grey, as if someone had coordinated all of their outfits when they dressed that morning. They slid leather briefcases onto the table almost in unison, Lydia noted with a half-smile as she fought not to fidget. Synchronized bean counting, she thought as the clicks of briefcase locks spread down the table. Should be an Olympic event.

The six Board of Trustee members were easy to pick out. They sat on the same side of the table as the administrators but the cut and quality of their suits were a step above. The overhead lights glittered on diamond studded Rolexes, and Mont Blanc pens clicked as they opened the folders in front of them. These were all prominent business people and they took seriously their roles of protecting the community's trust in their hospital.

No sign of Elliot Weiss, Lydia noted with relief.

"I'd like to proceed." Carol made eye contact with Lydia and inclined her head in a regal nod. Lydia was glad now that Gina and Nora had come to show their support. With this crowd, she'd need all the help she could get.

"I understand the case in question was videotaped," Carol said. "Let's proceed with that first. Then we'll move on to a brief," she paused for emphasis, "question session."

The lights dimmed but before the tape could be started the door opened and Elliot Weiss stood there, his features silhouetted in harsh angles by the lights behind him. Lydia looked up, dismayed by the grieving father's haggard appearance.

He looked around the room as if in a trance, then froze as his eyes locked onto hers. His stare was frighteningly empty, filled with a despair that was impossible for her to face. Lydia was prepared to handle the surgeon's anger and accusations, but she had no defense against such hopelessness.

One of Weiss's colleagues led him to a chair as if he were a blind man. Lydia was grateful for the darkness in the room as she wiped a tear away.

Then the video began and she relived the fateful minutes leading up to Jonah's death. She flushed with embarrassment during the point where she yelled at Nora and felt everyone's faces turn to her when she pronounced Jonah dead. Thank God, they stopped the tape before it showed Elliot Weiss's reaction to his son's death.

"Who would like to go first?" Carol asked.

Lydia swallowed hard, trying to ignore the acid burning in her stomach as the lights came back up. Now comes the hard part, she thought, getting to her feet and praying that no one noticed her legs trembling under the table.

A tall, willowy blonde dressed in surgical scrubs under her starched white coat stood. This was Leslie deGeorge, the second in command on the trauma service, Lydia remembered from the initial introductions.

"Dr. Fiore," she began in a deceptively friendly tone, "exactly at what point did you realize that you were in over your head?"

And the battle began.

"I would have appreciated backup from my surgical colleagues," Lydia replied in an even tone, "as any Level Two trauma patient would have warranted."

The response didn't faze deGeorge. "I see, so in your medical opinion, Jonah Weiss's death was the fault of the trauma surgeons? Surgeons who never had the opportunity to examine or perform any interventions? Is that your position, Dr. Fiore?"

Lydia realized it was a mistake to try to cast any blame on the surgeons. DeGeorge was right, she had been the command doc, any fault lay solely with herself. "No," she replied. "I'm saying that Jonah Weiss received the best possible care under the circumstances. Care that–"

"This is your best possible care?" deGeorge retorted. "If so, then this committee need not waste anymore of its time!"

"If you'll allow me to finish," Lydia went on, trying to maintain her calm. Carol made no move to halt the inquisition. "This was obviously a complicated case, but as you saw in the video everything possible was done to properly diagnose and treat Jonah Weiss."

"Excuse me, doctor." A distinguished looking man with salt and pepper hair rose. Dr. Rheinquist from cardio-thoracic surgery. "But isn't that rather like my telling a family that the surgery was a success but the patient died? Surely you have more to say for yourself. Why didn't you open the boy's chest?"

"In cases of blunt trauma, emergency thoractomy has not been show to increase survival," Lydia told him, quoting a fact that she was certain that he knew as well as she.

"But it may have bought him enough time for the surgeons to arrive and successfully resuscitate him," Rheinquist replied, a variation of the surgeon's credo that a chance to cut was a chance to cure.

Not if he died of cyanide poisoning. Lydia bit her lip before she could blurt it out. Until the lab results became available, she had no proof.

Which meant that she had no defense. Except for her actions on the video.

A knock came at the door and Isaiah Steward entered. "I'm sorry that I'm late," he told them.

Lydia blinked in surprise. What was he doing here? She glanced across the table at Mark who gave her a quick wink.

"Actually, Dr. Steward, I think this would be a good time to hear the autopsy results," Carol said, her eyes on Elliot Weiss. Several people looked in Elliot's direction, but the surgeon made no move to leave the room.

"I'm only here at Dr. Cohen's request," Isaiah began. "Even though my findings will soon be made public, I must ask you to all treat this as confidential information in an ongoing investigation."

He took his glasses off and peered into them as if looking for a flaw in the lenses. The entire room grew silent at his announcement and chairs shifted as they leaned forward to stare at the pathologist.

"Post mortem examination of Jonah Weiss revealed the manner of death to be homicide and the cause of death to be cyanide intoxication," Isaiah intoned as if he were reading today's stock quotes.

The room buzzed with excitement as several people jumped to their feet to ask questions. Even Carol Wierschesny seemed shaken. Lydia felt a weight lifting off her chest, taking her first deep breath in days.

"Was Jonah killed by the same person who poisoned the women at the church?" one of the internists asked.

"There's no chance that he received the cyanide here at Angels is there?" a worried administrator interjected.

"If Dr. Fiore was able to diagnose cyanide poisoning in the women at the church, why didn't she correctly diagnose Jonah Weiss?" Leslie deGeorge demanded. The crowd grew silent once more, all eyes on Lydia.

"Stop it!" Elliot Weiss had risen to his feet. "Just stop it," he repeated. "Don't you understand? I should have been there but I wasn't and that will haunt me until the day I die." His voice caught and Leslie deGeorge moved to his side.

"It's all right, Elliot. I can deal with this," she assured him. He slumped back down into his seat once more.

Lydia stood, alone at the end of the table, the conversation swirling around her. Gina and Nora joined her.

"Guess that leaves you off the hook," Gina said.

"Not quite," Isaiah replied in a tone cutting enough to silence everyone else. "I was reviewing the medical records of the sole survivor of the Friendship Fellowship Church poisonings before I came here. While I was in the CCU, the woman expired."

"Wanda's dead? What happened?" A sudden wave of grief swamped Lydia. Wanda had been fine, how could she be dead?

"The cardiologist said her potassium level was acutely elevated to almost twice normal."

The other medical professionals all nodded at this, their gazes darting from one to another with apprehension.

"Dr. Steward," Carol said, "would you mind translating for us lay people?"

"Certainly, ma'am. Going from a normal level to one that high in so little time could only come from someone administering potassium to the patient in question."

"You mean someone poisoned Mrs. Owen while she was under our care?" Carol blanched beneath her thickly caked makeup and shoved her Angel's coffee cup away from her as if fearing a similar fate.

Lydia was bouncing on her toes, questions barraging her mind. Like Sandusky had said, she'd assumed the Sons of Adam were behind the attack. Who else would have motive to kill a Jewish gay rights activist and a church filled with African-American women?

What if she was wrong?

She stared down the length of the table, lasering in on Isaiah Steward. Maybe there was one other person with a motive, one person who would profit from Jonah's death being blamed on the Sons of Adam, one person who'd just confessed to being in the CCU at the time Wanda died.

Isaiah met her glare with one of his own. Hatred washed off him as he stood and raised his hands for silence.

The conversation died down. Isaiah and Lydia continued

their silent battle as if they were alone in the room. Isaiah favored her with a smile that showed his teeth, bared as if ready to taste blood.

"Not only did Mrs. Owens die while a patient here at Angels," he continued in that Sunday-preacher voice of his that was so damn self-righteous it made Lydia's teeth grate. "But according to several witnesses, Dr. Fiore was the last person in her room before she died."

CHAPTER 31

GINA KNEW FROM LYDIA FIORE'S COLORING that she must have some African-American or Hispanic blood. Maybe both. But she'd never seen a person actually spontaneously combust before. Okay, maybe not combust, but she swore she could see sparks flying from Lydia. Hot blooded was right.

Lydia's body went ramrod rigid, her weight shifting, fists balling at her hips, elbows pulled back like she was ready to throw a punch. A dark red flush climbed up her neck. Even her hair stood on end, making her seem taller, more formidable. Her eyes blazed at Isaiah Steward and Gina was very happy not to be in the path of Lydia's flame-thrower glare.

Gina wanted to learn how to do that—even her folks couldn't have ignored it.

Steward didn't. He actually took a step backwards, arms raising up, before regaining his composure. The rest of the room was crackling with conversations as the real-estate lady tried to regain control of the meeting. Good luck with that.

"Did she kill my son?" Elliot Weiss had gotten to his feet, turning first toward Steward and then to face Lydia. "Did you kill Jonah?"

His voice wasn't loud but it carried enough power to silence everyone else.

"Dr. Weiss, please," the real-estate lady said. "This isn't the time or the place for accusations."

Weiss ignored her, stalking past his colleagues, heading towards Lydia. "Did you?"

Lydia pivoted to face this new danger. Before she could say anything—and Gina was holding her breath, waiting to see exactly what she would say—Mark Cohen intercepted Weiss.

"She didn't kill anyone, Elliot, and you damn well know it." Mark pointed a finger at Steward. "You of all people should know better than to speculate in public about something that could damage a person's career and reputation."

"What about Jonah?" Steward demanded, leaning forward to brace himself on the table top. "What about those dead women? Someone needs to stand up for them."

"Don't you dare even say my son's name! You deserted him, betrayed him." Weiss's veins began to pop out, and Gina wondered if he was going to stroke out right there in front of them all. Wouldn't that be a hoot? If Lydia ended up saving his life.

"You're the one who deserted him, Elliot. All I did was love him."

Silence fell over the room as Weiss opened and then snapped his mouth shut again. Several of the administrators bobbed their heads back and forth like spectators at a tennis match waiting for the next volley. Weiss's colleagues all managed to look anywhere but at the surgeon or his son's former lover.

"Excuse me," Lydia said. "But we seem to have a larger problem here."

Now all eyes were on her. Gina watched as the same expression of calm and control that Lydia had yesterday during the fight in the alley appeared. That, I'm in charge and you'll all listen to me, expression.

And despite everything, despite being a pariah, practically accused of murder, everyone turned to her and listened. How in hell did she do that, anyway?

"We need to protect our patients. Tighten security on all medications—from the time they leave the pharmacy until they reach the patient's bedside. Have nurses working in pairs, double—triple checking medications."

"She's right," Nora put in. "I've worked the units. Anyone could have gotten hold of potassium chloride, it's not locked up."

"It will be now," Mark said, addressing the other department heads. "All of you need to contact your charge nurses and start working on increased security. And you," he speared a glance at the administrators, "need to be ready to free up some budget for overtime and anything else it takes." Several opened their mouths to protest but he ran over them like a steamroller. "Don't give me any crap. Patient safety comes first."

"What about her?" Weiss asked, not even bothering to mention Lydia by name.

"This is a police matter now," Steward said.

Mark frowned. Gina saw a quick silent communication pass between him and Lydia. Lydia gave a small shrug and nodded.

"Dr. Fiore will stay on probation. No patient care until this matter is resolved. And I move that any vote on this matter be tabled until the police have a chance to adequately investigate."

Realtor Lady perked up at an opportunity to be the boss again. "I have a motion on the table. Does anyone second?"

"I will," Elliot Weiss said. "On the condition that Dr. Fiore be barred from stepping foot back inside Angels of Mercy until we've decided her fate."

"All those in favor?" Hands rose from all around the table. "Motion carried, this meeting is adjourned."

The room quickly emptied except for Gina, Nora, Lydia and Mark. Elliot Weiss was still apoplectic, had to be practically pulled from the room by Leslie deGeorge. Isaiah Steward disappeared in the throng, which was probably a good thing if he didn't want his ass kicked by Lydia or Mark or both.

Nora was doing her mother hen thing, already on the phone to the ED nurses, telling them to secure all the med carts and IV supplies.

"Wow," Gina told Lydia. "You sure know how to work a crowd."

To her surprise, Lydia sat on the table top, shaking with laughter, head rolled back. Then, even more amazing, Mark sat down beside her and joined in.

"Jeez, Mark. Thanks for making me feel so welcome during my first days here at Angels."

"This is nothing. You should see us when we roll out the red carpet for a real VIP."

"I guess the encore will be when the police haul me out of here in cuffs or charge me with murder."

"Jerry won't let that happen," Gina said, staring at the two of them, Mark swiping his eyes and Lydia holding her sides. She felt left out, like they were sitting at the grownup table and she was still relegated to the children's. "Not unless you really did do it."

That sparked more laughter. And reminded her that she had better pray Jerry didn't come down to the ED and find her there—she'd promised him that she'd take the day off to recuperate after the attack yesterday.

Like she would have missed this for the world.

Nora hung up the phone and turned to them. "Mark, we need to get back to the ER."

"What's up?" Unlike Gina, Mark was already off duty, so he should have been on his way home.

"It's your wife. She and your daughters had a near-miss with a car earlier."

Mark and Lydia both jumped down from the table. "Are they

all right?" he asked, already moving fast toward the door.

"They're fine, just some scrapes and Natalie sprained her ankle."

"Damn it, why didn't they call me?"

"Your cell phone's off."

"I turned it off for the meeting." He paused outside the door. "Lydia—"

"It's all right," she said. "Go take care of your family. I can take care of myself."

He nodded and sprinted down the hallway. Lydia turned to Gina and Nora. "I owe you guys. Big time."

"We didn't do anything," Nora said. "Never even had a chance to tell them what happened."

"Yeah, and why isn't anyone all over Isaiah Steward?" Gina put in. "He should have never have done that autopsy."

"Not to mention the fact that he was also in the CCU when Mrs. Owens died." Lydia shook her head again. "Look, I may not be around, so I just want to thank you both now. For standing up for me. It means a lot."

She walked away, not looking at all defeated, still with that same rapid stride Mark Cohen also shared. The mark of a leader.

Gina stared after her, seeing that the back of Lydia's shirt had the word "Physician" printed on it in large neon letters. The shirt looked worn, as if it had seen its fair share of disasters. She couldn't help but wonder if Lydia would ever be able to wear it again.

"Guess we'd better get back to work," Nora said with a sigh and Gina knew she was thinking the same thing.

CHAPTER 32

LYDIA FELT AS IF EVERYONE IN THE ER was staring at her as she walked out. She fought the urge to close her eyes or avoid eye-contact, instead facing everyone head on. After all, she had done nothing wrong.

Still, by the time she reached the wall of heat that greeted her in the ambulance bay, she felt guilty as sin. She couldn't resist the urge to turn back, look up at the chrome and glass tower, and wonder if she'd ever return.

"Ready to talk yet?" Pete Sandusky's cheerful bellow assaulted her. Back in civilian clothing, he was lounging against the wall, hugging the shadows like the blood-sucker he was.

Play nice, she reminded herself. After all, even leaches had mothers. And he had helped her out, answered her questions. "No comment."

"Come on, doc. Spare me the self-righteous martyr routine. Tell me your side of the story and I'll make sure the world knows what really happened."

She shook her head. "Do people really fall for that? You're going to tell whichever story will get you the biggest headlines, the best book deal, whatever."

He looked aghast, flattened one hand against his heart. "Doc, you're insulting my journalistic integrity. That hurts."

Rolling her eyes, she turned on her heel and began to walk away. He quickly caught up to her. "So, here's what I'm thinking. Tomorrow this city's going up like a powder keg. The Friendship Fellowship Church is holding an all-night vigil and memorial service. The Sons of Adam are planning marches all over the city, including in Friendship. Who knows what GOAD has planned. The politicians are shouting at each other, calling on the feds to intervene, but they can't do anything since a judge upheld the permits for the rally tomorrow—thanks to the good ol' ACLU arguing for the right to free speech."

"Sounds like you got your story. Now leave me alone."

"C'mon, doc. You owe me. I can't get boo from the cops or the medical examiner. I need someone to go on the record that both Jonah and the ladies at the church were killed by the same poison." He stood in front of her, blocking her way.

"I don't owe you anything. And I certainly am not going to provide you with information that might add fuel to the fire."

"Maybe you don't owe me anything," he conceded. "But maybe I know something you'd be interested in knowing too."

"Like what?"

"Seems like the Sons of Adam are the obvious suspects, right?"

To anyone who didn't know Isaiah Steward also could have killed both Jonah and Wanda. She nodded suspiciously.

"What if they're innocent? What if this was all a big cover up, and what if I told you that Isaiah Steward was a member of the Friendship Fellowship Church, used to sing in their choir? Until Jonah forced him out of the closet, that is."

Lydia froze. "You think he killed all those women?"

Sandusky was practically bouncing up and down in his eagerness to scoop the traditional media. "To cover up Jonah's murder. He'd know the routine, what time the ladies got there. And I saw him upstairs in the ICU before the goon squad dragged me out." He leered at her. "So, what do you say, doc? Ready to help me out?"

Help him orchestrate either a race riot or the public lynching of a man who may be innocent? "You need to call the police, tell them everything you know."

Her phone buzzed. It was Jerry Boyle. One thing about the detective, he had damn good timing. "Lydia, where are you?"

"Outside the ER."

"Stay there, I need to ask you some more questions."

She bet he did. Wondered what had taken him this long to get to her if Isaiah was right and she was a suspect in Wanda's death. She thought of Wanda's face, so peaceful, so trusting in her God—she didn't deserve this. None of the victims had. Shoving her phone back into her pocket, she saw that Sandusky was still waiting for an answer.

"You're going to have to keep looking for a source. I'm not talking to you anymore."

"Ah, doc, don't be like that. C'mon, let me buy you dinner. Anywhere you want."

"Go away, Sandusky."

"You're my best lead. I'm not letting you out of my sight."

"You want I should take him in for harassment?" Jerry Boyle's voice came from behind them. "I don't mind, it'd be doing a public service."

"Well, if it isn't Pittsburgh's favorite flatfoot, how ya doin' Boyle?"

"Tired, hungry, frustrated and too freakin' hot. Which makes me think maybe I should lock you up before my mood gets even worse. A few nurses up in the ICU said they saw you, trying to sneak a picture of Wanda Owens."

Sandusky held his hands up in surrender. "I vacated the premises as soon as I was informed that I was trespassing. Like any law-abiding citizen would."

"Yeah, well, just keep on vacating then. Before I change my mind."

Sandusky shrugged dramatically. "Whatever you say, Detective. Only doing my job—just like you." He jogged off, waving good-bye to Lydia and throwing Boyle a middle-fingered salute.

"What'd he want with you?" Boyle asked her.

"Confirmation that Jonah and the women in the church died of cyanide."

"Hmpf. He didn't get it, did he?"

"Do I look like I'm stupid? From what he said, the city's getting ready to riot already. If he went with a story suggesting that the Sons of Adam or some other group was targeting minorities..."

"Ka-boom. Yeah, that's pretty much what the brass is worried about. Tried to get an injunction against the rallies tomorrow, but thanks to Mickey Cohen—"

"Don't blame Mickey for doing her job. Speaking of which, you here to arrest me, Boyle?"

"Arrest you? No." He edged a glance her way as they walked. "Not unless you want to confess something?"

"At the Executive Committee, Isaiah Steward said—"

"Isaiah Steward is a pompous ass. Look, you've been up in the CCU. The place is a madhouse, and Wanda's room was in the side hallway—anyone could have gone in there and spiked her IV."

"Anyone who knew where to find potassium chloride."

They both looked at the hospital tower looming over them. "That's still a lot of anyones," he said with a sigh.

"Sandusky seems to think Isaiah could have done it. Said he had a witness who saw Isaiah in the bar with Jonah right before he died and that Isaiah was a member of the Friendship Fellowship Church." She didn't add that she shared the blogger's suspicions about the assistant medical examiner. Except she couldn't figure out why he'd risk exposing himself by killing Wanda.

"That man is a menace. Now the whole city will know before

sundown."

"So you don't think it was Isaiah?"

"I'm not paid to think. Or speculate. My job is to ferret out the facts and build a case." He wiped sweat from his forehead with the back of his hand. "I do want a statement from you. What Wanda said while you were talking with her, if you saw anything while you were there."

"Nothing helpful." She filled him in on her conversation with Wanda, leaving out only the part about Wanda praying for Lydia.

"Doesn't sound like she remembered anything more than she gave us in her initial statement."

"Boyle, why would the killer take the risk of going after her here at Angels? I can't believe anyone would go to all that trouble just to keep Wanda from giving a description—everyone knows how inaccurate eyewitness testimony can be, and you already had a statement from her."

He met her gaze, gave her a small nod of approval. "My question exactly. We're looking into her husband's, Commander Owens's, old cases, see if there was some kind of revenge motive. But so far we can't find anything to tie him and Jonah together. He hasn't worked active investigations for years, his job is pretty much administrative."

Fatigue clouded her brain. Somehow she also felt a hint of guilt, as if she were betraying Maria's memory by standing here chatting with a cop like he was a friend.

Which, despite his job, seemed to be a role Boyle had accepted. He gave her a scrutinizing look. "I heard about what happened with the Executive Committee. I'm sorry that they've taken such a hard line, Lydia. Once I have this case solved, I'll do everything I can to help you get your job back."

Blindsided by his generosity, Lydia felt her cheeks flush. "Thanks, Boyle. I appreciate that."

"Least I can do after everything you've been through. And I'd love to see Isaiah eat his words." They reached his car and he paused, his face cop-neutral once again. "As long as you didn't actually kill anyone, of course."

As he drove off, Lydia wasn't sure if he was joking or not. Cops. You never knew where you stood with them.

CHAPTER 33

NORA SIGNED OUT AT THE END OF HER SHIFT but didn't feel like going home to an empty house and a lonely dog and a long night imagining dead ladies in a church, jumping at shadows and reliving bad memories. Instead, she went up to the fourth floor where the ICUs, ORs and surgical call rooms were, hoping to catch Seth who was on call.

Starting in the CCU, she found the unit still buzzing about Wanda's death and the hastily implemented security measures. Mr. Perch, the firecracker guy Gina saved, was doing better, snoozing away and oblivious to the drama going on around him. One of the nurses told her that psych had already signed off saying poor judgment wasn't equivalent to suicidal intent.

Seth was nowhere to be found, but Amanda was in the PICU, sitting in a rocking chair, feeding a baby a bottle. With her blond hair and loving gaze, you could have easily mistaken the medical student for the baby's own mother. Nora sighed, wondering if she would ever have babies. Beautiful babies who looked like Seth. The thought made her smile, remembering Amanda's prediction that he was going to propose to her tomorrow night. Anticipation trilled through her as she dared to imagine the scene. The fireworks lighting up the sky nothing compared to the light in Seth's eyes....

"Hi, Nora," Amanda said, her voice light and sweet in contrast to the constant buzz of the machinery surrounding her.

"Is this your meningitis kid?" Nora asked, stroking the infant's fine hair, automatically feeling its fontanel. Nice and flat, that was good.

"Shannon," Amanda said, her smile widening as the baby thumped a hand against her bottle. "They took out her central line today and she'll be going down to Peds as soon as they have a bed open."

"Another save for Dr. Fiore."

"She's really good. I hope she can come back to work soon." Amanda's voice was filled with hero-worship.

"I doubt it, not after what happened today."

Amanda looked up at that. "I was asleep all day. What happened?"

"Lydia was on a ride-along, ended up countermanding orders and treating a patient herself."

"Oh no." Even the medical student recognized the enormity of Lydia's actions. "Is the patient all right?"

Nora pursed her lips, then stuck out her tongue at the baby who seemed to be fascinated with her. "She saved the patient's life. But later the woman died from a potassium overdose."

"Here? At the hospital?"

"In the CCU. Right after Lydia visited her, apparently. So don't be surprised when you hear people talking about her."

"I don't believe in gossip," Amanda said with a righteous frown. She glanced at Nora and her frown deepened.

"Something wrong?" Nora asked.

"No. I'm just going to be late for my shift if I don't get going."

Nora watched as Amanda expertly burped the baby and returned her to her bed. "Haven't seen Seth, have you?"

She was surprised when Amanda stiffened. The medical student didn't answer, merely shook her head, busy adjusting the baby's blanket.

"Guess I'd better go find him. Have a good shift." Nora blew the baby a kiss and turned to leave.

"Nora?" Amanda's voice stopped her.

"What?" She wasn't sure why, but something in Amanda's expression made Nora's stomach do a slow flip-flop. "Is something wrong?"

"Er. No. Nothing. Have a good night." Amanda sped away before Nora could ask her anything more.

EVEN AFTER VISITING SHANNON, Amanda was still a few minutes early for her shift. She was examining the board, checking out the patients waiting to be seen when she saw Gina talking earnestly with Mark Cohen. Gina broke away and greeted Amanda.

"Hey, you're early," Gina said.

"Had an appointment at the clinic. Didn't seem like much sense to go home after. What's up?"

"Let's see. The Med Exec Committee kicked Lydia out—"

"What? You're not serious." Nora hadn't mentioned that part.

"Wait. It gets worse. While we were in the Med Exec meeting, Mark's wife and two daughters came in because while she was picking the girls up at school some idiot almost ran them over."

"Oh my. Are they all right?" No wonder Mark looked so distressed. Sounded like Amanda had missed a lot while she had slept.

"The girls are fine. We're waiting for Natalie's CT results, but it looks like she just has a sprained ankle."

"Poor Dr. Cohen."

"Yeah, he's not too happy with the world right now. Which

reminds me. I thought maybe you'd like the chance to finish that college kid's tour of the hospital. The grand tour. Answer all his questions, tell him how things really are, not Jim's BS. You can start your shift as late as you want, I already cleared it with Mark."

"Won't that leave Jim with all the scut work?"

Gina smiled. "My thoughts exactly."

"You're the boss."

"I certainly am. And this boss is out of here."

"How's your head?"

"Nothing a long, hot bath and a glass of good wine won't fix." Gina started towards the locker room. "Oh, and if you see Seth, tell him to call Nora. He didn't go home last night and she's been worried sick about him. He hasn't answered her calls—the scrub nurse says he's been in the OR all day, but they should be wrapping up for the night."

Amanda looked away, stricken by indecision. Maybe she should have told Nora what she saw last night, Seth naked in the call rooms with another woman. "Can I ask you a question?"

Gina stopped in the doorway of the locker room. "What's up?"

"What would you do if you knew something—saw something—that might hurt a friend, but could also keep them from making a big mistake?"

"Amanda, don't make my headache worse. What are you trying to say?"

"I saw Seth last night, naked, in the call rooms. With a woman," she blurted out, the pressure releasing from her chest as she shared her burden.

"Seth? Naked, with a woman?" Gina pursed her lips. "No shit. Did you ask him what was going on?"

"Lord, no! Gina, he was *naked.* Of course I didn't talk to him. What should I do? Tell Nora?"

"Hell no. She'll hate you if you're right and there is something going on and will hate you even more if you're wrong." She shook her head, her braids jangling. "Let me handle it. The son of a bitch. I can't believe he'd do that to Nora."

"Maybe there's an explanation—"

"If there is, it sure as hell had better be a good one." Gina pushed the locker room door open, then looked back. "Hey. Tell me one thing. Is he as well-equipped as they say?"

Amanda's cheeks burned with embarrassment. "Gina!"

Gina only laughed, letting the door shut behind her.

Bob Brown came rambling down the hall, almost knocking a nursing assistant off her feet as he rounded the corner, his fingers fumbling with his visitor's pass as he clipped it to his jacket. Then he saw Amanda and came to a stop.

"Hi, Bob. Guess it's just you and me tonight."

"Great. Gina said you'd be able to show me the operating rooms?"

"It's not as dramatic as it sounds," Amanda assured him as she led the way to the elevators, her mind still on Seth and Nora. "Not at all like what you see on TV or anything. And they'll be shutting down except for emergencies because of the holiday tomorrow."

"Oh." His face slumped in disappointment.

Poor kid seemed never to smile. She wondered if his research on stress in night-shift workers wasn't causing him more stress than it was worth. He seemed jittery, anxious as they rode up in the elevator.

"Are you working tomorrow?" Bob asked her.

"Believe it or not, I actually get the day off. But I'll probably be back to watch the fireworks from the roof. Angels has the best view. You should join us."

That coaxed a smile from him. "Thanks. I think I will." Then he looked down, scuffing his feet as if embarrassed or uncertain. "Maybe we could go together? I could pick you up, we could do dinner first?"

Amanda felt her cheeks flush. She liked Bob, even if he was kind of earnest and tended to stare too long and hard at people with those spooky pale eyes of his, but she didn't really like-like him. Not that way.

He looked up at her, not blinking as he met her gaze. He wasn't smiling either. Just staring as if the weight of the world depended on her answer.

She faltered, took a step back even as the elevator came to a halt and the doors opened. He didn't move, simply waited for her answer.

"Uh, I think I'm supposed to meet some friends at a picnic," she stammered. Damn, she was so bad at lying, she was sure he saw right through her.

He said nothing, merely shrugged and walked past her out of the elevator. His shoulders were hunched so tightly she could see the outlines of his scapulas, like two tiny angel's wings bunching the fabric of his jacket.

"Bob, I'm sorry," she called out, jogging after him.

"No worries," he said, his grey eyes now the color of molten steel, his voice just as devoid of emotion. "Let's start with the operating rooms, shall we?"

CHAPTER 34

LYDIA DIDN'T BELIEVE IN LUCK OR FATE OR DESTINY. Instead, she'd always had a deep-seated belief that if she gave everything she had to the important things in her life, everything would work out all right. So she threw herself into her work, her patients, had fought for every inch of hard-won ground distancing her from Maria's legacy. Yet here she was, surrounded by blood and death once more.

After leaving Angels, she returned to her motel and choked down a protein bar despite the fact that her appetite had long since fled. Her mind was churning worse than the surf at Redondo on a winter's day. Her body cried out for movement, action. She changed clothes and headed out for a run.

She opted to forsake the crowds and congestion of Penn Avenue for the relative solitude of Schenley Park. It felt good to be alone, no one to judge her, to spy on her, to witness her vulnerability. Soon she was hypnotized by her rhythm, able to break away from the weight of the day's events.

The sound of pounding footsteps behind her caught her attention. She popped the safety off her pepper spray, glad she had brought it tonight. The footsteps grew louder, drew close. She kept her pace, gauging the distance, then stopped and pivoted, pepper spray raised.

"Hey, it's only me." Trey Garrison came to a halt beside her, hands raised in surrender. "Jeezit, don't shoot. I've been calling your name last half mile, but you kept going faster."

She glared at him, adrenaline still rocking her. He wore a pair of black nylon running shorts, New Balance shoes, and nothing else. Sweat beaded over his chest and dripped from his brow. He wiped his forehead with the back of his hand, his smile widening. "You always this serious about your running? You must have been clocking seven minute miles."

"I was thinking." She wheeled and resumed her pace.

He ran beside her, his longer legs effortlessly eating up the ground.

"I think better alone," she said, hoping he'd take the hint.

He shrugged and flashed her a grin. "Don't mind me."

Annoyed, she pushed her speed. He stayed with her at first, then slowly fell behind. Soon, she was moving so fast the trees and the path became a blur. The blood rushing through her head drowned out all thoughts of dead women or Jonah Weiss. It felt as if, if she could just force herself a little faster, push a little harder, then she could break free of everything holding her down. Leave everything behind.

Tears flowed down her face, mingling with sweat and further clouding her vision. Running away. Was that the only thing she was good at? Running from one disaster to the next in a futile attempt to find–what?

What was she searching for so desperately?

A tree root buckling the pavement almost sent her sprawling. She tripped, spun off the trail and grabbed at a tree trunk to regain her balance. She stood there, dizzy, breathing hard, tears knotting her throat as she clung to the tree.

Maybe the question wasn't what she was running from, but what she was running to.

Strong arms wrapped around her and she fell, sobbing, into

Trey's embrace. He held her while she cried so hard her insides felt scraped raw. Finally, she was empty of tears, and although still shaking uncontrollably, she pushed away from him to stand on her own.

Her cheeks burned. She *never* cried. At least never in public. What made it worse was that she hadn't been driven to tears by the thoughts of the deaths she'd witnessed today, but rather by her own confusion, the feeling that her life was spinning out of her control.

How selfish could she get?

"Guess maybe you should've come to that stress debriefing after all," Trey said, his hand stroking her shoulder.

She shrugged it off and turned away.

"It was a good one," he continued. "We talked and cried and told bad jokes and tore the scab off that sucker, dissected it until it bled dry. Bottom line, Lydia, was that we did nothing wrong, there was nothing more we could have done."

His words hit Lydia like a sneak attack. Her mind reeled as she put all the pieces together—the death of Wanda and the church ladies, what happened in the alley yesterday, her talking with Jerry Boyle last night. What Sandusky had said earlier about cover-ups. She bent over, her breath escaping her.

"I'm sorry," she gasped, almost unable to get the words out.

"About what?" His voice was quiet and earnest as if he really wanted to know.

She was silent, unable to find her voice past the knot in her throat. Images of the church women, reaching out to their God as they lay dying crashed down on her in a tsunami of guilt.

She pushed away from Trey, blindly stumbling toward the path. He took her arm and guided her to a side trail and a bench above the parking lot. Across the street a large building shaped in a series of gently curving arches and made entirely of glass glowed against the twilight sky like a Victorian fairytale.

"Phipps Conservatory," Trey said, his voice neutral as if he wasn't witnessing her impending breakdown. "You know, plants and flowers and stuff. I just like the way the glass looks when it's all lit up at night."

Lydia's legs cramped with the sudden stop, but it felt good to surrender to gravity. She slumped forward, hands dangling between her legs, her gaze fixed on the Victorian-style building. It seemed to float, a magnificent palace of light. As she stared, she made out the dark, irregular forms of plants and the humans roaming among them. Her vision cleared, her pulse stopped echoing through her head and she could breathe again.

"You want to talk about it?" Trey asked, his hand resting on her knee, offering comfort.

She shook her head, sweat beading off her hair. The conservatory blurred as if threatening to vanish into another dimension, then cleared again once she blinked.

"Why are you here?" Her voice sounded scratchy, brusque.

Trey took no offence. "Heard about what happened to Wanda. I was worried about you. Your motel clerk said you asked about good running paths—"

"You thought you'd come save me." A chuckle dry as dead leaves escaped from her. "Thanks, but no thanks. I can take care of myself."

"So I see." He raised his hand and at first she thought he was going to wipe her tears, which would have been more humiliating than words. Instead, he tapped the canister of pepper spray still clenched in her fist. "Truth be told, I had ulterior motives."

She turned her head to meet his eyes. Even in the dim light, they sparked with gold. "Ulterior motives?"

He nodded slowly, his gaze never leaving hers. "I kind of didn't want to be alone tonight." He straightened and shrugged one shoulder, making light of his confession. "Gecko has his girl, and the chief said I couldn't stay and work a double, so–"

"You thought of me." She was making a habit of finishing his thoughts for him. She remembered the way they worked so well together earlier, as if they were both on the same wavelength. Maybe Trey hadn't had such a bad idea after all.

"C'mon," he said, pulling her to her feet, wrapping his arm around her shoulder. Despite the heat and humidity, it felt good, like it belonged there.

"Where to?"

"I know a place not far. We'll have our own stress debriefing."

"What if I don't want to?" She had no idea why she was arguing with him, she definitely wanted to continue to share the warm comfort he offered. Being with him wasn't the usual see-saw control battle she felt with most men. It was as if they were on equal ground.

He paused, his face hidden by shadows. His fingers traced her cheekbone, smoothing away any trace of her tears. His touch was so light that she didn't mind at all. "What *do* you want?"

His words so closely echoed the thoughts haunting her that for a moment she couldn't answer. His hand slid down to rest on her arm, not pulling her close, but simply waiting for her response.

The air filled with the intoxicating smells of damp grass, testosterone and the tang of sweat. Fireflies lit the darkness, creating a magical illusion. She was tempted, sorely tempted.

Would she lose him once he learned the truth, that six women had died because of her?

CHAPTER 35

GINA HAD SURPRISED JERRY, waiting at his apartment with samplings of his favorite foods: ribs from Blue Lou's, fries from The O, falafel from Leena's, wings from Fat Heads, and for dessert, apple dumplings with caramel sauce. She knew he'd never come to her place, not while working a murder case. Just like she knew that he'd skipped lunch and dinner before dragging himself in at ten past nine.

She was waiting for him, cold beer in each hand, as soon as he opened the door. He took the beer, saying nothing, used it to wipe the sweat from his forehead before taking a long drink.

"Guess you had a rough day," she said, moving in for a kiss.

He ducked away, shedding his hopelessly wrinkled jacket, his fingers tugging his tie loose before taking another swallow of beer.

"They interrupted Jerry Springer twice with updates. I thought I saw Lydia there," she lied.

Jerry remained silent, drinking and staring at her. She'd chosen her outfit carefully, splashing on a coat of purple nail polish to coordinate with her orchid print halter top and white linen short-shorts. She'd left her sandals, Manolo Blahniks today, beside the door, the better to show off her pedicure.

He finished his beer and set it down. Still saying nothing.

"I brought dinner. All your favorites." She gestured to the dining room table. "Had to run all over town to get them all."

Another lie. She'd bribed one of the drivers from the car service her parents used and sent him after everything. But she'd made the phone calls herself.

Instead of looking at the food, Jerry just kept staring at her. This was bad. Definitely bad. Gina felt her pulse jump up a notch.

Jerry was always patient about hearing her stories from work but never eager to share details from his job, but this was different. Different even than his, "I'm just waiting for you to spin out enough rope to hang yourself with" silence that she'd seen him use with potential suspects in the ER. This was more like an "I'm so angry if I open my mouth I'll start spitting nails" kind of silence—something she'd never seen from him before.

"You didn't watch Jerry Springer today, Gina."

"Like hell I didn't. Ask me anything." She'd watched it while doing her nails. Just in case.

"I don't need to. I know you worked your shift today. You promised me—"

"A promise doesn't count when it's made under duress."

"Duress?"

"I seem to recall someone threatening to handcuff me to the bed if I didn't promise."

"You had a concussion, were up all night, you were in no shape—"

"I'm fine. And I don't need you trying to run my life for me." She planted her hands on her hips and pushed her chest out, straining the fabric of her halter top. Saw his gaze slant down and knew she had him. Men, they were so easy to manipulate. Especially when you knew them as well as she knew Jerry. She stepped forward, close enough to trail her nails down his shirt, ending by snagging his tie.

"C'mon, we'll eat in bed." She began to walk away, pulling

him with her. "I'll bring the food. You bring the cuffs."

LYDIA ALLOWED TREY TO LEAD HER DOWN to the street where his truck was parked. She loved that he drove a red Ford Ranger, bright and shiny. It suited him.

He unlocked his door, then walked with her around the truck to the passenger side to unlock her door and see her safely inside. He didn't help her up or anything patronizing, merely stood there, watching.

"I've climbed Half Dome at Yosemite," she told him. "I think I can handle a pickup truck."

He was silent, his gaze capturing hers. "I think you can handle just about anything." He slammed the door shut and walked around to the driver's side.

"You need to take it easy on yourself," he said as he drove. "You can't be responsible for the world."

She gave a small snort. "Says who?"

"C'mon, look around you. You really want to be responsible for this crap?"

"Maybe I don't belong here," she said, her mind trying to replace the grey-washed streets before her with the sight of the Pacific. "You ever been surfing?"

"Nope. Never been to Yosemite or Hawaii or Paris or any place exciting either. Doesn't mean I wouldn't like to visit, but sure as heck wouldn't want to live anywhere else."

"Why not?" She turned in her seat, challenging him. "What's keeping you here? A woman? Or women?"

Trey's shifted uncomfortably. "It's not like I have a harem or anything. There's no one permanent."

"The man has a short attention span, is frightened of long

term commitment, and still lets his mother do his laundry. Trey, you're a walking beer commercial. You'd better watch out, someday you might just start to grow up. Maybe even settle down."

There was a long silence. His eyes creased, mouth tightened as he studied the traffic. She was surprised he didn't throw her words right back at her—after all, other than a mother doing her laundry, the description fit her just as well as it fit him. At least it used to.

"We're here."

He pulled into the driveway of a Craftsman bungalow that looked like it dated from the 1920's. A river stone façade graced the front, with a wide porch, complete with porch swing. It sat at the end of a long drive lined by mature hemlocks and maple trees, giving it the illusion of being the only house for miles, despite being in the heart of the city. A wrought iron fence stood at the edge of the property, between the house and the cemetery beyond it.

Neither of them moved. Lydia was almost afraid to—the house, the setting, the twilight sky, the man beside her, they all felt part of a dream. Very far away from the real world where women died reaching out for God and finding nothing.

Trey jumped down from the truck and jogged around to open her door for her. She took the hand he offered, didn't let it go once her feet were back on the ground.

"Is that the hospital?" She pointed to the rows of lights visible above the far corner of the cemetery. In the dark, the lights appeared as random squares, hovering high in the sky then disappearing as the foliage of the cemetery drowned them out.

"That's Angels," he confirmed. "Your motel and Penn Avenue are over there to the left."

"You do live close."

"It's not my house. I'm only fixing it up—almost done."

"Except the painting."

"Yeah, how'd you—"

"You were wearing some yesterday when you came to the

ER." She paused. "Trying to talk some sense into me."

"Failing miserably."

His tone was light-hearted, but she couldn't help but think of her own recent failures.

"It was my fault," she said, her voice dropping down so low that she could almost hope he hadn't heard her. "Those women, they're dead because I started asking questions."

"You can't believe that," he finally said, his voice firm, refusing any argument. "You can't think that way, Lydia."

"What should I think?" she demanded, emotions still colliding—guilt, rage, frustration, fear—all conspiring against logic. "Jonah dies. I ask questions, tell the police about my suspicions. Next thing I know, there's six more dead."

His breath came out in a whoosh as he shook his head. "Or maybe there's just some nut job with a bottle of cyanide running loose. Any way you look at it, you can't blame yourself, Lydia. Although, I must admit, you sure do have a flare for pissing off the wrong people."

She shot him a hard glare. Despite his attempt at levity, his gaze was filled with concern.

"Don't try to sugarcoat it, Garrison. Those women would still be alive if I hadn't pissed off the wrong person—or people."

He frowned, lay one hand on her shoulder and squeezed it gently. "Lydia. That's not what I meant–"

His body was inches away, his scent filled her senses, and she knew talking wasn't going to make her feel any better, take the pain away. Nothing would. Sometimes the only way to face death and destruction was to spit in its face and grab whatever joy you could. That was one thing Maria had right.

She reached out, pulling him closer. His mouth covered hers, her fingers raked over his back, her elbow slammed the side of the truck as she struggled to press every inch of her body against his.

It wasn't an answer, but maybe with Trey she could at least

find some relief. For tonight that was enough. Just to know she wasn't alone.

CHAPTER 36

THE COOLING TRUCK ENGINE TICKED and pinged beneath Lydia, its hood radiating almost as much heat as what she and Trey were creating. She wrapped her leg around his, pulling him closer. As their kiss deepened, tongues intertwined, she ran her hands over his back, enjoying the feel of his muscles rippling beneath her touch.

One small corner of her mind hoped he understood and forgave her for using him. Sex, raw, hot, primal, was so much better than spending the night huddled in a bathtub hiding from ghosts.

His pelvis pressed against hers, revealing his arousal in no uncertain terms. She guessed he didn't mind her using him after all. He was ready to take her right there in the driveway. She pulled away, just far enough to allow the night breeze to cool the sweat from her face and whisper to him, "Condoms."

A noise like a growl caught in his throat, but he nodded his head. Tugging her hand, he pulled her to her feet, twirling her in a dance move. She ended up with her back pressed against his chest, her arm and his wrapped around her in front, his other hand on her hip. He half marched, half carried her into the carport stacked with tools and building supplies and through the unlocked door into the kitchen.

When their feet hit the smooth tile floor, he pirouetted her out of his arms but kept hold of her hand. "You have some fancy moves for a medic," she told him with a laugh.

He was busy rummaging through kitchen drawers. The only light was the one above the oven. The room was empty except for a small microwave and a stack of paper plates and napkins. No table or chairs, no dishes, no plants or cooking paraphernalia. When he'd said he was just camping out here, he was right.

She broke free of his grasp and stepped through a large curved archway into the dining room. To the left was another archway, leading into a living room. Again no furniture, just a large expanse of wood floors. There were no lights here, but enough moonlight shone through the windows that she made out a stone fireplace taking up most of one wall in the living room and large French doors leading outside to her right in the dining room. Chandeliers hung from both rooms and a staircase took up the far wall of the living room.

"Ah-hah," came Trey's exuberant cry from the kitchen. He reappeared, dangling a strip of condoms from his fingers, holding the other hand across his chest as he cha-cha'd his way towards her.

"You really can dance."

"I'm a man of many, many talents and hidden depths," he told her in a fake Latino-machismo accent, accompanying his words with a waggle of his eyebrows.

"Yeah, right. Why don't you come here and show me some of that talent." She reached for his waistband, but he danced away.

"You don't believe me?" He stood tall and proud and she could almost imagine him wearing a tuxedo, getting ready to start a tango. "I'll prove it to you. For every time I make you moan with passion, you will owe me one dance."

In response, she crossed her arms, tugging her sweaty sports bra over her head. She posed for a moment, arms stretched up, made certain she had his complete attention, then leaned over without bending her knees to take her shoes off. Tilting her head, she kept her eyes on his while she completed her striptease and shimmied out of her shorts. She kicked her clothes away and leaned back against the arch.

"I didn't come here to dance."

This time he didn't resist when she reached for him and reeled him in close.

"We'll see about that," he told her with a grin, his teeth flashing in the dim light.

JERRY HAD, OF COURSE, INSISTED ON STARTING WITH DESSERT. Afterwards, the ceiling fan whooshing above them, cooling the sweat from their bodies, Gina still had caramel sauce matted in her hair.

Jerry pushed himself up against the headboard, one hand drawing curlicues on her shoulder. "Thanks for dinner. And for putting up with my lousy mood."

She slanted a grin at him. "Worth it. I wanted to thank you for watching over me last night."

"Easiest duty I ever pulled."

He didn't mention her crying jag or the crazy, desperate way she'd needed him last night. God, she despised acting so out of control.

Gina curled her fingers in his. She loved his hands, the hands of an artist or pianist or something. Jerry could have been an artist—his photography was brilliant, but she'd never been able to convince him of that. Just a hobby, he said. She reached over him for a chicken wing, tore it in half and fed it to him.

"I'm sorry I got upset with you. About working today." He leaned down, kissed her, then licked away the dipping sauce his lips left behind. "I was just so worried about you. And after seeing those women—"

"Hey," she said, smoothing her hand over his arm, feeling the tension that had returned. "You don't need to think about that. Not tonight." Then she sat up straight, straddling him. "I didn't get a chance to tell you about my good news. I get to ride with Med Seven tomorrow."

"What?" He sat up, almost bouncing her off his lap. "You're not starting your ride-alongs until next month."

"Switched shifts with Marty. He wanted the holiday off. Isn't it great?"

He didn't look very excited. Or happy. His mouth curved down, chin jutted forward. No, not happy at all.

"What's wrong?" she asked. "You'll be busy at work all day."

"Maybe you should call in sick. There's something brewing out there—"

"You sound like one of the witches from Macbeth." She sat up on her elbow, her fingers tracing arcane patterns in his chest hair. "You know how jazzed I've been to get out there with the medics. It's the biggest perk of being a third year. That and running codes."

His sigh rattled through him. He sat up, pulling her hand to his lips and kissing it. "All right. Guess I'll have to give you your birthday present early."

She bounced up, clapping. "Really? I love presents. Let's see it."

He walked over to the closet. The view from behind was almost as nice as the view from in front, she thought as she watched him lift a gift-wrapped box from the floor. He returned and handed it to her. Damn thing was heavy, much too heavy to be jewelry or clothing.

"What did you get me, weights? It's too flat to be a bowling ball."

"Open it."

She shook it, puzzled as she received a solid thud for her

efforts. Finally she tore the wrapping, scattering bits of colorful paper among the remnants of their dinner. "I don't believe it."

Carefully folded inside the box, giving off a faint chemical odor like a new raincoat, was a black ballistic vest.

"I hope you like it. Janet Kwon helped me order it. I figured she'd know all about the proper measurements and such. It's custom made. Try it on."

His expression was earnest and his speech pressured, not giving her a chance to answer. She unfolded the Kevlar vest and saw he had her name embroidered over the left breast.

Tears welled up behind her eyes and for once not only had he absolutely taken her by surprise, he'd also left her speechless. The thought and work and planning that had gone into this gift, it overwhelmed her. Only Jerry, dear, sweet Jerry would think of something like this.

"It's designed for tactical medics, so you have all sorts of pockets for your stuff. And I got the extra-lightweight ceramic plates. They cost more, but you'll be able to move faster, won't be so sore at the end of the shift. And the inner layer is breathable, will wick the sweat—"

She grabbed him by the shoulders and planted a firm kiss on his mouth, shutting him up. Then she hopped out of bed, modeling her new ensemble.

"I love it. I've never had a more thoughtful present."

"So you'll wear it?"

"Are you kidding? I can't wait to show it off. I mean who else has a guy go to all the trouble of custom-designing a bulletproof vest for them?"

He sank back with relief. She twirled around, zipping and unzipping, pulling Velcro apart and re-sealing it, grinning like a kid at Christmas.

"So," she stopped, raising one foot onto the bed and leaning over him. "Have you ever made love to a woman wearing Kevlar before?"

"No ma'am. That's a new one on me." Before she could reply, he grabbed her waist and pulled her squealing down onto the bed.

CHAPTER 37

STARS SWIRLED ABOVE LYDIA. She felt so relaxed, her muscles melting into liquid, the night sky so clear, that she imagined herself falling into the galaxies colliding above her.

It reminded her of nights spent on the beach with Maria. Even during times when they had money, they'd invariably end up camping on the beach. Lydia never minded. A canopy of stars like diamonds, the lullaby of the Pacific, the sand as a pillow, the scent of freedom filling the air—what kid wouldn't love that?

Lydia stretched out a hand, brushing Trey's arm. He lay snoring softly, face down in the grass. After their first time in the living room—fast, frenzied, furious sex up against the wall, leaving them both gasping and laughing and energized—he'd brought her out here to the patio and true to his word, taught her how to waltz.

She laughed at the memory. Naked dance lessons? From a paramedic no less.

But it had been like something out of one of her mother's fairy tales, dancing under the stars, making love on the grass as if they were the only two people on Earth…

Lydia's sigh emptied her. She felt the hard ground beneath her, the tickle of the grass, the smell of dew. This was no fairy tale.

And it had been only sex, nothing more. A release, a primal reflex, a joining of bodies.

Except. It had felt like more. Much more.

She banished the thought. She'd seen Maria give her heart over and over again. The woman had fallen in love more often than she'd changed her shoes. And always she'd been left alone, broken, with only Lydia to put her back together again.

As far as Lydia was concerned, love was more dangerous than Ebola.

Trey made a small sound, shifted his weight, curling one leg protectively over hers. As if, even in his sleep, he understood exactly what she needed.

The thought terrified her. She eased her body away from his and stood up. And was surprised to see a strange pair of eyes staring back at her. A large animal sat up on the picnic table, green eyes glowing in the dark. It had a rather squared off shape, short fur that glinted in the moonlight and appeared speckled or patterned. It's head was small, shaped like a cat, but it was much bigger than the common cat.

It made a noise. Definitely unlike any cat she'd ever met. The sound it made was a harsh, squawking noise more like a parrot than a feline.

As she stirred it raised one paw, like a dog offering to shake. It stretched its neck sinuously, then butted its head against her arm.

She raised her hand, scratching behind its ears. Its fur was thick and soft like a cat's. A vibration rumbled beneath her touch, then a purr like a roaring locomotive emerged.

"Ah, you found No Name," Trey said, standing behind her, both hands on her shoulders. She noticed he kept her between himself and the cat. If it was a cat.

"No Name? It's yours?"

"Hell no. Darn thing won't come near me unless I'm using the hose. It loves playing in water—once followed me into the shower."

That didn't sound like any cat she'd ever heard of. "I thought cats hated water." She paused in her motion, eliciting a spine-tingling growl from the animal. "What exactly is it?"

"Damn if I know. I called the zoo 'cause in the daylight it looks something like a baby leopard or panther or something. They said they weren't missing anything and not to worry. It lives in the graveyard, maybe it's a mutant."

No Name head butted her again. Lydia resumed her scratching. The purring—if that was what you could call it—returned, and the cat arched its back, its tail thumping the table with enough force to rock it.

"Looks like he likes you."

"Great. What do I do now? I don't want to get some kind of mutant crazy panther mad at me."

No Name made the decision for himself. He shook himself before strolling across the table, away from Lydia, allowing her fingers to trace the length of his body. Then he leapt to the ground in a soundless pounce and disappeared.

"Problem solved," Trey said, circling his arms around her and nuzzling the side of her neck. "You ready for another dance lesson?"

"WHAT DID Y'ALL BRING US?" Amanda asked the paramedics as they rounded the corner with a college-aged woman on their stretcher.

"She's mine," Jim Lazarov said, pushing between her and the medics as they wheeled the patient into the exam room.

Amanda watched from the doorway. It was three-twenty in the morning. The ER was so quiet that after their tour of the ICUs and ORs, Bob Brown had left her to interview some ICU nurses. At least Amanda hoped that was why he had left. She hated to think that her declining his invitation had been the cause.

"Becky Sanborn. Nineteen year old CMU student," the medic said as they transferred the patient to the gurney. "Sudden onset of aphasia and possible seizures."

"Possible seizures?" Jim said doubtfully. "C'mon, either they are or they aren't."

"Your call, doc. Ain't like any seizures I've ever seen." The medics pulled their gurney out, handing Jim a run sheet as they went. "She's a patient of Dr. Stone's."

The woman lay there, silent, staring up at the ceiling, the only thing moving the rise and fall of her chest.

"Ma'am, ma'am, can you squeeze my hand?" Jim raised the woman's hand over her face, let it drop. It slapped the woman in the face and rolled limply to dangle from the gurney. The woman never blinked.

He pulled back the sheet that covered her legs. She wore a tank top and boxer shorts, typical college girl pj's. Jim pulled out his reflex hammer, struck it against her patellar tendon. No response. "What is this, a weird form of Guillan-Barre?"

"Jim, look," Amanda said, drawing close and pointing at the girl's left thigh.

Beneath her skin was movement, like the wriggling of a hundred snakes slithering down her leg then vanishing.

"What the hell? Page Lucas Stone."

Twenty minutes later the neurologist was at the girl's beside, hair rumpled with sleep and sheet creases still evident on his face. He didn't seem to care, all attention focused on the patient before him.

"This makes no sense," he said, finishing her examination. "There's nothing localizing. She has normal DTR's in her arms and right leg, absent in the left, but the aphasia and paralysis are more consistent with a caudate nucleus hemorrhage." He gave his head a little shake, drumming his reflex hammer against his own leg as he spoke. "Amanda, when's CT going to be ready?"

"They're ready now."

"Good, you go with her, I'm going to pull my clinic notes and I'll be right up."

"She's Jim's case." The intern had ordered her to wait on Lucas. Probably didn't want to face the wrath of an attending called in at this ungodly hour. "He'll be here any minute."

"CT's ready now, take her up," he snapped. Then his tone softened. "Sorry, but if we don't discover what's going on with her fast, she's going to end up on a vent in the ICU or worse." His eyes narrowed, staring at her with an intensity that made her rock backwards. "Besides, I want you on her case."

"Me? Why?"

"Because when Becky first came to me three weeks ago, she had the same symptoms you do."

CHAPTER 38

NORA STOOD BEFORE THE ER DOORS, already sweating despite the fact that it wasn't even seven in the morning, almost turning around and going back home. She could wait until tonight, she'd be seeing Seth for certain then.

Her fingers clamped tighter on the picnic basket she carried. It was a peace offering. For rushing him. But she needed answers. She bit her lip, nodded to herself. She could do this, she was strong enough to handle the truth—whatever it was.

As she walked inside, she was surprised to see Lucas Stone, looking distinctly sleep-deprived, standing at the nurses' station.

"Good morning. What are you doing here?" Lucas asked Nora as she passed him on her way to the elevators.

She stopped and balanced her picnic basket on the counter. He peeked under the red-check napkin she'd used to cover the assortment of muffins and bagels.

"Looks good," he said with a smile. "How did you know I skipped breakfast?"

Nora batted his hand away. They both knew the last thing germophobe Lucas would eat would be unwrapped baked goods. "They're for Seth. He was on call last night and I wanted to surprise him."

"Wait." Lucas left his chart and rushed out from behind the counter. "I think maybe he's in the ICU. Let me page him, ask him to come down here." He reached for the phone. "That way it will be a real surprise."

"No, that's all right." She grabbed her basket of goodies and strolled down the hall. "I'll page him from his call room."

Lucas started after her but was interrupted by a nurse asking for a TPA dose for his stroke patient. Nora got on the elevator, relieved as the doors slid shut before he could join her.

Poor guy, she knew Lucas was lonely. But she and Seth had planned today for months—she'd had to put her day off request in ninety days in advance and he'd switched his call day so they could be together. Last year, the Fourth had been the first time they'd made love, the first time she'd begun to believe that she wasn't just another disposable woman in a long line of interchangeable partners, the first time she'd seen him cry.

Last Fourth of July she discovered his secret—fireworks made him bawl like a baby. It was almost a year later before she trusted him enough to tell him hers.

She jabbed the elevator button. Damn thing was moving too slow, she should have taken the stairs. Shifting the basket from one hand to the other, she dried her sweaty palms on her khaki shorts. The elevator chimed its arrival on the fourth floor where the operating rooms and ICUs were located. Stashed in a forgotten back hallway was a string of small call rooms. She knocked on the one reserved for the trauma resident and got no answer. Went inside. No Seth.

Probably on rounds. Hmm…except his lab coat was still there, his cell phone on the bedside table. She set the basket down and used the landline to dial his beeper. As she waited for the machine to process the page, she looked around. The bed was rumpled, a copy of the latest *Annals* lay face down beside the pillow. That was funny, he'd left his shoes—both his street shoes and his surgical clogs.

Where the heck was he without any shoes? Distant thunder began to sound in the pulse beating at her temples. She dropped the phone back into its cradle.

The sound of a beeper going off joined the pounding in her skull. It wasn't in this room, was next door. Her face felt tight and she knew she was frowning. She forced herself to relax, he was probably giving last minute instructions to an intern.

Following the sound was easy—the rooms in this non-patient area had no sound proofing, consisted of thin layers of drywall thrown up to give an illusion of privacy. She traced the sound not to the intern's call room on the right but rather to the anesthesia call room on the left.

She knocked but there was no answer. The pager went off again. She placed her hand against the doorknob and held it there as if feeling for heat, for unexpected danger. The sound of a toilet flushing came from the room.

Ahh...that explained it. His bathroom was broken. Relief rushed through her as she pushed the door open.

And froze in the doorway. Seth lay naked and asleep on the bed.

A tall blonde, also naked, emerged from the bathroom. Karen Chisholm, one of the nurse anesthetists.

"Someone keeps paging him," Karen said, strolling past Nora and grabbing Seth's beeper, turning it off. She looked down on Seth, then perched on the edge of the bed, one hand trailing down, feathering his chest hair. "Poor baby had a hard night."

Nora wanted to scream but couldn't.

The blonde was smiling. She had perfect moviestar teeth to go along with her perfect moviestar body. She and Seth would look, well—perfect—together. Her fingers kept roaming, stroking Seth's naked skin and the inevitable happened.

Seth moved slightly beneath her touch, made a sound of

contentment. Karen laughed.

Her laughter was as perfect as the rest of her—the kind of laugh men fell in love with, not too high pitched, not too shrill, not too twittering. Musical.

"You bastard!" Nora's grip on the brass doorknob grew so tight the door rattled in its frame.

Seth's eyes fluttered then popped open. Wide open. As was his mouth, although no sound came from him. He tried to sit up, tried to push the blonde away, tried to jump out of bed but a leg got tangled in the sheet and he ended up hopping on one foot, the blonde knocked to the ground, his leg trailing behind him on the bed, his mouth opening and closing, his hand reaching for Nora just as she slammed the door shut.

On him, on the blonde, on their future.

DAMN THE MAN, by the time the sun came up, Lydia owed Trey two tangos and a rumba. She didn't even know what a rumba was. But it had felt good, waking curled up against his warmth; inhaling the scent of moist grass, damp earth, sweaty man; feeling his breath stir the hairs on her neck.

She'd woken up, nerves jangling with the feeling that she'd missed something. Her conversations with Sandusky and Boyle kept replaying themselves over in her mind and she knew she was close, but couldn't quite figure out what was bothering her. She left Trey sleeping, thinking that she'd see if there was anything in the house she could fix for breakfast. But No Name—she still wasn't entirely certain the damn animal was a cat and not some kind of dwarf-cougar—darted inside the house with her.

In the daylight, the animal was a soft tan color with large dappled chocolate brown and orange leopard-like markings. She pulled on her still-damp clothes and gave chase. No Name decided it was a game of Marco Polo, responding to her efforts with its goosebumpy screech that passed for a meow.

Before she could catch it, her cell phone rang. "Yes?"

"Lydia, thank God you're there." Mark Cohen's voice sounded pressured. "I need you to get over to Angels right away."

She placed one hand against her chest, feeling her heart stutter at his words. "What happened? Is there another cyanide victim?"

Mark didn't answer right away, instead she heard him bellowing orders in the background. No Name came out of hiding, curling himself against her bare legs as if trying to lend support. Trey also appeared, walking through the French doors, naked, his brow furrowed as if puzzled over why she was dressed and talking on the phone instead of still by his side. He ran a hand over his face, then stepped close, holding one hand out to her. She took it, grateful for the comfort.

"Mark?" she finally found the strength to ask.

"It's Mickey. It's bad." His voice broke. "Real bad."

"I'll be there in five minutes." She hung up the phone and reached for her shoes, wondering what could have happened to the wheelchair-bound lawyer. Trey was already stepping into his shorts.

"What happened?" he asked.

"Mark Cohen's sister, Mickey—"

"Your lawyer?"

"Yeah. He said she's bad off, wants me to come to Angels."

"I'm coming with you." He grabbed his keys and they ran out the door, all thoughts of crazy cats and breakfast abandoned.

CHAPTER 39

AMANDA SCRAMBLED, trying to stay out of the way and help at the same time as Lucas and Mark called out orders, one man on each side of Mickey Cohen's body.

"Secure the airway before the gavage."

"Get me a gas."

"Hyperventilate. And push those fluids."

"I need another line."

Amanda fought to keep her balance while people jostled her on either side as she swabbed Mickey's wrist for an arterial blood gas. She got it on the first stick, quickly drew the blood and stepped back to allow a nurse apply pressure. Dumping her syringe into a cup of ice, she spun around and collided with Lucas, almost losing the cup with its precious specimen.

Lucas's stony mask slipped for a brief moment and she saw how frightened he was. She knew Mickey had overdosed on phenobarbital but she had no idea how bad that was until she saw the look in his eyes. He steadied her hand holding the cup and syringe, steadying her at the same time. "Run this to the lab and don't drop it."

She nodded and raced out the door, this time almost bowling

over Bob Brown. The college student frowned at her, jumping back like she was contaminated or something. Sometime during the night he had changed into scrubs, maybe he had something spilled on his street clothes? Before she could say anything, he brushed past her to crane his head into the resuscitation room. Amanda ran down the hall to the lab. The tech waited at the window, already notified by the ER that stat labs would be arriving.

"Art gas," Amanda told her.

The tech plugged the heparinized syringe into the machine. "The phenobarb level should be back any minute. I had to send it upstairs."

As the computer printed out Amanda's blood gas results, the phone rang. The tech grabbed it, blanched, but wrote something down. She ripped off the blood gas results and handed both pieces of paper to Amanda. "Tell them that's only the preliminary phenobarb level. They're going to re-run it to confirm."

Amanda nodded and sprinted back to the ER. At the doorway to Mickey's room she found Lydia and Trey who both looked like they'd been out for a run, wearing shorts and sneakers. Bob had vanished.

"The gas looks good," she announced, handing the results to Mark who nodded as he read them. "The phenobarb level is 107."

The room fell into silence as the medical personnel exchanged glances. "They're going to re-run it," Amanda supplied, hoping that might help.

"Hemoperfusion," Lydia said, stepping into the room. "It's her best hope."

"It could also kill her," Mark argued, obviously torn.

Hemoperfusion basically drained a patient's blood and filtered it—a radical procedure that risked complications like stroke and blood clots. And death.

Lucas shook his head. "No. Lydia's right. Call the ICU, I want the tech there and a hemoperfusion unit primed by the time we get upstairs."

The nurses grabbed the equipment they needed for transport. Just as they were pushing Mickey through the door, Jim Lazarov appeared, a bagel in one hand, cup of coffee in the other.

"What'd I miss?" he asked, watching the parade accompanying Mickey pass him by. Then he spun on Amanda. "Did you steal another case?"

LYDIA WATCHED THE ELEVATOR DOORS CLOSE behind Lucas and Mickey as they headed up to the ICU. She exchanged a glance with Mark. They knew the odds, but neither could bring themselves to say it out loud.

Trey broke the silence. "Shit, doc. I'm so sorry."

They walked in silence down to the family room where Danny, Mickey's assistant, sat on the edge of a vinyl chair peppered with cigarette burns. The bright red "No Smoking" sign above his head was the only color in the neutral room.

"She's going up to the ICU," Mark told Danny. "It's touch and go. Phenobarb is a long acting drug. It's hard to get out of the system."

Danny hunched his shoulders, still not meeting Mark's eyes. "Is she going to be all right?"

"It's too early to tell. The hemoperfusion might save her, if we got to her in time. But," he looked away, blinked hard, "but there's a chance of permanent damage."

"You mean—brain damage?"

Mark nodded. "So what the hell happened?"

"It's my fault." Danny's hands dangled between his knees, his face twisted with misery.

"You gave my sister those pills?" Mark asked, his voice had

the impact of a well-aimed right hook.

"Take it easy on him," Lydia said, stepping forward to stand beside Danny.

Mark ignored her. "This damn sure wasn't an accident or a suicide attempt. Mickey didn't take those pills herself. She had bruises over her face and neck—someone forced them down her throat."

Danny jerked his head up as if he'd been slapped. "Of course I didn't give her those pills. But it's my job to be there for her and I wasn't."

"Where were you?"

"Someone tried to break into my girlfriend's apartment. She called in a panic and I went over there." He pushed his glasses higher onto his nose as he looked up at Mark, meeting the older man's stare.

"I would have called you, but it was four in the morning and Mickey was doing fine and you know how independent she is..." His voice trailed off and he hung his head once more, seemingly absorbed by the industrial grade beige carpet.

Mark frowned and paced the room. His staccato steps, dancing around the furniture in the claustrophobic room, carried the grace of an ex-boxer. "It's those damned Sons of Adam. Or someone angry that she went to court for them yesterday. Or some other nutjob client."

"That could be half of Pittsburgh," Trey said.

Lydia let the men do the talking. She slumped against the wall, busy thinking. Why would anyone target Mickey? "Mark, what can I do?"

"Huh?" His chin jerked up as if he hadn't understood her.

"Why did you call me? What can I do to help?"

"I'm supposed to be working, covering Nielson until nine. You were the closest, so..." His face clouded. "Oh God, Lydia. I wasn't thinking. You shouldn't even be here."

"I don't mind. What are they going to do? Fire me twice? But there could be some serious consequences for you."

"Hell with the consequences. Hell with the Executive Committee. This is my family we're talking about." Mark stood in a fighting stance, fists gathered at his side, obviously frustrated by his lack of an opponent or any real information.

Lydia lay her hand on his arm, felt his muscles bunch beneath her touch. "I'll go change into scrubs and get to work. You go be with your sister."

"Thanks Lydia," he said, his voice rough. He started out the door, Danny trailing after him. "I don't understand," he muttered as much to himself as to anyone. "Why Mickey?"

"Why any of them?" Lydia said to Trey as they followed.

CHAPTER 40

NORA SLAMMED THROUGH THE STAIRWELL DOOR, her feet propelling her down the steps so fast that she went flying into the concrete wall at the turn. She caught herself, leaning against the wall, her weight on her fists.

She wasn't crying. She didn't cry—not since that New Years when her tears had been scorched away. Permanently.

This pain was nothing like *that* pain. Seth was just a guy, the world was full of them. And if all of them were lying, cheating, bastards like him, then she was better off without any of them.

She pounded the sides of her fists against the concrete but felt no better. Felt pretty damn pathetic in fact.

Taking a deep breath, tugging her familiar mask of control over her face, she continued down the stairs, taking them one step at a time, planting each foot in the center of the tread, proceeding in an orderly manner as she planned. Go home, pack, find a cheap motel—maybe crash with Gina and Amanda? Or at Elise Avery's place? Elise was a flight nurse, never home anyway.

What to do with DeBakey? She couldn't stand leaving the dog behind; he was as much her dog as Seth's. Mulling over that conundrum distracted her from her feelings and the memory of the sight she'd just witnessed.

Nora rounded the final corner at the bottom of the stairwell and was surprised to see Amanda and Jim Lazarov there.

Jim had Amanda backed up into the corner, their heads bowed together in earnest conversation. As Nora drew closer, she could hear his voice, low, threatening.

"You've poached your last patient," he was saying. "I'm going to make sure you fail this rotation. I warned you—"

"How about if I give you a warning?" Nora chimed in, grabbing Jim's shoulder to spin him away from Amanda and toward her. Amanda looked awful—cheeks sunken, eyes flat with fatigue, but she still managed to give Nora a faint smile.

"Nora, I can handle this," she said.

"Handle what?" Jim challenged them both. "In case you ladies forget, I'm the only doctor here. I call the shots and neither of you can do a damn thing about it."

Nora shook her head at the intern's brashness. She felt a brittle smile stretch her lips. All of the morning's frustration and anger were now about to be unleashed, and for once she didn't care about losing control.

"That's right," she said in a soft voice, one that a bully like Jim might mistake for cowering. He straightened, looking pleased at her concession. She took one step forward, placing herself between him and Amanda, then one more, now almost touching him. "You're the doctor. Who could forget?"

"Right," he said, hunching his shoulders as if he were the one on the defensive. Good, because that was right where Nora wanted him.

"Nora," Amanda interrupted, a warning in her voice that barely penetrated the roaring in Nora's head.

"Quiet, Amanda. Jim's the doctor and he was talking. Telling us all about the things he was going to do to make our lives hell if we didn't do exactly what he wants."

Even Jim wasn't dense enough to ignore the danger in Nora's voice. He groped behind him for the door handle, but found only solid concrete. "Look, I'm sorry—"

"No. You're not," Nora continued in the same psycho-killer calm voice. She'd copied it from a bad slasher film, but no need for Jim to know that. "You're not sorry at all. If you were, you'd start thinking more about taking care of your patients and less about competing with nurses and medical students. If you were, Doctor, you'd realize that since you are a *Doctor*, you're now subject to the laws of the state of Pennsylvania, the ethics code of this hospital and the rulings of the Medical Board. Which leaves your behavior wide open to a number of remedies. Anything from reporting you to Mark Cohen, to filing a complaint with the Medical Board that will follow you for the rest of your career, or suing you for sexual harassment."

Jim's face went paler than his starched white coat. "You wouldn't, you couldn't—"

"Try me, Dr. Lazarov. Just try me."

Nora stepped away, backing up her words with a no-shit glare that made the intern gulp. He shifted his weight, his gaze dropping to study the floor.

"Um, I'm sorry. I apologize," he mumbled.

"Apologize for what?" Nora asked.

"Er, for, er, any misunderstanding. It won't happen again." As he spoke, he backed up, flailing for the door. He reached it, pushing it open and barreling through. Amanda followed, laughing as she called out, "Apology accepted!"

Nora joined her in the hallway. Amanda turned to her, still smiling. "That was great, Nora. You are a goddess!"

"Don't put up with shit like that," Nora told Amanda, hoping that the medical student recognized that she wasn't just talking about petty bullies like Jim. She placed her palm against her throat, felt as if she was out of breath. "Don't you ever."

LYDIA WALKED TREY OUT TO HIS TRUCK. "Good thing we didn't make any plans for today," she said, wondering why the thought made her feel a bit wistful. That was silly. They'd had some good—okay, great—sex. But that's all.

He stopped beside the front bumper, his fingers almost brushing her arm. "I want to make the rounds of my crews this morning. Check in and make sure there's no problems for the chief on call."

"And you call me hyper-responsible."

"Actually, I was telling you, because…" His face looked serious as he shuffled his weight from one foot to the other.

Was he actually nervous? Lydia wondered. The unfettered man who seemed to live his life like a beer commercial? "Spit it out, Trey. I won't bite."

"All evidence to the contrary," he said with a chuckle that seemed to bolster his spirits. "Actually, I wanted to invite you to my folks' picnic this afternoon. You know, food, fun, forget about all this?" He gestured at the hospital behind them. "I'm going over there before the fireworks, I can come by and pick you up."

"We'll see." She paused, uncertain of her own conflicting feelings. "Last night was great, but let's face it, I may have already outlasted my welcome here in Pittsburgh."

As she said the words aloud, she was surprised to feel her chest constrict with regret. An image of Trey's house flashed before her. She'd explored it last night and it had been perfect. The first building outside a hospital that had felt like a home for as long as she could remember.

He trailed his fingers through her hair. "You can't run away yet," he said, his voice not quite as light and joking as it was before. "You still owe me three dances."

An ambulance parked beside Trey's truck honked, the medics hanging out the open doors, grinning at catching their chief out of uniform and in a compromising position.

"Yeah, well." He looked over at the ambulance. "Aw, to hell with it." He grabbed her hard by the shoulders, raising her onto her tiptoes and kissing her thoroughly.

"I'll pick you up around three." Still gripping her shoulders tight, he bent his head so that their foreheads touched. "Promise me you're not going to do anything except go back to your room and get some rest. No chasing after killers, no rescuing strangers in dark alleys, nothing except you and an empty room and a locked door. All right?"

Lydia still wasn't sure about spending the entire day with Trey and his family. She was already more than overwhelmed with the new people in her life and it seemed that each one brought with it new responsibilities.

"All right?" Trey repeated, one finger tilting her chin until she met his gaze.

"Sure. No problem. As soon as I finish Mark's shift." A yawn pounced, overcame her before she could stifle it. "Sleep sounds like an excellent idea."

"I'm just full of good ideas."

Instead of answering, this time Lydia kissed him. The cheers of the medics finally broke them apart. Trey's dimple was showing as he waved to her before hopping into the driver's seat of his truck.

Lydia watched him drive off and ran back into the ER to change into scrubs and take over Mark's patients. What the heck had she gotten herself into? Her life had been so simple back in L.A. Now she suddenly had a guy taking her home to meet his mother.

GINA WAS CURSING THE HEAT, cursing the damn heavy bulletproof vest, cursing tenements with no elevators and people who abandoned their parents to go picnic and have fun during the holiday, and yes, after dropping the damn gurney on her foot for the gazillionth time, cursing the fact that she'd chosen her black Vicinis instead of the Timberland steel-toed work boots she'd been told to wear.

The Vicinis looked so much nicer—at least they had when she pulled them on this morning. They added a touch of elegance and style to an otherwise blah outfit. Navy cargo pants—from JC Penney!—and a plain white tee. At least that had come from Saks. The work boots were too heavy and clunky, made her feel fat.

Of course after a morning of well-being calls and scooping drunks and dope-heads from back alleys, her once lovely calf-skin hand-tooled Vicinis were now dented and smeared with layers of vomit, piss, and lord only knew what else. And Jerry's vest, which she had thought looked so sexy in a secret-agent-assassin kind of way, well, it was just plain hot and heavy. The bottom rubbed against her hips, scraping them raw, the armpits pinched anytime she moved and her breasts felt like they were being squeezed to the point of bruising.

"How you doing, doc?" Ollie, the rotund and perpetually cheerful medic sitting across from her asked.

In between them lay their patient, a morbidly obese man complaining of chest pain after eating a dozen brats for breakfast washed down with an six pack of Rolling Rock.

"Why?" Gina had asked the man, ignoring Ollie and Gecko's warning to never ask.

The patient had merely grinned at her, clutching his chest with one hand, wiping crumbs from his sweat-stained wife beater with the other. "Brats and beer—what else you gonna eat on the Fourth? They was good, too."

As they were hoisting him into the ambulance, he'd asked, "If'n they don't think it's anything serious, yinz think I could be back home by lunch?"

His EKG and vitals were stone cold normal and he now lay

sleeping, blowing snot bubbles with each sonorous snore.

"I'm fine," Gina told Ollie. Just fine. Fine and dandy. Oh yeah. "Is it always like this?"

"Worse because of the holiday. No Meals on Wheels today, no visiting nurses or the like, so lots of diabetics and old people will be messed up. Some just lonely, so they call us." He shrugged good-naturedly, resembling a cherub with his chubby dimples. "S'all right, it's what we're here for."

Not Gina. She was here for trauma, crashing myocardial infarctions, ruptured aortic aneurysms.

The action and rush to save patients who would be lost if they had to wait to get to the ED. This checking on grandma and porked-out heartburn patients was for the birds. Not to mention the three drunks and OD they'd hauled in already today.

"I thought working the Fourth, we'd be getting some blast injuries, maybe some burns—"

Ollie laughed. "No worries. That will come later, when everyone's good and drunk and hauling out their illegal fireworks."

"Don't forget," Gecko called back from his position in the driver's seat, "those protest rallies start at four. They'll be diverting most the ALS units downtown, so we'll be stretched thin. That will liven things up some."

As if in agreement, their patient expelled a loud burp, releasing a noxious cloud of partially fermented beer and bratwurst that made Gina's stomach rebel.

She leaned back in her seat, getting as far away from the toxic fumes as possible, and unzipped her vest. A sigh escaped her as her poor, squashed breasts were released from their prison.

Please Lord, just give me one good trauma. Anything to make this day go faster. Just one little car crash, a small gunshot wound. Hell, she'd settle for a kabob skewer impalement. Was that too much to ask?

CHAPTER 41

AMANDA LET NORA BUY HER BREAKFAST in the hospital cafeteria, but she made careful note of the price. She'd pay everyone back when she could—she hated accepting charity even if it was from friends.

She shivered as she carried her tray over to a table drenched in morning sunshine. *Not* a symptom, just fatigue, she was always cold after working nights. Her monthly check up with Dr. Nelson was next week. She hadn't told him about her symptoms yet—she didn't want to be taken out of the study. The two hundred dollars a month that being on his research project paid was the difference between eating and not eating.

But if Lucas was right about Becky Sanborn....She shook her head. Lucas was a supercilious, over-dramatic, worry wort, that was all. He was wrong. Dead wrong.

"Earth to Amanda," Nora was saying, waving her hand in front of Amanda's face. "I was asking how your night was?"

Amanda startled. "Sorry." She stifled a yawn. "Guess I was day dreaming."

"I hope not about Jim Lazarov. What did you do to piss him off this time?"

"Gina asked me to give Bob, the college kid doing the night-shift article, a tour of the hospital, which made me late for my shift."

"Leaving Jim to play catch up."

"Right. And then we had this strange neuro patient brought in—a college girl with weird symptoms that just don't add up. Lucas is—"

"Lucas? Since when is Dr. Stone, Lucas?" Nora asked, arching an eyebrow at Amanda.

Amanda cleared her throat, wished she could erase the warmth that flushed her neck and face. "Believe me, it's not what you think. He's such a know-it-all, totally not my type."

"He may not have the best social skills, but the reason why he acts like he knows everything is because the man is a certified genius."

"Really?"

"Yeah. He and Seth grew up in the same neighborhood, they've been friends for years."

Amanda noticed that Nora suddenly seemed fascinated with her food after she mentioned Seth, and remembered how upset she'd been earlier when she came down the stairs.

"Well, the genius has met his match with this patient," she said, keeping the subject steered away from Seth. Whatever was upsetting Nora, she wouldn't make it better by telling her about seeing Seth the other night. "She's a real puzzle. I should go check on her before I go home." She took a few bites of her lumpy oatmeal, feeling homesick for her mother's cheese grits. "Anyway, Jim was pissed because Lucas assigned me to her case. And then this morning, Dr. Cohen's sister—"

"Mickey? Oh no, did she have another seizure?"

"Worse. Overdose of phenobarb."

Nora straightened at that. "Did she try to kill herself? I know her MS is getting worse, but she never seemed the type."

Amanda glanced around, she wasn't one to gossip. "Actually, Dr. Cohen talked like maybe someone had tried to poison her."

"Like the church ladies and Jonah? Why?"

"I don't know, but he was real upset. Enough to call Lydia in to cover the rest of his shift so he could go up to the ICU with Mickey."

"Lydia's here? In the ER?"

"Working until Dr. Nielson gets in at nine."

"Damn. Mark better hope that Elliot Weiss doesn't get called down to the ER—he's on call for surgery today. He'd explode if he knew she was working."

Nora's phone buzzed. Again. Amanda had noticed that it had rung a few times while they were waiting in line for their food and Nora had switched it to silent mode. Nora checked the caller ID and shook her head.

"Something wrong?" Amanda asked. "Why were you here so early anyway?"

Nora looked out the window for a long moment. "I came to surprise Seth. But," she took in a deep breath and her mouth twisted into a smile that seemed closer to tears than happiness, "I was the one who got the surprise."

"What happened?"

"Let's just say that I don't think he was planning to propose to me tonight. I found him naked in a call room with another woman."

Amanda dropped her spoon and reached for Nora's hand. Nora flinched, pulled away. "I'm so sorry. And I'm the one who put that idea in your head. I wish I'd never said anything about him proposing."

"It's not your fault. You only said what I wanted to hear." Her phone vibrated again.

"Is that him who keeps calling?"

"Yeah. Looks like he's back at our place, so I'm going to hang out here until I figure out what to do, where to go."

"There's plenty of room at our house. Gina won't mind. She'll probably be with Jerry anyway."

"Thanks, I appreciate it. After we finish eating, I think I'll go up to the unit and check on Mickey, see if Mark needs anything."

"I'll go too. I want to see if Lucas has figured out anything about our patient, Becky Sanborn."

"WHAT THE HELL IS GOING ON?" Gina heard Gecko mutter as he hit the air horn and the siren for the fifth time during the run. The address was in Friendship, only twelve blocks from Angels, but it was taking forever to get there.

The ambulance lurched and Gecko swore again. Ollie didn't seem to notice, merely shifted his weight, but Gina grabbed her sissy strap and held tight as the ambulance swerved again before bouncing onto the curb and back down again.

She risked releasing her grip on the overhead strap to crane her head forward and peer out the main windshield. The streets were teeming with people, mainly young men, and they all seemed to be shouting and angry and pointing at the ambulance.

One man took a stance in the center of the street, blocking the ambulance and forcing Gecko to slam the brakes. The man's mouth opened and closed as he screamed something lost in the yowl of the siren.

Then he hurled a liquor bottle directly at them. Gina flinched as it struck the windshield dead on, causing a small star shaped crack in the thick glass. The bottle bounced back to the pavement. Gecko hit the horn again and kept driving, hunched over the wheel as he worked to not hit anyone.

"D'ja call for police backup?" Ollie asked, his voice calm, unperturbed.

"No joy. They're tied up down on the Point, said there was a demonstration out of control."

"Oh, as compared with a good old fashioned riot up here?" Gina said, watching as two boys lit a garbage can on fire. She zipped Jerry's vest up as high as it would go, the snug tightness of the Kevlar suddenly welcome. "Thought they said we were being called to a church, some lady fainted?"

Gecko turned the corner. "Mother of God," he muttered. "Not again."

A brilliant white-washed church rose up over the teeming mass of people crowding the street in front of it. People were everywhere—hanging off the balconies and fire escapes of the adjacent rowhouses, a few parked out on rooftops and porch roofs.

Those who lined the church steps were dressed in formal clothes, sober, dark colors, the ladies wearing broad-brimmed hats, the men in suits, all carrying candles or small bunches of flowers.

The others, those in the street especially, seemed to be a more motley collection. Several wore gang colors but seemed to have come to a mutual truce as they turned to engage their new common enemy: Medic Seven.

CHAPTER 42

LYDIA FINISHED DISCHARGING THE PATIENTS Mark had left her. Other than the guy with heartburn and a hiatal hernia that Gina and Med Seven had brought in, the ER had remained quiet.

Nielson was due in a few minutes to relieve her. In the meantime, she took advantage of the calm and tried to collect her thoughts. Why these people? she thought as she made a list of all the victims on a blank page of chart paper: Jonah Weiss, Wanda Owens, Maryam and the other four women, Mickey Cohen. What did they have in common? She added the names of the others connected with the case: Isaiah Steward, Elliot Weiss, Alonzo Hampton, Matthew Kent, Pete Sandusky. Then she considered and added Mark Cohen, his wife and daughters.

It was a long list. She began to draw lines, connecting people.

Jonah knew Isaiah and Mickey. Isaiah knew Jonah and the ladies at the church. Hmm...probably Mickey as well from his involvement with GOAD. So, Mickey knew them all. And if she did, probably Danny did as well. But what motive could Danny have? She massaged her temple, trying to still the pounding there. What motive did any of them have?

Matthew Kent and the Sons of Adam could have hated any of the victims just on general principles. Pete Sandusky probably also knew them all, he seemed to know about everyone in this town….

"You're forgetting someone," Jim Lazarov said from behind her.

Lydia spun in her chair, not really caring that she almost rolled over his foot. The intern annoyed her, always sneaking around, trying to hide when there was real work to be done, delegating scut to the nurses—and she'd only had the privilege of working with him for a few hours.

He yanked the paper from beneath her hand, scrutinized it. "I love puzzles—it's the whole reason I went into medicine. You're missing someone who is linked to all these people."

"Who's that?" Lydia asked, her curiosity getting the best of her.

"You." Lazarov handed the paper back to her. "You've had contact with all of them. Guess maybe it's true what they're saying about you," Lazarov said, whistling through his teeth as he strutted away.

His words echoed the fears she'd expressed to Trey last night, that her asking questions had made the killer target more victims in order to try to hide his tracks.

Lydia balled up the paper before consigning it to the trash can. Idly, she rapped her pen against the computer keyboard.

She decided to check on her patients. First, the baby she and Amanda had sent to the Pediatric ICU. Lydia was pleased to see that she was doing much better and there were no signs of any permanent damage from the meningitis. Next, she pulled up Mickey's chart to check on her. It was better than calling upstairs and interrupting Lucas or distracting Mark.

Mickey was stable, but that was about the best anyone could say. From her labs and orders, it looked like Lucas was probably fighting a losing battle unless the hemoperfusion began working. Of course, if Mickey was targeted by the same person who killed Wanda Owens, then surviving the phenobarb overdose may not be enough.

She spun around in her chair, rolling her neck, anything to stave off boredom and fatigue. She eyed the computer once more. It was against the law to violate patient privacy by using it to check any patients not her own—unless their information was part of the public record.

Knowing she was violating the spirit of the law if not the letter, she still gave it a try. There was a good chance the record she wanted wouldn't be available in the hospital database anyway. Sarah Kent.

She got lucky and was able to access Sarah's medical record and death certificate. Mark Cohen and Elliot Weiss had been the physicians of record. She made a mental note to ask Mark about the case later—now was definitely not the time, not with his sister fighting for her life.

Sarah's injuries had been incompatible with life. Her spine crushed, severe full thickness burns, massive head trauma, it was a miracle she had survived the transport from the scene. Nothing helpful in the record of Sarah's care in the ER. Except the date of her death nagged at Lydia: July first, last year.

"Most dangerous day of the year," she muttered as she leaned back, tapping one foot against the chair leg, re-considering the names on her list. Yesterday, she'd worried that her prying had led to Jonah's killer targeting the church ladies merely to send suspicion in the direction of the Sons of Adam, had even wondered if Isaiah Steward was involved. But, what if the five women who died at Friendship Fellowship weren't the real targets, only collateral damage?

What if the real target was Wanda Owens herself? That might explain why the killer had risked coming to Angels to finish the job afterward.

Lydia fished her list out of the trash and smoothed it out. The squiggles of lines between names resembled a tangled spider's web. When she tried it again, this time placing the three victims who seemed specifically targeted in the center, the result appeared less chaotic. Still no discernable pattern or answer, but definitely not random.

What would Wanda Owens, Jonah Weiss, and Mickey Cohen have had in common? Besides the fact that they were all patients at Angels? She wished she'd paid more attention to her epidemiology courses in medical school. This was like tracking back an epidemic to Patient Zero.

She brought up Wanda's chart and scrutinized it. Nothing obvious.

Lydia leaned back and considered as she stared at the acoustical tiles above her. A volatile gay rights activist, a religious black woman, and now Mickey, a disabled Jewish civil-rights lawyer. Jonah and Mickey had been close, but where did Wanda fit in? Maybe Mickey had once represented Wanda? Or maybe even the Friendship Fellowship Church? Maybe some kind of violation of their civil rights?

She was just getting ready to call Danny to ask him when the nurse standing near the EMS radio gestured for her attention.

"What's up?"

"Sounds like Med Seven is caught up in a riot. They're under attack."

Lydia jumped to her feet. "Tell them to get out of there."

"Can't. Their radio just cut out."

"THIS IS THE SAME CHURCH?" Gina started.

"Same one." Gecko hunched his shoulders and gave a small grunt that reminded Gina of a Frenchman she had once slept with, the Gallic equivalent of "what-the-hell?" She couldn't see his eyes behind his Oakley's, but she had the feeling he was rolling them in disbelief.

Gina realized she was holding her breath, waiting to see what would happen. As if in slow motion, the crowd turned toward them: a large, shaggy beast who had spied a particularly savory piece of meat.

"That's him!" a boy shouted, pointing at Gecko. "He's one of them!"

"Killers! Killers!" The mob surged forward, battering and rocking the ambulance with enough force that it lurched from side to side.

"He saved her life!" Gina yelled, hanging onto the sissy strap for dear life. "He didn't kill anyone."

Ollie actually looked a bit perturbed and clutched the gurney, anchoring himself. "Doesn't seem like they care about that."

The sound of breaking glass and fists thumping against the windshield echoed through the small space. Gecko was talking furiously on the radio, arms flailing as he gestured to the men who had climbed onto the hood of the ambulance and had their faces pressed against the glass.

"Gina, why don't you move up front?" Ollie asked. "Let them see you."

Gina felt her heart thud, bouncing off the ceramic breast plate of her bullet proof vest. "Are you crazy? Why?"

"Because," Ollie had to shout to make himself heard over the deafening roar of the crowd. People had climbed to the roof and now were jumping up and down, adding to the thunderous cacophony. "You're black."

Gina did a double take. Felt as if she'd been slapped by a wave of ice water. Yeah, she was African-American. But…she glanced again through the window at the faces flattened against the glass, turned grotesque with fury.

Until this instant, she hadn't even realized that the faces were all various shades of brown. She had nothing in common with these people, couldn't even understand half of what they were shouting or why they were attacking an ambulance come to offer help to one of their own.

Was sharing a skin color enough to save her, Ollie and Gecko? What if it wasn't?

A man rushed through the crowd, waving a lighter and what looked like a stick of dynamite. The men surrounding the ambulance cheered. He laughed and held the stick up in triumph as he lit it.

Then he vanished behind the ambulance. The crowd drew back, some running for cover.

Ollie fumbled his seatbelt off, lunged for the door latch.

Before he could reach it, a loud explosion rocketed through the air. The ambulance shuddered. Gina covered her ears, fell to the floor, wondering if Jerry's vest was bombproof as well as bulletproof.

CHAPTER 43

GINA'S EARS WEREN'T JUST RINGING. Instead, a rampaging stampede of buffalo galloped through her skull. She opened her eyes, mainly because she couldn't tell if she was right side up or not, and realized that despite the noise clamoring in her head, everything else had remained the same.

The ambulance was right side up and in one piece. Ollie was sprawled along the bench, and Gecko was crouched in front of Gina, his mouth opening and closing.

"Just a M-80," she finally made out his words, his voice sounding hollow and echoey, "big bang, no boom."

He helped her upright. She swallowed hard, popped her ears. The rushing noise cleared, leaving in its wake a headache that boomeranged from one side of her skull to the other.

For one brief moment there was relative quiet. No siren, no horn, no thumping, no screams.

Then a polite knocking on the front door of the ambulance rattled through the air. Gecko pivoted back into the drivers' seat and Gina followed, slumping into the passenger side seat. A tall, grey-haired man in a black suit with a clerical collar stood at the door, brandishing a bible in one hand and a microphone in the other.

"I'm Reverend Ainsley," he said in a baritone that was both

soothing and serene. "Are you here to help Sister Shirley? If so, I would like to facilitate her medical assistance and offer you an escort."

Gecko exchanged glances with Ollie who had climbed forward, wedging his portly sized body between the seats. Then he lowered the window a few inches.

"Nice to see you Reverend," he said. "We sure would like to help out, but I'm not all that sure how safe it would be. If you get my drift."

"Fear not," the Reverend assured him, sounding like an Archangel bearing glad tidings. He stood on the running board and waved his hand. Other men and a few women marched forward, aligning themselves as an honor guard, parting the sea of angry men. "We will guarantee your safety."

Gecko nodded and rolled the window back up. "What do you think?"

Ollie's Adam's apple bobbed up, then down again. His shrug echoed through rolls of fat and he said, "Why the hell not? We help them, they help us, and everyone's happy."

"Except them," Gina said, her gaze centered on the mob that waited, subdued but still simmering, beyond the lines of Reverend Ainsley's people.

Gecko pushed his sunglasses higher up on his nose. "Hey, at least we're getting time and a half."

NORA HAD ALMOST ESCAPED. She'd checked in on Mark and Mickey, found Mark busy talking with Jerry Boyle, had held Mickey's hand for a while, and tried to reassure Danny. Amanda's neurology patient was almost as bad off as Mickey—it looked like Lucas hadn't yet discovered what was causing her coma or seizures.

As Nora watched Amanda with the patient, she couldn't help but wonder if the medical student was more interested in the patient or in Lucas. No business of hers if the kid was setting herself up for heartache. Some days Nora wondered if she'd ever been that innocent.

Nora was just leaving through the main hospital lobby when her cell phone rang. It was the ER. She sighed, retraced her steps and returned to the ER.

"In case no one's noticed, today's my day off," she announced, gesturing to her shorts and casual attire. Nobody seemed to care. "Who paged me?"

Elise Avery came rushing around the corner. "Nora. You're here, great."

Nora looked at the tall blonde with suspicion. "Why don't I like the sound of that?"

The cobalt blue of her Nomex flight suit highlighted Elise's blue eyes and pale skin, making her look like a Nordic goddess. Not even the flattened hair from wearing her helmet in the helicopter could make her look squalid or ordinary.

Elise pulled Nora down the hallway to huddle beside a linen cart. "I just flew in an assault victim and there's no SAFE nurse here with the holiday."

A Sexual Assault Forensic Exam would take hours. Nora was shaking her head before Elise could even finish. "No, no way, not today. Elise, I just can't—"

"Please. Nora. She's just a kid, nineteen. Went out to water the plants on her stoop—that's all, just watering some freaking begonias and these four punks drag her down an alley and—"

Nora held her hand up, stopping the flight nurse. She wanted to wince at the images bombarding her, but instead she hunched her shoulders, tightened her jaw. "Who's on as attending? Most of them are really good with assault cases."

Elise wrinkled her face in distaste. "Nielson and some prick of an intern. I can't let this girl be further traumatized. Please, Nora."

Bad as it was for the nurse or physician performing the SAFE exam, it was a lifetime for a freshly traumatized victim. Unless you had the skills to both collect the evidence and start the road to recovery.

Nora shook her head again. "Yes. I'll do it. Let me change into scrubs. What's her name?"

"Mercedes. Mercedes Howard. Thanks, sweetie. I knew you wouldn't let me down." Elise's radio sounded. "Got to go. It's nuts out there—the natives are getting restless. You should be glad you're not working today."

Right. Except for the next several hours of performing an invasive and humiliating examination on a traumatized nineteen year old.

"You owe me," she called after Elise as the flight nurse hustled down the hall to the elevators that would take Elise back up to the helipad.

EVEN THOUGH NIELSON HAD RELIEVED HER, Lydia waited with the rest of the ER staff to learn Med Seven's fate. When the crew came trundling through the door, escorting their patient, applause broke out.

"What happened?" Lydia asked Gina after the resident left her patient in Nielson's care. "Was it the Sons of Adam?"

Gina still looked shell-shocked. "No," she said shaking her head so hard her braids threatened to come loose. "Just a bunch of angry black people. Angry at us, angry at the people at the memorial service because they *weren't* angry enough, angry at the heat. Just plain angry." She paused. "It was like it was a sport—they were having fun. I've never seen anything like it."

"You okay to go back out?"

Lydia watched as the resident collected herself, assuming her usual cocky façade. "I'm fine. I'm not going to be scared off by some loud mouths with a bunch of firecrackers."

"If you say so."

Gecko called to Gina, and the resident moved to leave.

Lydia walked out with them, heading back to her motel. "Gecko, you take care of her—I want her back to work in one piece, you hear?"

"Yes ma'am!" the medic said, snapping a mock salute at Lydia. "Hey, word's out that you snagged the Chief. You take care, I want *him* back to work in one piece!"

He and his partner sniggered as they closed the rear doors behind Gina. Lydia just shook her head. She'd forgotten that gossip was to street medics what oxygen was to normal people.

"No promises," she said with a laugh. "You all be careful out there!"

They whooped the siren at her as they pulled away.

She was crossing the hospital driveway when Mickey's assistant, Danny, roared toward her on an old-fashioned motorcycle. No helmet, she noticed. And he didn't seem to be paying much attention to the road in front of him. She stepped out, waved her hand to get his attention. "Hey, where are you going? Did something happen to Mickey?"

He swerved the bike, seemed uncertain whether to acknowledge her or not, but finally stopped, his feet balancing the motorcycle as the engine idled. "I'm, uh, just moving my bike. I left it in a no parking zone."

"Right. You left Mickey because you're worried about a parking ticket." Lydia stepped in front of him, blocking his path, giving him a challenging stare.

He wouldn't meet her gaze. His weight ping-ponged back and forth from one foot to the other. "I have to do something." He hunched his shoulders in a defiant shrug, finally raised his head to look her straight on. "I can't do anything for her, not even the doctors can. It's my job to take care of her, protect her. This never should have happened."

"Danny." Lydia put a hand on his arm, felt the anger and frustration shuddering through his body. "It wasn't your fault. Getting yourself hurt isn't going to help Mickey. She'll want you there when she wakes up."

"She may never wake up. She might even," he stumbled over the word, "die."

"She might." She gave him time to think on that. "Is this what she'd want you to do? Tell me where you're going."

He stared past her, face angled up to take in the patient tower above them. "I have to do something. I can't just stay here and watch her die—don't ask me to do that." His voice became pleading, reminding her just how young he was. He'd shouldered a lot of responsibility when he'd signed on with Mickey.

"No one is asking you to do anything."

"Then you can't stop me." He clenched his jaw so tight she could see his muscles bunch. "I'm going."

"Going where? Danny!"

He ignored her shouts, revving the motorcycle's engine, speeding away, barely missing an on-coming minivan. Lydia glanced in the direction of her motel, where bed and sleep and her promise to Trey lay.

She sprinted across the street to where her car was parked, pulling her cell phone free as she went. The mood Danny was in—who knew what he might do? Probably something stupid and reckless enough to get himself hurt or worse.

She wondered at Danny's behavior as she called Mark. "Is Mickey all right?"

"Still unconscious but the levels have begun to drop. Why?"

Lydia jumped into her SUV and pulled out of the motel parking lot, turning in the same direction Danny had gone. "I just saw Danny, chasing out of here like he was after the devil himself. I don't know where he's headed, but he's in trouble. Any ideas? Maybe Boyle can have him picked up?"

There was the sound of the phone being passed as she scanned the traffic ahead, searching for Danny.

"Kid hasn't broken any laws," Boyle said. "Where's he going?"

Lydia spotted Danny a block ahead, stopped at the light. "I don't know, but I'm following him."

"Lydia, don't be stupid."

"I'm not. I just want to stop Danny before he does something stupid. Or gets hurt."

There was a pause, then he relented. "Call me if he does anything we can bring him in for, give him time to cool off. And don't do anything to provoke anyone. This town is a powder keg today."

She hung up and hit the accelerator, burning through a yellow light. Within a few minutes she left the city behind and was surrounded by rolling hills and idyllic fields punctuated by grazing cattle and cylindrical stacks of hay. In the distance, shimmering in the August haze, the motorcycle lay down a golden trail of exhaust, winking like a sunbeam. The air smelled of fertilizer, freshly mown grass and smoke from a distant BBQ.

L.A. it wasn't.

NORA GLANCED THROUGH MERCEDES'S CHART, taking note of the injuries Elise had documented during her assessment.

Poor kid. Multiple abrasions, lacerations including one to her left cheek, abdominal wall contusions but no signs of internal bleeding, broken finger, two missing teeth, as well as vaginal and rectal bleeding. Sounded like she'd put up a fight—but against four men, she'd had no chance.

She took the chart down to Mercedes's room and was surprised to find Jim Lazarov outside the door speaking to a policeman. "Thought your shift was over."

Jim whirled at the sound of her voice, his face darkening. "Pulled a double because of the holiday. What are you doing here?"

Nora nodded to the cop, a uniformed officer named Murphy. "I'm going to do the sexual assault exam."

"I thought if there were no SAFE nurses around, the regular ER staff did them," Jim said. "This is my patient, and Dr. Nielson told me to do the exam."

"Look, doc," Murphy broke in, "if it's the same to you—"

"No," Jim snapped. "It's not. I've been accused of neglecting my patients and now when I'm trying to do my job, you horn in and—"

Nora didn't let him finish, instead grabbed him by the arm. "Excuse us a moment, Murphy?"

Murphy shrugged. Nora motioned Jim down the hall to the nearest empty exam room.

"Lady, I don't know what your problem is, but you can't have it both ways," Jim started. "Either I'm doing my job or I'm not. And you have no right to talk to me the way you did earlier, making threats, being insubordinate—"

"This is the wrong day and wrong patient to be crossing me," Nora interrupted him.

"I don't care. I've been up all night and I'm not taking any more of your crap!"

"My crap? Listen here. Do you have any idea what that girl has been through? Do you?" She leaned forward, fists balled, face heating and words spilling out so fast she couldn't stop them. "Do you know what it's like to be terrified, forced to beg for your life, forced to do things you never even imagined, humiliated? And then when the pain doesn't stop but only gets worse you find yourself screaming, begging to die just to make it all stop?"

Her voice spiraled into a crescendo that crashed from the walls. Jim backed away, palms up in surrender.

"You're crazy. You want the exam, want to waste a few hours of your holiday on a whore who got more than she was asking for, good for you. I'm out of here."

Something inside Nora broke at his words. She launched herself across the room, ready to hit him, tear his face off, do some serious harm.

But he was out the door, slamming it behind him before she got close. She fell against the door, chest heaving as she tried to compose herself. Stumbling to the sink, she splashed water on her face, washed her hands. Even though she hadn't laid a hand on him, she felt contaminated by his presence.

CHAPTER 44

LYDIA LOST SIGHT OF DANNY'S BIKE AS HE SPUN around a curve on the two lane highway she'd followed him onto. By the time she reached the same area, he was gone. She swore, hit the brakes and did a one-eighty. A plume of dust marked where he'd turned onto a dirt lane, ignoring the "trespassers will be shot" signs.

She had a sinking feeling she knew exactly where Danny was headed. The Escape bounced over the rutted dirt road as Lydia sped up. Finally, she came to a locked metal gate. Far beyond, she could see the roof of a barn, several large houses and smaller, whitewashed buildings.

Welcome to the Kingdom of God, a sign soaring over her head read. Barbed wire fences twisted out beyond the gates in both directions. The Sons of Adam's compound.

Danny's bike lay on its side, abandoned beside the fence. Lydia parked and jumped out of the SUV. A tingling crawled over her, as if unseen eyes were watching, telling her to run. She would have, if it wasn't for Danny and his pig-headed, reckless fury. What the hell did he think he would accomplish here? How would confronting the Sons of Adam save Mickey?

The compound appeared distinctly un-sinister. Bucolic even.

Except for the utter lack of human life. Cows and sheep grazed in fields beyond the houses and several acres were planted with crops. Laundry hanging on a clothesline swung on the breeze like flags at a parade.

The tranquil scene set Lydia's teeth on edge. She had to resist the urge to run.

"Danny," she called when she spotted him walking through the grass towards the compound.

He stopped, hunched his shoulders and turned around. "Lydia. Get out of here!"

"Only if you come with me."

He stood there, shaking his head, so she tried again.

"C'mon, Danny. Looks like there's no one home."

A rushing sound like the whistling of the Santa Ana winds whisked through the tall grass to Lydia's left. A blur of grey pounced on Danny, driving him back into the barbed wire along the path. The dog had its mouth open but no sound emerged; it attacked in stealth mode.

Danny cried out, falling below the dog, dragged down out of sight in the high grass. Lydia grabbed her pepper spray and climbed over the fence. She raced toward Danny, calling his name, trying to distract the dog whose jaws were clamped on Danny's leg. The dog didn't budge even when she drew close enough to tag it with the pepper spray.

The dog whipped its head as the capsaicin burned its eyes, but still didn't release its hold.

The grass rustled as a second dog shot out, leaping into the air and crashing into Lydia. She landed face first in the dirt, the canister of pepper spray flying.

Lydia held very still, afraid even to breathe. Sharp claws dug into her shoulders and thighs while a stream of drool dripped into her ear. From her peripheral vision she saw yellowed fangs emerging from the muscled jowls of a very large, very black dog. It was difficult not to envision those big teeth clamping down on her exposed neck.

"Good work boys," a man's voice called out as a Jeep stopped on the lane.

Lydia recognized the voice. Hampton. Matthew Kent's comrade in arms.

"Don't move, folks," he continued amicably, "or you'll find yourselves missing some vital parts."

Rough hands searched her, poking into the pockets of her scrubs. She strained her gaze to the side, saw two men giving Danny equal treatment, moving with practiced motions between his body and the dog that pinned him. She recognized one as the man who had attacked Gina with his baton two days ago.

"Release," Hampton called. The dogs immediately leapt away.

Lydia slowly rolled over, making no sudden movements that might trigger a response from the dogs. Hampton crouched down, praising both dogs. He rested a shotgun on one knee. Her stomach roiled and she resisted the urge to squeeze her eyes shut as she all too easily imagined him aiming the gun at her and pulling the trigger. Damnit, what had she done? Anger at her own stupidity flared through her. She forced herself to meet Hampton's gaze.

The other men flanked Danny. Several deep scratches colored Danny's arms, but otherwise he seemed okay.

"Don't know if yinz remember me, Dr. Fiore," Hampton said as she rolled to her feet and stood, the small act of defiance helping to keep her fear at bay. "Name's Hampton."

"I remember you."

He raised an eyebrow and grinned at her as if surprised that he'd made an impression. "Thought maybe that knock on the head might have caused some amnesia or something. Cuz you didn't remember what Wilson told you back there, now did you?"

She said nothing, met his gaze head on. Damned if she was going to let him see her cower. She gauged the distance back to her car. If it weren't for the dogs and the shotgun, they might make it.

Hampton shifted the shotgun to his arm, not quite but almost pointing it at Danny. "Just what brings the Nancy Drew of Angels of Mercy Medical Center all the way out here?"

Danny answered before she could, straining to pull away from the men who held him. "We just had to see the bastards who poison helpless women, leaving them to die!"

The dogs didn't like his tone and became instantly alert, but Hampton ignored him.

"Keep him here," he instructed his men. "I'm taking Dr. Fiore down to the compound, give her the grand tour."

His tone was one of a gracious host as he swept an arm before him, directing Lydia into their Jeep.

"Leave her alone," Danny shouted.

Hampton paused, the shotgun cradled in his arm. "I'm sure your friend will be safe if you come with me. Otherwise, no guarantees. Your call, Dr. Fiore."

Like she had a choice. "I'll be fine," she told Danny, joining Hampton in the Jeep.

He put it in gear and they sped off, gravel and dust flying, obscuring her view of Danny and the others.

"Brother Matthew is anxious to see you," he said as they drove over a hill toward the large white farmhouse beyond.

"Why? Does he need lessons in how to poison more innocent victims?" she snapped. Immediately she regretted it, remembering what happened to Gina when Lydia let her defiant impulses get the better of her. Staying quiet was the best way to protect Danny—and herself.

Hampton chuckled. "Now see, you have us all wrong. We didn't poison nobody. I guess Brother Matthew wants to put your fears to rest, is all."

Lydia saw what he was doing. Divide and conquer. Hampton held Danny's life as hostage against her good behavior. Which left few options.

She wished she could get a handle on what Matthew Kent and his people wanted. If the Sons of Adam were responsible for the poisonings, they couldn't leave any witnesses behind, would have killed Danny and her right away, buried their bodies under an outhouse somewhere. Not that the idea appealed to her. It was comforting that they were still alive. But what did Kent want from her?

"Relax," Hampton said, effortlessly following her thoughts. "No one's going to hurt you or your friend. We owe you one. For taking care of Jonah Weiss. Permanently."

He glanced over at her with a superior smile that she ached to wipe from his face. Permanently.

Instead, she folded her hands in her lap, hiding their trembling, and crossed her ankles to stop her feet from tapping. The essence of Zen calmness.

It didn't fool Hampton. He chuckled and pulled the Jeep to a stop in front of a large whitewashed building that eerily resembled the Friendship Fellowship Church. Lydia tried her best not to think of the gruesome sight she'd found in that house of worship.

Matthew Kent barreled through the door, smiling and reaching out a hand to help her from the Jeep.

"Dr. Fiore, I've been expecting you. It's so good to see you again," he said, rattling her teeth as he shook her hand with the vigor of a lumberjack. He seemed taller, larger than life, here in his own surroundings.

"Welcome to the Kingdom of God. Just as Adam did, we exist to serve." He finished with a deep bow worthy of a French courtier.

"The doctor's companion is being looked after?" he asked Hampton, confirming Lydia's suspicions that this rustic retreat was well fortified and guarded by surveillance.

"Yes sir."

"Very well then," he said, taking Lydia's arm in his. "Allow me to give you the grand tour."

They strolled past a large Quonset hut containing several old vehicles including a combine, tractor, ambulance, and fire engine. Tools and equipment lined the walls.

"My son, Ezekiel, is a real tinkerer. The boy can fix anything." The next building was a windowless barn. "For our livestock," he said. "And there, past the silo, is the children's house. That way they're close to the animals for their chores. The cottages across the compound are for married couples. The congregation builds them as a wedding present."

He stopped and stared down at her, concern wrinkling his brow. "I'm sorry. I forgot. You never had a real home, did you?"

His words sent a chill racing down her spine. These people knew entirely too much about her. Obviously, despite their rustic trappings, they were well-connected.

She ignored his comments and glanced in the direction of the white clapboard house with the wide veranda. "The children don't live with their parents?"

"Not after their third birthday. That way they can begin their schooling and parents don't have to worry about child care. So many of our fold still work outside the community."

"So you're not completely self-sufficient."

"Actually, we are. But it's important that we carry our message into the world outside. People there will need us when the Revelation arrives."

"The Revelation?"

"When the good Lord returns to his Kingdom on Earth and grants us the dominion that is our birthright."

He said this with a serious face, his eyes so wide that the whites seemed impossibly large, giving them a luminescent glow. "Let me show you our Sanctuary."

Like a gentleman, Kent held the door to his church open for her. The interior was white-washed with pale pine benches lined up like soldiers preparing for battle. She hesitated before crossing the threshold, remembering what had awaited her at the last church she'd entered.

Beside the door, along a wall covered with white drapes, was a small alcove. It was a shrine, its only ornamentation a large black and white photo. The woman in the photo seemed to stare at Lydia, her eyes narrowed in a disapproving glare that followed as Lydia drew closer. Dressed in a stark white shirt, her light colored hair twisted back, her lips thin and pinched in a tight line, she resembled the female model for American Gothic.

"This is your wife, Sarah?" she asked, wondering what the death of this stern-faced woman had triggered.

"Yes," he said in a low voice, one hand reaching out to graze the photo-frame.

"I read her chart. No one could have saved her, not with those injuries."

He slowly turned, as if reluctant to transfer his attention from his dead wife back to Lydia. "Of course not. Sarah was meant for a higher purpose. God called her home. No man could change that. Surely you don't believe you can interfere with God's plans, doctor?"

He dismissed her and her abilities with a wave of his hand. "Only God has power over what happens to his people. There's no need for the likes of you to try to meddle–you'll never succeed. Look into your heart, Dr. Fiore. You'll see that those who died under your hands were divine retribution."

"Retribution for what?" She knew better than to argue with a maniac like Kent, but she couldn't resist probing his psyche.

He ignored her, instead striding down the center aisle to the front of the church. There was no altar, but a wide platform several feet higher than the rest of the floor obviously served as a pulpit. Kent bounded up the steps to it, leaving her standing below as he took his place beneath a large crucifix suspended from unseen cables and lit from a skylight, making it appear to float in mid air.

Kent's version of Christ wasn't the emaciated, battered, world-weary image that populated most Catholic Churches. Instead his Lord was muscular, head held high, alert to any trespasses against his followers, a battle-ready warrior who bore an uncanny resemblance to Kent himself.

Just what she needed. The man didn't just believe he was doing God's work, he believed he was God. He prowled the stage, his arms swinging wide as if he was gathering energy from the very air itself.

"Doctors," he scoffed. "They would have had no power, not over my Sarah. She was consecrated to the Lord, doing His work. My only remorse is that she died surrounded by heathens." He froze, leaned forward to stare down at her, his grey eyes burning with passion.

"Sit." His voice wasn't loud but held an edge of command very different than before.

"I'm fine," she said, already tired of having to raise her head to look him in the eye. She didn't want to put herself at more of a disadvantage by lowering herself onto the bench behind her.

His entire body straightened, raising to a height that seemed impossible without his growing a few extra inches. The light from the skylight that bathed the image of Jesus above him caught him in its beams as if sharing some heavenly essence.

The result, when combined with that eerie gleam of his grey eyes, was intimidating. As it was meant to be.

"Sit down, Dr. Fiore."

If anything his voice was quieter than before, but she somehow found her knees buckling, bending to his will as she sank onto the bench.

Which scared the hell out of her. She realized that when he spoke of divine retribution causing the deaths of Jonah and the others, he meant retribution for something she had done. That his righteous and almighty God had smote them down because of her.

"I know you, Lydia Fiore," he continued, his gaze blazing into hers. "Know who you are, what is in your heart."

A shadow passed over his form as clouds blocked the sun. He couldn't have timed it better–it gave the effect that his voice was coming from the crucifix rather than the mortal who stood below it.

"Daughter of a junky whore. Your mother, she left you, abandoned you. Why, Lydia? What was in that dark heart of yours that even your own mother fled from?"

CHAPTER 45

AMANDA WOKE FACE DOWN IN A PILE OF CHARTS. She blinked slowly, wiped a trail of spittle away from her chin and looked up.

Lucas Stone stood in the doorway of the dictation area, smiling down at her and holding two cups of coffee in his hands. The delightful aroma more than compensated for waking up to his face, she decided, wordlessly taking the cup he offered.

"Thought you were off at seven," he said, taking the seat beside her.

"I was. What time is it?"

"Almost noon. What are you reading?"

"I was going through Becky Sanborn's chart. It makes no sense. She's been in perfect health all her life, runs marathons—"

She heard the tightness in her voice and knew it was because Becky's case scared her. And it was all Lucas's fault.

Telling her they had the same disease—whatever that was. True, some of the symptoms had been disturbingly similar, but Becky's deterioration had been frighteningly rapid.

"Find anything I missed?" he asked.

He kept staring at her and she didn't like it. Was certain he was cataloguing every move she made, dissecting her more thoroughly than a lab rat.

"No." Why was it so hard to admit? Because she wanted to prove him wrong, to prove that there was nothing wrong with her.

"Hey," she continued as the coffee finished waking her. "How's Mickey doing?"

His face went from engaged, filled with light and interest, to brooding. He was silent for a long, long moment. "Hanging on. If I can't get her back soon, she won't make it."

Amanda felt her gut tighten. Not just in sympathy for Mark Cohen and his sister, but for Lucas. It was all too obvious that he took his work and his patients to heart, that losing someone was like losing part of himself.

Alarms jolted them both upright. Lucas was the first to the nurses' station.

"Is it Mickey?" he asked.

"No," the nurse said, pushing the crash cart past them. "It's your other patient. Becky Sanborn. She's in full arrest."

LYDIA WAS FROZEN, caught by Kent's compelling voice and the memory it triggered. The morning Maria died. She and Lydia had argued.

Maria had been gone for two days, nothing unusual, and staggered in that morning while Lydia was getting ready for school. She was already furious with Maria for stealing the rent money Lydia had so carefully hidden, and the sight of her mother, clothes and hair mussed, lips swollen, makeup running, sent her over the edge.

"What the hell were you thinking?" she'd demanded in a voice so shrill and loud that Maria had covered her ears with her hands. "You're going to get us kicked out. Again!"

"It's all right baby," she crooned, capturing Lydia in her arms.

She stank of booze and aftershave. "We don't need this shitty apartment anyway. We'll go camp out on the beach, look at the stars, I'll tell you your fortune, your dreams–"

"No!" The single syllable rocked Lydia out of Maria's embrace. "No, not again. I like it here, I want to stay this time."

Tears punctuated her pleas. They had been in this stinky one room apartment whose only window opened onto the back alley and the garbage dumpsters for almost six months–a personal record for the two of them. This was by far the best place they had ever had. It had a real refrigerator, even if it only came up to Lydia's waist, and a microwave. Most importantly it had its own bathroom with a real door, a door with a lock, not just a sheet thrown over a curtain rod.

Lydia was twelve and although she lagged behind the other girls in the hormonal changes that came with puberty, she heard them talk, knew that soon there would be mysterious and frightening things happening to her body. That small cubbyhole of a bathroom with barely enough room to turn around and a shower that flooded the entire space was her safe haven. She wasn't about to let it go without a fight.

"No," she repeated to Maria. She crumbled onto the air mattress that was their only piece of furniture, hugging her knees to her chest. "I don't want to go. I just want to be normal. Have real furniture, a place I can ask friends over."

Maria sank down beside Lydia, her fingers stroking Lydia's hair. "Honey, you know that kind of life isn't for us."

"Why not? Why can't you get a real job? Why don't you marry one of those guys, take some of their money instead of always giving ours away?"

"It's only money, sweetie. And Glen really needed it." She seemed honestly puzzled by Lydia's anger.

Maria had more love in her heart than any one person could handle and even if the rent was due, if you asked her for money, she'd give you her last cent. She'd never think twice about it–or about the consequences to her daughter. After twelve years of the same routine, Lydia was sick of it.

"Well, so did we. I'm not doing it, not again." Lydia squirmed out of Maria's arms and stood, looking down on her mother, fists on her hips. "If we get kicked out, I'm going to go to Children Services, tell them to send me to your parents in San Francisco. Or maybe tell them to find my father."

Lydia watched the blood drain from Maria's face. Her mouth dropped open but the only sound that emerged was a tiny mewing noise like a sick kitten.

Why couldn't Maria understand that all she wanted was a bathroom with a door that locked?

Maria reached out a hand, fingers grasping only air. "Lydia. You can't. It's too dangerous."

Her mother's pleading and tears didn't sway Lydia. She'd seen it too many times before. Maria often played the guilt card, explaining how she'd given up drugs when she was pregnant with Lydia, how she'd sacrificed everything for the life of her child, leaving her family and Lydia's father.

She would never tell Lydia who her father really was, and anytime Lydia asked about him or her heritage, Maria would move them abruptly as if speaking of it was enough to bring trouble down on them.

Later that day, Maria had been waiting for Lydia as soon as school let out, not even carrying the duffle she usually used to pack their meager possessions. Instead, she had seemed terrified, dragging Lydia down unfamiliar alleys until they came to Saint Augustine's, then hiding her behind the drapes enclosing the confessional.

Images of blood, of a man's arm raising and falling, again and again, mixed with Maria's screams in Lydia's mind. She always knew somehow it was her fault. Maria had told her, begged her not to speak of her father, and look at what happened.

Slowly, she realized that it wasn't Maria's voice she heard

slicing through her mind, but rather Matthew Kent's. She blinked, her eyes feeling scratchy and dry. She'd been staring at the cross above him, had fallen into a trance.

"We're all sinners, us sons of Adam," Kent continued in that same insidious tone that made Lydia's teeth ache with ancient, unshed tears.

"Confess your sins, Lydia. Only then can you be forgiven them."

Sucking in a deep breath, Lydia cleared her mind of childhood fears and memories. Blinking again, she got to her feet. "What do you want?"

He remained in shadows, his voice swirling around her like a riptide trying to pull her under. "Confess, Lydia. Cleanse your soul. Together, we'll do the Lord's work."

"Like poisoning defenseless people? I don't think so."

There was a long silence, her opposition taking him aback. He stepped forward from the shadows. Suddenly he appeared merely human again. A frown creased his brow, as if by challenging him unscathed, she had passed a test he'd expected her to fail.

"I explained, that was not our doing."

"You expect me to take your word for it? After you sent your buddies to scare me off when I started to ask questions about Jonah Weiss's death?"

He shook his head slowly as if he were the one emerging from a trance. "No, no, you don't understand. I wanted–I needed Jonah Weiss alive. It is much easier to raise an army against the forces of evil when the devil can be seen. I am sorry about my men going too far. They were only meant to warn you, to give me time to investigate on my own without interference from the authorities."

He seemed to shrink beneath her inquisition. She continued, "So it was just a coincidence Jonah was killed on the anniversary of your wife's death?"

He looked up startled, as if he hadn't considered this. His

breath whistled through the air as he swung his head around, searching the empty church for something or someone. "You believe Sarah's death has something to do with this?"

It emerged less a question than a statement. He began shaking his head vigorously, hands raised, palms out as if warding off evil spirits. "No, no. It wasn't us. You must believe me."

Then he focused his gaze on Lydia once more. This time she could swear there was true fear in his eyes. "You need to leave. Turn your back, forget all about this and go far away."

"I don't think so. What's really going on around here, Matthew?"

"You're in danger, you must go." His voice gained in intensity as if he were trying to sway her will with the sheer force of it. "Or others will get hurt."

Lydia stepped up onto the stage. Now they stood on even ground, only a few feet separating them. "What are you implying?"

"I'm not implying, I'm telling you. You came here a stranger, but in only a few days you've developed quite a following, doctor. The boy out front," he jerked his head toward the windows and the landscape beyond where Danny waited. "The girl you defended in the alley, your friends in the ER, the paramedics—everyone you've touched, they're all in danger if you persist in this. Are you willing to risk their lives?"

Fear seared her gut. "If you hurt them–"

"Not me, doctor. Not me." His voice rose, echoing through the empty space. "Whoever doing this is the devil's spawn, lurking in shadows, slinking like a serpent among us. God's work is done out in the open, for all to witness and give glory to his name!"

His words crescendoed in a thunderbolt of self-righteous wrath. He stared past Lydia, his shoulders bunched together as if preparing to battle an unseen force.

She jumped back, down off the stage, anxious to place as much room between herself and Kent as possible. She edged away, not turning her back on him. He raised both fists high, still addressing his invisible foe.

"Run, doctor. Leave now! Unbelievers such as yourself cannot witness God's judgment without burning themselves. Believe me, the sinner who has perpetrated this insidious evil will burn in the eternal flame of righteousness. He will be brought to justice and cleansed!"

Lydia reached the door. She yanked it open, happy to escape to the sultry summer heat and the heavy odor of manure. Kent's words followed her out, hammering the air.

CHAPTER 46

IDIOTS, GINA THOUGHT as they swerved to avoid a car speeding down the wrong side of the road. They'd delivered their patient, who looked like she'd suffered nothing more serious than a fainting spell, and now were scrambling to answer their next call. Communications were down to cell phones since the crowd back at the church had torn off their radio antenna and Gecko was debating taking them back to the House for repairs once things slowed down.

This call was in Homewood, an area with a history of violence so bad that parents had to walk their kids several blocks out of the neighborhood because school buses refused to enter it. It seemed the festive rioting had spread here as well.

Fires dotted their route, at first just dumpsters and garbage cans, progressing to entire cars smoking and in ruin. The streets were clogged with streams of men and women, many carrying children, running away. Several stopped the ambulance, banging on the doors, begging for rides until they realized that Med Seven was going the wrong way—into Homewood.

As soon as they passed Murtland, most of the people they saw were driving like maniacs and shooting guns at each other.

"Maybe we should turn back," Gina suggested.

"This from the only person on board in a bullet proof vest," Gecko scoffed. "Come on, Gina. I know Mrs. Fenner. She's a sweetheart, real brittle diabetic and blind. We can't leave her alone in all this."

"Besides," Ollie put in as Gecko swung them around a burning Firebird. "We're here."

They came to a stop. Gecko rushed around back, opening the ambulance door. The sounds of breaking glass and shouting men filled the air.

"Here's what we're going to do. I want you two to guard the ambulance. I'm going to run in, get Mrs. F and I'll be right out. We'll do our assessment and treatment en route."

Ollie obviously didn't like that idea. "No way, man. I'm not letting you go in there alone."

He raced after Gecko, both of them disappearing into a grey shingled row house. Leaving Gina behind. Shit. What the hell was she supposed to do?

A car sped past, clipping the rear fender of the ambulance, hard enough to send it rocking. Gina braced herself, heard gunfire in the distance.

She double checked the door locks. Couldn't see anyone on this block, although up ahead fresh flames billowed, releasing greasy black smoke. Another car set on fire. She bit her lip, one finger nail scratching into the flesh of her forearm in soothing repetition, counting off the seconds.

Urgent pounding on the back door made her jump. She hit her head on the low ceiling and cursed. "Gina, it's us, open up!"

She unlocked and pushed the ambulance door open. Ollie hopped in, stretching to take a frail and skinny black woman from Gecko's arms. With her help they slid Mrs. Fenner onto the gurney. Gecko raced to the drivers' seat.

"Everyone good?" he asked as he gunned the engine and spun them into a three point turn. "Let's blow this popsicle stand."

HAMPTON DEPOSITED LYDIA AND DANNY outside the gate and left them there. Lydia turned to Danny. "Let me see your leg."

Danny gave her a look of fury sliced with terror. He lurched away from her, stepping into a clump of orange daylilies, hunched over, vomiting.

Lydia rushed to help him. Once he finished, she guided him to a clean patch of grass shaded by trees. He sank to the ground, rubbing his mouth with the back of his hand.

There wasn't much she could do except sit there, her hand on his thigh so he knew she was ready to listen. After several minutes his eyes lost their glassy, thousand mile stare.

"Sorry, doc. Sorry about dragging you into all this." He closed his eyes. His entire body was trembling. "I haven't felt this way in a long, long time. I forgot how–" His voice broke, his hands clenched into hard fists, drumming against the ground beside him.

"Awful?" she supplied. "It's the adrenaline. It effects everyone differently."

Danny opened his eyes, his gaze rambling from grass to sky to the bushes and back.

"It's just I get so angry and scared and it kind of grows in me, takes over until I just have to either hit something or..." He glanced back at the spot where he'd gotten sick.

"I know what you mean."

"You do? But you're so calm, so in control–"

She almost laughed. "Don't you believe it. When I'm really, really scared I get so mad it's like that old saying, seeing red. Only it's not just seeing, it makes me deaf and stupid as well. I charge in without thinking."

"You weren't scared back there? Not even when Hampton started waving that shotgun around?"

She nudged him. "I was more afraid you'd do something stupid, Sir Galahad. What would I tell Mickey if I let you get yourself killed?"

"C'mon doc, admit it. Those guys got to you, too."

She pursed her lips as if considering it. In the past, she had faced worse than Matthew Kent when it came to the threat of physical violence. But did his warped threats against the people she cared about scare her? Hell, yeah.

"Let's just say they hit close to home," she allowed, not wanting Danny to see just how shaken Kent's words had left her.

That seemed to sooth his macho ego. He leaned back, letting her examine his leg. A lot of bruising but the skin wasn't punctured. Lydia marveled at the dog's control.

"How old are you?" he asked, twirling a long stem of grass.

"Thirty. Why?"

"Just wondering. You've got one of those faces that looks really old sometimes and really young others." She almost laughed, but he seemed serious. "Mickey's like that, too. I'm twenty-two," he continued. "I've seen a lot of shit growing up in West Philly, time in juvie and at Rockview. But it's nothing compared with what Mickey has gone through. You know, last year she had a relapse and couldn't walk or use her right hand, but she still won that Brownfield case? Took her months to recover from that. Lucas says her form of MS is relapsing progressive, so each time it's worse."

She nodded. It was one of the most serious forms of MS. After each relapse the patient never fully regained the function they'd had previously. "She's already been on interferon?"

"Yeah. Makes her sick as a dog. She's tried it all. But here's my point." He rolled his shoulders. "Through all this shit, she almost never misses a day of work, even if she has to work from her bed. I can't figure it. Is there something about her work that she loves it that much? Or is it that if she gives it up, then she admits defeat? 'Cause if it was me, I'd be hitting the road and enjoying myself up to the bitter end."

"Maybe it's a bit of both?" Lydia hazarded a guess. She couldn't see Mickey as someone who would quietly surrender anything to her illness, and it was clear the lawyer was passionate about her work. "She just started using the wheelchair full-time, didn't she?"

Danny sighed, looking older than his twenty-something years. "Yeah. A few weeks ago things started going downhill. This is the worse I've seen her."

"How long have you been taking care of her?"

"About two and a half years. I finished my training as a paralegal, but no one would hire me." He looked up at Lydia sheepishly. "I was kind of wild as a kid and have a charge for assault on my sheet. Then I saw an ad for free room and board in exchange for light housekeeping and helping a handicapped attorney. It was just the break I needed."

"You love her."

"She's old enough to be my mother," he protested. Lydia stared, challenging him. He shifted, straightened his posture. "Well, yeah, I guess, maybe. I mean, it's not like how I feel about my girlfriend. It's different. I never had anyone need me before, you know?"

He gazed past her at the hazy outline of the mountains rippling into a clear blue sky. "I used to dream about living in a place like this," he said, indicating the landscape with a sweep of his hand. "Someplace quiet, where a man could think. But I couldn't leave Mickey." He sighed. "Hope she's okay." He pulled out his cell phone. "No service."

"It will be hours before they'll know anything."

He watched a dragon-fly skim along the tops of the tall grass. "What do you dream of, Lydia?"

"I don't. I have plenty to handle just taking care of what's right in front of me."

"C'mon. Everyone has dreams." He turned to scrutinize her, as if he could read her inner thoughts and hopes. "Ahh."

"Ahh, what?" She asked, climbing to her feet and brushing away all talks of dreams.

"I know what you're afraid of. You think if you let yourself believe in anything, it will hurt too badly when it doesn't happen."

Lydia ignored him, started back toward the road.

"What happened, Lydia?" he called out as he scrambled after her, limping slightly. "You shouldn't feel like that. Everyone's got to have dreams. It's what makes life worth living."

"You can't ride with that leg. And," she added when he looked ready to protest, "I'm not letting you out of my sight." Together they rolled the bike into the trees along the side of the road where it was hidden from sight.

"We can bring Trey's truck back to get it," Lydia promised him as he got into the Escape's passenger seat.

Despite his rocky background, Danny was at heart just a kid, an eternal optimist. He knew nothing about a world where mothers and friends and teachers and the families the state assigned you to were torn away as soon as you started to care too much, to rely on their presence in your universe.

The pavement sped by, a blur of black as they drove back into the city. The events of the past few days weighed down on her like a wet blanket, blurring her mind. She couldn't help but think of the passion she and Trey had shared last night. It had been so long since she had felt that way, that free....

Matthew Kent's words drove the image away. If whoever was behind the killings was coming after her next, then she had to leave, put distance between herself and anyone who could get hurt.

She couldn't risk it.

"Danny, promise me you won't go back there. That you won't go after Kent or the Sons of Adam."

"What? Leave it to the cops? No way."

"I'm serious. Promise me."

"Why? What did he say to you?"

"That more people are going to get hurt. You have to promise that you'll stay with Mickey. Keep her safe."

He blanched at that, his hand reaching for his cell phone. "You mean I wasted all day, and she could be," he faltered and gulped, "worse?"

They were close enough to the city that this time he was able to get through. He asked for Mickey's nurse. Instead he must have gotten Mark Cohen. "Is she all right?" he asked. "Yeah? No, that's okay. I can definitely stay with her tonight. Thanks." He hung up, his expression one of relief. "She's better. The hemoperfusion is working, he thinks she'll be all right."

"So you're going to watch her?"

"Yeah, I promise. No more crusades." A few minutes later Lydia pulled into Angel's front drive and Danny opened the door, ready to hop out. "Hey, Lydia. If I'm watching Mickey, then who's gonna watch you?"

"Don't worry, I can take care of myself." She squeezed his arm in encouragement.

He froze, twisted back to face her. "You're not thinking of doing anything stupid, are you?"

"No. I think Kent was right. I need to leave before anyone else gets hurt."

"You can't do that, it's like letting them win."

NORA WAS FINISHING UP the last of the photographs needed to document Mercedes's injuries. Some victims talked nonstop, asking questions, re-living the attack, venting. Others cried the entire time. Mercedes was in the stoic group: silent, compliant, as if she wasn't really even there, only her body.

"It's almost over," Nora said.

Mercedes shrugged, her eyes blank.

"Is there anyone I can call for you?" Nora asked. She'd tried to get the girl to talk, help her to start processing what had happened, but other than monosyllabic answers to direct questions, she'd gotten nowhere.

Mercedes shook her head, clutching the clean scrubs Nora handed her.

"You can get dressed. Wait here while I finish all the paperwork and then I'll be back with your medicine. Okay?" It was as if Mercedes's silence was propelling Nora to fill the void with meaningless words. Of course it wasn't okay, nothing would be okay for Mercedes for a long, long time.

Maybe never.

Nora grabbed her specimens, box of evidence, bags of clothing, and left. Some days, the bad ones like today, she wondered if she was doing more harm than good.

Rachel, the charge nurse on days, grabbed her as soon as she signed over the evidence to the police officer waiting. "Have you heard? There are riots going on all over the city. I'm worried—those demonstrations downtown aren't supposed to start for another hour. We're going to be in the middle of a full-blown disaster by then."

Nora eyed the patient board. Nothing remarkable and only a handful of people in the waiting room, mainly routine, minor injuries. Rachel was prone to exaggeration, but she'd heard what happened to Gina and Med Seven earlier. "What did Dr. Nielson say? Does he want to implement a mass casualty protocol?"

Rachel rolled her eyes. "Said there's no need since we already have the ORs cleared because of the holiday. But what about critical care beds, getting additional staffing, everything else that we'll need?"

"Who's on in charge on Four today?" When the ORs weren't in use for scheduled surgeries, usually one nurse supervised the ICUs and the OR.

"Gary. He's pretty new, never handled anything like this before."

"I'll go talk with him and start opening up beds. And I'll see if Mark can step in, maybe get the ball rolling in case things get worse. Does Dr. Weiss know?"

Rachel shook her head. "I didn't want to disturb him—not with how he's been with his son and all."

"I'll ask Mark to talk with him, maybe call in some of the off duty surgical residents." Which meant a good chance her brilliant plan to avoid Seth was about to flop. Not a whole lot she could do about it.

"Thanks, Nora."

"Yeah. Let's just hope we're worrying about nothing."

CHAPTER 47

TREY WAS WAITING AT THE DOOR TO LYDIA'S MOTEL ROOM when she pulled up. His Chief's uniform: pressed navy slacks, polished shoes, white uniform shirt with gold trim on the lapels, matched the officious scowl on his face.

"Where the hell have you been?" he asked as she jumped out of the SUV.

Lydia snapped her chin up, in no mood after her confrontation with Matthew Kent to placate his obviously ruffled feelings. She stalked past him and unlocked the door to her room.

He followed her inside before she could slam the door shut like she wanted. "Are you all right?"

She shook her head, her back to him as she rustled through her bags of clothing, searching for something to replace the torn and stained scrubs she wore. Anger made it hard to focus on anything, the urge to hit something was so strong it made her hands shake.

"What happened? Did someone hurt you?"

She couldn't tell if it was concern or anger that colored his voice. Either way, she didn't need it. She whirled on him, ready to vent her own fury on the nearest target: Trey.

He stood perfectly still, his gaze dropping from her eyes down to her clenched fists. His face creased with worry, and he blinked hard. She bounced on her toes with the effort of restraining herself, unable to voice the feelings rioting within her.

Trey gave her a small nod, then he stepped into the fray, wrapping his arms around her. He held her, ignoring her half-hearted attempts to escape.

A strangled noise of futility emerged from her before she finally stilled. He pulled her tighter still. "Tell me," he whispered. "Please."

She opened her mouth, but still could find no words. Just the awful empty feeling that fear and fury left in their wake. He kept holding her tight, stilling her motion, until she eventually, unwillingly, relaxed against his body.

"There's nothing to tell," she finally said, her voice sounding disturbingly normal. "I saw Matthew Kent. Says he didn't kill anyone. He did admit to sending the men after me and Gina, but he's never killed anyone. Although he most definitely is insane. And I think he knows who did kill Jonah and those women."

She broke free from his grasp, resuming her search for a clean pair of shorts. Trey backed off, almost tripping—the first time she'd ever seen him off balance. She shoved the thought aside, she had to keep moving. Standing still was how you became a target. If she'd learned that sooner, back when she was young, Maria might still be alive.

"That's all? You just talked?"

"Yeah." She hesitated, unsure of how to describe their eerie stand-off in the sanctuary. "We just talked." She glanced over her shoulder at him. "You can leave now."

"No. Pack your stuff. You can move in with me until this is all over."

She had no idea what had come over Trey and wasn't certain if she liked it. What happened to her peace-loving, teddy-bear of a man? Suddenly he'd become as ferocious as an untamed grizzly.

"What makes you think I'd be safer there?" she snapped. "Maybe I should just leave Pittsburgh all together."

"It might be for the best," he allowed, but his shoulders hunched as if he wasn't all too happy with that option.

She stared at him long and hard. The air conditioner chugged away in the corner, the only sound. The room seemed to grow smaller, cave in on itself as Trey waited for her answer.

"No. I'm staying." The words emerged slowly—probably because she wasn't entirely sure about her decision. She narrowed her eyes at Trey, not liking the way he made her doubt her first instincts.

Trey shook his head, both hands rubbing the back of his neck, as if shaking off a chill. "If you're staying, you'd better get changed," he said as she wondered what he was really thinking, the way he wouldn't stop staring at her. "My folks are expecting us."

She glared at him. Was he feeble-minded? She was in no condition to sit and chit-chat, make nice with his family. "You don't really expect me to go eat hotdogs and watch fireworks when there's a killer on the loose?"

Both his hands flew out as if he intended to grab her and carry her to his folks' house. Then they fell to his sides, empty. "I do. And you will."

"Just because we had sex gives you no right to tell me what I will and won't do!" She leaned forward, hands on her hips, assuming her best she-who-must-be-obeyed frown. "Get out, now!" She pointed at the door, a tank top fisted in her hand like a weapon, her body rigid with anger.

Her glare had no effect on Trey. He laughed, grinning at her. "I finally have you figured out, Lydia. You always get your way 'cause you out-stubborn everyone else. Including me. Not this time. I'm not letting you out of my sight again. Not until this is over."

Lydia spun on her heel, marched into the bathroom, and slammed the door in his face.

Usually when she went all raging bull, people ran and ducked for cover, avoiding her at all costs. Not Trey. He'd held her, whispered to her, shared his strength.

As she showered and changed, an unfamiliar warmth settled over her, soft and gentle as a worn blanket. Trey wanted her to stay. She didn't frighten him, couldn't scare him away despite trying.

What did that mean? she wondered as she rejoined him. He said nothing, merely held the door open, waited while she locked it behind her, then escorted her to his truck.

"Why'd you change your mind?" His voice broke into her thoughts as they drove toward his parents' house. "About staying?"

"Something I realized. Those women yesterday, they weren't killed because of anything I did. They were targeted because Wanda Owens was there. Wrong place, wrong time."

"Told you it wasn't your fault."

"Matthew Kent told me to run, said it was the only way to protect—well, to stop anyone else from getting hurt. But the killer isn't after me, he could care less about me. So there's no reason for me to run."

She paused. Hoped she wasn't setting herself up for heartbreak by asking, but couldn't help herself. "Would you really have stopped me from leaving?"

"No."

Lydia's stomach curled in on itself, somersaulting with disappointment.

"I would have gone with you. Protected you."

Her mood swung back to a gleefulness that felt child-like. She couldn't remember the last time she had felt this way. "Really?"

She didn't like the need that bled into her voice, so she quickly sat up straight, trying to project independence, self-reliance. It used to come natural, no need to force it, but suddenly it was hard to hide her feelings from Trey.

"Protected me? I just told you, I'm not in any danger. Besides,

I can take care of myself. Have for a long time."

His posture tensed, out of proportion to her words. He hunched forward over the steering wheel as if piloting the Titanic to certain doom.

"What is it?" she asked.

"You might still be in danger. Harold Owens," he finally said, his words clipped. "He's dead."

Lydia jerked forward, her seatbelt ratcheting against her body. "No. What happened? When?"

"This morning. Boyle said people had been leaving gifts on Owens's porch all night—food, flowers, candles. This morning Owens picked one up and—"

"It was a bomb."

"I don't even know if my dad knows yet. He and Owens know—knew—each other. I'm hoping I'm not the one who has to tell him."

She squeezed his arm, trying to offer him whatever strength she had left. They stopped at a red light. Trey turned, stared at her with a strange expression on his face. Fear, longing—she wasn't sure. When she met his gaze, he abruptly focused on the rearview mirror. "A Fat Albert. Haven't seen a rig like that in ages."

Lydia glanced in her side mirror, saw the profile of an outdated ambulance three cars behind them. Trey was trying to distract her. And she didn't think it was because he was worried about his father. "When I was late getting back to the motel, you thought I—"

"I thought you went for a run, were being inconsiderate and rude," he said firmly as if denying the truth to himself. "I swear, woman, I'm going to buy you a watch."

Yeah, right. Like her lack of punctuality was the issue.

"I never wear them." She gave him a break, let him change the subject. "Can't. They just stop. Maria said it was because my chakras were out of whack or something."

He shook his head, still not looking at her. "Or something."

Traffic thinned out once they passed a park bristling with picnicking families and groups playing volleyball and softball. They entered a residential area with modest two story homes on nice sized lots, much nicer than the cramped rowhouses clustered around Angels.

Trey turned into a driveway in front of a white-pillared colonial house with a well-kept lawn and inviting flower beds brimming with roses, lavender, and lilies. "Home sweet home."

CHAPTER 48

AMANDA WIPED HER EYES with the back of her forearm before resuming chest compressions. Her gloves clung to her, a coating of sweat between her skin and the latex acting like glue. Splashes of Betadine and blood colored the gloves brown and red, the results of her getting an arterial blood gas and then helping Lucas insert a central line after Becky's IV blew.

Her shoulders and hands were cramped from doing CPR and she knew she'd pushed too hard that last time, had felt a rib snap beneath her palm, but still Lucas wouldn't give up.

When she looked up at him, he appeared haunted, eyes focused only on his patient and the monitor above her, as if the rest of the world had vanished. He didn't even acknowledge Mark Cohen when the ER doctor came over to ask if they needed help.

The nurse had shown Mark Becky's chart and he had just walked away, shaking his head like it was a lost cause.

Even Amanda knew it was too long. They'd gotten Becky back twice in the last three hours, but this time she'd been down thirty-seven minutes.

"Stop CPR," Lucas ordered. "Check her pulse."

Amanda gratefully rocked back, raising her hands from Becky's naked chest. Nora Halloran joined them, sent over by Mark, no doubt, and quickly looked over the code record.

"Dr. Stone," she started in a gentle tone.

"What?" He whirled on her, weight flung forward, fists balled as if she were the enemy.

Nora stood her ground, met his eyes and shook her head sadly.

"No pulse," the nurse called out.

Lucas opened his mouth, ready to fling another order, but Nora stopped him with a hand on his arm.

"Lucas," she said. "Enough."

His chest expanded as he drew his breath in, he seemed to grow larger than life, and Amanda almost could believe that he might have some weapon strong enough to overcome death.

There was a pause as all activity around Becky's bed stopped. Everyone looked at Lucas.

His gaze dropped, eyelids half shut, and he blew out his breath, his cheeks caving in, his shoulders slumping and suddenly he was once again simply a tired, all too mortal human.

Just like the rest of them.

"Call it," he mumbled. "Time of death 3:24 pm."

GINA FOUGHT TO START AN IV on the old lady but her veins were for shit. "What's her D-stix?" she asked Ollie.

"Forty." He leaned forward, yelling into Mrs. Fenner's ear. "Open up, Millie, I need you to swallow this."

She nodded, her eyes still closed, and opened her mouth wide, her dentures slipping. Ollie squirted a tube of frosting and Mrs. Fenner sucked at it greedily. Her eyes fluttered open, revealing cloudy, sightless corneas. "That you, Ollie, child?"

"Yes'm. You mixed up your insulin again. Here, have more

frosting, that will bring your sugar back up until we can get you to Angels."

The sound of squealing tires approached them from behind. A car horn sounded, unrelenting. Gina glanced out the back window. "Pull over, they're trying to ram us."

"It's not us they want," Gecko said, swerving them up onto the curb and hitting the brakes, narrowly avoiding a lamp post.

Gina climbed past Ollie into the front seat and watched through the side mirror. A white man in shorts was pounding on the front door of a house, while pushing a black woman down behind a porch swing—as if trying to get her under cover. "What the hell are they doing?"

Gunfire sounded from another car as the first one passed them.

The second car, a black Jeep with a sunroof that two black men crowded through, gleefully firing automatic weapons at the first car. They sped past the ambulance just as the first car jumped the curb and hit the brick wall of a row house.

The Jeep kept going, honking its horn as the men standing in the sunroof cheered. Gina saw no movement from the crashed car. "Should we go help?"

"No," Ollie's voice came from the rear. "Wait. They always come around twice."

"Tell him that," Gecko said, pointing to the man who was now sprinting down the porch steps. "He's asking to get shot, fool."

They watched as the man raced to the crashed vehicle, obviously trying to help the driver. He'd just gotten the front door open when the sound of squealing tires rounding the corner behind them filled the air.

Gina had no idea what she was doing, had no idea why she was doing it, just knew she had to do something.

She was out the door, pounding down the pavement before Gecko's shouted protests even registered. She heard the Jeep speeding toward her, but her vision was filled with the sight of the half-naked Good Samaritan half a block away.

Her breath thundered in her ears as she ran. "Down!" she screamed. The Jeep was almost level with her, the sound of the men's laughter shivering through her awareness. "Get down!"

With one last burst of power she tackled the man, driving him to the pavement, pulling her arms up over her head and praying that Jerry's Kevlar would shield them both as the bullets began to fly.

CHAPTER 49

TREY HAD NEGLECTED TO MENTION that he was related to Norman Rockwell. Or at the very least that his family had inspired the heartland artist's work.

As they approached the front door, it opened, revealing a beaming black woman in her late fifties. She flung the screen door wide and rushed to embrace Trey. She was a bit shorter than Lydia, the top of her head hit Trey mid chest, but that didn't stop her from encircling his broad torso with her arms.

"Mom," he said, mirroring her smile and unleashing his dimple. "This is Lydia Fiore. The new doctor at Angels I told you about."

"Lydia, welcome, welcome. I'm Ruby. Please come in out of the heat."

Before Lydia knew what happened, she'd been bustled inside, the door irrevocably shut behind her. The foyer was wide, with a slate floor that continued down the hallway into the kitchen, a generous staircase on the left, and two arches on either side revealing a formal living room on the right and a dining room on the left. The wall along the staircase was lined with photos: a wedding photo of Ruby and a tall black man who shared Trey's hazel eyes and dimple, school photos of children and several of men and women in uniforms. Police uniforms. Seemed like Trey's father wasn't the only police officer in the family.

Lydia darted a glance at Trey. He had stopped, head bowed as he spoke in a low tone to his mother. "Does Dad know—"

"About poor Harold? Yes. He's being his usual stubborn self, won't talk about it."

Trey blew his breath out and started down the hall to the kitchen. "Smells good, Mom."

"My baked beans," Ruby said. She raised a lid on a huge stock pot, releasing an enticing aroma. As she reached for hot pads to carry the heavy pot with, Trey beat her to it.

"I'll get that. Let you two get acquainted."

Lydia whipped her head around to glare at him. He gave her a grin. "Don't worry, Lydia. She doesn't bite." Then he vanished from sight.

She tried to follow, but Ruby Garrison tilted her head, studying her, blocking her way. The sounds of children squealing with laughter, of women talking and the clank of glassware accompanied the sound of a sliding glass door opening and closing. Then it was just Lydia and Ruby.

Ruby had short, dark curly hair, speckled with a hint of grey. Her eyes were brown and nothing seemed to escape their notice as they took an exacting inventory of Lydia's appearance.

Lydia felt sweat gather beneath her arms, plastering her shirt to her sides. She ran her palms along her shorts, finally jamming her hands in her pockets.

Most of her elementary education had been in Catholic schools—the nuns and priests were far more sympathetic to Maria and far less demanding of details such as social security numbers, transcripts, and photo ID's than public institutions. Lydia had met some tough nuns, nuns who could peer into your very soul when they wanted.

Ruby put them all to shame.

Only a few moments had passed since Trey left, although it seemed like hours to Lydia. Ruby touched her on the arm as if guiding a skittish child and steered her to a chair at a large oak kitchen table.

"Thought you might enjoy a few moments of peace and quiet and something cold to drink before meeting the rest of the family." Ruby surprised Lydia by saying as she turned to get them both glasses of lemonade. "We're a rather large and boisterous group. Can be overwhelming if you aren't used to that kind of thing."

The kitchen and family room took up the entire back half of the house. Windows and sliding glass doors lined the rear wall, revealing several men huddled over a smoking stainless steel grill approximately the size of Lydia's last apartment. Several women lounged beneath an awning, while children of various ages giggled and shrieked as they ran through a sprinkler and onto a slip-and-slide.

Movement and noise and color all blurred as Lydia tried to count, losing track after four adult women, five men including Trey, and an uncertain number of kids. Ruby set the glass in front of her and took the seat beside her.

"Looks like fun from inside here," she said with a smile in her voice. "But don't be deceived. It's hot and muggy and the mosquitoes are fierce. You're not missing a thing."

Lydia nodded, not taking her eyes from the scene. Something knotted in her stomach, the feeling of blowing out your birthday candles and making a wish even though you knew it could never come true. Still you tried, blowing as hard and fast as you could.

She shook her head. Until you outgrew all that childishness, that was. Maria had never outgrown it, constantly scampering across sidewalks to pick up pennies or blowing on dandelion puffs. But Lydia had abandoned all that foolishness long ago.

Still...She hid her yearning by turning to take a sip of

lemonade. It had a refreshing tang.

Then she almost choked, remembering the lemonade the ladies of Friendship Church had drunk with fatal consequences. She set the glass down with a clatter. Pieces of seeds and pulp floated among the ice cubes.

"This is good," she finally told Ruby who was staring at her. "It tastes different."

Ruby smiled—actually, other than a mournful frown at the mention of Harold Owens, she hadn't stopped smiling since they had arrived. Maybe she always smiled? Laugh lines bracketing her mouth seemed to imply that was a possibility. Now her smile became approving and she leaned toward Lydia conspiratorially.

"The secret is peppermint. I add a few peppermints to every pitcher. Sugar free of course, on account of Denny. That's Trey's father, he has diabetes."

Lydia spun the glass between her hands, considering before taking another sip. "Peppermint? I'll remember that."

She looked around the room. Like the foyer, it was filled with mementos and photos crowding shelves, the front of the refrigerator, hanging on the walls. Lydia's attention was drawn to the photos of police officers: an older man, his arms around two tall younger ones and a woman in the center. She licked her suddenly dry lips. "Your family has a lot of police officers."

Ruby chuckled. "Trey didn't tell you? He's our black sheep—always a rebel, that boy. Guess that's what comes from being the middle child and youngest son. Denny retired from the Sheriff's department last year. Trey's two older brothers—that's them out there arguing about how to cook their burgers—are both with the state police. And Shondra, our youngest, she and her husband live in Cleveland and she just graduated from their police academy."

"Trey has two brothers and a sister?" Being in the middle of all that would certainly explain his peacekeeping skills.

"Two brothers older than him *and* two sisters younger." Ruby waved through the window to a very pregnant woman sitting in the shade with her feet dangling in a kiddy pool. "That's Patrice, most of that horde of screaming children belong to her. Well three of them, with the fourth coming along any day now. The others are divided between Marcus and Thom who each have two and Shondra who has two step kids. Her husband's in Iraq, so they came here for the holiday weekend."

Lydia bobbed her head knowing it would be hopeless for her to keep it all straight. The oldest man, Denny she guessed, turned and tipped his beer bottle in their direction, nodding. Ruby pushed her chair back and stood.

"Looks like they're ready to eat. Come on, Lydia," she said in an encouraging voice. "Just think of it like one of those gruesome pile-ups on the parkway. What does Trey call them? A mass casualty. Can't be worse than one of those."

GINA FELT LIKE SHE'D FALLEN INTO THE TWILIGHT ZONE, or at the very least into a time warp. The crack of bullets, sparks of metal, shards of flying glass seemed to go on forever as she huddled over top of the man.

She wasn't even sure if he was alive. He could have already been shot, could be lying there dying below her, she had no idea.

Her eyes were squinched shut, as if opening them would be inviting a bullet. Her hands clenched tight, gripping Jerry's bulletproof vest. Jerry. God, what if she never saw him again?

Finally, it was over. Only a ringing in her ears remained. The man shifted his weight below her, pushing her off.

Gina's head throbbed, her headache awakened, returning full force. She climbed up, shrugging back into her vest. The man was reaching into the car, trying to assess the driver. Idiot. Didn't he see the brains splashed against what remained of the windshield?

"Gina!" Gecko shouted. "Hurry, they'll be coming back!"

"C'mon," she yelled at the man, who tried to resist her.

She sprinted toward the ambulance only to stop as he disappeared back up the porch steps. He reappeared, carrying a toddler, a cute little girl with cornrows, wearing red shorts and a Pirate's T-shirt. Two other kids ran down behind him, followed by a woman in her twenties, also carrying a crying toddler.

"Help them," the man cried as he sprinted past her.

Gina scooped up one of the kids, reached the ambulance just as the man deposited the girl into Ollie's arms and turned back. He and Gecko sprinted back to the porch, both emerging holding pre-school aged kids.

The sound of gun fire and squealing tires threatened to out run them. Gina shoved the kids into the back of the ambulance, forming a strange bucket brigade with Ollie playing catch.

"Hurry!" she shouted as the Jeep rounded the corner, men now hanging from every window, obviously enjoying their target practice.

She climbed into the ambulance, swinging one door shut and holding the other ajar. Gecko came in sight first, grabbing her outstretched hand and jumping on board, crowding past her.

The other man tossed one last child into her arms, then flew past her just as bullets ricocheted against the ambulance walls. Gina tried to swing the door shut and almost fell out of the ambulance. A man's arms pulled her inside, toppling her on top of him as she fought to shield the child in her arms.

This time, even though he wore no Kevlar, the man rolled her over, sheltering her and the children with his body until the weapon fire ceased. Then he lunged for the open door, slammed it shut and leaned against it.

"Everyone all right?" he asked even as he began to run his hands over the children and then Gina who was trapped on the floor between the gurney and the bench seat.

"Leave me alone. I'm a doctor," she snapped at him, irritated by this Good Samaritan who seemed impervious to fear and bullets. She was about ready to wet herself, she was that scared.

"So am I," he said with a grin, leveraging her to her feet. He grabbed the sissy strap, leaning over her as he called up to the front seats. "Home, James!"

"I hear ya," Gecko shouted back with a chuckle. He jammed the ambulance into gear and punched the gas, bouncing them off the curb and back onto the street. "Next stop: Angels of Mercy."

CHAPTER 50

RUBY HAD SAID TO TREAT THE GATHERING like a mass casualty and she was right. Lydia kept herself at a bit of a distance, observing, listening, smiling and everyone pretty much just swirled around her, having fun despite the stranger in their midst.

Soon, she found herself relaxing and enjoying herself as the kids played a game of freeze tag on the lawn.

"How do you want your burger?" Trey asked her, gesturing with two overflowing plates. "You can have medium rare with cheese or well done without cheese."

"Medium with cheese, please."

"Thought so."

He set the plates down and slid onto the picnic table bench beside her. He had added baked beans, chips, coleslaw, corn on the cob, pasta salad and watermelon to both plates, a mountain of food that threatened to slide into her lap. It was more food than Lydia usually ate in a day, but it smelled so good, she found her stomach growling in anticipation.

"I thought you were a vegetarian," she said as Trey took a healthy bite out of his burger.

His brother, Marcus, sat across from them and snorted in

laughter. "Trey? A vegetarian? You got to be kidding."

Trey flushed and swallowed quickly. "I am. Usually." He glared at his brother as if daring him to defy him.

Marcus' wife, whose name Lydia still hadn't learned, slid in beside her husband. "He means that they all promised Ruby to eat healthy. Low fat. Ever since Denny had his heart attack."

She nudged her husband in the ribs and scooped half his French fries off his plate and onto hers. "Just Trey is the only one of the boys who actually pays attention to his health. They all have high cholesterol, you know. This one is already taking medicine for it."

"C'mon," Marcus said, rescuing a handful of fries. "It's a holiday. No rules on a holiday."

"You think I don't see all those Burger King wrappers you leave in your car?"

Marcus, a good six foot-four, two hundred twenty pounds of muscle and attitude, slumped his shoulders in defeat.

"Busted," Trey sang out.

"Yeah, well that's the difference between us cops and you guys," Marcus retorted. "We need real food to do our jobs, can't make it on that veggie crap."

"Do your jobs. Right. You sit on your butt all day clocking speeders."

"Hey, now," Ruby's voice rang out, cutting through the brotherly rivalry. "You two behave yourselves. The kids are going to put on a concert for us."

Everyone swiveled as the children set up a portable karaoke machine. It came well stocked with tunes, and the kids took turns belting out everything from hip-hop to Motown. Lydia watched, matching offspring to proud parents by the gleams on their faces. The youngest was maybe four or five, the oldest ten, and all beamed at the attention.

Suddenly the laughter and the smiles and the outpouring of love, the essence of family, overwhelmed her. What would it have been like to grow up in a home like this one? She remembered what she had told Danny, that she didn't believe in dreams.

She'd lied. She had a dream, one so deep she kept it hidden it from herself.

She dropped her fork, planted her palm flat against her stomach as if trying to hold something in. Trey sensed something was wrong, turned and whispered, "You okay?"

Lydia nodded. "I'll be right back."

Before he could say anything more, she fled inside the house, found the powder room beneath the stairs in the main hallway and locked the door behind her. Her vision wavered as she leaned against the sink.

Lydia turned the water on as tears began to choke her. Sucker punched by the sudden onslaught of emotion, she allowed her tears to flow for a few moments. Then she blew her nose, splashed water on her face and dried her hands.

This was silly, getting all teary over something she couldn't change. It was her future she had to think about, not her past. She took a deep breath, filling the empty void in the pit of her gut, steeling herself to return to the bright and noisy crowd outside.

"You all right in there?" Trey's voice came from beyond the door.

Lydia opened it. Trey stood in the doorway, blocking her exit.

"Thought you might need some fortification," he said, one finger trailing her damp cheek before coming to a rest at the corner of her jaw.

"What'd you bring me? A shot of whiskey?"

He leaned forward, his hips nudging her back, and shut the door behind them. He tilted her chin up and kissed her.

"Nope. Just me."

His warmth enveloped her, overwhelming any memories or wistful thoughts. Instead there was only the man, solid and real and so very sexy, holding her tight against his body. She stretched her arms up to encircle his neck, bringing him even closer, suddenly hungry again. Ravenous, in fact.

He responded in kind, making a small noise as she planted her mouth on his, before lifting her up onto the vanity. His arms cradled her, protecting her from a nasty collision with the faucet.

"I'm sorry I worried you earlier," she told him, wondering at her urge to apologize, to set things right with him.

He nuzzled a ticklish spot behind her ear. She giggled then shivered as his mouth moved down her neck.

"What about the picnic?" she asked, trying her best to ignore the heat building within her.

"What picnic?"

He shifted his position, allowing her to wrap her legs around his thighs. His pelvis rocked against her and she arched back, banging her head against the mirror and almost sliding into the sink.

A clatter of glass and metal coming from the kitchen interrupted them. Trey jerked upright, face flushing like a kid caught playing hooky. Just to torture him, Lydia grabbed his shirt, pulled him back for one last frenzied kiss.

"I've got it, Denny," Ruby's voice broke through their passion, accompanied by the sound of the door sliding shut and more clatter.

Trey swore under his breath and straightened his shirt, backing out of the tiny room. He winked at Lydia, mouthed the word, "later" and closed the door. She hopped down from the vanity, made a show of flushing the toilet and running the water for a minute before opening the door.

Ruby was in the kitchen, a bucket of empty bottles in her arms. She glanced at Lydia as if it was just a coincidence that she'd picked that exact moment to leave the party and clean up the recycling. "Everything all right?"

Lydia didn't have to force her smile. "Fine, thanks. It's been a long couple of days is all."

"Uh-huh. That's exactly what Trey said as well."

Lydia found herself avoiding Ruby's piercing gaze.

"You know, you're all he's talked about for two days. Usually I don't even hear about one of his girls until they've broken up." Ruby led her into the living room. "Why don't we sit in the cool air for a few minutes. It's too darned hot out there."

She sat on the camelback couch in front of a large picture window facing out onto the front porch, patting the cushion for Lydia to join her. "Tell me about yourself."

Lydia walked over to the fireplace and examined the photos and awards that lined the shelves surrounding it, hoping to buy herself some time before she needed to answer. One was a plaque from the Realtor Association.

"Rare Gems Realty," Lydia said. "Trey used that name when he was helping me get rid of a pesky real estate agent." She turned to Ruby. "Are you the Rare Gem in the name?"

"Yes. I started RGR, but I can't take all the credit. Everyone in the family has worked for there at one time or another. In fact, since he retired from the Sheriff's Department, Denny works for me, finding properties."

"Trey said he moonlit renovating properties. Do you specialize in places that are damaged or dilapidated?"

"On the contrary. Our properties are usually very well loved by their former occupants. But that's the problem—most new buyers don't want to deal with the memories attached to death scenes."

Lydia glanced up at that. "Death scenes?"

"We take properties where people died on the premises or that were the scenes of crimes and we place them with buyers who not only appreciate a bargain but who also will respect the history of the property."

Lydia remembered how the scent of cigars had permeated one corner of the living room in Trey's house. "The house Trey is working on now, a man died there, didn't he?"

"Yes. Poor man, wandered around that house all alone after his wife died last year. Then he fell asleep in his recliner, smoking one of his cigars—"

"And caught on fire." That explained the darkened area of the floorboards in that same area. Although there didn't seem to be any other structural damage. "Is that house for sale?" Lydia could hardly believe she was even asking. A few hours ago she had been determined to leave Pittsburgh. Yet, she felt herself tense, waiting for Ruby's answer.

A shadow flitted across the window and Lydia saw a man's figure pass by.

"You have company," she said as he moved toward the door then back again to the window.

Ruby twisted in her seat. "Now, who can that be?"

The window exploded inward, showering them with glass as a rock flew through the air. Ruby screamed and fell onto the couch, clutching her head. Lydia ran to her but before she could do more than take a step, she felt a whoosh of air followed by tremendous heat and flames.

In an instant, the couch and curtains were on fire. And so was Ruby.

CHAPTER 51

NORA SHIFTED HER RADIO TO ONE HAND and sifted through patient assessments with the other. Some holiday. Finding Seth in bed with that nurse anesthetist, Karen, was looking like the highlight of her day so far.

Disaster—yeah, that pretty much described her day. How the hell was she going to find beds for all these patients and get them moved?

She crossed two names off her list and entered the SICU. Then her day went from bad to worse in one blink.

"What the hell did I do to piss Weiss off?" Seth was grumbling, talking to no one in particular, his head down, scribbling on a chart at the SICU nurses' station. "If there really is a disaster, I should be in the OR. Not counting bedpans and jumping every time some nurse says Boo!"

"It's counting beds," Nora told him as she approached the desk. He flinched at her voice, looked up then looked away again. *Nice to see you too, Seth.* "And I believe the nurse you're to jump to would be me."

Seth kept his head down, pretending to re-calculate a Lasix order. "They called you in too? Why aren't you in the ER?"

"They already have a charge nurse in the ER. What they were lacking on this disaster of a holiday was someone to run the OR and critical care units. So here I am. In charge and in no mood to take any of your crap."

He winced at her tone, met her gaze for the briefest of seconds, just long enough for her to see the wounded look in his eyes. What the hell right did he have to look hurt?

Anger flared in her but she choked it back, concentrated on what her patients needed.

"How many beds can you give me?" she asked, all business.

"Four trauma, three SICU."

"They're all trauma tonight."

"This shit is for real? No drill?"

Nora set her clipboard down with a clatter. "You didn't hear about Gina? Riding in Med Seven and attacked by a mob. And there's fires, fights breaking out all over in East Liberty, Homewood, Garfield. Gangs deciding today would be a good day to go to war, some of those Sons of Adams loons raising hell. Sorry to interrupt your love fest with Karen, but yeah, Seth, it's for real."

"Gina's all right?"

"I guess, they headed right back out. And the cops are spread thin—Jerry Boyle said most of them are tied up Downtown. The Staties and Sheriff are lending a hand, but the roads are tied up and it's a royal mess getting anyone to this part of the city."

"So we're basically on our own," he said. "Just like *Fort Apache, the Bronx*. Damn."

"You can say that again." She hated that she knew he was speaking of the original movie, not the remake, hated that part of her was already missing him, their shared love of movies, the way they had been together. Damn him, how could he throw that all away? How could she have let him? She knew the kind of man he was.

Her radio squawked. It was Lucas Stone asking for her help

in the Medical ICU. She turned and walked away from Seth, hoping Mickey hadn't taken a turn for the worse. She reached the doors, couldn't resist one quick glance over her shoulder at Seth.

He was already gone.

BLACK SMOKE ROILED THROUGH THE AIR, choking Lydia. Fire swept up the curtains, raced across the couch and down to the floor.

Lydia ignored the blaze and the broken glass, throwing herself onto Ruby. She rolled them both off the couch and onto the carpet. Glass crunched beneath her, biting, stabbing, but Lydia kept her arms and body wrapped around Ruby, working to smother the flames that had blossomed on Ruby's arms and legs.

The stench of kerosene clogged her nostrils. The flames were stubborn, sticking to Ruby like a deadly second skin. Lydia grabbed a knitted afghan from a chair and wrapped it around Ruby, finally extinguishing the fire.

In the few moments it had taken to save Ruby, the room filled with smoke in a red-hot, roaring conflagration. Ruby was screaming, her words incomprehensible over the blare of a smoke detector. Lydia gathered the smaller woman into her arms and carried her in a hunched over crab walk, blindly feeling her way through the blinding smoke.

Shouts and screams now permeated her consciousness. She banged into a wall, followed it until she hit an opening where carpet changed to tile and fell into the kitchen, never releasing Ruby. There, strong hands raised Ruby from her grasp. Lydia collapsed onto her hands and knees, coughing and retching.

The sounds of a hose, swoosh of a fire extinguisher and rush of footsteps swirled around Lydia punctuated by the shrill tones of the smoke alarm hammering into her brain. Someone dumped water on her before she even realized her clothing was on fire. A pair of hands pulled her to her feet and then carried her out through the sliding doors.

Her vision was blurred with tears, her eyes burning as if she'd been swimming in gasoline. She blinked, then blinked again. Trey's form began to separate itself from the bright colors rushing around. Now the sounds of sirens could be heard.

"Ruby?" she croaked, her throat constricting with the effort. She hadn't just swum in gasoline, she'd swallowed it and breathed it in as well. No, not gasoline. Kerosene.

A Molotov cocktail. Kerosene and soap flakes. That was why it had clung to Ruby so greedily.

"She's fine," he assured her.

Her vision cleared and she saw that the kids had vanished—probably rushed to a neighbor's for safety. The hose was now going into the house and when she looked past Trey into the kitchen she saw the floor was covered with water and the wading pool lay upside down. There were no more flames to be seen. Marcus and Trey's other brother were pulling cushions from the furniture, tearing down the curtains, searching for any remaining hotspots.

On the other side of Trey, Denny and Shondra bent over Ruby who was sitting in a chaise lounge, holding one arm extended away from her, coughing as Denny wiped her face with a wet towel.

"Let me see her," Lydia said, pushing Trey's hands aside.

"How about if I check you out first? I couldn't carry you both, had to grab her and come back for you. You definitely swallowed some smoke in there."

Lydia stood, felt a rush of pain as she leaned a palm against the side of the house for support. Both her palms had superficial burns as did the backs of her calves. She coughed and gagged on a wad of mucus, didn't spit it out because she didn't want to see if it was tinged with charcoal—she didn't have time to worry about herself, it was Ruby who had taken the worst of the fire.

Trey held her elbow as she wobbled over to Ruby, almost tripping on the hose. Ruby was crying, her eyes reddened. A gash on the side of her scalp was bleeding steadily. Her left arm was already blistering with partial thickness burns, but they were less extensive than Lydia had feared.

"Ruby, are you all right?"

Ruby nodded, reaching out with her good hand to clench Lydia's. Lydia winced against the pain but didn't pull away.

"Thank you," Ruby gasped, breaking into another spasm of coughing.

"You saved her life," Denny said, both hands on his wife's shoulders and looking like he wasn't going to let go anytime soon. "Thank you."

"What happened?" Trey asked. Lydia looked up and saw that his brothers and sister flanked him, all staring at her with cop eyes: hard and suspicious.

They had a right. She'd been so very wrong, thinking that Matthew Kent was mistaken about her being in danger, about her endangering anyone she came near.

"A man. He threw a rock through the window then," she took a breath, choked back a cough, "he threw a Molotov cocktail."

"Why would anyone want to burn down our house?" Denny said, now also giving Lydia that same suspicious glare of mistrust.

Shivering, Lydia remembered Matthew Kent's warning. He'd told her that anyone she was near was in danger. How could she have ignored him?

"He didn't care about your house. He wanted to kill me."

CHAPTER 52

GINA HAD BECOME A HUMAN JUNGLE GYM. The squealing, laughing children had somehow decided she was the second best thing to missing their picnic and fireworks and were now climbing onto her back, launching themselves against her legs, and trying to tickle her.

Kids. They didn't seem to care that a few minutes ago they'd been dodging bullets.

They were in one of the larger suture areas of Angel's ER. Gina managed to check the kids for damage while pretending to give them raspberry kisses and checking for potatoes in their ears. Fine. Not a scratch on them, thanks to the Good Samaritan sitting across the room, bouncing the youngest toddlers on his knees while their babysitter had her scalp laceration repaired.

"You always go for jogs in the middle of a riot?" Gina asked.

"Wasn't any riot when I started out," he said, his face serene as if shit happened and why should he care?

Gina wanted to slap that Dalai Llama smirk off his face. "What kind of doctor are you?"

"Immunology."

"Here?"

"Sure here. I've been an attending for the last two years."

Idiot still hadn't given her his name, she noticed. Even though he knew hers. It made her feel distinctly at a disadvantage despite the fact he was the one who was almost naked.

One of the kids was dragging her vest across the floor. It was too heavy for him to lift.

"Hey, that's not a toy," she said, taking it from him. She looked up and saw Jerry knock over a stool in his rush to get into the room.

"Gina, are you all right?" he said, absently shuffling kids until he was the one next to her. He gave her a quick hug then held her at arm's length, appraising her. "What happened?"

She loved the way the kids immediately transferred themselves from her to him. Now, there was a real kid-friendly grownup. Jerry was a natural with children.

She braced a hand against his chest, then tugged him close, kissing him firmly.

"You are the most wonderful man in the world," she told him, wondering why she was so acutely aware of the stranger's gaze on her. She glanced over her shoulder, saw the stranger staring and just to spite him, kissed Jerry again, this time raising a flush of scarlet that raced up to Jerry's ears.

"You wore your vest, right?" he asked, taking the heavy Kevlar from her.

"Yes, but I didn't end up needing it," she lied, already deciding not to worry him with the escapade with the gang-bangers and the bullets and the Good Samaritan.

"Who are you?" Jerry asked the stranger, his tone sharp as if he sensed there was something going on. Then he went rigid. "Gina, what the—"

She yanked the vest from Jerry, holding it high. A bullet glinted from where it was buried in the fabric. Her fingernails bit into her palms as she fought back the urge to vomit. "Oh my God."

"That would have hit you right in the spine," Jerry said,

yanking up her shirt to examine her. "I don't even see a bruise. Does it hurt anywhere?"

His fingers pressed against the knot of muscle between her shoulder blades and Gina winced. She'd seen patients come in with gunshot wounds and not know they were shot, but she'd never expected it to happen to her. Shit, shit, shit...she should be dead right now. Her vision blurred for a moment, then focused on Jerry's comforting form.

"Lucky thing I have such a thoughtful guy around to protect me," she said, tossing the vest to one side and pulling him close for another kiss.

This time the kids clapped and cheered, obviously thinking it was some sort of game.

By the time they parted and Gina looked up, the stranger had vanished. And with him the damaged Kevlar vest.

"Have you guys heard?" Gecko poked his head in the door. "Someone just blew up the fireworks barge Downtown."

"Was anyone hurt?" Gina asked.

"No, it was out on the river. The Sons of Adam are taking credit for it. But the whole of Downtown and Oakland are pretty much cut off, the roads are a mess, and there are more riots breaking out."

Jerry grabbed his cell phone. "Call your supervisors. I'll get Mark Cohen. We're going to need to coordinate a response."

"Trey just got here with his folks and Lydia. Someone tried to burn down their house."

Gina couldn't believe it. Of all people, only Lydia could turn a Fourth of July picnic into attempted arson. "Are they all right?"

"Trey's mom has some partial thickness burns, but Lydia saved her. She's a bit banged up herself."

"GET THOSE SCISSORS AWAY FROM ME," Lydia snapped at the hapless intern who insisted on treating her as a trauma alert and wanted to cut her clothing off. Her voice broke and she sputtered into another coughing fit.

She had tried to tell him she was a physician, but he obviously thought she was a mental patient or intoxicated. And, after running the gamut of admissions again—this time they questioned her California identification and lack of insurance—she was ready to launch into someone. This idiot made a damn fine target.

"Ma'am, you need to calm down," he told her, again, brandishing the trauma shears once more.

Ma'am? Her patience exhausted, she didn't feel up to babysitting this intern. The ink on his MD degree was still wet and he wasn't even from the Emergency Medicine program. The embroidery on his lab coat proclaimed him a resident from Internal Medicine. She hoped the fact he was with her meant more senior personnel were attending to Ruby.

En route, the medics' radio had broadcast an alert about the explosion on the Allegheny River. Trey had gotten a few details; whatever he'd heard had left him grim faced and as soon as he saw his mother safely to an exam room, he'd run to the nurses' station to use their communications equipment.

Deciding she'd be better off treating herself than letting this idiot touch her, Lydia jumped down from the gurney and began to rummage through the stainless steel supply cabinet, searching for a tub of silvadene or a few bio-occlusive dressings to slap on.

The intern backed away, looked aghast. "You give me no choice, I'm calling security."

"What's going on in here, Harrison?" Mark Cohen asked, entering the room.

He glanced over at Lydia, who now stared into the mirror above the scrub sink. She tilted her head back, crossed her eyes and pushed her nose from side to side, trying to see inside her nostrils.

Harrison, the intern, watched her with apprehension, backing away to stand behind Cohen. "Approximately thirty-year-old woman rescued from a house fire," he intoned, presenting the case. "Paramedics report partial thickness burns to all extremities and possible smoke inhalation."

Lydia ignored him and, satisfied with the appearance of her nose hairs, ripped a paper towel from the dispenser, leaned over and forced herself to hack up a wad of phlegm.

"Patient appears disoriented, won't follow commands and is combative," Harrison continued, his tone growing more confident as Lydia peered into the paper towel, closely examining her sputum. "I recommend soft restraints, Haldol and a psych consult."

"Oh really?" Cohen replied as if seriously considering Harrison's suggestions.

Lydia watched him in the mirror as he crossed his arms and gave her a wink.

"Yes sir. She won't even let me examine her." Harrison's tone was one of aggrievement.

"She won't? Did you ask her why?" Mark continued, the voice of reason. "Excuse me, ma'am, but could you explain why you won't allow this fine young first year resident from the medical department examine you?"

Mark was having difficulty in restraining his laughter any longer. Lydia could see why.

Her hair had been singed and bristled haphazardly; her clothing was wet, dirty and scorched; her face red, eyes redder; eyebrows partially burnt off, giving her a maniacal wide-eyed expression; and she was peppered with tiny cuts that didn't require any treatment but had left smears of blood like war paint, completing her transformation into a wild woman.

"Yes, you may," she said politely, resuming her seat on the gurney. "First of all, Young Harrison here has no idea of the basic principles of trauma resuscitation. Second of all, he wanted to cut off my clothing without assessing if it was necessary. You get those shiny new trauma shears as a graduation present or something?" she asked the intern who stood gaping at her. "And finally, he treated me rudely. Even the worst psychotic deserves compassion, Mr. Harrison."

"Harrison, meet Dr. Lydia Fiore, our new Emergency Department attending," Mark told the flabbergasted young man.

To his credit, Harrison held his ground although he was blushing furiously. He looked from Mark to Lydia and back again as if now doubting the department chairman's sanity.

Lydia bet he couldn't wait to get back to the "fleas"—internists—upstairs on the medicine ward. At least those attendings weren't nuts, his expression said, all they did was to pimp first years mercilessly with questions about arcane medical trivia.

"Don't worry, it's a long story," Lydia told him, feeling sorry for the kid. Jeez, he was just a kid—hard to believe that only four years separated them.

Harrison cleared his throat and stepped forward, offering her his hand. "Er, I'm pleased to meet you, Dr. Fiore," he said, his voice steady although his grip was a little shaky.

"Run along, now, Harrison. I'll take care of Dr. Fiore myself. And I'll talk to you later."

Harrison nodded mutely and beat a hasty retreat.

"No singed nasal hairs, no charcoal in my sputum," Lydia told Mark, now all business. "Give me a pair of scrubs, some Silvadene and gauze and I'm out of here. Is Ruby Garrison all right?"

"She's fine. None of the burns will need grafting. As soon as the nurses have her dressings done, we'll get her home."

Mark pulled up a stool so that he faced her. "I'm more concerned about you. Danny told me about your trip out to the Sons of Adam. And Trey said you think the man who did this was trying to kill you."

"How's Mickey?" Lydia changed the subject.

She had already asked Trey to call Jerry Boyle. As soon as she got Boyle headed in the right direction, told him about her meeting with Matthew Kent, she was out of here. Out of this hospital, out of this city, out of sight. She had no intention of anyone else getting hurt because of her.

Mark's expression lightened. "She woke a few hours ago. They kicked me out because they were going to extubate her. I want to get back upstairs to talk with her, but I just activated our disaster protocol."

"The explosion Downtown?"

"No real casualties there—police and fire had enough men that they controlled things quickly. But there's worse brewing in the neighborhoods in this section of the city. Several drive-by shootings and small riots in Homewood, Garfield, and East Liberty already. It's only going to get worse."

As he spoke, he'd deftly cleaned and debrided a few of the more extensive burns. He was good, Lydia barely felt it.

"I'm glad you're here," he continued. "I'm going to need every pair of hands I can get."

She waited until he finished applying a dressing to her left arm, then stood. "I can't stay."

"What do you mean you can't stay? Don't worry about the Executive Committee or Elliot Weiss. This is a disaster. As soon as the streets clear, we're going to be inundated with patients. How can you ignore them?"

"Yeah, I'd like to hear the answer to that one, too."

Lydia jerked her head up at the sound of Trey's voice. He stood in the doorway, arms crossed over his chest, lips tightened in disapproval.

"Mark, could Lydia and I have a minute?" Trey asked, stepping into the room and closing the door behind him.

"Sure, I want to check on Mickey before I have to deal with

incoming patients." Mark darted one final worried glance at Lydia and then left.

Lydia had thought she'd seen Trey angry before. But it was nothing like the scowl that twisted his features now—squeezing his eyes at the edges, a V of a crease etched deep between his eyebrows.

"How's your mom?" she asked.

The second hand on the overhead clock made a complete sweep before he answered. "Fine. Thinks you're the best thing since sliced bread. So does my dad."

She hopped back onto the gurney, looked down, anywhere but at Trey. Her Teva sandals had held up pretty well, a few scorched areas in the fabric, and one heel strap broken, but that was it. She kicked her feet. Air brushed against her burns, made her skin feel tight, dry. Left an aching deep in the tissues.

Or maybe that was an aching deep in her heart. Damn, she hated this.

"They think that? Really?" The words broke through her guard. "I told them it was my fault."

"Not like you planned to have a maniac try to torch their house." His tone didn't give an inch. Sounded bruised, hurt and disappointed.

"Is Jerry Boyle here yet?" Best to get this over with. Give her statement and get the hell out of Dodge.

"Haven't seen him. Patrice is going to run Mom and Dad home, the rest of us are being called back onto duty."

"Riots, fires. Sounds like it's going to be a long night."

"Yet, here you are. Running away." His voice was charged with electricity.

She snapped her head up. Almost surrendered to the ferocity of his glare but forced herself to meet it head on.

"Of course," he continued. "That's what you're good at, isn't it, Lydia? Running."

"That's not fair," she protested, then bit her lip. She hated whining–most especially her own. "I don't have a choice."

"Sure you do. There's always choices. All depends on what you really want and how hard you're willing to fight for it."

"Look what good comes of trying to fight." She gestured at her raw hands and her smoke-damaged, water-logged clothing. "If I go, maybe it will stop before someone else gets hurt."

She slid down from the gurney, ignoring the pain that jarred through her body. She stepped toward the door.

"I'm thinking it's too late for that." He didn't budge from his position blocking the exit. "What do *you* want?"

"I told you," she said through gritted teeth, restraining an impulse to haul off and hit something. Or someone. Like a too-smart for his own good paramedic. "I have to go."

"Why?" he persisted. "Think you're really gonna stop what's going on around here by taking off?"

They stared at each other in silence. His eyes were sparking with gold again, just as they had last night. Lydia remembered how he made her laugh, remembered the house on Merton Street, the way it seemed to welcome her. Just as Ruby, Lord love her patient soul, had welcomed a troublesome stranger into her home. Just as Gina, Nora, and Mark had all risked their careers to defend her. She'd only been here a few days but already had so much to lose by leaving.

"What do you want?" Trey repeated, stepping to Lydia, placing his palms on her shoulders.

She shook her head, her gaze dropping to the floor. Facing his question was more frightening than facing the fire. How could she tell him how she felt when she was too scared to admit it to herself?

"You're not going to find what you're looking for out there." Trey jerked his head toward the door, his gaze never leaving her face. "Thought someone as smart as you would have figured that out by now."

Lydia remained silent. He waited a beat, giving her one more chance, then dropped his hands.

A sigh rumbled through him. He stepped away, hands hanging empty.

The door swung shut behind him. Lydia's teeth clamped down so hard her ears popped. Her vision grew bleary but she couldn't blink. All she wanted was to go home.

But to do that, you had to have a home to go to–the one thing that had been wrenched from her time and again her entire life.

She couldn't bear the pain of losing everything. Not again. Leaving by her own choice was the only way to prevent that from happening.

She could always find another hospital, another house, another town.

So why was she standing there, feeling like if she didn't blink, if she didn't move, if she didn't do something, that she was going to burst apart, explode into tiny, broken, combustible shards, a human Molotov cocktail?

She blinked. No tears. Just an unbelievable knot tightening her gut and threatening to choke the life from her.

Then she ran. Out the door, one Teva's loose heel flapping against the linoleum, hoping she wasn't too late.

CHAPTER 53

JERRY LEFT, TALKING ON HIS CELL PHONE, trying to get SWAT team members flown in to protect firefighters, while also coordinating a safety zone around the hospital. Gina tried her best to make herself helpful in the Emergency Department. Better that than thinking about what had almost happened out on the street earlier. No, she was absolutely, positively not going to think about that. She was an EM doc, she was in control. A few street punks weren't going to rattle her.

She'd quickly disposed of a number of minor injuries and helped the nurses shepherd the walking wounded down to the cafeteria to free up the ED's resources for more critically injured patients. Which now left her with nothing to do. She began pacing the circumference of the nurses' station. It was too damn quiet.

The calm before the storm, the nurses had told her. They were scurrying around, all with jobs to do, even if it was to only get paperwork ready, while Gina paced with empty hands.

She did *not* do waiting well. Waiting led to thinking and thinking was not something she wanted to do right now.

Trey Garrison emerged from the side hallway and Gina ambushed him. "Where are all the patients? Why isn't anyone here? This is a disaster, isn't it?"

Trey smiled and shook his head at her. She saw one of the nurses flash him a sign, jerking a thumb towards the door, and knew they were trying to get rid of her. "C'mon Gina. Let's get out of their way. This is how disasters are. At least a well-run one with enough advance notice. Hurry up and wait."

They strolled outside. Gina coughed against the smell of smoke. Oily, black clouds shifted in the breeze, circling the hospital. Like they were surrounded.

From the streams of people walking toward Angels and the cars lining up to pull into the parking garage down the block, it seemed like the hospital was the last refuge for many. The security guards were doing a good job of making sure everyone avoided the ED unless they required immediate care, shuttling the crowds in through the main hospital entrance.

Gina spotted a familiar figure on crutches, hobbling from the ambulance bay towards them, waving frantically. "Mr. Perch, what are you doing here?"

He pulled up to a stop beside them. "Dr. Gina, I'm so glad I found you. I saw him, I saw the killer!"

She and Trey exchanged glances. "Calm down, now. What did you see?"

"Yesterday, I saw the doctor who killed that woman. But the cops, they never talked to me—I tried to tell the nurses and my doctor, and they said they'd tell the police, but, I don't know. Anyway, they let me out today, and I called Sally to come pick me up, and I was waiting over there," he nodded towards the exit from the ambulance bay. "That's when I saw him again. Young kid, I didn't know they made doctors that young. But he parked an ambulance in the tunnel there, beside the ER and walked into the hospital. It was him, I know it was him."

"This doctor, you saw him kill Wanda Owens?" Trey asked. He seemed better able to interpret Mr. Perch's unique conversational style than Gina.

"Yeah, I was going down for my kidney test. The nurses had me parked in a wheelchair facing backwards, down the hallway. That's when I saw the dark-haired lady doctor leave and the young doctor go in. He had light hair, was real skinny, wearing those blue pajamas."

"Scrubs."

Mr. Perch nodded. "Then he came out and a few minutes later all heck broke loose and everyone's running down the hall. They came and took me away for my test, so I didn't know she was dead until after and the cops had already left. Then today I saw him again."

"Driving an ambulance?"

"C'mon, I'll show you." Mr. Perch pivoted on one crutch and began hopping back into the ambulance bay. Trey and Gina followed him. "It's that one there. The old one."

It was an out-of-date van converted into an ambulance. Except for the windshield, its windows were painted over but there was no sign of anyone in the front.

"A Fat Albert," Trey said. "Just like the one I saw earlier—"

Gina watched as he sprinted towards the ambulance. She chased after him, leaving Mr. Perch juggling his crutches behind them. "Trey!" she shouted. "There's someone back there."

Trey darted around the back of the ambulance and emerged pushing a man in front of him. They stepped into the light. The man was tall, skinny, with light-colored hair, just like Mr. Perch's description, but too old to be the killer Mr. Perch had seen.

"I'm Matthew Kent," he said, shrugging off Trey's arm. He wore a dress white shirt, creased black slacks and appeared pretty harmless, especially alongside the six-foot tall medic.

"I'm looking for my son, Ezekiel," he continued. "I think he might try to kill Elliot Weiss."

AMANDA JOINED LUCAS AT THE NURSES' STATION, watching as he filled out the boxes on Becky's death certificate. He'd already done the other cumbersome tasks that surrounded death: completed the code record, dictated the resuscitation and death notes, tried to contact the next of kin. She wished she could do more to help. Becky had no family in town; they were still waiting for her parents to arrive from Ohio but with the roads blocked it might take a while.

Lucas dropped his pen and rubbed his eyes with the heels of his palms.

"Will an autopsy show what was wrong with her?" Amanda forced herself to ask. She wasn't altogether certain she wanted to know the answer.

"Maybe. I hope so." He glanced at her, his gaze raking over her as if examining for flaws.

"I'm fine," she said, wishing he'd stop looking at her like that. Like he knew her inside and out. "Honestly."

His mouth scrunched up and she knew he was getting ready to argue with her, harass her about setting up another clinic appointment. Before he had the chance, Nora Halloran knocked on the counter, getting his attention. "You paged?"

"We're ready to extubate Mickey Cohen," Lucas said.

"Great. I'll call Mark."

"Jerry Boyle wanted to be here as well, in case she was ready to talk."

"Do you think she'll be able to? Talk, I mean," Nora asked, pausing with her radio half way to her lips. "I mean, Mark said her levels were off the charts."

A weary sigh spun out from Lucas. "We'll see. But we got to her early. She's responded much better than I expected."

He pushed back from his chair and stood. "Amanda, do you

want to help me extubate her? Then we'll see how her neuro status is."

"Sure." She followed him to Mickey's bed on the far wall of the unit. Lucas grabbed the bedside chart, eyed her vitals. He double-checked the hemo-perfusion cannulas that drained Mickey's blood.

"Levels are still on the high side. We'll need to wait to take her off." He turned to Mickey and grasped her hand. "How you doing, sweetheart? Ready to get that tube out?"

Mickey opened her eyes, nodded, her face filled with pain. Amanda hid her wince. Being tied to a bed, unable to speak or communicate—she couldn't think of many things worse. It was like her childhood nightmare of being locked in a coffin, no one hearing her screams.

She helped Lucas set up for the extubation. Nora joined them. "Mark's on his way."

"Good. Now Mickey, when I say three, you cough hard," Lucas ordered.

Amanda helped raise Mickey's head, she couldn't sit all the way up because of the hemo-perfusion, and steadied her as Lucas removed the tube. Mickey began coughing, at first weakly, then with more vigor. Nora slipped an oxygen mask over her face.

"You okay, Mickey?" Lucas asked after listening to her breathing and having Nora check another set of vitals.

"What the hell is going on?" Mickey's voice came out as a muffled squeak that triggered another coughing spasm. She collapsed back against the pillows once more.

Lucas and Nora exchanged a glance and Lucas smiled down at Mickey with relief in his eyes. "You won't believe this, but those are the best words I've heard all day."

Mickey just glared at him as if he were the one at risk for brain damage. Nora left for a moment and returned with a cup of ice chips.

"Was it the MS?" Mickey croaked.

"No," Mark Cohen said as he and Jerry arrived. "It wasn't."

He held Mickey's hand and Amanda swore he was blinking back tears. "I'll explain everything. But first Jerry has some questions."

"Do you remember anything?" Jerry asked, gently inserting himself between Amanda and Mickey so that Mickey could easily focus on him. His voice was gentle, as if trying to give her time to find her own answers.

She frowned, shaking her head vigorously, eyes creased with confusion. "No. Nothing…" her voice faded. Nora handed Mark the cup of ice chips and he fed a few spoonfuls to Mickey, who gulped them eagerly. "I was fine. Dinner was fine. Then I went to bed—"

The monitor alarmed as her heart rate hit one-forty. Jerry jerked back, but Lucas merely reached up and silenced the alarm.

Mark stroked Mickey's arm. "It's all right. Nothing can hurt you here."

Mickey calmed and her heart rate returned to normal. She squeezed her eyes shut in an effort to concentrate. "I heard a sound. Then the smell of grease and motor oil. No air, there was no air—" She raised a hand as if warding off a blow.

"Kent," she whispered and opened her eyes once more.

"Was it Matthew Kent?" Mark demanded. Jerry clamped a hand on his arm, trying to pull him away, but he shook it off. "Is he the one who did this?"

"Not Matthew." Her voice sounded thin, as if it might be swallowed by the emotion swirling around the bed. "The son."

"Ezekiel Kent," Jerry said, leaning forward. "Are you certain?"

"Yes. He told me," she faltered, licking her cracked lips. "He said it was because of his mother. He forced me to take pills. A whole bottle." Tears welled then broke free, streaming down her cheeks. "He said I was lucky. I would die in my sleep. Said I should thank him for being merciful. That he was the Angel of Mercy bringing," she choked and continued, "bringing redemption to the families of those who murdered his mother."

"Ezekiel Kent forced you to take the phenobarb and said he was trying to kill you." Jerry looked at her for confirmation, his expression neutral, not pushing her.

Amanda edged back to stand beside Nora. They exchanged glances. She had only heard bits and pieces of the story, but seeing the terror on Mickey's face, made her shudder. Mickey took more ice chips then squeezed her eyes tight as if the memories were too painful.

"He said he killed the others, the church women and Jonah. Said," she reached blindly for Mark's hand. "He said it wouldn't be so easy for the rest. Said his mother's killers would die in fire and blood, screaming for mercy."

CHAPTER 54

LYDIA LOOKED FOR TREY but couldn't find him anywhere. She knocked and stepped inside Ruby's room, hoping he was there. That's how bad off she was, willing to bare her soul in front of Trey's parents.

Trey wasn't there. Only Ruby, Denny and Patrice, who was leaning against the bed frame, one hand massaging her back.

"Are you all right?" Lydia asked, hesitant.

"Lydia, come in, come in," Ruby called out from her position on the stretcher. Her wounds had been dressed and she looked like a mummy with the bandages swathing her arm and both legs. "I'm fine. Just waiting for my papers. But I'm worried about Patrice. I think she's having contractions and is just too darn stubborn to admit it."

She cut a look at Denny who stood beside the stretcher, obviously worried about both his wife and daughter. "Gets that from his side of the family."

"Mom, I'm fine. It's just Braxton-Hicks, not real contractions. After three babies, I know the difference."

"I'm afraid you'll all be stuck here a while. There's been some disturbances—"

Ruby waved her hand. "The boys told us all about them. We

don't want to add to your worries any. As soon as I get my papers we'll head down to the cafeteria with the rest of the patients. But still," she glanced at Patrice, worry creasing her forehead.

"Mother, stop babying me. Just because I'm the only one in the family who doesn't carry a gun—"

"Except for Trey," Denny put in, then went silent once again. Lydia thought she detected a hint of wounded pride in his voice.

"I'll go tell your nurse what's going on. See if someone can check Patrice."

Ruby patted her hand as if Lydia were one of the family. "Thank you dear. We would appreciate that."

Lydia took a step toward the door, then turned back. "I'm so sorry about your house. It's all my fault."

"Your fault? Don't you believe it. Those bastards are probably thinking they can start to target cops at will."

"Denny," his wife said, obviously trying to calm him. "Remember your blood pressure."

He waved her words away. "You know it has to be them. I mean me and Harold, both targeted on the exact same day, who else could it be?" Denny's gaze darted around the small room as if searching for a hidden enemy.

"Who are you talking about?" Lydia asked.

"The Sons of Adam, of course. It was a year ago, almost to the day that Harold Owens and I stopped Sarah Kent before she could blow up half of Pittsburgh."

"Commander Owens was involved in Sarah's death as well?" Lydia said, a cold hand snaking around her throat, squeezing it tight.

"Yeah. Harold was off duty, picked up the call as he was driving home. He was burned pretty bad, but not enough to force him off the job. Not like me."

"You and Commander Owens, Elliot Weiss and Mark Cohen—" Lydia felt as if she'd been bowled over by a Macker, sucked under the water and tumbled along the ocean's bottom. She bolted for the door. "Stay here. Don't leave."

"Lydia, what's wrong?" Ruby asked.

"I think someone is targeting the men involved with Sarah Kent's death. Them and their families."

Denny's hand slid to his hip as if he expected to find a gun there. Patrice gave a low moan and her knees buckled.

"Mom," she said through clenched teeth. "I'm thinking maybe this is for real."

"Wait here," Lydia said as Denny and Ruby helped Patrice up onto the bed. "I'm going to go get help. And call the police."

She ran out to the nurses' station and found a nurse who said she'd move Patrice into the ob-gyn room as soon as possible.

The other patients had been cleared out—either admitted upstairs or moved to the cafeteria to wait until the crisis was over. Everyone was hustling around, preparing for the impending onslaught of casualties, but there was no sign of Jerry Boyle or any other police officers.

Boyle's cell was busy as was Trey's. Mark Cohen had said Mickey was awake, maybe Boyle was up in the ICU with her?

Lydia raced up the stairs to the ICU floor. She was passing the surgical ICU, heading toward the medical ICU, when the doors to the operating room swished open. She looked up, startled to see a young man wearing scrubs but no hospital ID passing through.

He froze, his face breaking into a glorious grin as if she was the answer to all his prayers.

It was the boy from Friendship Church. The one who had glared at her with hatred in his eyes.

"Dr. Fiore, we finally meet," he said with a ghastly smile that chilled her. "I'm Ezekiel Kent."

Instead of offering a hand for her to shake, he pulled his arm from behind his back and aimed a gun at her heart.

CHAPTER 55

ADRENALINE SURGED THROUGH LYDIA'S NERVES, sparking beneath her skin.

"I think you've been looking for me," he said, his voice a sing-song as if he'd pitched it to match an unheard cadence. "Isn't this fortuitous?"

"What do you want?" she asked, stalling for time more than anything.

She couldn't let him get past her, to patient areas where people could get hurt. At least the OR was empty, cleared out for the impending mass casualties. She edged forward, hoping to herd him back into the contained area. Then she'd figure out what to do next.

"What do I want?" he said, his eyes locked onto hers. They were pale grey, so pale that the color blurred into the whites, making them look impossibly round and inhuman. "Nothing, Dr. Fiore. Only the eternal damnation of Satan's spawn, the resurrection of the true believers and the arrival of the good Lord's Revelation. Are you prepared to deliver any of those to me?"

She decided it was a rhetorical question and remained silent. He gestured with the gun. "Let's go find Elliot Weiss. I believe he's in his office."

Last thing she intended was to let him wander the halls with a gun. Any staff or family member could stumble into things, get hurt. "I don't know where his office is."

"It's the hall near the elevator. Back near the call rooms."

Other than the elevator lobby it was an area that wouldn't be highly traveled. Lydia reluctantly began to march in that direction. The gun nudged against her spine made for excellent persuasion.

GINA STARED AT THE LEADER OF THE SONS OF ADAM. "Right. Like we're going to lead you to a man you're trying to kill."

Matthew sighed, arms slumped. "Not me, my son. He hates me because I preach violence as the last defense, thinks I haven't appropriately avenged my wife's murder."

"Murder?" Trey asked. "Your wife was smuggling enough weapons to start a war."

"She believed in following a more militant path. A point of contention with us throughout our life together. I'm afraid Ezekiel has followed in her footsteps. Along with some of our other converts."

"Like the men who attacked Lydia Fiore? And who are currently instigating riots throughout the city?"

"Hampton. My second in command. He blew up the fireworks barge and launched teams to start the riots. But there's nothing I can do about that right now. However, I can, with your help, stop my son from killing again."

"You know about the others?" Gina asked.

"I figured it out. After speaking with Dr. Fiore. Quite an impressive lady—for an unbeliever."

Trey had his head tilted to one side, eyes squinted as if trying to decide something. Gina thought it was a pretty easy call: grab

Jerry, let the cops deal with Kent.

"You have a picture of your son?" Trey surprised her by asking.

Kent nodded, pulled his wallet out and slid a photo from it. Trey held it up for Mr. Perch.

"That's him. That's the one. I knew he was no doctor."

"We need to get copies of this photo to security and the cops," Trey said, starting for the ED doors. Kent followed him.

"Thanks, Mr. Perch," Gina said. "It'd probably be best if you go wait in the main hospital lobby."

"Sure, if you say so, Dr. Gina."

Mr. Perch turned to hobble away. Gina rushed to catch up to Trey who was ushering Kent through the metal detector in the patient entrance.

Kent had his arms spread wide. "I carry no weapons other than the word of God."

"We'll see about that." Trey gave him a small shove through the entrance. The metal detector didn't even hiccup. Trey escorted Kent to the nurses' station. "Anyone know where Dr. Weiss is?"

"Up in his office," the desk clerk answered. "Said to page him as soon as trouble started. You want me to call him?"

"No thanks. We'll go up there." He turned to Gina, handed her the photo of Ezekiel Kent. "Make copies, let Jerry know that there's a killer in the hospital."

"Where are you going?"

"I'm going to go get Weiss, drag him someplace safe."

"Shouldn't you leave him," she indicated Kent, "here?"

Trey looked around the empty ER. "No. I can handle him. And if we run into his son, he may come in handy. Tell Jerry to meet me on the fourth floor."

Gina turned the photo over and got her first good look at it. Sonofabitch. It was the college kid who'd been hanging around, following Lazarov. Bob Brown, he'd said his name was. Hell, they'd given him tours of the entire hospital—if he was trying to hide, he'd know exactly where to go.

THE SURGICAL OFFICES WERE ALIGNED ON THE OUTSIDE WALL while the call rooms were on the inside wall of the corridor. Lydia knocked on Weiss's door. Ezekiel shoved her forward before Weiss opened the door the whole way.

Lydia stumbled into Weiss, who had been stretching a hand out toward the door, holding his reading glasses and a copy of the latest *Annals of Surgery* in his other. No hope of a weapon there.

She allowed her momentum to carry her farther into the room, hoping to spot something she could use to overcome Ezekiel and his gun without getting anyone killed. A letter opener, a scalpel, a laser pointer for chrissake. But Weiss's office was as devoid of personality as the man. Bookshelves lined with volumes standing at rigid attention, all exactly one finger's width from the edge. A Spartan desk holding only a large blotter, legal pad, pencil caddy, and computer. A number 2 Ticonderoga seemed a poor choice to go up against a Smith and Wesson. Maybe a nice thick *Schwartz's Principles of Surgery*?

"Get out of my office before I call the cops!" Weiss snapped at her. Then he turned to Ezekiel. "Who the hell are you?"

Hello? Was the man blind? No introductions necessary when you're the one holding the big, deadly gun.

Ezekiel seemed as disconcerted by Weiss's lack of respect as Lydia was, raising the gun and taking aim between Weiss's eyes in answer. "You killed my mother."

"I don't know what you're talking about. Give me that gun before I call security."

"My mother," Ezekiel insisted, the gun never wavering.

Lydia inched to one side, leaving Weiss as the central target. No sense both of them getting killed with the same bullet. If Ezekiel did fire, maybe she could tackle him before he could shoot her. Of course, there'd be no tackling until absolutely necessary, not with Weiss in point blank range.

"Your mother got a name?" Weiss said, flipping his *Annals* onto the desk as if they were debating the merits of splenectomy versus a salvage procedure.

Ezekiel reddened, his eyes now almost glowing as the rest of his face turned crimson with fury. "Sarah Kent."

"Sarah Kent?" Weiss repeated as if racking his memory. His eyes were vacant and Lydia wanted to scream at him to remember the woman or at least pretend to.

Ezekiel saved her. "Don't you say her name! You're not fit to utter it, you heathen bastard!" He steadied his aim, preparing to shoot. "On your knees."

"No. I'll do no such thing." Weiss sneered at Ezekiel, ignoring the gun with haughty arrogance.

"Fine." Ezekiel had obviously reached the end of his patience. "Then I'll kill you just like I killed your son."

Lydia bit her lip and braced herself, waiting for the shot.

CHAPTER 56

AMANDA EMERGED FROM THE ELEVATOR on to the first floor and headed to the ER. Lucas dogged her steps as if she might collapse at any moment, watching her closer than a hunting dog who'd treed a raccoon.

"I'll go see Dr. Nelson," she finally told him, hoping that would get Lucas off her back. Why did he insist on treating her like a child? She was almost a full-fledged physician. If indeed there was something to worry about, she'd deal with it. Herself. At a time of her own choosing. Without any interference from a smug, know-it-all like Lucas Stone.

"Amanda, if you have what Becky has—"

"Had." The single word echoed through the empty hall. "Had. And I don't. I can't. I hope y'all find out what killed her, really I do, but it has nothing to do with me. Honest."

She pushed through the double doors leading to the emergency department. Lucas kept following her.

"Amanda, you need to take care of yourself. Let me check you out. Run some tests." His voice was worried and when she spun around to face him, his expression was clouded.

"I am taking care of myself. And you have no right to try to interfere with me or my doctor. Now, I promise you that I will make an appointment to see him as soon as possible. And that's the end of it." He opened his mouth to protest but she held up her hand, met his gaze unflinchingly, and was surprised to see him shut it again. "Not another word."

With that she turned back around and continued onto the nurses' station. The Emergency Department was quiet, as if holding its breath. Nurses had stacks of disaster charts ready and waiting, the waiting room was empty, and the nurses and staff were all crowded into the triage area, going over their plan one last time. The only patient on the board was an OB patient who had been half erased with a notation: up to labor and delivery.

"Guess they don't need us yet," Lucas said.

Amanda looked around. The usually vibrant, non-stop area around the nurses' station seemed spooky as if it needed the constant motion to breathe life into it. Before she could say anything, an exam room door opened and a man poked his head out.

"We need a little help in here," he barked the words like an order, not a request. "Her water just broke and she wants to push."

Amanda looked at Lucas. After all, he was the attending. His eyes widened for a brief instant, then he walked over to the gentleman.

"Is it your wife, sir?" Lucas asked while sliding free of his lab coat and pulling on a Tyvek trauma gown.

"No. My daughter. It's her fourth child. They were supposed to take us up to OB, but," he swung his gaze around the deserted nurses' station. "Guess they forgot about us."

"Don't worry, we'll take care of it."

The man went back inside and Lucas turned to Amanda, handing her a trauma gown. "When's the last time you delivered a baby?" he asked.

"Last year, on my OB rotation."

"Good. You get in there, assess the situation. I'm going to get help."

"What? Me? But—"

"Hello, neurologist here. Last time I caught a baby was seven years ago when I was still a medical student. You're up, kid." He practically shoved her into the room, pulling the door shut behind her.

A woman wearing a patient gown lay on the exam table, her feet up in stirrups. She was blowing out, panting, squeezing an older woman's hand with one hand and her father's with the other. The older woman had bandages over her left arm and both shins, and fresh stitches over her eyebrow. Amanda spied a patient chart on the bedside table and grabbed it.

"Mrs. Hutchinson?" she asked, trying not to sound too overwhelmed.

"It's Patrice, please," the woman puffed.

"You're the doctor?" the older woman asked.

"I'm Amanda Mason. Let me just assess the situation, if you don't mind."

She scanned the vitals on the overhead monitor. Patrice's vitals were fine including a normal blood pressure. The baby's heart rate looked good as well. Hurrah for small favors.

Amanda glanced over her shoulder at the door, expecting Lucas to enter with an OB or at least a nurse midwife. Or someone.

"How far apart are the contractions?" she asked, pulling a pair of sterile gloves on. More for something to do than anything else. Surely help would arrive before she had to examine Patrice.

"Pretty close. And I feel like I really need to push."

"Okay, just keep breathing, that's good." Amanda squeezed some KY onto her fingers. "I'm going to do a quick exam and then we'll go from there."

Patrice's father glanced away but Patrice held his arm tight so that he couldn't flee. From the look on his face he wanted to.

Amanda totally understood, it was her first instinct as well.

She did the manual exam. The baby was fully engaged, almost crowning.

"Well, now," she said, snapping her gloves off and turning to set up the neonatal warming bed. "Looks like we're going to have a baby here real soon."

GINA EMERGED FROM THE OFFICE, carrying a stack of copies, only to find the ED deserted. She'd tried Jerry repeatedly on his cell but it went straight to voice mail.

Fourth floor, she thought as she entered the elevator. Next stop, OR, ICUs, and crazy kids on killing sprees...She rubbed the back of her head where the bullet would have hit if not for Jerry's vest, wished for the vest now.

Yanked her hand away from her scalp. As long as Ezekiel Kent stuck to poison, she'd be fine.

LYDIA WAS DOING HER BEST TO PREVENT Elliot Weiss from getting both of them killed, but the surgeon sure as hell wasn't cooperating.

"Down on your knees!" Ezekiel shouted, his face flushing crimson.

"No. I'll do no such thing." Instead of obeying, Weiss faced Ezekiel, challenging him. "I had nothing to do with your mother's death. She brought it on herself."

Suddenly the door slammed open and a man barreled through it. Lydia was shoved aside as Matthew Kent charged his son. "Ezekiel, stop!"

A gunshot boomed.

Trey rushed in right behind Matthew, plowing into Weiss, who scrambled to get out of the way. Matthew and his son struggled for the gun.

Weiss slammed Trey against the wall, blocking any exit for Lydia. She grabbed the only weapon at hand, the *Schwartz Principles of Surgery*, and tried to get a good angle to slam the heavy textbook down on Ezekiel's head. Weiss escaped from the room just as a second shot blasted, reverberating through the room.

Weiss stood frozen in the hallway. Lydia straightened, still holding the book at the ready, her gaze riveted on the two men at her feet. Matthew Kent groaned and scuttled away from his son's body, holding a revolver.

Ezekiel lay at his feet, blood blossoming from a wound in his stomach.

CHAPTER 57

Gina found Jerry with Mark and Nora in the ICU. "He's here," she gasped, thrusting her copies of Ezekiel's photo at them. "Ezekiel Kent. He's come to kill Elliot Weiss."

Nora scrutinized the photo. "That's Bob Brown, the college kid shadowing Jim."

"How did you get this?" Jerry asked.

"Trey and I found his father. He came here to stop Ezekiel."

"Matthew Kent is here?"

"Trey has him in Elliot Weiss's office. Said for you to meet him there."

Before they could move, shrill beeps began to emerge from the radios Jerry, Mark, and Nora all carried. "Sounds like the first wave has hit," Mark said. "I'm heading down to the ER. Nora, you're in charge here."

Jerry began down the hall in the opposite direction, headed towards Weiss's office. Gina was torn, wanting to go with him, knowing that if she was with him, no matter what happened, she'd be safe. She reached out, tugged at his arm, pulling him into the alcove near the family room.

"Hey, you okay?" he asked, scrutinizing her for a long moment.

She hadn't realized her lips were trembling until he brushed his finger over them. "Who me?" she answered, damning herself as her voice quavered. "I'm fine. I'm always fine."

He looked down at her, his face calm, an oasis. His fingers smoothed her brow, then he planted a kiss there. "Well, I'm not. It's been a helluva day."

The sound of a muffled crack came and they jumped apart. She looked past him in time to see Nora and Seth racing down the hall toward the surgical offices. A second crack sounded. Jerry pushed her further back into the alcove, his gun drawn.

"Stay here." He began to sprint down the hall, calling after Nora and Seth, but it was too late, they had already disappeared around the corner. He stopped, pressing himself tight against the wall, gun raised.

Gina cowered in the shadow of the alcove, stomach churning, the sound of the shots reverberating through her mind like a permanent echo.

LYDIA DROPPED THE TEXTBOOK, fell to her knees, feeling for Ezekiel's pulse. "He's still alive."

Trey stepped between her and Matthew. Making himself a target. A very big, impossible-to-miss target. She threw him a glare, but he shook it off, turning away from her to focus on Matthew.

"Give me the gun, Matthew," he said, stretching his palm out.

Matthew startled, jerked his gaze down to the gun as if he didn't realize he held it. He started to hand it to Trey. Then Ezekiel let out a moan.

"No." Matthew straightened, held the gun steady as if he knew what he was doing. Aimed it right at Trey's sternum. "No. Oh God, what have I done?" His voice shook with palpable grief. "I can't lose him, can't lose him, there's nothing left. Why? Why my wife, my son?"

His gaze darted wildly between Trey, Lydia, and Weiss who still stood in the hallway, transfixed by the scene unfolding in his office.

"It's a test," Matthew proclaimed, his voice regaining its strength. "Not of me. Of you." He aimed the gun at Weiss. "It's your chance at redemption. You can save my son."

Weiss was shaking his head but remained silent. Lydia kept her hands pressed against Ezekiel's wound. There wasn't much blood on the outside, not yet anyway, but his belly was already distending and she knew he was bleeding internally. She forced two fingers inside the bullet track and tried her best to angle them so that she could put pressure on the abdominal blood vessels. Immediate surgery was Ezekiel's only hope.

Trey tried again. "Matthew. You're a man of God, you don't believe in violence, remember?"

Matthew lurched back a step, keeping both Trey and Weiss in his line of fire. "I don't believe in your medicine either. But now, suddenly I'm a man of violence, the worst violence imaginable. God is testing my faith and your skills. He's giving us all a chance at salvation."

Weiss stirred as running footsteps echoed in the hallway. Nora Halloran arrived, Seth Cochran close on her heels.

Great, two more to worry about. Lydia tried to split her focus between Ezekiel and the group before her, but all she could see was the very large gun pointed right at Trey.

"What happened?" Nora asked.

"Stay where you are. He's going to save my son." Matthew raised the gun, aiming it at Weiss.

"No," Weiss said, his eyes narrowed, posture ramrod straight. "No, I won't." He raised his arms wide, making himself a larger target. "That monster killed my son. He deserves what he gets. You can't make me do anything."

Matthew's gun twitched, his finger slipping from the trigger guard. "I can. I will. You must. Or suffer God's wrath." Single syllables seemed the most he could manage, his lips pressed so tight they blanched to a chalky white. "Save him, damn it! Save my son!"

"It's all right," Nora said, her voice calm and soothing. "You don't need the gun. We'll take care of him. I promise, it will be all right."

Lydia rocked back, caught Trey's attention while Nora tried to coax the gun from Kent. She had her hands pressed against Ezekiel's abdomen but blood already covered them as if she wore scarlet gloves.

"Hurry," she mouthed.

"You're not going to shoot anyone," Weiss sneered. "You're a coward. You and your son."

Silence struck. Everyone staring at Weiss in a combination of dismay and disbelief. Only a surgeon could possess such arrogance, Lydia thought. Then she saw that Weiss's eyes were wide with pain. Pain and grief as if the reality of Jonah's death had only just now struck. Did he want to die? He looked like maybe he was ready to—and condemn the rest of them in the process.

"You all can go to hell," Weiss said, tears rasping in his voice.

"No. My son will live. He must be saved." Matthew punctuated his words with three shots fired at point blank range into Elliot Weiss's chest.

Weiss staggered back. He slid down the wall, leaving a trail of blood and two bullet holes behind.

CHAPTER 58

AMANDA ALMOST CHEERED when the door behind her opened. She spun around, hoping to see a full obstetrics team, but only Lucas entered. Beyond him the ER was swarming with people, as if a tsunami of humanity had suddenly crashed down at Angels of Mercy.

"Refugees from Homewood," he muttered in her ear. "Most of them are all right, but," he shrugged. "Looks like it's just you and me, kid."

Then he straightened and said in a normal voice, "Hi folks. I'm Dr. Stone. How's everyone doing?"

"You don't have to hide anything from us, Dr. Stone. I'm former Sheriff's department," Patrice's father said with authority. "What's going on out there?" He stepped toward the door.

"Dennis Garrison, you're not going anywhere," his wife ordered. "Not until after you see your grandbaby delivered safe and sound."

"Nothing to worry about. The ER staff has it under control," Lucas said although Amanda knew he had no clue what he was talking about. But it sounded good—calm, certain. "Let's focus on having this baby. How are we doing, Amanda?"

"I've got the pediatric resuscitation equipment set," she said, showing him the bag-valve mask, ET tube, meconium aspirator, DeLee suction catheter and bulb suction she'd set up under the warming hood. From the tightening around his eyes, she realized neonatal resuscitation was probably ancient history to Lucas. She felt a thrill of anticipation—despite his seniority, she was the one responsible for two lives here. "We're ready whenever Patrice is."

Lucas flashed Amanda a smile, squeezed her shoulder reassuringly. "All right. Amanda, you catch the baby and stay with it. I'll finish up with Mom."

As he spoke, he steered her into the stool at the foot of the bed. Patrice gave a cry of pain as another contraction tore through her and the baby's head appeared.

"There he is. Lots of hair on this one."

Amanda got into position, ready to help the baby. The room suddenly seemed far removed from the chaos of the ER as her focus narrowed to Patrice and her baby. She darted a quick look at the monitor. Everything looked good.

"Go ahead and push again Patrice. Push, push, push, push, push!"

LYDIA WATCHED AS ELLIOT WEISS'S BODY SLID TO THE FLOOR. Her ears rang with the echo of the gunshots and pounded with adrenaline. If she moved her hands, Ezekiel would bleed out within seconds. Her fingers clamped down on his abdominal aorta and vena cava were the only things keeping him alive.

"I need a gurney and an OR, now," she ordered, deciding the best way to keep everyone safe was to save Ezekiel. "Mr. Kent, I'm going to do everything possible to save your son, but I need your help."

Matthew responded to that. "Yes, of course. Anything."

"You're going to have to let this man," she nodded at Trey, "go to get us more help. I need a stretcher to transport Ezekiel and an operating team."

"Y-yes. That's all right."

Behind him, Seth and Nora dragged Weiss down the hallway. Hopefully to an OR of his own. Now her only problem was a spectacularly stubborn paramedic.

"No. I'm not leaving you," Trey said.

"You have to. Go. Now."

Something in her voice triggered Matthew to action. He whirled on Trey, raising the gun. "Do as she says."

Ezekiel moaned, one hand fluttering towards his belly. "Father, you stayed for the end."

"No son," Matthew said, tears choking his voice. "There's not going to be any end. These people they're going to save you."

Lydia watched as Ezekiel's eyes slid half shut even as a smile filled his face with radiance. "No one is going to be saved. Not after the bomb."

"Bomb?" Trey joined Lydia on the floor beside Ezekiel.

Ezekiel nodded weakly, his eyes closed now. "Six sharp, the Revelation starts."

"Where is it? Six o'clock, is that when it's set to go off?" Trey shook the boy but Ezekiel didn't respond.

Lydia pressed down harder, hoping to drive more blood to Ezekiel's brain, to help him regain consciousness again. No response. "What do you know about this?" she asked Matthew.

"Nothing. I swear."

Trey searched Ezekiel's pockets, removing a set of car keys and a folded piece of paper. "Plans for a truck bomb. It must be in that old ambulance. And if it's due to detonate at six," he glanced at the clock, "that's only eighteen minutes from now."

No way they could evacuate even the ambulatory patients that fast.

"You'd best hurry, then," Lydia said, wishing she could say more.

Trey was so close she could see his pulse throbbing at his neck. All she had to do was turn her head and she could brush it with her lips. Wished she could free a hand to touch him, hold him one last time.

She had to settle for the kiss. Trey, consummate rhythm artist that he was, anticipated her movement and turned his head in time to meet her lips with his. It was probably the shortest kiss on record and quite possibly the sweetest.

"See you soon," he whispered. Then he bolted out the door.

NORA STARTED CPR ON ELLIOT WEISS, even though it was obvious that it was hopeless. Blood spurted with each downward thrust of her palms.

"I need an OR, two large IV's, someone bag him, get me into an OR, now!" Seth shouted as he ripped open Weiss's shirt.

ICU staff scrambled to help. Gina showed up from out of nowhere, began bagging air into Weiss. They were on the floor at the elevator lobby, out of sight of the crazy man with the gun. Nora rocked back on her heels, breathing hard from the effort of doing chest compressions. She met Gina's gaze and shook her head. Gina stopped bagging.

Seth resumed chest compressions. "Weiss, hang on, damn you! I'm not going to be the resident who killed the Chief of Surgery."

The elevator arrived, depositing a burly security guard and two cops dressed in SWAT gear. They circled around Jerry Boyle, guns drawn.

Nora pulled Seth away from Weiss. "Give it up. He's gone."

"No." Seth struggled against Nora's grip. "We can crack his chest, transfuse him, repair—"

Gina shook her head. "He's already bled out." She nodded to the wide path of blood leading back to the scene of the shooting. "And there's a bullet palpable in his neck—you can feel that C-3 is shattered. No coming back after that. He was dead before he hit the floor."

Seth knelt, staring at his blood-stained hands. He looked like he might cry or scream. Nora wrapped both her bloody hands around his. He shook himself free, climbed to his feet. Gina remained on the floor at Weiss's head, kneeling, the useless bag-valve-mask in her hands.

Nora grabbed a gurney from one of the nurses rushing from the ICU. She began to push it down the hall, colliding with Jerry Boyle when he stepped in her path, forcing her to a halt.

"I have to go. There's another victim down there," she protested.

"And a man with a gun. Hang on," Jerry peered around the corner, exposing as little of his body as possible. "Here comes someone."

He raised his gun, eyes clear and focused. Then lowered it as Trey barreled around the corner.

"Lydia needs help. Kent won't hurt anyone else if we let her try to save his son." Trey's words toppled over each other in a rush. "We need to evacuate the hospital. There's a bomb. Set to go off in eighteen minutes."

CHAPTER 59

A BOMB? DID HE JUST SAY THERE WAS A BOMB? Gina staggered to her feet. This was exactly what her parents had warned her against. Inner city hospital, all sorts of unsavory types, danger lurking around every corner. Surely if their daughter was going to be a physician, she could chose a more appropriate specialty like plastic surgery or dermatology?

She remembered the Good Samaritan from earlier. He didn't have a bullet proof vest, didn't even have a shirt on, but he'd rushed into danger to help those kids and that driver.

She swallowed hard. She didn't have that kind of courage. Right now she wanted to barf her brains out, race home, have a long soak in the Jacuzzi, drink herself senseless, devour a gallon of Peachy Paterno ice cream, and screw the living daylights out of Jerry.

Except there Jerry stood, so calm and in command, surrounded by men with guns, men ready to obey his orders and lay their lives on the line. How could he love someone like her? A coward?

She climbed to her feet. Lurched over to the gurney, met Seth's eyes. "We need to try to save Ezekiel."

Jerry stopped mid-sentence, stared at her. "Gina, get out of here."

She pushed the stretcher a few inches forward. Seth grabbed the other side, pushing as well. "She's right, Jerry. Let us through."

"No. Seth. You can't," Nora said.

"I have to," Seth said. "It might be the only way to keep the guy with the gun from shooting Lydia."

Jerry gave Seth an appraising glance, his eyes narrowed. "You up for it, Seth?"

"I'm going, too," Gina said.

"You'll need a nurse," Nora added, grabbing onto the stretcher.

Both Seth and Jerry shook their heads.

"I'll go. Alone." Seth yanked the gurney away from Nora, not meeting her eyes.

"Can you get to an OR without exposing more people to the gunman?" Jerry asked

Seth nodded, already pushing the gurney forward, leaving Nora and Gina behind. "We'll go in the back way. The entrance is just down the hall from Elliot's office."

Nora's radio squawked for attention but she ignored it. Gina saw the grief crash down on her face, reached out to squeeze her free hand. Nora gave her a quick nod and grimace of a smile, then grabbed her radio and began ordering the evacuation, her gaze cemented on Seth.

"You two go the other way, stay out of sight but keep an eye on things," Jerry told the men with him. "We're off the page here," Jerry reminded them. The guy dressed in SWAT gear scowled, head cocked and one eye narrowed as if to say, way the hell and gone off, but he merely nodded. "If you have a better idea how to handle this, speak now."

Seth and Jerry edged down the hall, stopping before the corner. Nora followed.

Once again, Gina was left standing alone, empty-handed.

SUDDENLY NORA'S JOB HAD CHANGED from moving a few patients to accommodate new ones to evacuating over a hundred critical patients. Her mouth went dry as she gazed down the hall toward the ICUs.

She grabbed one of the OR nurses who'd been pulled to help with the disaster. "Clear the family room, get everyone who can be moved out of here."

The nurse looked stunned then nodded, began organizing the others. Nora glanced at Seth. He looked a wreck, eyes red-rimmed, at half mast, running on adrenaline and nothing else. How could Jerry let him risk his life? There had to be a better way.

Jerry was obviously out of ideas. "All right then. Primary concern is the doctors' safety. Anything hinky, you waste the hostage taker and let me deal with the fall out. Got it?"

The other officers nodded once more and jogged down the hall to the main OR doors, weapons at the ready.

Jerry snagged Seth by the arm, stopping him before he could wrestle the gurney around the corner. "You sure about this, Seth?"

Seth craned his neck over his shoulder, searching for and finding Nora's eyes. She thought he was going to say something. Instead, Seth clamped his mouth tight, gave a small nod, and rounded the corner, disappearing from sight. Nora released the breath she'd been holding and turned to Trey.

"How long?" she asked.

"Sixteen minutes," Trey said, sprinting past her down the hall toward the fire stairs. "It's in an ambulance parked by the ER."

Jerry holstered his gun and raced after Trey. Nora stared after them as she relayed the bad news to Mark. Sixteen minutes, one hundred and four ICU patients, most on vents, unable to be moved off the floor, not in time at least.

She jogged down to the ICU just as puzzled and terrified looking family members streamed past her toward the elevators. How many of their loved ones could she save?

"WHERE ARE THEY? WHAT'S TAKING SO LONG?" Matthew Kent's voice was jagged, had lost its mesmerizing dulcet tones. Just as he had shed his charisma as soon as he'd pulled the trigger and killed Elliot Weiss.

Lydia was certain Weiss was dead. That amount of blood on the wall and floor—no way he had survived. But she wasn't about to tell Matthew that.

"Probably getting the OR set up. It takes time. You know, with Dr. Weiss getting hurt right here, I'm sure he's fine. You can go ahead and drop the gun. We'll still do everything we can for your son. I promise you."

She stared at him, putting her heart and soul behind her gaze. She thought she had him, his hand holding the gun drifted down the slightest bit, but then Ezekiel spoke.

"Fool," he muttered, his voice stronger and more clear than his father's.

Lydia held her fingers on his great vessels, one twitch and she could let enough blood drain to quickly render him unconscious again. His eyes challenged her, dared her to do it, and Lord knew she wanted to. But she didn't, instead reinforcing her cramped hand with her free one.

"She'll never forgive you," Ezekiel continued. "You're corrupted, past redemption." His eyes fluttered, then opened wide again, as if he were gazing upon some wondrous sight. "It doesn't matter. She's here with me. Together we'll bring the Revelation."

Matthew looked around as if he could see his dead wife. He knelt and shook Ezekiel's shoulder. "What does she say?"

Ezekiel smirked, turning his gaze upon his father as if giving him a blessing. "She says you're all going to die a fiery death, just like hers." He closed his eyes, his face relaxing except for that damned superior smile. "You'll see, Father. There are two bombs."

CHAPTER 60

LYDIA'S HAND WASN'T MERELY CRAMPING, it was starting to go numb as she leaned her weight on it, pressing the muscular aorta and the more flabby-walled vena cava against Ezekiel's spinal column.

It was her only hope. By stopping the hemorrhage, she kept his blood volume high enough that the vital organs above her hand—including his heart, lungs and brain—functioning. Everything lower down was slowly dying, strangled by the lack of blood. She could care less. She needed to get him talking again.

She shifted her knee, jostled him, hoping for a response. His eyes moved beneath his closed lids, but nothing else.

The rattle of a gurney approaching put Matthew on alert. "Who's there?" he called out, brandishing the revolver like a bad guy in a spaghetti western.

"It's me, Mr. Kent. Dr. Cochran. The surgeon."

Kent opened the door and allowed Seth to enter. He watched as Seth carefully scooped Ezekiel's body up and onto the gurney, Lydia never releasing pressure on Ezekiel's wound. She saw him eye Kent's gun, tense his shoulders, ready to take action.

"Don't," she whispered.

He frowned, on the edge of disobeying her, but she shook her head. She knew exactly what he was thinking. There had been five shots and Ezekiel's weapon looked like an old-fashioned six shooter. Leaving at most one bullet. Except that Lydia knew from her experience in L.A. that there were other models, some that carried seven shots, some even eight.

Which changed the odds drastically. And the gun wasn't their immediate problem.

"Ezekiel woke long enough to tell me there's a second bomb. But he didn't say where it was," she told Seth as they moved down the hall to the OR. Lydia had to jog alongside the stretcher, both hands still clamped inside Ezekiel's abdominal cavity. "We need to get him awake again."

"How?" the surgical resident asked. "I'll need to intubate him, put him under for the surgery."

They pushed through the doors from the "dirty" part of the OR suite to the sterile area and headed down the hall to the two trauma rooms across from each other, OR One and OR Fourteen. Seth steered them into OR One.

"Open a vascular tray and get a couple Satinsky clamps. Then you're going to reach in and cross clamp his aorta and vena cava. Above where my hands are."

He scurried around the room, banging open glass and metal cabinets until he unearthed a vascular set. Hurriedly he unwrapped it. As he worked, she tried to distract Matthew Kent from the movement she saw outside the OR doors.

"Mr. Kent," she called out.

The man seemed to be drifting away. She was losing him. He couldn't tear his gaze from the blood that covered his son's scrubs.

"I need your help."

"He's going to die, isn't he?" Matthew said with a moan. His entire body shook as if an unseen wind had grabbed him and wouldn't let go. "Dear God, I killed my son."

"I'm doing everything possible to keep your son alive, but I need your help." She raised her voice, hoping the men outside heard.

"He said there was a second bomb. When he wakes up again you need to ask him where it is. Can you do that? It's very important."

Matthew didn't look up, kept staring at the gaping incision Seth was creating, expanding the wound she'd thrust her fingers into.

"Ready," Seth said from the other side of the table. He'd put on gloves and slowly slid his free hand into the incision, palpating her fingers. She raised one hand out of the way to give him more room, leaning all her weight on her other hand. The edges of Ezekiel's vertebra felt like sharp pieces of coral, digging into her palm.

"That's pretty high up," Seth said. "Too high to save—"

"Clamp it," she interrupted him before Matthew caught his meaning.

Damn surgeons, always thought a chance to cut was a chance to cure. Seth wasn't going to get a save. Not tonight. Ezekiel was already as good as dead, she was only trying to see that he didn't take everyone else at Angels with him.

"Got it."

Her other hand emerged with a loud slurping noise that made Matthew jump. Loops of intestine, already turning blue from lack of blood, escaped from the wound.

"You're going to help him, aren't you? You promised." Matthew's voice was now a plaintive mewl, barely audible.

"Yes. Dr. Cochran is going to pack the wound, repair the damage."

She shot Seth a hard glare that made him jump into action, grabbing lap sponges and looking for all the world like he was actually doing something. As he pretended to work, she grabbed a fourteen gauge angiocath from the anesthesia cart and started forcing fluids into Ezekiel. If that didn't work, she'd hit him with some epi. But damn it, he had to wake up and tell them where the second bomb was.

She glanced at the clock. Twelve minutes left.

Time was almost gone. She started a second IV line. Ezekiel's pulse was slower, stronger, all good signs. She knuckled his sternum, painfully. He blinked and opened his eyes.

"Ezekiel," his father said, collapsing over his son's body, hugging him. "You came back to me."

"Ask him where the bomb is," Lydia coaxed.

Matthew had totally forgotten about the gun, although he still clutched it like a talisman, warding off evil spirits.

"The second bomb, where is it?"

Ezekiel's eyes darted around the room, narrowed as he registered where they were. "Here."

Lydia whirled, looking at the myriad of hiding places the OR offered. They'd never find it in time.

"Seth, I'll take over from here." She grabbed a handful of lap pads, jerked her head toward the door. "You can leave now."

Matthew didn't even pay attention, he was sobbing, his free hand rubbing Ezekiel's hair. Seth looked up, his hands still plunged in Ezekiel's belly, trying to staunch the oozing. It was a losing battle. Even though the main blood vessels were clamped, the damaged organs were now shutting down, blood leaking everywhere.

"No. I'm not leaving you."

"Go. Now. There's not much time left."

An eerie chuckle emerged from Ezekiel. The boy was a living corpse, yet he still could have the last laugh.

"No time," he crooned in a ghastly sing-song. "No time for the wicked."

CHAPTER 61

NORA WATCHED SETH DISAPPEAR and wasn't sure whether to feel angry, sad, or frustrated. She'd almost run after him, but realized she couldn't help him. Not as much as she could by doing her job.

Instead she pivoted and strode into the Medical ICU. She took a deep breath, flagging down nurses even as the Code Orange alert began to sound. She saw several pause, glance at their code alert cards to confirm. Code Red, fire. Code Blue, cardiac arrest. Code White, blizzard. Code Green, Hazmat. Code Black, mass casualty disaster. Code Orange, bomb alert.

"Let's move, people. All families and non-essential staff out of here, now," Nora ordered, her voice steady but loud enough to carry through the room.

She began to patrol the bedsides. None of the patients up here were ambulatory, there would be no evacuating them. But some were stable enough that she could release the nurses caring for them, get them out of here, at least. Thank God, she'd already moved as many patients as possible because of the disaster alert.

By the time she reached Mickey Cohen's bedside, the unit was in chaos.

Nurses calmly giving report to the colleagues they were abandoning, tears streaming down their faces; family members saying vocal farewells to their loved ones, a few refusing to leave. Nora didn't fight them, saving her energy to hasten the evacuation and save as many as she could.

Eleven minutes, she thought looking at the clock. Damn it, if she only had more time.

Danny stood at Mickey's bedside. "You can't make me leave," he was saying, angrily swiping away his tears. "Of course I'm staying."

"Danny, you need to go. Now," Mickey argued. They both looked up as Nora approached. "Nora, make him leave."

Nora ignored them for a moment, watching the hemoperfusion machine spin. If something happened and one of the cannulas broke loose, Mickey would bleed out before anyone could stop it. "We need to clamp both lines, shut it down," she told the tech.

"I've already begun clearing the blood volume from the machine," he replied. "I was waiting, hoping for a doc, since I don't have any orders and can't—"

"I'll take responsibility," Nora said.

He frowned, but nodded. Quickly they re-routed all of Mickey's blood from the machine back into her body and clamped the large arterial and venous cannulas.

"Go on," Nora told the tech when the job was done. "Get out of here." She glanced up at Danny. "You, too. Last chance."

"No," he said, crossing his arms as if daring her to move him.

"Danny—"

"Forget it, Mickey. I'm staying."

"Okay, then. I need you to—" The sound of running footsteps interrupted Nora. A flushed security guard appeared behind her. "What?"

"There's another bomb. It's in one of the ORs," he said, panting.

Oh hell. The ICU and OR shared a wall—this wall. Nora

blinked then transitioned into urgent care mode.

"Okay, everyone!" She shouted to the few remaining medical personnel. "We need to move everyone away from this wall and get everyone out of here and down the hall to CCU. Now!"

As the staff jumped to carry out her orders, she ran through the back hallway to the utility closet where the emergency anesthesia and oxygen cut offs were. She flicked the switches, shutting down all the oxygen flow in the hospital and cutting off the flammable anesthesia gases. Some patients might suffer from the lack of oxygen, but hopefully it would keep the entire hospital from exploding.

Eight minutes.

Her hand shook as she realized she might be condemning people to death. She clamped it tight, tried not to think of Seth's face before he ran past her down to the OR.

She headed back into the ICU, determined to try to save as many of her patients as possible before time ran out.

"STOP PUSHING, PATRICE." Amanda had just delivered the baby's head, was in the process of gently rotating his face, giving Lucas room to suction the baby's mouth and nose, when the door banged open behind them.

"We're a little busy here," Lucas shouted, from his position beside Amanda.

Amanda switched her hands, ready to deliver the body with one more good push. At least that was the way it was supposed to work, unless there was some shoulder dystocia or a prolapsed cord or a hand in the way…

"You're not supposed to be in here," a man's voice came from the doorway. Amanda recognized that voice, the same voice that had been harassing her for the past two nights. Jim Lazarov. "Amanda, what the hell do you think you're doing?"

"If you don't know the answer to that—" she said, clamping her lips shut before she used language her mother definitely would not approve of. She kept her eyes on the baby's head cradled between her palms.

"Leave. Now." Lucas's voice carried the weight of authority.

"Fine," Jim said in an aggrieved tone. "But you should know, they're evacuating the entire hospital."

"What's going on?" Mr. Garrison demanded.

"Apparently there's a bomb. Some crazy guy wants to blow up the hospital." Jim's voice sounded almost gleeful. The door banged shut behind him. Other than the sound of Patrice's rapid panting the room was quiet for a long moment.

"Daddy," Patrice gasped, her body writhing with another contraction. "What did that man say?"

Denny exchanged a worried glance with Ruby, then rubbed his palm on Patrice's arm. "Nothing important, dear. Don't you worry about anything except having this baby."

"No nuchal cord," Lucas said, his voice steadying Amanda's nerves and keeping her focused. "Go ahead and push when you feel ready, Patrice."

GINA STARTED DOWN THE STAIRS, crowded with staff, family members, and ambulatory patients all running for their lives. She made it to the third floor, Pediatrics, when she spotted her Good Samaritan, now dressed in scrubs, forcing his way through the crowd, coming up the steps.

"Gina, give me a hand," he shouted over the echoes of pounding footsteps. He grabbed her arm, tugged her through the tide of humanity and pulled her onto the pediatrics ward.

"Thank God the census was low for the holiday," he said as he jogged down the hall to the long-term care unit. The critically ill children, like Amanda's meningitis baby, would have been the first patients evacuated from upstairs in the PICU. But these kids, these were the ones dependent on technology, many of them had spent their entire lives inside the hospital walls. Some no longer had family who visited, their only family the hospital staff who cared for them.

A harried-looking nurse was working to bag two trach-dependent kids at once as her colleague arranged them onto a pediatric back board, strapping them down tight, a head at each end. The better to transport two at once, Gina saw.

"These two are ready to go, Dr. Ken," she said and Gina realized that her Samaritan, "Dr. Ken", must have already made at least one trip out, ferrying kids. "But that still leaves the twins and Ashley."

"You guys get out of here," Ken said. "I brought reinforcements."

"We'll set up everything outside and meet you there." The nurses shrugged into backpacks filled with emergency equipment and lifted the backboard, each one using one hand to bag oxygen into the children as they held on to the board with the other. It was a good thing the kids weren't very large, Gina thought, holding the door for them as they exited.

Ken moved over to the three remaining patients. Two infants, maybe ten months old, both with narrow heads, tracheotomies, and feeding tubes. And one older patient, it was hard to tell how old, since her face was chubby like a pre-schooler's but her limbs were atrophied and contracted. She also was on a ventilator.

"Help me get the twins set and then I'll give you a hand with Ashley," Ken said, rolling a sheet into a wide-based sling and tying it around his neck. "Okay, let's do Sammy first. Disconnect him from the vent and lay him in the sling. He's only on C-Pap, so he can stay off the vent longer. Just as long as he doesn't brady down on us. But you're not going to do that, are you, Sammy boy?" he crooned as he helped Gina position the baby.

Gina felt overwhelmed by the task. The twins were obviously extremely premature and had to have some severe complications to still be dependent on the ventilator. But there was no time to waste on hesitation. "How early were they?"

"Twenty-four weeks. They were triplets, but Abe didn't make it. So now it's just the two of them, but they're fighters. Aren't you guys?" Sammy squirmed in the make-shift baby carrier but Ken stroked his head and he quickly quieted. "Okay, now give me Jacob and position him so I can cradle them against my chest but still bag him with my free hand. That's it. Good. You're a natural at this, Gina."

Was he kidding? She felt like ET, lost on a strange planet. She hated working with kids, especially ones as fragile as these. "We don't have much time."

"Sure we do. Now this is Miss Ashley," he said, directing her to the little girl with blond curls. "She's real particular. Jostle her the wrong way or don't mind your manners and she'll throw one of her hissy fits."

"Hissy fits?" Gina asked, trying to figure out how to even pick up the girl whose arms and legs were flexed into place.

"Yeah. Death spells, the nurses call 'em. Miss Ashley is a budding drama queen. Likes to stop breathing until she turns black and goes into a full arrest. She's been coded more than any other living patient in Angels' history."

Not a good record to set. Gina froze, one arm under Ashley's knees, the other getting ready to disconnect her from the ventilator. "I don't think I can do this."

"No time to argue, Gina. Just connect the bag, scoop her up. Your arms are nice and long, reach over and breathe for her."

Gina followed his direction and suddenly she was cradling the little girl against her chest. Ashley's head flopped to one side, landing on top of Gina's breast, leaving a puddle of drool in her wake.

"Good work. She likes you. Okay, let's move out!"

Gina always considered herself a pretty graceful person, a good athlete, but the effort of walking, squeezing the bag to force air into Ashley's lungs, monitoring her patient's coloring and watching where she was going, turned her into a staggering idiot. And she only had one patient. Ken had two to juggle and he made it look easy.

He led the way to the stairwell, walking at a brisk but steady pace. The number of people on the steps had dwindled to a trickle and those few stood to one side to let Ken and Gina pass with their precious cargo.

They emerged into the ED and headed out the ambulance bay doors. Just in time for Gina to see Trey and Jerry speed by in the old-fashioned ambulance Ezekiel Kent had arrived in. Jerry looked like he was trying to fiddle with something on the dashboard.

She froze. The bomb. Jerry was in the van trying to defuse the bomb.

Ashley went rigid and Gina realized she'd been so stunned that she'd forgotten to bag the girl. She hastily squeezed the bag rapidly and Ashley settled down again. She rushed to catch up with Ken, just in time for a man to jump out and blind her with a camera flash.

"The hero of Angels," the man said. "I'm Pete Sandusky. What's your name? I'm gonna make you famous."

Hero? She brushed past Sandusky and joined Ken and the pediatric nurses. All she did was carry a baby down the steps without dropping it. Jerry was out there, riding in a bomb about to go off. Numb with terror, Gina handed Ashley off to the waiting pediatric nurses and ran after the ambulance. She was just in time to see Trey steer it into the cemetery, bouncing across the grass and over grave markers into the open area in the center.

She knuckled her fist against her teeth. Jerry was going to die, she was never going to see him again, she just knew it.

THE GURGLE OF A BABY CRYING FILLED THE ROOM as Amanda raised the squirming, slime-covered newborn onto Patrice's abdomen and quickly clamped the cord with Lucas's help.

"Congratulations," she told Patrice, blinking away beads of sweat. "Let me dry him off, make sure he's nice and warm."

She stood back, finally able to take a deep breath. The picture before her—mother, child, and proud grandparents—was the most absolutely perfect thing she could ever imagine. Amanda turned away, swiping tears with the back of her wrist, grinning and feeling relieved and triumphant all at once. She'd done it! And without a flicker of a tremor or twitch. Lucas was wrong—if she could make it through the stress of delivering a baby and surviving a bomb scare without any symptoms, then there was nothing wrong with her.

"Thank you, thank you," Patricia said, still catching her breath. "He's beautiful. Look how beautiful he is."

Amanda changed places with Lucas, added a dose of Pitocin to Patrice's IV, and then gently disengaged the beaming mother from the baby and rushed the boy over to the warmer.

Grandma watched every move Amanda made while grandpa seemed thunderstruck.

"He's perfect," Amanda assured them. She quickly dried him off, covered his head with a stocking cap and wrapped him in a blanket from the warmer. "Now, let's get him out of here." There was no way she was leaving the baby here with a possible bomb. Lucas could finish delivering the placenta and take care of Patrice while she got the baby and grandparents out of the building.

Before the others could respond, the lights went out and the entire building shook. A roar of thunder rumbled through the ceiling, jarring loose a cloud of plaster and dust. Amanda hugged the baby to her, crouched against the wall in the darkness.

CHAPTER 62

LYDIA WATCHED HELPLESSLY as Ezekiel faded once more into unconsciousness. Seth was furiously trying to staunch a new bleeder, refusing to look at her or listen to her commands for him to leave.

She was just about ready to ask the two police officers outside the door to haul his ass out of there, but she had to get the gun away from Matthew first. The preacher was sobbing, his chest heaving, but he still had a firm grip on his weapon.

"Matthew," she said softly, one hand on his shoulder. "I think its time for you to say good-bye. There's nothing more we can do."

He shook his head. "No. No. You promised—"

A blast rocketed through the room, blowing the steel door off its hinges, hurtling it past Lydia. She was knocked off her feet, watched helplessly as the gurney with Ezekiel flew across the room, taking Matthew with it, carrying them out into the hallway. She lost sight of Seth as an instrument cabinet blew open then fell over her, the open metal doors saving her from being crushed.

Her ears rang so that her head felt caught between two cymbals. The concussion of sound and howling wind blew a thick, smoky haze into the room. Then the final blast wave screamed past, echoing down the long hallway with a banshee's shriek.

An ominous silence descended. Lydia thought for a moment that she'd gone deaf. The pressure in her ears built, forcing tears of pain from her, then mercifully released as her eardrums burst.

She swallowed hard and finally was able to make out the distant sounds of alarms overtop the pounding in her head. Debris flew past, buffeting her, but she was relatively protected by the metal cabinet.

Dust filled her throat, triggering a coughing spasm. She crawled out from under her shelter and looked up. The roof was still intact, at least over her. But the door leading to the main hall was now a gaping jagged hole filled with blue sky. The explosion had originated in the OR across the hall and had had enough force to demolish it and the outside wall behind it.

Lydia lay there, gasping for breath, fear still with a stranglehold on her heart. The smoke was beginning to clear. Every blink left her tearing with pain. Corneal abrasions from the debris, ruptured ear drums, strained shoulder, assorted scrapes and abrasions, but she was alive.

She looked around for any sign of Seth or the police officers. Saw Seth's foot under a pile of acoustical ceiling tiles, a fallen fluorescent light fixture lying across them.

The main lights were out but the emergency lighting was on. That meant the damage was localized, she thought as she crawled through the debris toward Seth. Which meant the bomb hadn't triggered the anesthesia or oxygen lines. Thank God.

The addition of the flammable gases would have turned the entire fourth floor into a raging fireball.

Before she could reach Seth, he shoved the debris aside and sat up, coughing. His face was a mask of grey dust.

"You okay?" he asked as he pushed himself free of the light fixture.

"Fine." She stood, blinking away a wave of vertigo and tottered out into the hallway.

The long corridor had acted as a particle accelerator or giant wind tunnel, amplifying the blast. Although the OR across the way was demolished, more frightening was the twisting columns of metal and the jagged opening leading into the Medical ICU.

Seth joined her. "Jesus. Nora."

"Go," she told him. "I'm going to look for the police officers who were outside the door."

He nodded wordlessly and began to claw his way over the jagged mound of debris that opened into the ICU. Lydia peered down the hallway. The opposite end, where it took the sharp bend to the OR central nursing area looked relatively intact. Broken glass, over turned equipment carts and lighting fixtures hanging by wires. No signs of any victims.

She heard a moan from the OR where the blast had originated. As she stumbled over the threshold, she slipped in a mass of liquid that could only be Ezekiel Kent's blood. She couldn't see where his body had landed, but didn't really look.

Large pieces of ceiling tile and drywall littered the floor, twisted lengths of metal supports and rebar jutted into the air, looking naked and exposed without their sheaths of insulation and plaster. Electrical wires bristled from the edges of the gaping hole.

No fire that she could see or smell. From beneath a pile of warped acoustical tile a hand was moving. Matthew.

She dropped to her knees and began dragging debris off him. Blood seeped from both his ears, indicating a possible skull fracture. His legs were wedged between the remains of the concrete supports for the outer wall, his feet dangling precariously out into the empty space. Of more concern was the piece of twisted re-bar jutting through his lower right chest, impaling him to the floor.

GINA HAD WATCHED IN HORROR as the ambulance pulled to a stop in the middle of the graveyard. Trey and Jerry had bailed out and took off running at top speed, heading back toward Angels. Ken joined her, putting his hands on her shoulders, holding her in place when she tried to run towards them.

Jerry and Trey were almost to the gates when the ambulance exploded. A fountain of dirt and rocks and shards of granite blew into the air, accompanied by a blast of heat that threw Gina to the ground, Ken covering her with his body. The roar that followed was loud enough to knock Gina's teeth together.

Debris rained down on them and within seconds, a second, less powerful explosion sounded. Gina fought against Ken, determined to look around and make sure Jerry was all right.

"The hospital!" Ken was shouting. "They blew up part of the fourth floor."

Screams drowned out anything else he was saying. He climbed off her, pushing himself upright and then bending over to help her up. People were racing in every direction: away from the hospital, away from the cemetery, colliding in the street between, uncertain where to go to find safety.

"Jerry!" Gina screamed, craning her head to find him. She couldn't see past the mob of people. She began pushing and shoving, dodging chunks of sculpture, headstones and building debris. Glass was everywhere, sparkling on top of debris. The macabre image of blasted bits and pieces of decades old corpses crunching beneath her boots flit through her mind, but even that ugly thought didn't stop her from trying to find Jerry.

She only made it halfway across the street before the sheer wall of humanity blocked her way. Tears blinded her, she was turned around, not sure which way to go. Suddenly she found herself in Ken's embrace, holding him tight, tears flowing unfettered. "Help me," she gasped. "Help me find him."

He gently freed himself from her arms. "I think he found you."

She raised her head and turned around. Jerry was covered with mud and grass, blood coming from one ear and a small nick on his forehead. Trey looked just as bad. Then Jerry met her eyes and flashed a smile so brilliant it outshone any diamond she owned. He swiped his hand over his face, smearing more dirt than he cleaned, and ran toward her, scooping her up in his arms.

"You weren't worried, were you?" he said, laughing like a loon.

She pummeled her fists against his chest. "You idiot! Don't you ever do anything that stupid again. Driving off with a bomb? Who do you think you are, Superman?"

He laughed some more then kissed her so hard she could taste mud and grass.

NORA SHOOK HER HEAD, trying to stop the screaming in her ears. The blast had thrown her across the room, skipping her like a stone until she'd slammed into the wall of the nurses' lounge. She'd sat there in darkness for a moment, then the lights had returned, revealing a scene of destruction.

The shared wall between the ICU and ORs was gone. A jagged hole half filled with debris all that remained of the bed space she and Danny had moved Mickey Cohen out of less than a minute before.

Gagging on dust and phlegm, she struggled to her feet. Thanks to the help of the two policemen, only two patients in addition to Mickey remained in this room. The rest had been moved down the hall to the Cardiac Care Unit.

She waded through debris, most of it paper and office supplies with the occasional acoustical tile and overturned chair thrown in. The first patient she reached was an end-stage COPD patient, ventilator dependent. His monitor still chirped from where it was bolted to the wall above his bedside. His oxygen level was low, but he'd only been getting room air since she shut down the O2 flow. Heart rate a bit fast, no surprise there. Her own was ready to launch into orbit.

She pulled the debris from him, surprised to see that her arm was bleeding. She didn't remember cutting it. "How you doing, Mr. Olsen?"

He blinked up at her, snaking one hand out from under the blankets she'd thrown over him to protect him. Gave her a thumbs up.

The gesture made her smile, then she was laughing, crying, unable to stop herself as she turned to the next bed space.

Mr. Henderson, persistent vegetative state, in the ICU for pneumonia that had put him on a vent. His monitor had been ripped from the wall, and now dangled between his bed and Mr. Olsen's. She tugged on his blankets, coughing as acoustical tile snowed down on her from above. For some reason the ceiling took a worse hit here than elsewhere.

She freed him. Felt for a pulse. Steady. He was as well as could be expected, the ventilator doing most of the work of living for him. Poor thing, she thought. It might have been a blessing for him if he had died. But it wasn't her call to make. His family had fought and won to have his living will overturned and they insisted that everything possible be done.

"Help," Mickey's weak voice cut through the haze. "Danny's hurt. Please help."

Mickey's bed had spun ninety degrees with the force of the blast and rammed into several other empty beds, one turned onto its side.

"Where is he?" Nora asked once she uncovered Mickey and ensured that she was all right, no damage to the clamped cannulas.

"He was on top of me, trying to shield me," Mickey whispered, her voice fading. "Then he was gone and the bed was spinning..."

"Nora! Are you all right?"

Nora whirled. Seth was crawling through the jagged hole in the wall. His scrubs were torn, he was covered in dust turned to mud by his sweat, but he was safe.

She hadn't even allowed herself to think of him, had locked the certain sight of his battered and torn body away, ready to grieve when she had a chance, but here he was...safe and whole.

He lurched over the debris and caught her by the waist, hugging her so tight it was a struggle to breathe. "I was so worried about you," he said, his voice raspy. "I couldn't think—"

She pushed him away, shaking her head, fury tightening her muscles into thin wires that she feared would snap with the tension. "No. Don't you dare say that to me. You have no right to worry about me, not ever again. Not after what I saw this morning. We're done."

"But, Nora—"

"I'm not discussing it. Either leave now or help me find Danny," she told him. "He must be trapped."

He opened his mouth, then snapped it shut, shoulders hunching. In silence, they searched the area around Mickey's bed. Two of the empty beds had collided with Mickey's, probably what spun her bed sideways, Nora thought as she fought to free the logjam.

Then she saw what was causing the obstruction. Danny. He was pinned to the floor, tangled between the mechanisms under the beds, his neck at an unnatural angle.

"Seth," she pointed, her back to Mickey, trying to shield her from the sight.

Seth looked where she was pointing and immediately wedged himself between the beds, crawling down to check on Danny. A few moments later he stood up again, shaking his head.

"He's gone."

"LYDIA, YOU ALL RIGHT?" Trey's voice called out from the intact end of the OR hallway.

"Down here," Lydia yelled.

She closed her eyes and bowed her head for a quick moment, the sound of his voice piercing through her crisis-mode armor. Tears squeezed free but she shook them away and was composed moments later when Trey and Gecko arrived. Trey's hair was matted with leaves and twigs and mud, but other than that he seemed uninjured.

"How you doing?" he asked as he craned his neck over the edge of the abyss beside her and Kent, assessing the situation.

"Nothing a long, hot bath won't cure," she said, surprised by the light-hearted feeling that ambushed her at the sight of him. She was smiling like a crazy woman, but she didn't care.

"Glad to hear it."

"Help me secure his airway. Watch his c-spine," Lydia told him, grabbing the stethoscope hanging from his pocket and focusing on her patient. "Everyone else all right?"

"Yep. Except that a few of the city's founding fathers are now resting in pieces. Jerry and I kinda blew up part of the cemetery." His dimple was showing as he met her gaze.

Gecko glanced down at Matthew's still form. "You sure he's worth it? After all, he's what started all this."

"Yes. Get moving," she ordered. Didn't matter who Matthew was or what he'd done. He was a patient and he was going to get her best whether he deserved it or not.

"Your call."

Gecko began bagging air into Matthew while Lydia listened. No breath sounds on the right. She felt his trachea. Definite shift. Tension hemo-pneumothorax. His right chest had filled with blood, collapsing his lung and now putting pressure on his left lung and heart. Needling it wouldn't be enough. He needed a chest tube. Now.

"This is going to be one bitch of a rescue," was Trey's professional assessment as he examined the re-bar and the precarious position of Matthew's body.

"You love this shit and you know it." Lydia grabbed a scalpel and a handful of gauze.

"Besides," Gecko added, "we're on time and a half, so who cares?"

"Give me that ET tube, I'm going to use it as a chest tube. This isn't going to be pretty," she said as she used Trey's trauma shears to cut off Matthew's shirt.

The wind caught it and it fluttered through the air, down into the debris scattered four stories below. She gingerly climbed over Matthew's legs to reach his right side. The wind gusted through the metal framework of what remained of the wall, blowing with it the stench of melted plastic.

She looked down. If she fell, she'd land in a chasm of jagged and deadly looking debris.

She swayed, her balance still off. Trey's hands caught her waist, holding her safely in place. "I got you, doc."

After pouring Betadine over Matthew's chest, she sliced through the skin and muscles above the fifth rib. Using a pair of hemostats to separate the tissue, she probed the hole with her finger and pushed through the lining of the pleural cavity with a pop. She threaded the ET tube through the tunnel and quickly secured it. A free-flowing stream of blood poured from it, cascading down four stories onto the debris below. Trey hauled her back onto solid ground.

Trey lifted the stethoscope from Lydia's neck and listened as Gecko bagged air into Matthew's lungs. "Better, almost equal."

"That ought to keep him alive until we can get a saw and extrication gear up here."

"So he'll live?" Gecko asked.

"Long enough to make it to jail." She met Trey's eyes. His dimple was showing, the one clean area left on his grime-streaked face.

"Nice work, doc."

CHAPTER 63

LYDIA WOULD NEVER HAVE GUESSED Ruby Garrison had recently been in a fire. Ruby wore slacks, a knit sleeveless sweater, and a lightweight chiffon blouse that hid her bandages and still looked cool and professional. The smile she flashed deepened into a grin as she waved Lydia into a chair.

"I'm sorry to drag you into work on a weekend," Lydia said. "We could have met next week."

"Nonsense. And have you wasting money on that musty motel room? Besides, I had to come in anyway to open the dance studio while Patrice is on maternity leave." She nodded at the glass doors across the hall from Rare Gems Realty.

"Patrice runs a ballroom dance studio? Is that where Trey learned to dance?" Lydia was surprised by the blush that warmed her face, hoped Ruby had no idea at the cause.

"Denny and I love to dance. We taught all our kids—the boys more reluctantly than the girls, of course. And I taught it to all the children at our church's Sunday school. Amazing how well behaved rowdy young men can become when you teach them manners and comportment."

Lydia smiled at the old fashioned word.

"Poor Trey," Ruby continued. "He had to partner his sisters

and all the girls. Complained about it, but now it's a nice sideline for him."

"He teaches at his sister's school?"

"So do Denny and I. Told you this was a family-run operation." She opened a file and shuffled through an ominously large stack of papers. "Now. Let's get you settled."

Two hours later, Lydia parked her Escape in front of the house on Merton Street. She was renting it until they closed on the house later that month, but it was a done deal. Her house. Her home.

Sitting here, just looking at it, reminded her of that feeling of running on the beach, the ocean stretching out to the horizon, beckoning her to chase after a new adventure, new life. Only this time she didn't need to run anywhere. She was already there.

Home. Maria would've liked it, she decided, as she left the Escape.

A familiar red truck was parked across the street. Trey. She walked toward her porch, wondering about the implications of that and found him sitting on the swing, watching her with a lazy grin on his face.

He got to his feet, still saying nothing and she saw that he was wearing a white dress shirt and crisply pleated navy slacks.

"What's the occasion?" she asked, turning her key in her door.

"Heard from the studio that I had a new student. Thought I'd come over, give you your first lesson." He reached behind him, brought forth a large bouquet of irises and gladiolas. She straightened, looking from the flowers to him.

"Trey, I thought we agreed not to rush–"

"Relax, they're from my mom and dad. They send them to all their clients when they make a sale."

She took the flowers. Ruby worked fast. Just like her son. "Nice. Thank them for me."

He stepped forward, rested his hands on her hips, trapping the flowers between them. "I decided to get my own place too. Settle down. No more crashing at my folks."

She raised an eyebrow, squinting up at him. "Good for you. What about the others? Your harem?"

He surprised her by flushing. "No more crashing anywhere. Unless you invite me."

"Trey..." Now it was her turn to feel uncomfortable. Sex was one thing, but what they had could be so much more, she didn't want to risk a misstep.

"C'mon, Lydia. You owe me–"

"I know. Two tangos and a rumba." She allowed him to waltz her over the threshold into her house.

Their footsteps echoed on the wood floors as he twirled her around, releasing her to spin across the floor. She swore she could hear Maria's approving chuckle ringing through her ears.

Before she could catch her breath, the doorbell rang. Lydia turned in Trey's arms, startled by the melodic chimes. Trey kept hold of her hand as she dashed over to greet her first guest.

Make that guests. Nora Halloran stood there, juggling a lamp and a set of baking dishes. Gina nudged Nora over the threshold and entered herself, followed by Jerry Boyle, who was balancing an overstuffed chair on his head.

"Put it there, Jerry," Gina directed as she unloaded a stack of dishes into Trey's arms. "We heard you were moving, thought we'd help out."

Lydia stood silent, staring as Amanda joined them, hauling a braided rug. "It was Nora's idea."

"Actually it was Mark's idea," Nora said as Mark and his wife, Natalie, walked in, both carrying covered platters of something that smelled like spicy pork. "I just had the truck rented since I'm moving into Mickey's place."

"You are? What about Seth?"

"Forget about Seth. Besides, Mickey is going to need some help after she gets out of the hospital." She gave a sad smile. "Hope you don't mind that some of this stuff is Danny's. And Mickey sent his bike—said she thought you would appreciate it."

Lydia was stunned, pressed one palm against her chest, suddenly speechless.

"Hey, Lydia," Mark said, giving her a one-armed hug while Natalie kissed her on the cheek.

"Home cooking to fatten you up," Natalie said, elbowing her in the ribs.

Trey and Jerry went out for another load. Lydia glanced out the door, still thunderstruck. A U-Haul was parked beside the Escape, packed full from the looks of it.

"I don't know what to say," she stammered, blinking hard. She was not going to cry. A tear escaped and she swiped it away. Okay, not much.

"Now that you've got your job back, we couldn't have you sleeping on the floor and showing up for work all cranky," Nora said. "Besides, it's only the bare essentials, just enough to get you started."

"I'm sure you'll want to decorate with your own things," Amanda said. "It is a gorgeous house."

"Hey," Gina called out from the French doors. "Is this your cat? Very cool—he looks like a baby cougar or something."

"You girls get together, I promised Mickey some pictures," Mark said, holding up a small camera.

Gina struck a pose, Amanda encircled both Gina and Lydia's shoulders, while Nora hung on Lydia's other arm. The flash went off just as Lydia was unable to contain the laughter bubbling through her.

"Great shot," Mark said. "I'm gonna call it the Trauma Mommas of Angels of Mercy."

Lydia hugged her new friends tight, still laughing. Trey appeared in the doorway, looking concerned at first, then breaking into a wide grin at the sound of her giddy hysteria.

She'd arrived in Pittsburgh with nothing, traveling light,

ready to run away again if need be.

Now she was the proud owner of a mortgage, a dozen dance lessons—satisfaction guaranteed—a graveyard cat that looked like an escapee from an African jungle, and, to her complete surprise and delight, a new family.

Trey approached her, the other women giving him room, his arms wrapping around her waist, snugging her close.

"Welcome home, Lydia."

WANT MORE ANGELS OF MERCY?

Check out Amanda's story in CATALYST, available now.

ABOUT CJ:

New York Times and *USA Today* bestselling author of over forty novels, former pediatric ER doctor CJ Lyons has lived the life she writes about in her cutting edge Thrillers with Heart.

CJ has been called a "master within the genre" (Pittsburgh Magazine) and her work has been praised as "breathtakingly fast-paced" and "riveting" (Publishers Weekly) with "characters with beating hearts and three dimensions" (Newsday).

Her novels have twice won the International Thriller Writers' prestigious Thriller Award, the RT Reviewers' Choice Award, the Readers' Choice Award, the RT Seal of Excellence, and the Daphne du Maurier Award for Excellence in Mystery and Suspense.

Learn more about CJ's Thrillers with Heart at www.CJLyons.net

40069511R00246

Made in the USA
Middletown, DE
22 March 2019